Praise for Elliot Perlman's
Three Dollars

". . . a remarkably well-written first novel, funny, moving, and
constantly surprising. . . . It is impossible not to care what happens to
Eddie, Tanya his wife, and Abby, their adorable daughter . . . Perlman
is echoing Auden's cry, "We must love one another or die."
—*Time Out*

"Verdict: Encore! Bravo! More please."
—*Melbourne Sunday Herald-Sun*
and
Sydney Sunday Telegraph

". . . [a] wittily assured first novel. . . . [*Three Dollars*] gradually builds
into a study of a whole generation, a sad, angry, disconcertingly funny
reflection of the way we live now."
—*Times Literary Supplement, London*

". . . Perlman is a marvelous storyteller . . . . rich in observation and
pathos."—*The Observer*

"Funny and dramatic, literary yet accessible . . . what a find this is!"
—*Marie Claire*

"A compelling story, a great drama, even a great tragedy."
—*Sunday Age*

". . . one of the year's most pleasant surprises."
—*The Australian's Review of Books*

". . . [a] poignant tale. . . ."—*Australian Bookseller & Publisher*

"His novel doesn't have any answers but it puts the questions with
such deftness and sad humor that you'd laugh aloud if it weren't for
the lump in your throat."—*Adelaide Advertiser*

"Perlman's critique of the culture of greed is considerably composed
and rewardingly memorable."—*The Weekend Australian*

3 DOLLARS

3 DOLLARS

elliot perlman

MacMurray & Beck
Denver

First published by Picador/Australia–All Rights reserved

Copyright © 1999 by Elliot Perlman
Published by:
MacMurray & Beck
Alta Court
1490 Lafayette St., Ste. 108
Denver, CO 80218

Acknowledgments are due and are gratefully made to the following: DEATH OF A SALESMAN by Arthur Miller. Copyright © 1948, 1949, 1951, 1952 by Arthur Miller, renewed 1975, 1976, 1979, 1980. Reproduced by permission of the author c/o Rogers, Coleridge & White Ltd., 20 Powis Mews, London W11 1JN in association with International Creative Management, 40 West 57th Street, New York, NY 10019, USA. Published by Methuen, an imprint of Random House (UK).
J. C. Fogarty, "Bad Moon Rising" (Warner/Chappell)
Joy Division, "Shadowplay" and "Love Will Tear Us Apart" (Joy Division)

Printed and bound in the United States of America

1   2   3   4   5   6   7   8   9   10

Library of Congress Cataloging-in-Publication data
Perlman, Elliot
Three dollars / Elliot Perlman.
p.   cm.
ISBN 1-878448-88-9 (hc)
I. Title.
PR9619.3.P3619T48   1999
813'.54—dc21
99-14355
CIP

MacMurray & Beck Fiction: General Editor, Greg Michalson
Three Dollars cover design by Laurie Dolphin.
Cover photo by Michel Madie.
The text was set in Janson by Chris Davis, Mulberry Tree Enterprises.

For Janine, Lena and Harry

. . . a man is not a piece of fruit!
. . . You can't eat the orange and
throw the peel away—

Arthur Miller
Death of a Salesman

CHAPTER 1

Every nine and a half years I see Amanda. This is not a rule. It does not *have* to happen but it does. It has happened four times that I have seen her every nine and a half years which tends to make it more like a rule than an exception. But each time it is always and everywhere exceptional. Most recently was today. I had three dollars.

As children we were put in the same class at school although she was a year younger than me, and has been ever since. It was part of a pilot programme to have the brightest children from the year below put into a composite class with the brightest children of the year above and me. I don't know how I got into that class because I had not demonstrated a particular capacity for anything much. It was not that I was not interested in things but rather that I was interested in too many things. This interest in everything was completely internal to me, without external manifestations, and so went unnoticed by all adults except my parents, who were worried by it. I would just sit around and think; at least that's the way I remember it. Perhaps Amanda remembers it differently. I couldn't be bothered running around or even making much trouble. There were too many things to contemplate for me to be tempted into running at speed from A to B in order to get there sooner. While we were being taught about trains or mammals, I was wondering how it was the teacher managed to have the same smell every day, a musky smell that announced him long after he had gone and always would.

Amanda had a smell of her own and long, long hair that was whiter than it needed to be to pass for blonde. She smiled a lot and could have been mistaken for Heidi were it not for her tendency to get dirty. This worried her parents, particularly her mother whose severe Calvinist bleaching techniques were in constant battle with the toughest stains Amanda could find. The dirt from basketballs hugged her chest at recess and lunchtimes and had to be treated with the sternest pre-wash solutions her mother could obtain on the open market. The scrubbing and bleaching left their own stains on the felt letters that spelt *Amanda* on her t-shirt.

We were at a government school and Amanda's mother seemed to feel it was this, more than anything intrinsic to Amanda, that was staining the angelic Heidi shampoo commercial that left home so perfect each morning with her brothers. The family lived in a large Georgian-style house across the road from a plant, fruit and vegetable nursery by the canal. Her mother never set foot inside the nursery, preferring instead to buy the family's fruit and vegetable requirements in the shopping strip that called itself 'the village'.

Amanda's father was more of a presence than a person. She seldom referred to him and I think I only ever saw him once. He wore a dark suit with a crisp white starched shirt. Her mother must have loved doing *his* laundry or perhaps it was the housekeeper who had this privilege? He was a cross between Fred MacMurray in *Double Indemnity* and Fred MacMurray in 'My Three Sons'. His pronouncements were never heard, just heard about. His status in the family was seigneurial. And not only in the family: he was the first person I had ever come across with a job that had a two-word name. He was a chemical engineer.

Amanda would say it from time to time, not boastfully but matter-of-factly, 'a chemical engineer'. It sounded good but we didn't know what it meant. My father worked for the council in ways he could never bring himself to discuss and I never pressed him. He wore a white shirt and tie too but it was more crumpled than Amanda's father's shirt, something Amanda might have noticed on one of those evenings at our place after school. But what were the chances of an eight-and-a-half-year-old girl noticing something like that? Only her mother was sensitive to pleats.

There were quite a few afternoons at our place when a group of us would hide from each other, not just Amanda and me but also a few of her friends and some of mine. I tried to make it about equal. My mother would make afternoon tea for us. Sometimes Amanda and I would hide in my parents' wardrobe. We all hid in different permutations and combinations but I never took anyone else but Amanda into the wardrobe. We wouldn't say a word, we would just wait in the dark, bunched up and the sides of our knees pressed against each other as we sat on my parents' shoes. In the warmer months she wore my beach hat, the one with my name embroidered on it, and when her parents took her away with her brothers to Coff's Harbour for a holiday she called me on the public phone, feeding her pocket money in, coin by coin.

'It sucks here,' she said and I, never having been there, agreed and was delighted to hear it. My sister Kirsten had a

David Bowie album I had learnt by heart while watching her and her friends colour their faces. I quoted a line from it to Amanda in Coff's Harbour and told her to write it down when she got off the phone and to carry it around with her. *Be elusive but don't walk far.*

I had no idea what it meant.

It was through Amanda that I first learned of the precariousness of things and of the arrogance of certain memories in demanding your attention out of turn. When her mother called our place for the first time ever I expected her to want to speak to my mother, or at least to my older sister who had just started secondary school and had taken to wearing make-up when she went up the road for bread or milk. But Amanda's mother told me that I would do. Amanda would not be coming back to school after the summer and there was to be no more playing. I remember she asked me to have a good day. That was the end of the first time I saw Amanda.

When I saw her today I had three dollars. This might not be so bad under certain circumstances. I cannot imagine what they might be but I was not under them.

CHAPTER 2

Childhood summers are always better than adult summers. I have heard a variety of explanations for this: memory improves the past by natural selection, it is the origin of the specious; children have nothing they have to do during summer so every scorching day is like a year in which each day is long and free; and the recently elucidated El Nino effect acts surreptitiously to give your current summers to other people.

My mother was hanging washing on the clothes line in our back yard. It was a very still, hot day, the kind made for remembering. I watched her for a moment or two without her noticing me. I had not yet realised that I wanted to talk to her. When I started kicking the soil at the base of the birch tree nearest the clothes line with my heel she asked from behind a sheet what it was I wanted to talk about.

'Do you want any help?' I volunteered, not in a hurry to indulge my urgent need to tell her about the phone call from Amanda's mother.

'No thanks, Eddie. I'm just about finished here,' she said, securing a t-shirt to the line. She did not persist with her inquiry immediately, knowing instinctively how many beats to wait.

I picked up an old, nearly bald tennis ball which I kept on the patio as an aid to lengthy outdoor sessions of personal reflection and started throwing it in the air to myself.

'Did you hear the phone before?' I asked, breaking the silence I had myself imposed.

'No. Did you take a message?'

'No,' I said, now holding the tennis ball in one hand and digging the ground around the birch again.

'You didn't?'

'No. It was for me.'

'Really, for *you*. Who was it?' Phone calls for me then were unusual.

'Mrs Claremont, Amanda's mum.'

'Amanda?' she asked still with a few sheets between us, unconcerned.

'No, her mother.'

'Her *mother*? What did she want?'

'Amanda's not coming back to school after summer,' I said matter-of-factly.

'Her *mother* rang to tell you Amanda's changing schools?'

'She won't be playing with me anymore.'

'At school?'

'Anywhere.'

My mother pulled back one of the sheets to look at me. I knew this even though I was again watching the ball in mid-air. She waited for me to catch it and ran her fingers through my hair, knowing she was comforting me for more than I understood.

In addition to the promise of a summer's worth of unjust boredom and the gnawing hollow of a child's loneliness, my mother saw something else when she examined me there under the sun, something resulting from choices other people, possibly even she, had made or else had been unable to make, choices which were connected to me only by virtue of their remote consequences. She seemed to be scanning the back yard slowly as if surveying our patch for either the first or else for the last time. Then she asked whether I would like to join her in the kitchen for a cool drink. But before I could accept we heard my father calling her from inside with restrained urgency.

I was left by myself to nurse my anger at the capriciousness of adults that had in the space of an hour led Amanda's mother to expel me from Amanda's society and my mother to lose interest in palliating the expulsion. Ready to curse the world that bore me by slamming the ball hard into the uncaring back fence, I was stopped by the shock of my uncle's sudden appearance between me and the fence I had so nearly punished.

'Hi, Eddie,' he said quietly, sheepishly. 'You can throw it to *me* . . . if you like.'

George Harnovey was my father's brother. Born in 1922 and seven years older than my father, he had stories from the Depression and the Second World War which he used to bring over along with soft-centred mints for Kirsten and me, claret for my father and muscatel for my mother. He would also bring over Aunt Peggy. Much younger than he was, she had, from all accounts, enjoyed the 1960s more than anyone married to George had any right to expect. That day he stood empty-handed.

'Alright, *don't* throw the bloody thing,' he trailed off. He sat down under the birch tree and I went over and sat with him. When I said hello he kissed me and I handed him the ball. He was unshaven and his eyes were streaked with red.

He smelled of beer so much that thereafter beer would always smell a little of him.

'You're a good boy, Eddie,' he said to himself, and then turning to look at me he whispered, his eyes moist and plaintive, 'Do you think anyone saw me coming in?'

Before I could answer that I had not understood his question he started again, 'What you need here . . . is a verandah, good and wide. Did your father ever tell you? We used to . . . used to have a verandah at Dad and Mum's . . . along three sides of the house. Marvellous.'

He took out a handkerchief from his pocket and dabbed at his forehead before blowing his nose. Then he left it lying in his hand, squeezing it from time to time.

'Along three sides with vines growing up the supports to the guttering . . . wisteria and . . . er . . . passionfruit I think it was. See the world from a verandah. We lived on 'em.'

I did not yet know that my father had invited George to stay with us for a while. But just by looking at him, unshaven and bleary-eyed, I could tell that not only was he no longer the avuncular raconteur, the family's town crier bringing news fresh from the first half of the century but, as Auden put it, here was a man who had already spent his last afternoon as himself.

Unlike George, my father had never sold a camera, nor any photographic equipment in the back of a pub. Nobody had ever seen him crouching in the back of a utility extolling the virtue of some instant rolled lawn which he could get a little more of if required. My father had never gone rabbiting as a child nor had he ever been a carpenter who mistook himself for a property developer until the bank reminded him what he was. By the time George had been disabused by the bank manager he was not a carpenter anymore. But there had been a time, forever ago, when

Peggy thought she was marrying a property developer. She always had a delicate way with lipstick and mascara.

'She used to do my nails . . . can I tell you . . . She used to cut my hair,' George told my father one night in my room when he thought I was asleep. 'Said I was good with my hands. Used to do my nails . . . I was never any good with my hands . . .'

I closed my eyes and listened, imagining Peggy cutting my hair. She had a way with *her* hands, and her voice. I knew it even then.

'She wasn't . . . faithful . . . y'know,' he whispered. 'Could've stood some of them. Not the last two.'

It should have been the summer indelibly marked by the arrival of my first dog, an eight-week-old Golden Retriever, or at least the summer Kirsten began to entertain at home with her door closed, the summer she began to play spin the bottle with old friends I could not recognise from their latency period, the summer she began to kiss, audibly, a fearless hero at her school named Joe Geraghty. At the very least it should have been the summer someone explained to me why Amanda was going to go to a school for 'young ladies', as her mother had put it, and why people everywhere seemed not to need me. There was summer enough for all these things and yet it became known to all of us, solemnly thereafter, as the time George had stayed, the summer with George.

As the days progressed after his arrival the furnace at the end of the hall that was my bedroom became a confined place of whispers and drawn curtains, discarded singlets and half-eaten meals left on trays propped up on a worn leather suitcase beside his bed. George slept, or at least stayed in bed, most of the time. I learned that the stubble on a man's face can measure the change in his circumstances, and that his circumstances can change until he no longer recognises himself.

The cheerlessness of my own circumstances hit my mother one bright afternoon when she came to my room to replace an old meal with a new one. George was asleep and I was on the floor with a scattering of balsa-wood, some ice-cream sticks and glue, trying to read the instructions to one or other model aeroplane by torchlight. I whispered my concern that the glue might dry if I took it outside under the sun. It was a day or two after that my mother came home with an eight-week-old Golden Retriever from the Lady Nell 'Seeing Eye' Dog School. She told me the dog was mine but only for a year.

My father told Kirsten and me that George was not well. When he told me this his voice took on a solemnity which clarified nothing for me, nothing except that I had to be understanding of an ailment which he was not going to explain or even define. He showed very little interest in my dog or in the circumstances of Amanda's disappearance. He was so distracted by his brother that Kirsten, without the least subterfuge, was able to transform her bedroom from a Laura Ashley Garden of Eden, a haven for soft toys and meetings of a girls' only Friends of Narnia society, into a junior secondary school version of a cat-house. It was only the likelihood that George would be disturbed by the immoderate laughter emanating from the entertainment across the hall that led to a dramatic scaling down of Kirsten's late night socialising. But I could have told my parents that George did not sleep at night. He just lay there and, for much of the time, I watched him.

Once my father had discovered this for himself he and George began having regular whispered bedside conversations into the small hours of the night. Presumably they thought that they wouldn't wake me, or, if they did, that I wouldn't understand them. It was during those hot whispered nights that I heard how George had borrowed against some properties to pay for a parcel of speculative shares; minerals, gold. I heard how good it had looked. When the price began to fall George thought he would wait for the market to 'come to its senses'. And it was still going to, he begged my father to believe, but the bank would not wait and the shares kept falling. He was unable to pay the interest. It was then, without telling Peggy, that to buy more time he mortgaged their house as well. When he wouldn't answer the bank's correspondence or return their telephone calls the bank sent a representative over to the house to inquire personally. But George was out trying to raise another loan and the bank representative, a young man named Fitzspiers, ended up telling Peggy much more than she could tell him.

Peggy said nothing of Fitzspiers' visit to George but began calling at the bank to find out exactly what her husband had done with his money. The house was in George's name, the properties had been owned by his business. The usual legal niceties of confidentiality were dispensed with by Fitzspiers who must have been ahead of his time in taking the position that the debtor's young wife had a moral claim to a full disclosure of her husband's debts. Still she said nothing to George and he, frantically arranging meetings with all sorts of people at odd hours, said nothing to her.

A man cannot lose when his gain is tied to the loss of a man who cannot win. Fitzspiers could wait. A bank takes stock of its assets in units of time greater than an hour but when a man owes more than he has, he knows it by the minute, every minute. It would have been trespass had Peggy not invited him in. Fitzspiers drank Scotch, Peggy gin and tonic. They waited for George to pull up in his

Zephyr sedan. Fitzspiers' superiors regarded his patience as a sign of his dedication to the recovery of a bad or doubtful debt. Peggy regarded it differently.

She knew how to please men. George's voice endowed the word 'please' with a significance I did not quite understand. He had heard this before he had even met her, about her knowing how to please men, but as he explained to my father, when you love someone you choose not to see what you don't want to see. He asked my father if he understood what he meant. I did not hear my father's response.

'You see, she's not . . . really,' he whispered, '. . . she's not . . . a whore.' George sat up. 'It was greed,' he whispered.

'Your greed?'

'Hers. *I* didn't want that much. You're my brother. We've never needed that much . . . I didn't . . . only her. I needed her. Things had to keep getting better for me to keep her.'

'Do you believe that?'

'Don't you?'

He explained with conviction that a man is, both to the world and to his wife, the sum of his material effects, his house, his furniture, his car, his business, his clothes, and that no one could be fairly blamed for seeing it that way. Certainly not Peggy.

'You know her hair wasn't really blonde. She didn't bleach it but it was actually more like . . . gold. Really . . . it was . . . like wheat, the colour of wheat in the afternoon. It hung down as far as her coccyx so that sometimes when she was naked you still couldn't see all of her. She'd wanted to be an actress. Really . . . like wheat. Her skin was so smooth. In bed I would rub my nose along the small of her back. I died inside her. Part of me never came out, never left her. So sometimes . . . I really thought that whatever she did . . . was alright . . . because I was . . . still with her. Isn't that . . . pathetic.'

Lying still as a corpse, I listened to every word George whispered and could see it all for myself. I could hear the music, Sergio Mendez, blanketing out the sound of his car. I felt the weight of the car door as it closed shut. Then I could hear Peggy's laughter as it turned into moans. She knew how to *be* pleased too.

From that time on, I have remembered it as though I had been there. My father must have been certain I was asleep or else he would not have let his brother continue. But only the crickets interrupted his brother's whisper. Perhaps he was watching it happen as every word took the air, just as I was. I could see it all. I imagined the night hot and still as the night I was hearing it.

———————————

George had missed Fitzspiers' car but I had seen it. I wanted to warn him not to go any further, as though had he seen it, it would not have happened. I liked Peggy very much.

Her hair hung down her back. Her shoulders were bare, her back to the window. From the street the man from the bank could not be seen. Nor could he be seen from the front lawn. But we knew he was there, George, my father and me. George knew it but he kept coming closer, drawn further in horror but without anger. He could not be angry because it was his own doing, he reasoned. He had brought it on himself. Moths and mosquitoes fought each other for prime position around the porch light. With real estate, position is everything. We knew Fitzspiers was there, facing us, on his knees, his head below the window with her seated on a dining chair between him and us and the flickering insects. George could not talk. Breath left him and he stopped where he was. Having seen enough, he stayed there watching more. You could see the world from his verandah.

This was the way he told it and the way I saw it. He drank before this but he used to sleep then as well. My father was watching his brother simply shift along an old continuum. The bank did sell the house. There were papers to prove it, documents recording a 'mortgagee sale', as it was called. All that was left for him, he felt, was to make an ageing nuisance of himself at bingo or else wander the night streets in the hope of being granted permission to weep an old man's regret into the silicon breasts of a bewildered transsexual prostitute. Having lost his house he came to the house of his younger brother and there on a makeshift bed in my room he wept for Peggy. And I, separated from him by the width of a single bed and almost forty years, had no choice but to breathe in as much of his grief as I could stand and to store the rest for a rainy day.

Kirsten was sounding so much older than she had before she took up with Joe Geraghty just a few weeks earlier. If she was not with him she was attached to the telephone in an approximation of the alternative. My mother was having trouble disguising her displeasure at the relationship. Was it the intensity, the suddenness, Kirsten's youth or her sudden need to address both our parents by their first names that so bothered my mother? Or was it Joe?

Joe was at our place the evening George walked into the dining room for dinner. It would have been the first time George had eaten with us since he arrived. From the way he looked it could have been the first time he had eaten at all. His face was gaunt and the skin around his substantial beard was pale and veined the colour of an onion. The sun had started to set.

If he could have drawn from the well of empathy for him in that room he might just have been able to stay. Instead, overwhelmed by the shame that was the fruit of his former vanity, and with his face wet from tears, he turned and fled back to bed.

'George,' my father went after him. He emerged alone some fifteen minutes later, and as we ate in silence, he called Dr Byard.

'I can't do any more for him,' he said to my mother in despair. 'All that's happened . . . I mean . . . it's not *that* bad. He shouldn't be . . .'

My mother rose to steady my father to his seat at the table. From the kitchen she brought out a plate of food she had kept hot for him in the oven.

It was not *that* bad but it did not need to be. Peggy's leaving, her infidelity, the loss of his house and his business, as bad as these were, these were simply the inevitable way-stations to a place I would one day learn about.

> *O the mind, mind has mountains; cliffs of fall*
> *Frightful, sheer, no-man-fathomed. Hold them cheap*
> *May who ne'er hung there.*

Gerard Manley Hopkins knew all about it but my father did not. He kept searching for the reasons his advice and his patience were of no use to his brother.

Dr Neville Byard was somewhere between my father's age and George's age. He was our family doctor and had been since Kirsten was born. His hands were always smooth and cool so that it seemed that just by touching a fevered forehead he could reduce your temperature to normal within

seconds. Periodically we waited in our sickbeds for his lay-
ing on of hands. He had immaculately manicured fingernails, even better than my father's fingernails which
occasionally attracted a speck of grey under them after he
had been repairing something for us. His hair was shiny but
trimmed so short it looked to be painted on. He had made
the taming of nasal hair into an art-form. But more than his
personal grooming, my parents relied on his thus far unfail-
ing capacity to alleviate their anxieties over any itinerant
ailment that dared to trespass upon their children's anatomy.
He had assured my mother that baby Kirsten's apparent
inhabitation by wolves was more accurately described as
croup and would be gone within three days. (Her asthma
was to prove more stubborn.) He had put a stitch in my
chin after a collision with a renegade swing.

But by the summer of 1970, Neville Byard was no longer
the smiling but phlegmatic doctor my parents had always
appealed to when we were ill. He had changed in those last
few months between my outbreak of chicken pox and
my parents, who did not see him socially, had no way of
knowing when my father picked up the telephone to call
him about George.

My Golden Retriever barked her small dog's bark even
before the two knocks at the door. Dr Byard never rang the
doorbell, as though there was something apocalyptic and
maybe even therapeutic in the sound of a hand against
wood. He could better control the sound which announced
his arrival this way than by trusting a doorbell of some third
party's design and installation. After instructing me to put
the dog out, my father took the good doctor into the
kitchen. Kirsten and Joe had long since retired to her bedroom where Kirsten could all the better discuss how she
really felt.

Neville Byard was a more reserved man than the one my father had expected to be confiding to about his brother. I noticed it immediately. He barely looked at me, whereas usually, even when it was Kirsten he had come to see, he would always say hello to me and ruffle my hair with his wrist, never with his fingers. He had always made things better. I watched him through the kitchen door as my father gave his account of all that had happened to George and its effect on him. Before they were finished I took my pup to her basket where she curled up with me beside her, both under my bed.

Then the door opened briefly letting in both a thin shaft of light and Dr Byard with his black satchel. He came in alone and sat down quietly on the edge of my bed, on top of me and the dog and opposite George.

'George, I'm Neville Byard, your brother's GP.'

George said nothing.

'I think we've met . . . once or twice before . . . It was a few years ago. Perhaps you don't remember. Things were different for you then, I understand, for me too . . . actually very different. Your brother suggested that we might have a chat. He thinks you might be suffering some form of depression. He thought I might be able to help you . . . Actually I don't think he realises . . . quite how much . . . I know about it . . . Last year Russell, my eldest, turned twenty. Like so many of the young lads today, I suppose, he didn't possess any burning ambition to do anything in particular on leaving school. He'd had various jobs, part time, but nothing . . . nothing you could call a career. Although he had talked about . . . well, it was more than just talk . . . taking up engineering at RMIT. But . . .'

Dr Byard paused for a few moments.

'He got the letter, George, soon after his twentieth birthday. He was to report to the CES for a medical. He'd been conscripted. I wasn't there when the letter came. I was at the surgery but my wife got the mail and there was the letter from the Government addressed to Russell. He was in his room playing the guitar. Not really my kind of music but . . . you know how it is, he liked it . . . always played it, right from the time . . . pretty good at it really, I suppose. So I'm told.

'He *had* talked about enrolling not long before . . . in engineering, I mean . . . but he . . . well, he had just finished with his girlfriend. Russell had been mad about this girl, Louise, lovely girl and . . . anyway she ended it . . . I don't know why but he was heart-broken. You can imagine, George, it had been . . . what had it been? . . . well since before he'd finished school so . . . that makes it over two years and then all of a sudden . . . well I don't really know how sudden it was. I don't blame her. She was a lovely girl. But when they broke up he just . . . he didn't seem to have much enthusiasm for a while and he didn't mention engineering . . . I don't think . . . not after Louise. Then he was twenty and before we knew it we were getting his letters from Puckapunyal.

'Ten weeks' basic training at Puckapunyal. I would imagine it's the same for everyone. "Fit or dead" one of the drill instructors told him. Ten-mile runs, twenty-mile marches in full pack, constant pressure, weapons training, physical training, the whole bit. Russell said some of them would just whimper at night till they fell asleep, and if they woke in the middle of the night, once they realised where they were, they would start to whimper again. That's what Russell said.

'The drill instructors apparently got them in groups to watch each of them fire directly into forty-four-gallon drums filled with water. Then they'd take the recruits around to the other side of the drums just to show them the gaping holes where the bullets had passed through and the water was gushing out. Told them this was what they'd look like if they got hit. It served no didactic purpose, George. Prepared them for nothing but fear.'

George knew about fear.

'We saw him for the week between Puckapunyal and the infantry training centre in New South Wales. Having no skills, George, they put him in the infantry. If he had any engineering he wouldn't have gone there. If he'd had *any* engineering, even if he hadn't finished his course, he could have got out of the whole thing. But . . . he spent his week at home staying in his room, playing his guitar and crying. Broke his mother's heart. Well, there was nothing I could do by this stage. Nothing.

'He spent about a month and a half in New South Wales. I can't remember the name of the place. Was it Ingleburn? Anyway, after that his letters started coming from Queensland, the land warfare centre at . . . er . . . Canungra. Each time they moved him he left the people he'd met for a place where he didn't know anyone. After three weeks at Canungra he had a week of what they call "pre-embarkation" leave. He came home.

'Well, his mother took one look at him and burst into tears. He had lost so much weight. He looked quite different physically. Again he spent every day and every night of that week's leave at home. Except the last night. He went over to visit Louise. She'd been seeing some other fellow by all accounts. Shouldn't have gone. My wife tried to tell him that.

'From Melbourne to Richmond air base and from there they flew him out in a Hercules transport to a place called Thanh Son Nui near Saigon. I can't see my skinny son Russell in a Hercules transport but that's how he got there. From there to Nui Dat where he joined a battalion, 3RAR. He didn't know a bloody soul there, George, not a soul.'

Dr Byard ran his palm slowly over the outside of his leather satchel. I could hear him do it. From under the bed I could see the heels of his shoes, always black, and the grey socks growing out of them to beyond the inside hem of his trousers. The dog beside me sighed in her sleep. She seemed to find his tone soporific.

'Is that the dog?' he asked.

George stayed silent.

'They keep the dog in here,' he said to himself.

'I don't know about you, George, but I've got no particular interest in the Orientals. Nothing against them really. In fact I knew a fellow in medical school . . . but he was . . . not Vietnamese. Very bright, some of them. Of course, I've got no time for Communism, but Russell and I . . . I don't think we ever talked about it. Probably never talked about it with anyone . . . unless he started asking questions in the army. I suppose not. Not the place for questions, is it, George? Maybe they talked about it on the way over, on the Hercules.

'My wife talks about him all the time . . . all the time but not of him in Vietnam. She talks as though he's still home. She prefers to dwell on his boyhood, on his youthful doings. She has many stories about him from that time that I had never heard before. From *that* time—I say it but it was only a few years ago . . . all stories of Russell are of his youth. Louise too. She's come around several times, a good girl. She speaks of a kindness in him to her and to her friends before her. Of course, I couldn't have known about that either.

'But my area is Vietnam. I've found people, it wasn't too difficult, who could tell me what happened. The first day he was there, the very first day, he was sent out on a night ambush. Apparently there were certain villages known to be sympathetic to the VC. At night some of the civilians would smuggle food to them. Do you know anything about clay-more mines, George? A man of your years could have seen action in World War II but I don't know whether they were using them then. Truth is, George, I don't know much about weaponry, only what I've found out 'cause of Russell.

'A claymore mine is a command-detonated mine made out of plastic. I think it's a green plastic. It has ball-bearings pushed into the explosive, which is a paste . . . with a plasticine-like consistency. Attached to the plastic covering are electrical leads connected to what they call "clackers". The troops are able to set them up, angle them in trees or dense foliage and then, when the VC are within range, they just hit the clackers. The explosion is instantaneous.

'Some of those claymore mines had been set up in trees on the route these villagers took at night when smuggling food to the Viet Cong. Russell was part of a group lying in ambush waiting for the villagers. Now apparently they have to wait in utter silence, not a word to be spoken, not a movement. You can imagine.'

What *was* George imagining?

'Well, they waited for a few hours in the middle of this Vietnamese jungle. I cannot imagine what Russell was thinking. What goes through a young man's mind at a time like that? I suppose only those who've been through it can know. His mother doesn't want to think about it, doesn't want to hear about Vietnam at all. She turns off the news or else leaves the room. Dwells on his boyhood.

'They waited for a few hours and sure enough a group of villagers came their way, men and women, with food under their arms. They had to be VC sympathisers moving about, George, because there was a curfew over the area at that time and no one else had any other reason for being there.

In the dark it was difficult to see which of them were men and which were women. They're so skinny anyway, it's hard to tell their womenfolk, especially at night. You know what I mean. But two or three of them—and this is apparently highly unusual—two or three of them, probably women, were carrying children, babies, on their backs.

'Well, Russell and his mates had been waiting for hours but when the commander saw the children with them he let them all pass without a scratch. You see, it was hard to imagine any of the villagers taking their babies along to smuggle food to the VC. And any attempt to question them would've divulged the Australians' position. So they let them go and continued waiting. They waited another . . . it was more than two hours before another group of villagers came the same way carrying more provisions. It occurred to the commander while they waited that the babies might be some new tactic or trick the villagers had come up with to lend a cloak of innocence to their movements if they were caught. It was possible, he thought, that these peasants were using their babies as insurance. They'd had experience of nine-year-old children coming into bars where the troops were relaxing and blowing themselves up. These people are said to be capable of things beyond our imaginations, George. My wife . . . she won't hear about it.'

I knew Mrs Byard. Her husband was right.

'Having mulled it over after the second group of villagers had gone through, the commander gave the order when the next lot came through. It was a smaller group that time. One child. Only one they could see. Russell was one of the boys who hit the clackers. Not one of the villagers survived. It was his first night in the country.'

He ran his palm over his satchel again. I imagined those perfect fingernails.

'You see, George, I've tracked down men here and there from his regiment, his company, from his platoon. I've been something like an investigative journalist or a historian these last few months. It's not so hard. You've just got to be persistent, keep ringing back. People understand. It's been time-consuming, at some cost to my practice but the more you find out the more you want to know. As futile as it might seem, George, I am . . . trying to put myself, trying to take for myself the view that he had of everything . . . to stand in the middle of it. Then maybe I could be there with him.

'A night lying in ambush doesn't entitle you to anything. It's part of the job, a job he didn't apply for. The next day, Russell was at a place called Binh Ba. It's a rubber plantation the French established before the war. He can't have had much sleep. I don't know how much sleep he had but it can't have been much. They take men in this kind of sleep-deprived state, he can't have been the only one, and subject them to open warfare.

'The very next day at Binh Ba his platoon were fighting in close, out in the open. Russell was in the open . . . like a field, they said. And children were running all over the place from a nearby school, trying to run out of the line of fire. Russell was yelling at the children, "*Dung ly, dung ly*", which means "stop" and waving his hands for them to get down. He must have heard the others yelling it at the children.

'Lying in the long grass he had to get up somewhat to make the waving motion. A child was running towards him, not knowing whether Russell represented safety or danger, I suppose. When the little girl got close enough Russell stood up and caught her, covering her with his body. At that moment, the moment he stood up to catch her, that's when he was hit the first time. He fell on the little girl and, in that position, the second bullet hit him and crushed his skull. He

was, after that, unrecognisable. You know, it was probably
our own fire.

'"Too much too late," his mother says. She doesn't want
to hear about it. Says it's just speculation . . . about his last
two days. I don't agree. There's blame in there, George. She's
angry . . . angry with me. And I've thought . . . I've tried to
find something I'm responsible for in all of this . . . in his
death. I never gave him the idea for any heroics. Anyway, he
was conscripted. It was not as though he was schooled in
war stories and military adventure. We never talked about
war.

'But there is one thing I've come up with. I wonder if it's
occurred to her yet. It will. Engineering. I did encourage it,
George, I really did. But not enough. I should have pushed
him. I should have made him enrol. I should have whetted
his ambition, George. Isn't that what a young man needs?
Enrolled in engineering, he could've grown older discussing the war over dinner like the rest of us. Ambition is
what a young man needs and I did not instil any in him.
Ambition. Every man needs it.

'My wife thinks these investigations of mine have been a
waste of time. It's true Russell and I had a fondness for each
other which manifested itself . . . at a distance. But I
thought by gaining, by *knowing* as much as possible of his
last two days . . . we could get . . . closer. I don't of course
know what he was thinking but it's a terrible thing for a
father to feel that, whatever his son was thinking during his
last two days, and this is in no way reprehensible, he probably did not think of his father once.

'I know what I know, George, about the claymore mines
and the night ambush, the civilians and about the next day
with the children running in the open at Binh Ba. At least
I know what I've been told. No one can say for sure about

Russell. He'd been there for two days. He didn't know anyone. Nobody knew him.'

There was a long silence punctuated only by my dog's
gentle breathing. Then, for the first time since Dr Byard had
entered the room, George spoke.

'I don't sleep. Have you got anything to help me sleep?'

From under the bed I heard the clasps of Dr Byard's
satchel opening. He placed something on the bedside table
and said nothing more.

I was not there to hear his report, if there was one, to my
father. Had he spoken honestly, not only would my father
not have been comforted or any the wiser, but he would
also have had to recommend someone to attend on Dr
Byard himself.

The next day, fresh and unashamed in the white light of
childhood summers, seemed to possess an innocence so
pristine as to make a lie of the previous day. I was first up
and gave myself breakfast. My parents had decided to take
us, which really meant me, to the beach. The invitation was
extended to Kirsten as well and she accepted, but unlike
me, she was not completely dependent on other people to
take her to places. I was still at that stage where each unac-
companied journey on public transport was the outcome of
some fiercely contested negotiation. It was planned that we
would get there in the morning and leave by lunchtime
when the sun would be directly above us.

For a while it seemed that I had my father back. The bay
was invitingly calm and he took me out past most of the
other revellers to a sand-bank of the kind he could always
detect but I never could. It was another part of the mystery
of adulthood and I could content myself with the belief that
if I simply stayed alive for enough rotations of the earth
around the sun the scales would fall from my eyes and I too

would be able to detect sand-banks from the shore. But as an adult now in his late thirties with only three dollars, it seems that this skill, along with many others, has yet to develop.

On the way out to the sand-bank he let me ride on his back when the water got too deep but on the way back in I rode all the way. There was French cricket on the sand with a bat and a tennis ball I had brought. He even took an interest in my sand castles, which warmed me the same way a good strong sun dries you so quickly after you have been for a swim. In decades to come, this type of concerted effort with one's children would be called 'quality time' but, like for so many things, there was no name for it when I was a child.

Kirsten had gone for a walk leaving my mother to alternate between reading and watching us. But the last of my sand castles, though better in terms of aesthetics and structure than the early ones, was paid almost no attention, my parents by then being deep in conversation. Kirsten had been gone for an hour and three quarters. My father went to look for her. My parents were each equally divided between concern for her safety and anger at her irresponsibility.

In the car on the way home it transpired that my father had found Kirsten sitting in some sandy scrub between the car-park and the beach proper. She was with Joe and a few of their friends. It had about it an air of premeditation. That was my mother's feeling anyway, a feeling to which she gave some voice on the way home in a series of rhetorical questions and accusations.

What had got into Kirsten? She used to be so reliable. Didn't she see enough of Joe? Hadn't they always welcomed him into the house? Whose idea had it been to have him to dinner last night? Was this the sort of influence he had on her? Don't insult them by pretending the rendezvous was a coincidence. At least confess the first lie. She had a good mind to forbid Kirsten to see Joe. She didn't want to do it. Kirsten was forcing her with this irresponsible behaviour. Don't speak to her that way, young lady! The tone, it was the tone. It had been such a lovely morning. Why was there always someone who had to spoil it?

The dog did not come to the door as she usually did when the car pulled up. I found her in my room, not in her basket under my bed but whimpering on George's bed. I tried to quieten her because George was asleep but she whined even more. My father came in to check on George. After looking at him and feeling his forehead he told me to take the dog out of the room and to get my mother. My mother came quickly and they closed the door. Kirsten was already in the shower by then. I was on my way back to my room when my mother opened the door and ran to the telephone calling out behind her for me not to go in there. I had never seen her move so fast and wondered who she was phoning. Whoever it was, they could do nothing for her. George was dead.

He had swallowed an excess of the sleeping pills Neville Byard had taken from his satchel the previous day. When he had taken them, how many he had taken and whether the excess was deliberate my father went over and over as though something could be salvaged depending on the answer. It was possible, perhaps even likely, that, still barely touched by sleep after one or even two pills, George had within a few hours absent-mindedly taken more. It was possible, perhaps even likely, that had someone looked in on him sooner, an ambulance could have been called and he could have been saved. But we had been delayed at the beach. My father discussed all these things with my mother. Kirsten and I listened to them from the other room where the clock ticked as if nothing had happened and the barometer lied that all was fair. That's when Kirsten started crying and she would not stop even when my mother assured her that she was not at all responsible for what had happened to George.

I did not cry then. Even when the ambulance officers went into my darkened room and started clunking around, accidentally knocking my aeroplanes to the floor, lifting George onto a stretcher, putting a sheet over him so that he could have been anyone, carrying him down the passage past the kitchen into the street where the neighbours were watching; even then I did not cry. I waited.

I waited till beyond the time my parents had taken Kirsten to see George buried a few days later beside my father's parents. I was left with a neighbour but through a gap in their fence I saw Joe Geraghty on his bike in the street near our place. I called out to him in a whisper. He pulled up beside the gap in the fence and I told him where Kirsten was. He thought for a moment, said he was sorry and then asked me if I wanted a ride.

He took me to St Kilda pier on his bike and bought me fish and chips. As we walked along the pier, Joe wheeling his bike, I told him about the way George used to be, about losing his house and the verandah. I told him about Peggy and Fitzspiers, the man from the bank. I told him about Amanda and the school for 'young ladies'. I told him about Neville Byard, Mrs Byard and Russell Byard and Louise, about claymore mines, and about the rubber plantation at Binh Ba where the children ran from their school to get out of the line of fire. And even then I did not cry.

At night in my room, which was suddenly bigger since George's makeshift bed had been removed, I thought about the mints he used to bring us and whether there is anything wrong with choosing the time you die. He disappeared in the dead of summer. The bay was still, the streets almost deserted. The seagulls rested on the public statues, the mercury rose in the mouth of his dying day. What instruments we had agreed the day of his death was a fine still day.

I got up to get a glass of water and found my father sitting in the lounge room in the dark. I got him a glass of water too and sat on his lap. He told me that Kirsten and I had always to take care of each other, that we should never give up on each other. I put my hand to his face in the dark. Then I cried.

CHAPTER 3

The first time I saw Tanya she was sitting outside, on her break, smoking, wearing desert boots, white socks, black jeans, heavy mascara and the smock provided by the supermarket which employed her. She had dark hair tied back and large gold circles for earrings that made her look like either a pirate or a Romany gypsy musician. As she stared down at the cigarette burning between her fingers, ignoring the talk of her colleagues around her, I was struck by the recalcitrant beauty in what Durkheim would call her '*anomie*'. I didn't know it at the time but she, like me, had just finished high school and was waiting to see which faculty at which university would metamorphose her into a solid pay-as-you-earn citizen.

I was not about to talk to this ethereal raccoon-eyed and deeply troubling girl however much I might have wanted to. I was still a few years away from Wordsworth—*What are fears but voices airy?*—*Whispering harm where harm is not*—because Tanya had not yet read Wordsworth and it was through her that he and I were introduced. She has always known more than me, about most things. Even on our wedding day it seemed she had done it all before.

I met her formally in a checkout. It took a number of attempts, all of them embarrassing, before my courage, my pitiful groceries—cottage cheese, Vita Wheats, celery, Coco Pops—and the hard-hearted, unfeeling, trolley-pushing hordes relented or else conspired to permit us to speak. I had hoped she was going to say something smart like, 'You going to eat all that celery yourself?'—something that would open the door for the kind of wicked repartee so common in the teen movies of the day. But neither of us watched teen movies until we were much older (when Tanya took a course in the semiotics of them), preferring instead the Bergmanesque tight shot of a languid drop of Scandinavian water reluctantly leaving its metaphor. I half grunted and handed her the cereal.

'You've been here before, haven't you?' she told me.

'Mmm. Coco Pops.' I smiled back; protoplasm with small banknotes, that's all I was. She stopped the conveyor belt and the cottage cheese was left stranded between the things she had rung up on the register as belonging to me and the goods of customers not yet reached. Tanya seemed oblivious to the queue that had formed behind me. She brushed her hair behind her ear with one hand and asked me,

'What's the difference between a commodity and something else?'

I had no idea what to answer but I knew it was possible to love her, if I didn't already.

By the time the university offers came out we were already taking each other seriously enough to have become co-conspirators in what really amounted to a form of subterfuge, each with respect to our parents and the issue of our enrolments at university. Our parents, or more specifically my parents and Tanya's mother, her father having died when she was eight, were made to feel that we were consulting them about our futures but in fact we consulted only each other.

That we would be attending the same university went without saying. That was really all that mattered. Nothing was more remote to us than the future and, in any event, any discussion of it seemed futile since we knew with certainty that, whatever we chose to study at university and however intensely we studied it, we would still, in the end, be the same middle-class, socially concerned, politically inactive, foreign-film-going, wine and cheese tasters.

———————

It was late one summer afternoon a week or so before enrolment. Tanya lay on the bed while, supine on the floor, I finished her old school library copy of *Antigone*. Her mother was out and her brother and his band had either stopped for the day or were taking a break. We had just made love. There was a slight breeze which I did not notice until the battle between the dad-king and the deities was done. I closed the book and looked up at her on the bed. There was no more beautiful woman in all of Thebes.

'I thought the son sleeps with his mother. Didn't you say that?'

'Same family, different play.'

'Same playwright?'

'Uh-huh. Well, at least whoever wrote *Oedipus* used the same pen-name or chisel-name but how can anyone really be sure about anything in the life of someone who died in 406 BC? Come here, Creon, my tragic king.'

I took the book and lay beside her and suddenly with a need to be overtly theatrical, I read aloud. '*I am nothing. I have no life. Lead me away . . .*'

'I said Creon, not cretin.'
Undeterred I continued.

'That have killed unwittingly
My son, my wife.
I know not where I should turn,
Where look for help.
My hands have done amiss, my head is bowed
With fate too heavy for me.

'How could he get away with starting a passage with *That*?'

'Sophocles? No standards. The guy was a hack. For a moralist he sure got away with murder.'

I lay face down and she started massaging my back, kneading away at the sinews.

'Do you know what you want to do?' she asked.

'Tonight?'

'Yes . . . tonight and then a bit later . . . at university.'

'I've narrowed it down to seven.'

'I'm still a bit that way too.'

She shifted on her elbow and looked over me into the middle distance.

'The sky is the limit you know,' I said, face buried in her pillow.

'What do you mean?'

'Well, not to put too fine a point on it, we've both done well enough to do anything we like, Medicine, Law, Engineering, Arts, Science—whatever we choose.'

'And if we *do* put too fine a point on it, what then?' she asked.

'The point being *too* fine meaning more fine than it should be?'

'Yes.'

'Tanya, I don't understand what you're asking me.'

'Do you want to spend your life behind a desk?'

'A desk or a bench, yes. Not all of my life. I'd like to mix it up a bit each day, a bit of desk, some couch and then bed. Without condescending to the particulars, I do see the rest of my life involving the exploitation of furniture. There's no way out of it. I refuse to perform surgery on a levitating patient. All it takes is one person in the operating theatre to cease suspending disbelief and we're all on the floor looking for the instruments.'

'So it's Medicine.'

'Tanya, I don't know. I was kidding. I haven't got any burning desire to be a doctor.'

'Then you shouldn't be one.'

'Alright then, I won't,' I said kissing her on the forehead.

'Are you patronising me, Eddie?'

'No, I'm not patronising you. I'm failing to understand you. Do I want to spend the rest of my life behind a desk? What does that mean?'

'Which side of the desk do you want to spend the rest of your life behind?'

'Well, if the room is air-conditioned, I won't mind having the sun on my back.'

'You see, if you, if either of us, spends our life behind a desk, away from the door and with a chair on the other side, waiting for people to seek us out, to seek out our supposed expertise, it will have an effect on us. We will be different people because of it.'

'You're saying we'll be *worse* people because of it?'

'Yes, I think so. There will be a kind of uptight righteousness about us. We won't be able to brook disagreement. We will have to be right all the time. Now assume we were to spend the rest of our lives together.'

'Assume away.'

'How could *both* of us never be wrong?'

'Well, we could never disagree?' I suggested.

'Yeah, but that's not likely and anyway I love disagreeing with you.'

'You do?'

'Yes. I like to try to change your mind with the cleanest argument I can muster, distilling my thoughts, filtering out my emotions, just for the sake of the competing propositions, I mean.'

'But, I love your emotions.'

'You're the first person I've ever known who feels about things but can put his feelings to one side for the sake of an argument. If I can't convince you of something then you convince me. This has never happened before. I love it,' she said.

'Maybe you should do Law, Tanya?'

'Law! It sounds so dry and, besides, I really don't want to be on the expert's side of the desk playing God and losing touch with the things I most like about myself. Then there are the hours, the stress, the fatigue and likely ill health from it all. I would never want to be a lawyer.'

'You could earn a comfortable living from it, comfortable or better.'

'Yes, but I don't think I would be comfortable with that. Would you?'

And there it was that I lay on Tanya's bed in her mother's home late one summer afternoon before enrolment, with a gentle breeze coming through the fly-wire screen and the beginnings of a Creedence tune from her brother's rejuvenated band, backed into a corner. No one expects that they will one day only have three dollars.

'Would you want that, money, I mean? Do you need money and do you need to tell people what to do in order to be happy?' she continued.

'No, of course not. But I'd like to be able to eat, to pay the bills.'

'To see movies when we want, buy all the books we want,' she said.

'To eat out, just occasionally,' I added.

'I can cook and I'd teach you.'

'Okay,' I said unconvincingly, being, as I was, unconvinced. 'What about music, Tanya? I'd like to be able to buy records.'

'Of course, and I want to travel a bit too. I don't mean we should starve in a dark room.'

Whatever the unreality, immaturity and plain stupidity of this conversation I saw almost none of it. I was too busy trying to hide my elation at Tanya's projection of us together. Who cared what I did for a living?

'Eddie, were you really thinking about Medicine?'

'I'd be lying if I said it wasn't on my list but it's not at the top.'

'What is at the top?' she asked. We lay on the bed, beneath her brother's opening to 'Bad Moon Rising', waiting for my answer.

'Engineering, I think. Maybe.' She rolled on top of me, took me in her arms and squeezed me within them. The room was warm and I was floating within her embrace. Even now it is hard to think of a time when I have been happier. Sophocles fell to the floor as she undressed me. 'Tanya, an engineer implies *some* expertise, you know.'

'I know,' she said taking off her t-shirt, 'but no one will care.'

We began making love again, the curtains gently swaying

in the open window and I listened to Tanya's breathing as her brother sang in the other room: '*Don't go round tonight for it's bound to take your life. There's a bad moon on the rise*'.

Tanya enrolled in Arts and I stood in the queues for Engineering. I didn't know anything about it but I had it in the back of my mind that if I majored in Chemical Engineering I would probably be alright. I was not, at the time, aware of the extent to which my enrolment in Engineering was externally influenced rather than an act of my own volition. University itself had always been the goal. I had achieved it. Now I was free to be single-minded in my pursuit of Tanya's recommendations. We were exchanging ideas and opinions all the time. There was nothing wrong with this. It did not, of itself, necessitate any loss. We seemed to work perfectly. It was chemistry working. We were hot. In most chemical reactions heat is either taken in or given out. By the First Law of Thermodynamics, an increase or decrease in heat must be accompanied by a corresponding change in some other form of energy. I realised that I might have my atoms rearranged but there would be no loss.

It was one of those summers everyone either has or years later remembers having had: bike rides at sunset, walks along the beach, cigarettes in the long grass behind the beach huts, shared beer stolen from her mother's fridge (bought by her brother for the band), poetry, prose for every occasion, hot chips with salt and vinegar, music and an exchange of windcheaters after quiet windswept sex in the most private of public places.

Hours were spent shopping without anything ever being bought. We went from one newsagent to another reading all the newspapers and magazines together, over each other's shoulder or sometimes just side by side, occasionally pointing out something of interest. The shop that knew us best was Williamson's Cards and Music. We must have driven Old Man Williamson crazy, asking him to play us one record after another, especially since we never bought any and he knew we never would.

At first, he played our requests over the system that broadcast our taste through the shop and into the street but after a little while he made us listen through the headphones. Since he had only one set of headphones we listened with one ear each. As bad as this was, it had to be better for Williamson than having one of us listening to both headphones singing aloud to the other one. It was usually me singing to Tanya, guitar solos and all, while she collapsed on the floor with laughter, gasping for air and begging me to stop. She was probably making more noise than I did singing.

Between the two of us we would have taken a few years off Old Man Williamson's life by driving his customers away. At least he didn't have to search the length of the store each time we asked to hear something. He seemed to have all our requests catalogued under 'T'. We wondered about this. Under 'T' we found The Clash, The Jam, The Cure, The Sports, Television and Tubeway Army before *and* after they split up to become Gary Numan.

Music was critically important to us at that time. It served as a link between popular culture, and that included its *alternative* allegedly avant garde face, and the private culture we shared only with each other. Since no one we met in those early days at university read Wordsworth, Keats, Eliot, Robert Frost or A.D. Hope, we paid lip-service to humility and gave our seal of approval to anyone who listened to Joy Division.

Tanya at least met people who read. No one in the Engineering Faculty knew it was an option. I had to keep it quiet myself. But Joy Division was something else. A shy apocalyptic punk poet meets manic but melancholy pop. This was the cutting edge and I was on to it early, pre 'Love Will Tear Us Apart'. Even some of the engineers could understand this music. It was urgent and when a shy young engineering student like me heard it at the awful parties Tanya took us to, final night parties for the cast of the University Revue and for the aristocracy of student politics, I would be transformed. I knew all the words and in an instant I was dancing like someone I could never be, someone I hoped Tanya would not ever want me to be. But there I was in the dark of an urban warehouse or suburban sharehouse dancing like Ian Curtis, the lead singer of Joy Division, arms everywhere, anywhere. It was not until years later that I learned he was an epileptic.

It did not matter that I had nothing to say to Tanya's new friends, because I alone knew which of 'Unknown Pleasures' and 'Closer' was recorded first and that Joy Division came from Manchester not London, that Martin Hannett was their producer and that they were once called Warsaw. And if this sort of erudition was what it took to impress her new friends, then it was something I did not mind regaling them with. It was not that Tanya needed me to be that person but rather that her friends did. It was the only way I could interact with them and Tanya seemed to want to be with these people, not all the time, not as much as she wanted to be with me, not then. Later the balance would tip and she would need these people and when she did, it was only the recognition of the fact that was hard. Changing her perception was more than hard, it was beyond attempt and I was at least smart enough to know that.

This is how it happens. An introspective young man finds himself enrolled in Engineering, deeply attached to a romantic headstrong gypsy-girl with new friends who seem to admire nothing in him but his own admiration and emulation of an apocalyptic epileptic Mancunian Sinatra. All of a sudden you have taken on an identity. Why have you become this? Where do you go from there? *To the centre of the city where all roads meet waiting for you.* You are, more or less obviously, waiting for her all the time, either physically or in your mind. I was written and authorised by Tanya and if I had been her I would have become bored with me too.

You can dress in black, waving your arms around at parties for only so long. It wasn't that I could not see myself but that I saw myself too clearly and I was desperately unhappy with the post-industrial parody of myself that I had become. The greater my despair the deeper I was driven into the ascetic jejune persona of the romantically anti-social recluse; my overt affect suggested that I understood pain better than anyone else which is how I came to be Ian Curtis's personal representative on campus. But what pain did I have? None but the usual angst of a young man, too often drunk, hungover or tired, struggling with his subjects and with an empiricist's fear of his own inability to measure the imperceptibly increasing distance between himself and the woman he loved.

Tanya never faltered in her step, guided as she was by the light of the tyranny of the new. She became increasingly involved in student politics, student theatre and what she called 'woman's business', a term which always reminded me of one of my mother's euphemisms for a hysterectomy. None of this seemed to affect her Nobel prize-winning exam results which had her tutors and lecturers courting her and bribing her with offers of paid research work during the holidays. She was in her element and believed that everything that was happening to her was a part of the evolutionary process that turns a caterpillar of the car-park and the checkout into a butterfly of Vienna-at-the-turn-of-the-century. I saw it as a subversion of all that I had loved about her for the better part of two years and the best part of my life. I felt shut out of her cocoon. Previously I had never felt lonely when I was with her, now that was when I was most lonely.

My subjects were threatening to make a fool of me. Engineering in all its guises was difficult enough but even more difficult was to be interested in it. I had lost interest in the university and felt that it was reciprocating. Only two years at university and already I had struck a reef. I took to wearing eyeliner at certain parties in the hope that it would make people suspect that I was bisexual and interesting. Perhaps even Tanya would think I was. She had time for people with all sorts of sexual preferences now. This increased my potential competition by fifty per cent. Nobody noticed the eyeliner or if they did they were too polite to comment. Nobody except Tanya, who whispered to me one night with a kindness which really hurt that she did not think Ian Curtis wore eyeliner and that if I had ruined her applicator she would kill me.

My concentration seemed to evaporate on contact with any of the required reading and I found myself attempting to learn by rote, a sure sign of quintessential floundering. I paced my bedroom repeating with emphasis that it is movements of the earth's crust along with subsequent weathering and rock displacement that provides for mineral formation and relocation into the sites where minerals are found. I always seemed to get stuck at the fault lines. I understood what they were but it was at this point that my attention would float off the page to a world where there was no fault and the original layers of rock formed by sedimentary or chemical processes were never distorted into folds to produce synclines and anti-clines but rather that we were always inclined towards each other, as we were at the beginning.

I knew that where the folding is sufficiently severe, the rock is frequently heavily fractured, particularly where it is under tension. But equilibrium on the surface of the earth was a thing of the past. At the end of four or more hours at my desk this was all I really knew.

CHAPTER 4

The second time I saw Amanda I was not certain that it was her. I was waiting in a queue trying to decide what I would order for lunch. It was spring. There had been almost a week of hot storms but now the sun was out and everything grew unrestrained. Exams were not so far off. People took the opportunity to wear t-shirts for the first time in months. My mind was more or less divided between the act of choosing either a baked potato with chives and sour cream or a hot turkey roll, and the quiet inarticulate indulgence of self-pity.

She was in another queue, the one with wheatgerm and I was not certain that it was her. When I reached the head of my queue I was still unsure. An older woman on the other side of the counter, whose name was Muriel, asked me what I wanted. She knew me by name because I went out with Tanya and everyone knew Tanya.

'Where's that girl of yours, Eddie?'

Where was that girl of mine, no longer with me in the long grass behind the beach houses, nor at Old Man Williamson's Cards and Music. Nor was she in her bedroom, at her mother's house, with a gentle breeze wafting sleepily through her chiffon curtain. How young I was to mourn the loss of Eden and if it had been lost why hadn't the fall announced itself with thunder and lightning or at least the discovery of infidelity? But then there had been thunder and lightning just the week before. It was the violent weather that had made the blossom's arrival so stark, now that it had finally arrived. With the hayfever. I had never noticed the arrival of blossom before. What did I want? It looked like Amanda but how could she just turn up towards the end of the year like this? Surely I would have come across her before now? People do not just materialise unless, of course, we don't want them to.

'Eddie?'

'Sorry, Muriel,' I said, still thinking.

'Do you know what you want?'

'It's between the baked potato and the hot turkey roll.'

'What's Tanya having? Buy them both and share with her.'

I had not thought of sharing. There was an idea. Sharing was always being promoted to children as the ideal method of problem resolution. But then any liberties *I* could take she could take too, and the prospect of someone else with Tanya was too painful to contemplate. Was she already thinking of me in part as a brother?

'She's at a meeting, Women's Business or Drama. I can't remember. What's today?'

'Looks like you're on your own for this one, Eddie.'

I knew that whatever choice I made I would regret it. I left Muriel after opting for a baked potato. The woman who might have been Amanda was no longer in the wheatgerm queue. I sat at a table with my potato and started reading a copy of the student newspaper.

All the articles had been written by Tanya's new friends. And in all of them the authors quickly demonstrated their profound inability to think and write. These were the elites of tomorrow. I bemoaned fallen educational standards knowing that none of her friends would agree with me because they were the products of it and stood to benefit from an across-the-board decline in erudition.

Was I any better than them, flirting as I was with the prospect of failing second year? How could that have been Amanda in the wheatgerm queue? I would have seen her before. Why? Why did I have to have seen her before? If something were not a cliché it had every chance of escaping my attention. I hated myself. How many neurons did I have to waste, how many did I have spare, that I could afford to devote so many of them to Ian Curtis and Joy Division? Old Man Williamson had the right idea, file everything under 'T' and don't ever tell anyone why. Where was that girl of mine? Idle hands make the devil's work. Or is it idol hands, or ideal hands? Where was that apparition, the hypostasis of Amanda? I hated clichés. I should've had the turkey. A bird in the hand was worth the whole wheatgerm queue.

When I met Tanya in the pub later that afternoon she was in organisational mode. I could see it immediately. Something had incensed her but she had already gone beyond being angry and was attempting to channel her outrage into the promotion of some new cause and it was only a matter for me to identify the cause and come down firmly on its side.

'Hi,' I said.

'Hi, Eddie,' she replied, a little distracted.

We no longer greeted each other with a kiss, not even in private. To kiss hello was too bourgeois. To kiss goodbye was too sentimental. To kiss during sex was time-consuming and also required having sex. I wondered if she'd noticed these little things. The old Tanya would have. She would have noticed them before I had. But now she was distracted by everything. I was pleased not to have to kiss her. There was a charge in the atmosphere that I could not help but inhale. It was as though we both knew that we were on the verge of some event or conversation which would, with distillation and in the context of some greater cosmological design, ultimately become an anecdote, perhaps one I could tell Amanda.

The showman chooses well his place and if this were to be my show I was not going to offer a kiss, to have Tanya turn away to one side, briefly favouring one vista of the Nottinghill Hotel over another. Besides, in the preparation of my baked potato, Muriel, it seemed, had substituted spring onions for chives.

'Has something happened? You don't seem yourself.'

In fact she seemed someone else, several people, and had seemed them for a while.

'You've just arrived. Are you already able to discern how I seem?'

'You've just confirmed it.'

'You're right. I'm sorry. I think there's a storm brewing,' she said.

'Where?'

'Here, on campus, and I'm in the middle of it.'

'What kind of storm? How are *you* involved?' I asked.

'Because of my involvement both with the student theatre and with the Women's Executive Committee. I am probably best placed to draw attention to it.'

'To what?'

'*Hamlet.*'

'*Hamlet*? Is there a storm brewing over *Hamlet*?'

'As you know, we're putting on a production of *Hamlet.*'

'No, I didn't know that.'

'Well, we're putting on *Hamlet* and the auditions are meant to have started already,' Tanya continued.

'And you've fallen behind schedule?'

'Yes, but that's not the problem. It's the director.'

'Isn't he any good?'

'How did you know it was a him?'

'Well you said your membership of the Women's Executive Committee had something to do with it so I just assumed that a difficult director was probably a male. Who is he?'

'Anatol Lerner.'

'Anatol Lerner? I thought you said Anatol Lerner was a catch, a *find*, a dream?'

'Yeah, well I thought he was.'

'So, what happened?'

'Well, he's got some really worrying old-fashioned and patriarchal ideas about *Hamlet*. They are already evident at the audition stage.'

'Really, like what?'

'He wants Hamlet to be a man.'

I sat up straight.

'Surely you jest!'

'Eddie, I knew you wouldn't take this seriously.'

'Tanya, for four hundred years Hamlet has been a man.'

'For Christ's sake, since when has tradition ever been a justification for anything?'

'Traditionally, always. Listen Tanya, Shakespeare wrote him as a man, a young man, with all the attendant oedipal hang-ups that young men keep somewhere between the head and the heart, to the side of the dashboard, often in the glove compartment.'

'Young women have oedipal hang-ups too. Anyway, I would play him as a man.'

'*You* would?'

'I thought I'd audition. What's wrong with that?'

'I didn't know you wanted to act.'

'Well, some of the others have been very encouraging. They say I should have more than just a behind-the-scenes involvement.'

'Really? Who?'

'Some of the others. Why are you so surprised?'

'Tanya, who's been encouraging you to try out for Hamlet?'

'No one. It was my idea to try for the role of Hamlet in particular. I like the role. Why do you think it has to be someone else's idea? I don't need someone to put ideas into my head.'

'No, certainly not Shakespeare.'

'They've been encouraging me to act and I was attracted to the role of Hamlet.'

'But who is *they*?'

'You mean who *are* they?'

'That's only what I mean if there is more than one.'

'Oh, now I see. Your questions betray your own insecurity,' Tanya shot back.

'I fear she doth protest too much.'

'Eddie, don't let your balls get in the way of the issue.'

'By that do you mean either strength or courage, because if you mean it literally then, with the exception of the possessive pronoun, that *is* the issue.'

'Look how you seek to objectify everything.'

'Hamlet is a man, Tanya.'

'But there is nothing to say he couldn't be played by a woman, if she did it well enough.'

'She would have to do it better than a man.'

'Yes, I accept that.'

'Why should we assume that a woman would do it better than a man?' I asked.

'That's my point, Eddie. We shouldn't assume anything. If

everyone was free to audition then Anatol Lerner could choose the best Hamlet we've got.'

'Who might be a man?'

'Who might be a man, right. But Lerner refuses to let any of the women audition.'

'How many women want to play Hamlet?'

'Well, just me at the moment, but once the floodgates have been opened—'

'Everything will be all wet,' I interrupted.

'I should have expected an attitude like this from you, Eddie.'

'I know, because I'm a man.'

'No, because you're so *you*, not because you're a man. Don't look for the easy way out.'

'Whose looking for a way out? I wasn't going anywhere. Is there support for your bid to play Hamlet?'

'The issue isn't whether *I* get to play Hamlet. This isn't about me and, yes, I do have support.'

'All from women, I'll bet.'

'No, not only women.'

'Name the man.'

'Eddie, now you're being ridiculous, childish.'

'Can you name him?'

'Is this because you think I'm lying about having the support of men on this issue or because you're asking an entirely different question, a paranoid question?'

'Why do you question the motive behind my question when neither of the putative motives extinguishes the enquiry?'

'I refuse to be cross-examined.'

'It's too late.'

'Then I refuse to be cross-examined further.'

'I want names.'

'Eddie, listen to yourself.'

She was right, I was being pathetic. *When routine bites hard and ambitions are low. And resentment rides high and emotions won't grow. Then we're changing our ways. Taking different roads, Then love, love will tear us apart again.* Ian Curtis understood how it happens. I was getting up to get a beer when she finally gave me that which I had not wanted and had half expected for some time.

'Gerard supports me.'

Harder or softer, in the course of a normal day I would gulp a number of times. Could she not have left this as something almost said? I didn't make a practice of talking to her about engineering. The practice of any one of civil, electrical, mechanical, mining and chemical engineering has had an immeasurable impact on civilisation throughout this entire century but none of these were topics I felt would bring Tanya any closer to an endorphin-release kind of euphoria, so she was never burdened with their contemplation on my account. But my consciousness was to be assaulted by the addition of a Gerard, a Gerard whose facial hair was a perpetual parody of some cult film-inspired retro fashion, a Gerard who was no doubt found not far into infancy under a park bench beside some discarded indeterminate citrus peel and faulty prophylactic, clothed, washed a couple of times, spoon-fed the leanest venison of pretension and packed off to university to torment me.

'Gerard supports you. I see.'

'Yes. He can't see why women should be excluded.'

'Let me understand Gerard's point, Tanya. Gerard cannot see why women should be excluded from playing the part of Hamlet in Shakespeare's *Hamlet.*'

'No. In fact he thinks I would make a very good Hamlet.'

'And although he might have been a chance for the role himself, he would, in a Walter Raleigh-like act of chivalry, bow to your greater thespian inclination, no pun intended?'

'None received.'

'I understand it now. He accepts your right to be Hamlet so long as he might be your Ophelia.'

———————

For some time we had been losing heat. My attempt to supply it directly through the agency of a none-too-fine mist of stifling, ill-concealed jealousy was unfortunately not a calculated one and if it had been it would have been a miscalculation. To be or not to be Hamlet was clearly not the question here. As it is with elections in the body politic so it is with lovers that the challenger always holds the promise of everything the incumbent has failed to deliver. Tanya allowed no decent time to elapse between me and Gerard. She did not get to play Hamlet, but with the looming threat of a general strike amongst the troupe, Anatol Lerner allowed her to audition.

It was a shame that she did not play Hamlet because she would have made a great Hamlet, being at the time unaffectedly crazy and one of the great auto-eavesdroppers of my small acquaintance, right up there with me. We were always hampered in our progress, separately and together, by the irresistibility of cupping our ears to the walls of our own mind. It was always less 'what was I saying?' than 'what was I thinking while I was saying it?'

CHAPTER 5

A knock at the door came one weekday afternoon in spring while I was at home, nominally studying. The last time someone chose to knock in preference to ringing the doorbell it had been Neville Byard. I got up from my desk to answer the door expecting anyone. Almost anyone.

I had not expected her and it was so clearly her, even after all those years, that her mere appearance on the other side of the front door sent me into a child's panic which I found difficult to hide. There was no time to consider my position *vis-à-vis* her, no time to adopt a policy. She had not changed, not enough.

'Hello, Eddie,' she said somewhat coyly as I opened the door. 'Aren't you going to invite me in?'

My aunt, my uncle's widow and a major contributor to his death, as the story had gone, stood before me looking barely a day older than the woman I remembered, the woman George had seen from his verandah. Though I had changed from a young boy into a young boy in a young man's body, Peggy had remained as she had been then, a woman to whom attention had to be paid.

'Look at you, Eddie Harnovey! What a man you've become.'

I invited her in and offered her a cup of tea. She followed me into the kitchen and made us both a gin and tonic while the kettle boiled.

'Any lemon, hon?' she asked.

She promised to tell me everything but not till we were seated comfortably with a drink. But even with a drink I was not comfortable. She sat opposite me in the lounge room. By then nearly forty, her hair was still long and the colour of wheat. The long skirt she wore had a split up the side which, unlike me, gaped unashamedly. I was meant to be studying and she was meant to be anywhere else but here. Unsure of how I ought to relate to her, I toyed with the idea of asking her to leave. But that was not really an option. As George had known too well, she had a way of capturing you. She was still fascinating.

'I'm your *aunt*. Isn't that funny? Do I seem like an aunt to you?'

George had told my father that she had wanted to be an actress. In many respects she *was* an actress. Even her lost opportunities cried twice as loud as those of other people; once for what could have been and once for your attention.

'Actually, Eddie . . . I'm glad you're the only one home. I didn't know what to expect. I wasn't sure I'd have the courage to come here till I'd knocked on the door. I didn't see much of your parents after George . . . died. I thought maybe your parents . . . I don't know . . . *connected* his death to me since he died so soon after we'd split up. But there were two sides to that story, you know. I don't want to speak ill of the dead, especially not George. I'm not sure how much your parents knew about him . . . I mean how much they *really* knew or what . . . they . . . thought of me.'

Looking at her closely I saw that her hair had threads of grey amongst the wheat and that the shadows on her face remained there whenever she turned her head.

'I'm not at all surprised to find you turned out such a handsome man,' she said sitting beside me and taking my hand in hers. 'Or that you're at university. What are you studying?'

'Engineering.'

'Engineering! You were such a clever little boy, always making those model aeroplanes . . . remember? . . . And reading, all the time reading books . . . And how's Kirsten now?'

'She's engaged.'

'Really?'

'Yes.'

'That's great. Little Kirsten's engaged. I can't believe it . . . I remarried, you know.'

'Yes, we'd heard.'

'Didn't work out.'

'I'm sorry.'

'Aren't you sweet. No, I haven't had all that much luck, not as far as men are concerned. Perhaps I bring it on myself. I don't know. Sometimes I look for patterns in what I've done but there aren't any, not really. Or if there are I can't see them . . .

'Engineering, that's great, Eddie. Isn't it?' She squeezed my hand.

It seemed incredible to me that this woman who had been my late uncle's wife was sitting beside me, holding my hand. She was still so young while he, an ambassador of the Great Depression, had been already dead for half my life. She'd had more than one husband since George and she would tell me about them. I wondered if she had found occasion to visit their nephews, to hold their hands and surreptitiously edit their memories of the deserted or the dead.

She had not had children and tried unsuccessfully to disguise a sadness in the telling of this. I realised how little I knew of her. She was a near mythical character to me, part of the story of my uncle's demise. I knew nothing of her past, her childhood, adolescence. Did she have any siblings? How alone was she? Wasn't she from somewhere else, from the country? We were meant to blame her and then feel good about ourselves for overcoming it, for approximating forgiveness. But that is much easier when she inhabits only the past or else some realm of myth. She was never meant to reappear in the flesh, looking much younger than forty, and sitting next to me, with a split up her skirt, sipping alternately tea and a gin and tonic.

'Vince was in the meat trade, slaughterhouses . . . sorry, *abattoirs*. He was very attentive, at first anyway, made great money but . . . I just got bored. He was a big man's man, you know?. . . Much closer to my age than George had been and I was . . . you know . . . lonely . . . I suppose, after George. But pretty soon it became clear, as he put more and more time into expanding his business, that we were never going to get any *more* to talk about. I was just some kind of . . . what do they call it? . . . trophy wife. Well, I'll admit it's flattering to be a trophy for a while but . . . Pretty soon there's not much difference in the way you feel 'tween being put on a pedestal or being driven up the wall to be stuffed and mounted! You know what I mean?

'I thought that maybe if I could get more involved in what *he* was interested in it might sort of save things. So I started dropping into his office . . . you know . . . visiting the abattoir. I mean I really do have quite a head for business.'

'And he didn't appreciate that?'

'No, he did not. First he said I was in the way. Then, 'cause I suppose I did get some attention from the meatworkers, he started accusing me of a million different things, wild suspicions . . . million different things, most of which, you know, were absolutely crazy. Once he even hit me, right there in front of everyone. It was awful. He was screaming obscenities at me and I was crying right there among the carcasses and the offal and whatever. He was just a trumped-up butcher with tickets on himself. And he wasn't gentle, you know? That's one thing you can say about George. He was always gentle. A lot like your dad as I remember, in that regard. How *is* your dad?'

'He's fine, the same. Hasn't changed, I don't think.'

'George was crazy about him. You know? It was really sweet to see two men, brothers, love each other like that. George was a very sweet man, larger than life in many ways. Lot of love to give.'

'What happened, Peggy?'

'With George?'

'Uh-huh.'

'I don't know, Eddie. He was a gambler, you know? I mean he gambled in business, in everything. Even I was a gamble for him. Well, he felt that way.'

'What do you mean?'

'Oh, you know, a much younger woman. He was always afraid he'd lose me. He'd tell me this. And nothing I could ever say would reassure him. The thing was, as much as he was afraid of losing me, he did everything he could short of moving state to send me looking.'

'Looking?'

'Looking for something . . . or someone.'

'What did he do?'

She thought for a few moments.

'Look, I lost my mother in childbirth and my father when I was five so I was effectively an orphan. I was put in a Catholic orphanage for girls in Ballarat. Everything there was run on fear. You know? You learned not to pee your bed at night 'cause of the beating you got in the morning. Jesus might've loved me but sure as hell no one else did. Imagine a six-year-old girl lying in the dormitory in the dark freezing in the middle of a Ballarat winter, shivering in her own piss, waiting, frozen, for the morning when you know you were going to get a beating. Even if you hadn't done anything wrong the nuns, or some of them, could still scare the Christ out of you. Get up to go to the toilet in the middle of the night and you run into a bald old woman with green teeth. You'd pee yourself where you stood.

'As I got older they seemed to pick on me because . . . I don't know . . . 'cause of my hair . . . 'cause I was pretty, I suppose. I stood out. I was nineteen when I met George. He was flattering but not in that sleazy way. He was older and gentle. I thought he was God. You know? He was funny. I would've done anything for him. I used to . . . used to cut his hair and take care of his nails. He was kind and so . . . positive. He was going to lasso the moon for me, like Jimmy Stewart in . . . er . . . er . . . you know that movie?'

'*It's A Wonderful Life.*'

'Yeah, *It's A Wonderful Life.* I love that movie.'

'Did you stop loving him?'

'No, Eddie, I still love him. But he never understood that. He could never take it for granted. He felt that he had to keep showing me new things, taking me to new places. Well, I won't lie. I *am* that kind, in a way.'

'What kind?'

'I do like new things, fancy places and all that. I like them but I don't need them, not like I needed him, his attention. We already had a beautiful house and every-thing. But he became more and more obsessed with mak-ing money. He was hardly ever home, always looking at this property or that, meeting with some agent or other. And when he was home he was always on the phone. I couldn't tell after a while if it was legitimate business or gambling or even other women. He said it was all for me, anyway. I couldn't believe that 'cause I didn't need it all that badly. I was missing him. But still he was happy, y'know positive, going to lasso the moon for me and all that. Then he started losing his money. I didn't know the details till the end but he just started throwing good money after bad, throwing away everything we had, like an idiot. I was young, Eddie. I probably did start to lose respect for him.'

Why had she come to my parents' home? Was she looking for those who had once shown kindness to her? Whatever they might have said privately all those years ago about the age difference, my parents had welcomed her to our family. And Peggy had not been around to see their bitterness, particularly my mother's, towards her after George's death. But she had expressed relief to find me the only one home. She could not have been as certain of my parents' fidelity as my parents had been uncertain of hers. She sat with her cocktail of tea, gin and tonic, still provocative with a beauty that was depreciating by the minute and a sadness that she fought against unsuccessfully. She did not have these prob-lems in the long summers of my childhood. I sat there think-ing of the folly of avoiding candour in a marriage.

Why had she come to my parents' home? How do you ask that sort of thing? All that I needed was patience. George had said she could have been an actress. Which actress could she have been?

'Don's been encouraging me to sing. That's how I met him.'

'Is Don your . . .?'

'We're not married but it's . . . fairly serious . . . on my part. He's in the entertainment industry. That's how I met him. I was managing a jazz club in town. Great little place. Do you like jazz?'

'Sure.'

'Well, you must come in some time. Only, I'm not there anymore. See, Don's gone to America. He's got business there. He thinks I've got a bit of a voice. George always said so. He left some money for me to get a ticket to join him there but since he left, the price of the tickets has gone up and I can't reach him. I've got an itinerary for him but it must have changed or something. I don't know what's happened exactly. He must've had to change plans. You know the entertainment industry! But if I can get to Los Angeles on time he'll be there to pick me up. However if he's waiting and I'm not there . . . well, he might think I've pulled out on him and that's not right at all. I've never been to the United States and this could be the start of a new life for me. You know?'

'Did you come to ask my parents for—'

'Not for money,' she cut me off, 'for advice. See, I quit my job at the club and I've got to get to the US or else . . .'

'How much do you need?'

'Four hundred and sixty-five dollars. That's departure tax and everything.'

Had he been there and heard everything that I heard, perhaps my father would have given her the money, if he had it. I did not know the details of my parents' savings except that things had always been tight. Had he been there and given her the money my mother would have killed him.

And she would have been right. How long had she gone without and made do in silence just to have Peggy glide into our consciousness long enough to remind us of George's failings, and while she was at it pick up a lump sum *ex gratia* payment after ten years? My mother was due to return at any moment from a day of helping people less fortunate than her. George would have given it to her.

I had managed to save four hundred dollars. I'd had various part-time jobs and had earmarked the money for a holiday with Tanya somewhere in the country after our exams. Since that was no longer going to happen it did not seem such a big sacrifice to walk down the passage to my room, find my cheque book and send Peggy to the United States. Four hundred dollars was not a momentous sum for me and perhaps it could change her life.

'It's all I've got,' I said handing her the cheque.

'You're an angel, Eddie, an absolute angel. You know I'll pay you back as soon as I team up with Don.'

'Thanks.'

'Thank you,' she said as I walked her out to our front gate.

'Do you think you'll come back?' I asked her.

'Maybe one day. Sure. For a visit. Not really that much here for me, 'cept you of course,' and she turned to face me, put her hands to my temples and kissed me flush on the mouth for a very long time. We stood there embarrassed, she still with the cheque in her hand. I felt the stare of the neighbours, the same ones who had watched George carried out into the ambulance on a stretcher with a sheet over him.

It was hard to get back to my desk and harder to concentrate once I was there. I kept thinking of George and of my childhood memories, of Peggy's story and even of her questions.

'What about you? You must have a girlfriend, Eddie?'

I had to agree. What would I tell my parents? Would I tell just my father, all of it, then, never? Had I done something wrong, something stupid? I was just sitting at my desk trying to study. The last person to knock on the door rather than use the doorbell had been Dr Byard. But it could not have been him. The Byards were moving away. My mother had told us this one evening after returning from the supermarket. She had heard it by chance that day directly from his widow.

CHAPTER 6

That it had been Amanda in the wheatgerm queue was confirmed early the following year when she made further by then unmistakable appearances in the same queue. For eighteen summers she had kept her skin out of the sun so it had the same softness then that it had when I first knew her some half of her life earlier. I could see this at a distance. Having pictured Amanda in my mind during various and increasing gaps in my sleep since Tanya and I had formally agreed that she would leave me, there was an anticipatory edge to the new year. It wrestled with the melancholy Tanya had left with me for safekeeping along with the tender inscriptions in books bought for me, handwritten notes secreted about my bedroom and her scent on certain once-favoured items of knitwear.

What had become of Amanda? What was she like now? I put off confronting her for a while, not so much out of regard for Tanya but out of regard for all that Amanda might conceivably come to mean to me. I applied myself to my education with the naive and futile vigour of the chronically immature, simulating interest at every turn.

Coming to know her lunchtime habits, I transcended

myopia to examine her from a distance before I was driven, as I knew I soon would be, by residual curiosity, lust and suppressed loneliness, to confront her in a disciplined and virtuoso performance of 'the casual me'. Her hair, being still that of a model in a shampoo commercial, long, strong and with a gleam enough to reflect whatever an admirer might want to see in it, had not changed from childhood. Her eyes, round and perfectly defined, had not changed and nor had her skin, since the day her mother had forbidden her to know me.

But the shape of her body was now womanly. Have I been conditioned to notice the synclines and anticlines of a woman's body or is it innate? I never judge women on the basis of their surface geometry, though neither can I pretend a lack of interest in it. But it is not the puerile interest of erotically disenfranchised men overly attached to their rain-coats, sad and dangerous men who learned certain limited things in their deprived schoolboy salad-dressing days and never anything more.

Unfortunately for all that it says about me, Amanda Clare-mont's breasts, or the thought of them, have always been a comfort to me. To say anything else would be less than hon-est. I do not look women up and down when I talk to them. I do not mentally undress them. I do not want them given nor denied opportunities in any sphere of human endeavour on the basis of their appearance. But Amanda's breasts, their firmness, strength of character, their propor-tion; I cannot be indifferent to them.

Because I had already seen her on a few occasions in the wheatgerm queue and because, height, curves and breasts aside, she seemed identical to my little playfriend of pri-mary school, it did not seem entirely unreasonable for me to come up behind her, place my hands over her eyes and say 'Guess who?' But it was sufficiently unreasonable, fool-ish and unworthy of the portent with which I wished the moment to be impregnated for me to jettison the idea, storing it instead for a second or third meeting with any children of her brothers at one of the, no doubt, many occasions to which I would be welcomed, finally and after all, another chemical engineer (almost), like Mr Clare-mont, the patriarch with the perfectly starched white shirts.

'Hadn't I grown into a fine young man,' her mother would surely remark as though I was not there. Amanda would blush a little and gently rebuke her mother for speaking *about* me rather than *to* me but I would, with full magna-nimity, reassure her that I was not in the least offended.

'Will it be Scotch?' Mr Claremont would beam from across the room before shaking my hand firmly. 'Although I don't remember it being your drink when we last saw you.' Everyone would laugh heartily at this and one of Amanda's brothers would be dispatched to the bar to pour me a Chivas Regal from a bottle the size of a small car. I would remark on the bottle with a quiet understanding of spirits, double and single malts, retail versus duty free prices, and Mr Claremont would explain, via a humorous anecdote involving the Ministers for Foreign Affairs and Trade, Min-ing and the Arts and Communications, how it was he came by the ostentatiously large bottle.

This would trigger recollection of an article I would have read concerning recent changes in the direction of government policy on joint ventures in off-shore mining operations and the extent to which approval is to be required from the Foreign Investment Review Board. Amanda, sensing the topic turning to politics, would attempt to pre-empt anything controversial being discussed by suggesting her father and I agree to disagree.

'Nonsense,' Mr Claremont would cry good-naturedly, his voice filling the room, adding that it would seem he and I were in perfect agreement and that she should not give me the impression that he was an uncompromising old so-and-so. In any event, he would be more than happy to hear my views on a range of related topics. Her mother would call out from the kitchen that we had better finish talking 'shop' because she would like us all to come to the table.

After dinner, between coffee and port, Amanda's nieces and nephews would ask me to play Twister, Monopoly and Go Fish with them. Amanda's brothers and sisters-in-law would tell the children to play quietly on their own and leave me in peace but I would join in with the children just for a while and hear Amanda's mother say confidentially to Amanda from the kitchen that I seemed very good with children.

At the end of the evening, one of Amanda's nieces would ask me in front of everyone whether I was going to marry Amanda. I would answer that I might have to if the little girl herself was unable to marry me. Everyone would laugh again and Mrs Claremont would say that it looked as though the little girl already had eyes for me.

That night in bed Amanda would tell me that her family adored me, each for different reasons which she would then outline. She would start once again to ask questions about Tanya and seek reassurance that Tanya never meant very much to me. I would tell her that she really would not want me to be the type of person who spoke ill of past lovers and that it was the present with which we should be concerned. This would not fully placate her but she would fall asleep in my arms nonetheless. The scent of her hair would slowly carry me off to sleep and I would have difficulty remembering the time before we were lovers.

On the day I chose to speak to her the wheatgerm queue was long, perhaps the longest it had been since the university was founded. Although I was then in third year, I had never myself been in this queue before. Just thirty feet from where I had been buying my lunch for two years, I felt quite out of place. I knew that I had to be in front of Amanda in the queue or she would buy her lunch and leave, for wherever it was that she went to eat, before we had a chance to speak. The plan was to wait for her to arrive and join the queue. I would beg someone to let me in some distance ahead of her. From there I would procrastinate, check the chalk menu for as long as it took, go through my pockets for change and let others behind me go ahead of me in the queue until she was directly behind me, next in line. At that point it would just be a matter of a chance sighting and, 'No, it couldn't be . . . Amanda? . . . Amanda Claremont?'

The young man who I asked to let me into the queue in front of him wanted to discuss it with me. Was I really so hungry that I would be willing to pay someone for the opportunity to eat alfalfa a little sooner? It was not a question of money but he wasn't prepared to believe that there was not a story to my urgent need to get in ahead of him. Was it a competitive thing? How much money would I be willing to part with in order to get ahead of him? Was it a part of a bet? He said that he would be prepared to leave the line altogether or even start at the back again if I would tell him the real story behind my desire to be in his place.

No one had ever wanted to be in his place before.

Without identifying Amanda, by name, description or by the school to which we had gone, I indicated why it was I wanted his place and how I wanted to engineer a re-meeting. He pressed me on the socio-economic differences between my family and Amanda's that would lead Mrs Claremont to terminate our friendship at such a young age.

Amanda was gaining ground in the queue. I was afraid she would see me or hear our conversation. Had it really been just a question of income differential or did my family lack certain social graces? Had my father ever been in trouble with the law? Had my father interfered with small children? Now the curious young man was letting people pass him. He said that this whole thing fascinated him. The girl's mother sounded like a nightmare. The girl had to be very beautiful to warrant all this trouble. Which one was she, the one behind us? Was I more ambitious than my father? How does one measure these things? He agreed to give me his spot and even to leave the queue entirely on condition that he be permitted to watch from within earshot. Since I had no way of stopping him from standing wherever he liked anyway and since Amanda was, by then, only two or three places behind us, the deal was done.

A little flustered, I continued according to plan. Please serve someone else. I'm still deciding. There she was, also looking up at the chalk menu. I could breathe her. She was wearing a tight white t-shirt, not at all grubby, and instead of felt letters spelling her name across her chest, she had those life-affirming breasts. The outline of her nipples and their brown pigmentation was clearly visible. Then I turned and spoke my first adult words to her.

'Excuse me, you may not remember me but—'

'Yes, I remember you,' she said sharply and without sentiment.

Yes I remember you could have been said a number of ways but it was only said one way, as though because of me Amanda had been sentenced to nine and a half years in her mother's kitchen to help prepare one unconscionably long evening meal and was now cutting me off like the unpalatable end of a Lebanese cucumber. The woman serving in the wheatgerm queue, who was not Muriel and did not know me, had grown impatient, perhaps with me, perhaps with the vegetative nature of her professional life, and insisted that I order without further delay.

Unfortunately there was a surplus of lentil burgers and when I ordered one it was ready immediately, leaving me no opportunity to discover what it was that Amanda had remembered about me that compelled her to demonstrate such an eschewal of nostalgia. Things had not gone according to plan. I had not gone through my pockets for change while waiting and now it hit me, with Amanda ordering her lunch beside me and the outraged keeper of the watercress, her reptilian hand stretched out toward me, that I did not have the money to pay for my lunch. Amanda was leafing through her smiling purse as my penury dawned on the cold-blooded woman, who asked me with rejuvenated contempt, 'Haven't you got any money?'

At this point the curious young man, having seen my distress from a distance, came to bail me out. He acted so swiftly it is hard to describe the shape of my shame. But Amanda had gone. The curious young man's name was Paul. He bought me lunch, agreed that Amanda was worth any strategem I was clever enough to think of, and invited me to come out with him and his girlfriend Kate. She was a History major and Paul was finishing an Economics degree which, he insisted, did not define him. His major was Economic History. The two of them got me through the rest of the year, listening to bands, seeing movies and laughing the anaesthetising laugh the lonely among us need more than food.

They had been together for some time but I don't think Paul ever told Kate the story of Amanda and me in the wheatgerm queue. If he did she never mentioned it. And this was all it deserved because at the end of those drunken nights on the threadbare floor of their rented house, the glasses left for the morning, when they had made up the couch for me, my shoes scattered upside down like derailed toy derby cars, it was Tanya I whispered about even as they closed the door.

CHAPTER 7

It was in Kate and Paul's living room, perhaps the most appropriately named room I had ever visited on a regular basis, that I opened a letter which I knew from the handwriting was from Tanya. This was the first contact in almost a year. It had arrived that day but, unable to read it on my own, I drove it over to their place early that evening to read it there. Paul was still at the library and Kate was working on a tutorial paper which she thought she might one day turn into a book. It was really the tentative title of her paper that had so taken her—*The Good and the Hurt: Irish Catholics in Australia.*

When I told her about the letter she gave me a beer and put the kettle on. After her tea Kate suggested I read the letter alone. She would be in the next room with Archbishop Mannix, Mary McKillop and B.A. Santamaria, when I was ready to discuss it.

> *Dear Eddie,*
> *It's trite to ask how someone is in the second line of a letter or to express a hope that they're well but I do wonder how you are and I do hope that you are well. It*

feels a little strange writing to you like this but it would
probably feel even stranger talking to you. I often wonder
what you are doing. Sometimes I think I have seen you
see me at a distance on campus and turn away. I never
thought that would happen.

My main purpose in writing to you is to offer my com-
miserations on the passing of Ian Curtis. I am sure you
have been deeply affected by it. I would have written
sooner but I only found out about it recently. Nobody
told me. Gerard doesn't really have his finger on the
pulse of the Manchester music scene although I know
now it's gone beyond Manchester. It would be naive to
ask why Curtis did it. He was a poet and, you'll see,
we'll still be talking about him ten and twenty years
hence. I am truly sorry.

> *Every best wish,*
> *Tanya.*

P.S. We're putting on a production of Antigone *by that*
old Greek hack. Of course, I'll be playing Hamlet!

With the help of Kate and later Paul, and after a few read-
ings, I managed to construe from her letter everything I
needed to nurture the fragile buds of an old hunger. But
whereas Kate said I should respond, Paul counselled me to
date other women. The letter, or at least my favoured interpretation of it, an interpretation I would still maintain Tanya
had left open, acted as a tonic of sorts and I did find it
within myself to approach my degree with renewed vigour
and to ask out other women.

I was catholic in my tastes, seeking the company of both
the good *and* the hurt, the educated, the uneducated, the
post-educated freshly unemployed and the barely educated

yet never been out-of-work fair and happy milkmaids. For a time it was the last of these I enjoyed the most. As long ago as the seventeenth century Sir Thomas Overbury spoke of that type of woman. *She knows a fair look is but a dumb orator to commend virtue, therefore minds it not. All her excellencies stand in her so silently, as if they had stolen upon her without her knowledge.* But after a while you get tired of that.

Then there were the pseuds; the pseudo-intelligent, pseudo-fashionable female equivalents of Gerard. This was the type of person who would say, 'Tell me what your house is like and I'll tell you who you are.' My house was exactly, to the atom, like my parents' house. I was still living with my parents and I suppose this did bespeak something of who I was. It was getting close to a time when I was going to have to make some decisions about my future. But one way or another I was going to be alright. After all, I was going to be a chemical engineer. I talked to a career guidance counsellor who advised that a master's degree would not be wasted. Counsellors really have the best jobs, no care and no responsibility.

My parents had begun to talk of retiring and of moving to south-east Queensland, a great place to rehearse for death. But I could not yet see them as old, trading in all their shoes for just one pair each of the white silent kind, the type specifically designed to minimise the wearer's perception of reality as he strolls across his patio holding a glass of chardonnay. Is this what they had been dreaming of, is this what they had worked for all their lives? They didn't know either.

Reviews of books and films that Tanya had written started appearing in the real world's newspapers, the ones where the weight of the editorial is leavened by the insubstantiality of the advertising. Paul said she was 'one to watch' but he knew that I had known this since I was seventeen. I generally agreed with her reviews so I took to only reading the books or seeing the films she thought were exceptional. She would be dismissive of her success, I knew, and it would not be entirely false modesty. She had her own idea of success, an idea of which I had a far from perfect emotional grasp. It enabled her, still an undergraduate, to deal confidently with editors while I was still unable fully to comprehend the concept of being or not being on the advice-dispensing side of a desk.

What the hell was I going to do with my life? How was it that I found myself on the way to devoting the least tentative of my daylight hours to the design and operation of large-scale chemical plants, mining operations and oil refineries? Contrary to a conceit among educators, most students do not have a passion for the careers they choose. Once I had been led away from the powerful side of a desk, keeping options open and avoiding embarrassment were all that mattered. Chemical engineering was preferable to the other branches of engineering because it drew more heavily on chemistry than on physics and mathematics, which I wasn't good at. I saw it as the cutting edge of the industrial revolution, albeit the first, not the second, with which I was ill at ease. It had given Amanda's family a standard of living high enough to exclude me from her life.

I was essentially just an egocentric pseudo-intellectual slob motivated only by facile romantic notions that were contrary to the very world-view upon which my future profession was predicated, but it would take two words to say what I did for a living.

The nights and days of eating, sleeping, dating, laughing with Kate and Paul, of attaining a required narrow technical understanding of things narrow and technical and a general understanding of things general, meant that I had eventually to become the plaintiff and Gerard the defendant. With Kate's encouragement and Paul's lack of discouragement, I finally responded to Tanya's letter.

On the telephone she sounded older at first and for the initial minutes of the call I wished I'd never met her. We circled around each other, sniffing, trying out different inflections in ways we could not entirely control. How were we? Fine thanks and you? The studies? Not bad, we supposed. Family? Pretty much the same. (Her father was still dead.) A book? Haven't read it. Really? You should. Okay, I will. Liked your reviews, well done. Thanks. You're welcome.

It was not till a second conversation that I enquired after my successor and all that he was doing for her. He had already self-administered the noose and I just had to let them play it out. I could sense it. Coffee? Yeah, okay. When was a good time?

She looked as sullenly quixotic as ever, dressed partially in black but with a magenta scarf and a hint of caprice. She was, coming out of it, adorable.

'Like the purple scarf,' I volunteered.

'Thanks. *Fuchsia*, actually.'

'Where'd you pick *that* up?'

'What, the scarf?'

'No, "*Fuchsia, actually*".'

By the time of our next meeting, Gerard had been dispatched to another era. After that he and all his muscle tone were spoken about disparagingly from a languid horizontal position without my having to say a word in a scene out of French new wave cinema: crumpled sheets, wine and a half-open window in the blue light of night.

'He didn't read. When he thought I'd made a good point he'd tell me that I'd hit the snail right on the head. He thought the Tallis Scholars were experts in Jewish prayer shawls. He's very bad with abstract concepts. And words. Abstract concepts and words, that's all. And logic and history. And irony. That's all. I had to convince him that it was no coincidence that the only Australian prime minister ever to drown in office had a major municipal swimming pool named after him. We went there not long before we broke up. In fact it might've hastened it.'

'Really, what happened?'

'I told him he belonged in the shallow end.'

'That's really cruel, Tanya.'

'I know. Do you think I'm a bad person? I hadn't expected him to get it.'

'Yes, I must say he always struck me as a strictly single entendre sort of guy.'

Gerard had really been of tremendous service to me, not merely (or perhaps I should say not *even*) in the Nietzschean sense of *whatever does not kill me makes me stronger*, because I do not believe that. Experience tends to suggest that whatever does not kill you is simply acting in concert with whatever does. We live in an age where all the utopias can be found on top of each other in the bargain basement bin of ideas and the last we heard of Superman he was trying to settle out of court.

But at the time of the renaissance of our relationship there seemed to be so many things to be thankful for and Gerard was one of them. Where would I have been had his genes and environment been kinder to him? Even so it was hard not to feel puny some nights beside my own memory of his physique let alone all that Tanya had to remember. Gerard was one of the first people I knew to deify cardiovascular fitness and make regular sacrifices at the altar end of the bench press. He was not in need of athletics or sport of any kind to change or make his life. His parents had plenty of money and had sent him to all the right schools, again and again. He just couldn't remember why.

It must have seemed strange for Tanya to meet Kate and Paul and find them such an important part of my life when, pre-Gerard, they had not existed. I had expected a certain reticence, perhaps more between Tanya and Kate than between her and Paul. Men love meeting their friends' new girlfriends. They can dance around them for a while, breathe them in and try to impress the girl but everybody knows it doesn't really matter much and that this is just a free introductory offer of charm on each of their parts. But while Kate and Tanya hit it off immediately, Paul was slower off the mark, playing just a fraction hard to get. And I liked this. He was a good friend.

He knew how much she had meant to me and how much her sampling and discarding of things had hurt me. That I had done it too and that it was necessary for both of us he also understood which is partly why he did not hold out for very long. Tanya is difficult not to like and I don't think Paul ever actively disliked her. By the time Tanya and I moved in together both Kate *and* Paul were ringing up to speak specifically to her. But for a time, the time it takes a leaf to hit the ground, or the time for which a small child can hold its breath, he was just marginally reserved. Like the best of friends he did not just want the best for me. He also lived a little through me. And of course, he had seen Amanda.

CHAPTER 8

Neither of us had ever lived with anyone before, not anyone with whom we were more significantly connected than
through DNA and with whom we were by virtue of that
connection entitled, required, to do our worst to and in
front of. Living with a partner is more fraught than you
might imagine if you have never tried. Whenever I had idly
thought about it, which was not very often, it had seemed
to me that all possible problems could be resolved merely
by negotiation and accommodation. Some people squeezed
the toothpaste tube from the middle, some squeezed from
the bottom. If you love someone enough surely you can
meet halfway? And if you can, your children will not be able
to blame you for their instability and you can regard yourself as a success, at least in your personal life.

   But the naivety of this is breathtaking. The scope for mis-
understanding, at which you gape open-mouthed after dinner
and before bed whilst the tiniest food particle is already irre-
trievably breaking down and turning your breath into an
irreconcilable difference between you, is astronomical. In the
morning, every word you speak and every kiss you bestow
cannot help but be putrid. If you had any inkling of how

offensive your breath had become you would agree with the only conclusion that could be drawn from your partner's behaviour, namely, that you are the world's greatest misfortune and should be taken out the back and hurriedly put down.

It's not just oral hygiene, there's the rest of your body. In the days when you lived apart you often knew in advance when you were likely to have to perform acts of the utmost intimacy and you could prepare accordingly. Living together, however, there is often no warning. If you do not have confidence in every orifice and protuberance it can affect your sexual performance and that, in turn, can affect everything else in the world.

From your body, moving outwards in the direction of other people, there are your clothes. How do you wash them, how often, what time of day, in hot or cold water? Do you mix whites and colours, ever, by accident or by design? What happens if you inadvertently destroy the favourite garment of the person who shares the bed with you every night, the person whose percussive nocturnal respiratory habits might or might not rival your sulphurous breath at times when you are ill and she knows it first. If you destroy the Taj Mahal of blouses, and she asks you how you could be so stupid, where is the answer? You really do not know how you could be so stupid. You are part-way through a Master's degree. You tutor bright young first-year students. If only you could answer. But you cannot think, so sleep-deprived are you, having not slept since before the Ice Age because the rhythm section of a tiny reggae band has sublet the space between your lover's Eustachian tubes and her throat so that it can rehearse between the hours of one and six each morning without disturbing the sleep of someone who matters, namely her.

———————

In the mornings, particularly in winter, we had got into the practice of waking early and holding onto each other for dear life. Falling in and out of consciousness, snatches of dreams whispered themselves in the dark like hallucinated newsflashes, repressed and unasked for, somnambulant. Occasionally reality reported in, coming in the form of the raw material needed for a later dream about rent or the gas bill. Still only firmly in our twenties, we suspected that we had begun to live the rest of our lives. There was nothing wrong with our lives, no present fear or horrible imagining which we were unable to shake off by lunch at our respective places of work. I had completed my Master's and was working for the Federal Department of Environment. Tanya was tutoring in the Politics Department where various academics were courting her by inviting her to write a Master's thesis in their particular area; 'one to watch', as Paul had said all those years ago.

We were there together. There was money coming in, not a lot, but more than we had as undergraduates doing shift-work at bottleshops, supermarkets, cafes and convenience stores. We were blue-chip tenants, the ideal unit, a young tertiary-educated childless couple both in employment, one car and no apparent impediments to our potential. We should have been eager to interrogate the future, grabbing at its collar, but at six o'clock in the morning, particularly in winter, as the barely audible radio told us the things somebody must have wanted to know, we would hold onto each other for dear life. Not that either of us had ever been prone to leaping out of bed to greet the coming day, not even Tanya who might have been expected to be a day-greeting leaper by people who did not really know her. But this was something else, something we couldn't even put into words, not at that time. There was a reservoir of grey which seeped toward the surface in the small hours of the morning. Small dread is grey. Anxiety is brighter. Grey dread seeps. Anxiety is chauffeur-driven to the centre of your consciousness. Perhaps it was a recognition or acknowledgement of the unmitigated indifference of the world, not merely to your well-being, but to your very existence.

Young people choose each other in the hurry-up years when perfect certainty is matched only by equally perfect disregard of the non-immediate future. They have no idea what they are looking for and no idea that that which they choose some triumphantly stupid night is not it. But just as most of us learn instinctively to negotiate the dynamics of riding a bike in gentle ignorance of the physical laws that make it possible, so without realising it, we seek someone who can foster the now-you-see-me-now-you-don't self-esteem you picked up for a song on the ground floor of your parents' lives. Instinctively you feel that someone else's confidence might mate with yours and that for once your offspring will not be the only beneficiaries of the union. In the first light of a winter morning the union might produce something else; two people might have a better chance of coping with that which is always there but which cannot be named and which usually disappears when the light is on.

'Eddie?' she whispered.

'Tanya.'

'Eddie, are you awake yet, sweetie?'

'Uh-huh. How did you sleep?'

'Okay. How about you?'

'Sleep?'

'Yeah.'

'Well. I slept well. How are you . . . in yourself?—Tanya—Tanya, are you awake?' I thought she had woken me and then fallen back to sleep but she was considering her answer.

'Ordinary.'

'A *bit* ordinary?'

'*All* ordinary.'

'Completely ordinary.'

'Yes, I think so.'

I paused before responding.

'You know it won't last. It'll go. There's no basis for it and you know that. You know that already and it's still half dark. Things are okay.'

She paused.

'I know they are.'

We hung onto each other. I knew exactly what 'all ordinary' meant because I had felt that way. She knew that I had and rather than smelling it in each other and fleeing for our lives we hung onto each other for them. We had a shorthand, a language other people did not have. Each of us had experienced attacks of the 'all ordinaries'.

The truth was that although I knew well the small grey ordinary feeling which lies in ambush some mornings and tries to keep you from getting out of bed, Tanya suffered more frequent bouts of it than I did. I was still partly buoyed by my job, not by the fascination of it (I was reading other people's on-site or field reports and then summarising them), but by the regularity of it.

How good it felt being required to turn up somewhere at a specified time to do something, albeit more mundane and less taxing than anything I had done at university, and to be capable of it. To be capable of it, isn't that what everyone wants? Each day, I would say 'good morning' to the same people I said it to the day before. There were 'in' jokes about the standard of the coffee, the football tipping competition or somebody's outrageous tie. Lunch was snatched hurriedly from the place next door, a little cafe where the

regulars from the department joked with the proprietor and
his staff, small jokes, small business, small change, but these
people were immensely important to each other. It might
be that none of them was aware of their importance, each
to the other, and it took me a little while to realise it myself
but with each 'good morning' they were reminding each
other, just slightly, who they were and that they were there.

Continuity in the form of running jokes (never really
funny) or repeated themes (never really deep) is reassuring
even to people who might not know how much they derive
from it and who might even deny that they derive anything
at all from it. If they who have never been without it really
understood its cohesive force, they might willingly pay a little more for locally made goods and ignore the prophets of
neo-classical economics who consign us to isolation in our
homes, forgotten even by ourselves. *Look out, here comes the
man with the dangerous ties. Stop expressing your personality
through your ties for Christ's sake. You'll get locked away.* What a
relief to find the mundane so rewarding.

It was nineteen eighty-five, the first year of the second
Reagan administration, the sixth year of the Thatcher reign
and the second year of what many would later regard as a
look-alike Labor government in Australia. Early that year,
Tanya had a strange experience first thing one morning as
we lay in bed. As usual the radio news woke us. Tanya lay
there listening to the reports of bushfires raging up and
down the eastern coast, the prime minister's limited offer of
drought relief, the sport and the weather. And then she
heard herself being mentioned. It was not by name, but she
insisted it was her they were speaking about and in the most
personal way. I had missed it, still half asleep, but we caught
it again an hour later. It was the first time we had ever heard
a report of share movements on the radio and it took a few

days and a call to the ABC to realise they were broadcasting international and local stock market movements. The Australian measure was known as the 'all ordinaries index', an index of the price of ordinary shares, those without special voting rights or other privileges attached to them.

'So, let me get this straight. They're telling the public hourly every day, whether overall, on average, the price of the shares in all the publicly listed companies in the country has gone up or down?' Tanya asked in astonishment.

'Yep. That seems to be it.'

'Eddie, why should the price of shares rise or fall?'

'Confidence.'

'What do you mean?'

'Well, if investors believe, for example, that something bad is going to happen to the company in question no one will want the shares in that company and if no one wants the shares then their price will fall.'

'But what if the investors are wrong? What if nothing bad is really about to happen to the company and their belief is based on faulty reasoning or superstition or just the prospect of a lot of other people panicking?'

'The price of the stock will nonetheless plummet. It's all to do with the investors' confidence, valid or not. The price of a share will rise or fall depending on whether the majority of investors think the majority of investors think it will rise or fall.'

'And *who* are the investors?'

'Theoretically, anyone.'

'But, in reality, who are they?'

'Mostly large institutions, banks, insurance companies, wealthy people who want to become wealthier. Or ordinary people with a little money to invest for an uncertain future.'

'How come you know all about this and I don't? It's not a science.'

''Cause I'm a man and even if we're not interested we're expected to know these things like we're expected to know how to play cards, how cars work and how come the moon doesn't fall out of the sky and crush everyone as they dream in their beds.'

'Why *doesn't* the moon fall out of the sky and crush everyone as they dream in their beds?'

'Confidence.'

Tanya predicted that the day would come when people would have difficulty remembering a time that movements in the stock market were not reported more frequently than the road toll or air pollution indices. She was right. The interminable repetition of sharemarket indices thereafter did not leave us unchanged. I would call Tanya at work and get a quotation of her 'all ordinaries index'. Was she up or down today? 'Slightly up but coming off a low base,' she might say.

CHAPTER 9

One evening I came home from a full day of saying good morning to people and found Tanya sitting cross-legged and barefoot in the living room watching a children's cartoon on television with the sound turned down. She had been crying. I threw my briefcase on the floor and fell to the ground to meet her, to hold her as tightly as I could in my nine-to-five sanctioned arms. It was summer and most of the staff in the Politics Department were still on one sort of leave or another. Tanya was a woman of leisure for another two weeks and, in the quiet and colourfully flickering glow of a small mouse's repeated torment, I could see that everything had gone all wrong. She said that she was sorry she was in the state she was in and I listened in silence as she recounted the triggering event in her day.

'I went over to Kate's today. Paul had the car so she couldn't pick me up and I took the bus. I was walking home from the bus stop. It was quite hot this afternoon and I was looking forward to getting home, putting my feet up to Vivaldi or perhaps that new Lloyd Cole and having a glass of iced tea. It was then that I came upon this young woman in a motorised wheelchair. She would have been in her late teens or early twenties. She was just sitting there, stationary at the bottom of that steep rise before Dandenong Road.

'As I approached her she saw me and started to make inarticulate hurt noises like the sounds of a wounded animal. They became louder and louder and more insistent, more exaggerated, a grotesque pantomime of all our private ceaseless sleeve-tugging pain. She clearly wanted me to stop. I could see that. I had to stop.

'With clumsy limited hands and arms which stopped and started violently without her seeming to want them to, as though she always had to work around them, she took what looked like a small calculator the size of a paperback out of a little zipped bag, like one of those chairbags primary school children have at the back of their seats to store things they've made. She stopped me, both with the sounds she made and with the message on her little computer. She seemed to want to talk to me, right there in the street in the middle of the afternoon. But I didn't want to talk to her. I was angry with her, Eddie. Her existence was causing me pain. I didn't even want to look at her. I told her I had to go.'

Tanya started to sob. It was difficult to understand all of her words. I told her to take a deep breath and wiped away some of the tears from under her eyes with the smooth of my hands.

'I told her I had to go but she motioned to me in something like a wave that she didn't want this, that she didn't want me to go, and she typed again for me to stop. Then she started to type that I should, or rather that she *wanted* me to help her. She seemed to expect it. It was as though she was angry with me for not having understood and helped her already. She looked so utterly pathetic with that stupid bag attached to both her and the chair like it was part of each of them. I asked her what was wrong. She signalled on the calculator-thing that her name was Rachael. I noticed how long and thick her black hair was. Like mine. Once she had given me her name, in that instant, it became hard to be angry with her. I said hello and told her my name and she repeated it, typed it in.

'She said that the wheelchair was out of power and that she couldn't make it up the hill. I wondered how she would have made it up the hill even with power. I wondered why she hadn't thought of this when she left wherever she had come from. I wondered where she had come from, why they'd let her go out into the hot streets so unprepared and helpless; now and always pathetic with her fucking chairbag. I wondered why she'd had to choose me, to pick on me, to target me.

'I asked her what she wanted me to do. Was there anyone that could be called? Yes, her mother. She gave me her mother's name, Sylvia . . . something . . . I can't remember now. She typed her mother's name and phone number and I took it down. But I couldn't just leave her there sweating into the bag so I offered to push her up the hill to Dandenong Road. She let me know she'd be alright from the top of the hill.

'It was hard work pushing her up the hill in the heat. She was so heavy and there was something so unendearing about the way she had asked for assistance, almost demanded it. But I felt guilty for resenting her and, anyway, how was she meant to act? It was hot and she was stuck as she must often be, stranded, alone, humiliated, vulnerable, dependent on the degree of development of the next person's super-ego just to get from one place to another. Why should she feel like apologising? She should hate all of us who waltz so blithely around the parquetry dance floors of our lives stumbling only every now and then, as she sees it, and over often imagined and trivial exigencies like the state of our skin, or our hair and over our eternally unsatisfied acquisitiveness and our occasional half-remembered loneliness. She should hate us all passionately for the trivial nature of our obsessions, self-obsessions which prevent us not only from helping her but even from mourning over all that she could have been and all that she is not. She should hate us at least as much as I hated her halfway up the hill to Dandenong Road.

'Partly in pique and partly in an attempt not to be patronising, I spoke to her as though she was anyone else, the person she was trying to be, an equal. Ultimately, however, she *did* want me to acknowledge the inequality of our situations for otherwise I'd have just as much reason to use all my guile to get her to push *me* up the hill.

'We reached the top and I pressed the button at the traffic lights. When it was green I pushed her all the way across Dandenong Road. It was too hot for reason, for humour, for people, too hot for anything meant to be dry. The road signs were wilting and we didn't speak until we reached the other side. Then she told me that she was on her way to visit her aunt. She had been on her way to visit her aunt when the battery gave out.

'Think about it, Eddie. I did. I tried to picture her aunt, what she would look like, the cool drink she would have for this girl, Rachael, when she got there. Would she hold it for her, tipping it into her mouth? What would they do? What would they talk about? It would be difficult for the aunt to understand her and when Rachael left to go home again or back to wherever it was she'd come from, the aunt would look around at her porcelain bric-à-brac and feel ashamed of the relief she always has when Rachael leaves. And Rachael, not yet fully down the drive would know this is what the aunt was feeling because when you have lived a couple of decades and people are relieved each time you leave a place, you cannot miss it every time.

'She said her aunt lived "just down there" and that she would be okay. Could I call her mother to explain what had happened and that she was on her way to her aunt's place? She asked me to get her mother to call Ann.'

'I thought you said her name was Rachael?'

'I know. That's what she said. Maybe her aunt's name was Ann. I don't know. Anyway I got home and rang the number she'd given me. A young woman with an accent, Turkish or Arabic, maybe Israeli, answered the phone. I asked for Rachael's mother, Sylvia . . . whatever her surname was . . . Sylvia *Leitch*, that's it, Sylvia Leitch. The young woman said that there was no Mrs Leitch living there, just her and her husband, no older woman. I explained what had happened with Rachael. "Oh," she said, "that explains it. We've been getting these inarticulate calls that we couldn't understand. It must have been this girl asking for her mother. But we've been here for six months or a bit more." '

Tanya let out a deep, slow breath against my chest. She cried until the tears were no longer able to meet the demands of her sadness and, in defeat, they nestled together in resignation at the back of her throat.

'Tanya, I understand how touched you are by the . . . utter wretchedness of this young woman's—'

'Rachael.'

'—of Rachael's life. But it doesn't involve you personally. Why are you crying?' I asked her gently.

'I know it doesn't. I don't know why. It's . . . the strangest thing. I just don't know.'

My drip-dry shirt, white at the first 'good morning' was creased now and wet down my chest. When I looked down

I could see the top of Tanya's head resting against one half of my diaphragm with my tie on her ear and the now damp cotton-polyester cover over the other half of my chest. My skin was pink through the shirt. I ran my fingers through her hair and rocked her slowly without saying a word until her breathing returned to normal. The silent mouse on television was still taking a beating but he never died. Not once.

'Thank God you're home.'

'Of course I'm home,' I said quietly in a way that I realised I had always wanted to say something like that. I could feel her eyes follow me as I went to the television to turn up the sound to give the mouse a voice and then into the kitchen where I picked up the telephone.

'Who're you calling?' she called but I pretended not to hear.

'Who did you call?' she asked when I returned after finishing and turned the mouse down again.

'Your mother. I invited her round for dinner and she accepted. I told her I'd pick her up at seven. She wasn't busy.'

Tanya put her arms around me and kissed me just below the ear.

'That's so nice, Eddie.'

'I thought that after that story you might feel like seeing her. Maybe we should take her out, maybe we should celebrate?'

'Okay. What should we celebrate?'

'We should celebrate our lives thus far. And our getting married. I want to marry you. We've been living together for nearly ten years, so we're probably compatible. If you want to marry me we only need to choose the restaurant for dinner. You can tell your mother over dinner but not before we've ordered. Does she like Chinese? Everyone likes Chinese.'

Now she was smiling.

'What about *your* parents? Let's invite them for dinner too,' she said, hugging me and running her hand down my back. I looked at my watch.

'I don't know, Tanya, my mother would have most of the potatoes already washed by now.'

CHAPTER 10

The third time I saw Amanda I was on the second floor of a department store in the city, a little lost, trying to find my way to men's formal wear on the fifth floor. She had been in kitchenware and had meant to be there. There was nothing there that she needed. It was not as if she had found herself at some earlier time in her kitchen or dining room cursing the absence of salad servers, a fruit platter or a decanter that could be purchased in kitchenware (although the really good decanters, the best ones, were kept on another floor in crystal, not far from silver, she told me). But, as I was to learn, she did need something, and she was there gathering her thoughts.

I was there to be measured for a dinner suit and had an appointment with a woman Tanya had spoken to whose name, she insisted, was Maria-Men's-formal-wear-can-I-help-you. Tanya would have come with me but she had back-to-back tutorials to give. She had even started giving guest lectures which she said made her feel a bit like the barrel girl who gets to host the show every now and then when the regular host is unavailable. We talked about the possibility of introducing a 'wheel' segment into her lectures, 'Tanya's Wheel', in which she might give away our car or a weekend for two staying with my parents at the home they dreamt of on the Gold Coast, looking at baby photos of me and going to Seaworld. This would make her lectures very popular with students and that was a much faster road to academic advancement than publication which required so much original work and so much liquid paper.

Amanda's hair was a little shorter than it had been the previous times I had seen her. She wore a matching aubergine jacket and skirt with pleats that would have made her mother proud, and under the jacket, a white ribbed singlet. Her face and her skin around the singlet were still as smooth as a little girl's and she had brought along those breasts to mortgage your house for. Even after I had seen her and registered that it was her, I pretended to the world and to myself that I had not seen her. I had an appointment. I was getting married. Amanda Claremont did not really exist. I should have known that by then.

'Eddie? Eddie! Eddie, is that you?'

I had to think about that. All I knew with certainty was that it was really her calling out, and not just to any member of the crowd in the department store willing to answer to my name, but to the favourite climbing tree that was too high, the porchlight so attractive to moths, the rocking chair on the verandah she was suddenly not allowed to rock on anymore, the fig jam she tasted only once or twice, enough to remember it fondly before forgetting; yes, it was me. Me. I was twenty-eight years old and six weeks away from marriage, a chemical engineer by profession, by trade, by accident, one of those good-natured young educated people for whom rented accommodation was invented, a person who did not so much look back fondly on his

childhood as who still dipped into it in his spare time. It was
not over. It was just that younger people had more time for
their childhood. But I was too busy playing other roles for
the most part by then. None of them was remotely connected to Amanda Claremont.

'God! I *thought* it was you,' she said kissing me on the
cheek.

'I'm not God. You've mistaken me for someone else.'

'Eddie, you haven't changed a bit.'

'I have so. I'm much taller than I was at nine. You see, you
have mistaken me for someone else.'

'We've seen each other since then, surely?'

'Yes, briefly at university,' I conceded, taking the opportunity to look at the floor.

'I remember.'

'That's pretty much what you said then too.'

I cursed her freshness, her svelte beauty, her clean designer
scent, her girl-next-door hair to which no doubt an advertising agency had the sole rights. And I cursed the well
inside me the depths of which she plumbed each time I saw
her. That time I was a stand-up comic. I could not help it.
I wanted to say something, anything for a laugh. But neither of us was laughing.

'It's so good to see you. You won't believe this, Eddie,
although I hope you do, but I've been thinking a lot about
you lately.'

'Oh you have, have you?'

It was meant to sound like Bogart and for the first couple
of syllables I think it did. But as it hung in the air I realised
it was more like Moe from the Three Stooges, right before
he says 'A Wise-guy, eh?' and knocks Larry's and Shemp's
heads together. My palms were moist and their heads would
probably have slipped out of my hands. I was neither

Bogart nor Moe. I was Curly Joe. I was Zeppo or Gummo, more likely. I was Pete Best, Syd Barrett and 'Jerker' Jenkin, upon whose back Jezza jumped to immortality in the 1970 Grand Final.

'Eddie, have you ever gone through a period in your life where your past keeps getting replayed in your mind at all hours, day and night?'

'Yes, but they said I'll get over it.'

'No, I'm serious Eddie, I don't quite know what it is, although I could guess, but lately I keep thinking about my life, my family, my past all the way back to my childhood. I've been thinking about you too, that I've really wanted to talk to you. Is that funny? It's as though I missed something, some particular richness in my life and I'm all the poorer for it. It might sound silly, I know, but it keeps coming back to me—you, that is.'

'Perhaps it's something you ate?'

Sid Caesar would have fired anyone who gave him a comeback like that. If only she *had* sounded silly, but it sounded like the sort of thing some people wait their whole lives to hear, like 'you've just won the car', or 'the house is now yours', or 'you know I'll never leave you'.

'Can we talk, Eddie? Do you mind? There's so much I want to talk to you about. Am I embarrassing you? Just a quick coffee perhaps, you're not in such a hurry are you?'

'Amanda?'

'Yes?'

'Is your life a mess?'

We drank coffee-flavoured milk water amidst the sturm and drang of food-trolley collisions, the crying of small children and the heightened fluorescent realism that is a department store cafeteria. She worked in administration and coming from what was to me an egregiously wealthy background, she was forced to earn more than she needed. It was that time in her development for her to be angry with her parents and all that remained was for her to figure out exactly why. I suggested that although I was late for an appointment and she was even later with her disapproval of her parents, I was quite sure that I could help her blame them for most things, particularly her mother, whom I blamed for the Cold War and cholera. Even after her cameo ignore of me at the university (I wanted to ask her about that), I could not be angry with Amanda but I was already late for my appointment to be fitted out by Maria-Men's-formal-wear-can-I-help-you. I told her that I had to go, that I was sorry if I appeared rude and that the coffees were on me. She followed me to the cash register.

'Eddie, I'd hate to lose touch with you. I'm serious, I really would like to talk to you. Not just about our childhoods. I'd like your advice on a few things.'

'You've no reason to put any store in my advice, Amanda. What do I owe you?' I said to the cashier with sudden embarrassment as I looked in my wallet

'What's the matter, Eddie, don't you have it?' Amanda asked.

'No. No. It's just that I always . . . well, I usually put everything . . . I was going to put everything on the credit card today 'cause I didn't get to the bank. Excuse me, can I put this on the card?'

'Credit card, sir?'

'Yes.'

'I'm sorry. There's a ten-dollar minimum limit.'

'Let me get this one, Eddie. You can get the next one.'

CHAPTER 11

The next one was lunch about ten days later at a restaurant not far from where I worked. It was, she said, time for her to tell me everything, or at least the most recent part of everything. I was uncomfortable just being with her. I had only ever eaten there once before, at one of the secretaries' going away parties. This secretary had had several going away parties—twice when she got pregnant, once when she took long service leave and once when she had her hysterectomy. It was for this last one that someone, feeling like a change, booked a table at this particular restaurant. Afterwards, everyone agreed it had cost too much for a hysterectomy, especially when you consider what we paid for each pregnancy.

'Look at you, Eddie, a chemical engineer!' she said smiling and then again, 'Look at you!'

'Well thanks, Amanda. Really. Don't look at me. Look at you.'

She told me she'd had a series of unsuccessful relationships, unsuccessful in that they had ended. She was working as the personal assistant to the chief executive officer of a mining company, or at least that was the way I translated her description of what she did. This was in part what she wanted to talk to me about. I thought that perhaps she might have thought she could get some privileged information with respect to the mining company out of me. After all, I *did* work for the government. I had even voted for it. But if this was her game she was out of luck. All I knew that she didn't know was that I was not privileged to any privileged information. It soon became clear however that my position in the Department of Environment was really not what this was about.

'I don't know where to start. It's sort of hard . . .'

'Amanda, you don't have to tell me anything if you don't want to. In fact, don't tell me anything even if you do.'

She took no notice.

'We work in groups at our level, in teams. I work very much with the CEO, as part of his group. Tell me if I lose you. Our group had been working on a pretty major deal—you've probably read about it—but that doesn't really matter, not for our purposes.'

'*Our* purposes?'

'It was one of those on-again off-again mergers . . .'

'Yes, the on-again off-again mergers—I think I read about that.'

'I was doing a lot of liaising, you know, *their* lawyers, *our* lawyers, that sort of thing. Eventually after weeks of long hours, late nights and weekend work, the deal was finally done. The group went out to dinner to celebrate, you can imagine the scene, an outrageously expensive restaurant, a lot of drinking, back-slapping, the whole thing. Are you with me, Eddie?'

'Yes, an outrageously expensive restaurant.'

'Right. So we're at the front in the bar section at first, having celebratory drinks. There's a lot of back-slapping and I'm talking with the company secretary, a man called Roger

Schauble—a nice enough guy in his late forties or early fifties, and all of a sudden I notice that he has his hand on my knee. Can you imagine? Imagine how I felt!'

I could *only* imagine how she felt. I had not touched her knee since I was nine.

'I didn't know what to do. I mean, I've had men make passes at me before.'

'Really?'

'Oh yes,' she said letting her drink moisten the inside of her neck, 'but they've always been gross drunken slobs, really revolting men.'

'All of them?'

'Most of them, yes. But this was different. Roger Schauble was a nice guy. He had two kids from a first marriage and was now in a relationship with another woman. There had been rumours that he'd been ill. Anyway, he left his hand there on my knee. I didn't know what to say and I just pretended not to notice. After a little while everybody got up to go in to dinner, to the table. Roger removed his hand and escorted me to the table. It was a long boozy dinner, wonderful place—I should take you there—at the end of the dinner the CEO, my boss, starts calling cabs for everyone. It turns out that Schauble lives in North Fitzroy. Well, I live in North Fitzroy too. My boyfriend has a place there.'

'Your boyfriend?'

'Yeah. Gerard has his own place there. He runs an import company from the ground floor and we live on the top floor. Anyway Roger Schauble finds out I live in North Fitzroy and offers to drive me home. He really shouldn't have been driving. We'd all had too much to drink. His car was parked in the underground car-park back at the office so we walked from the restaurant back into town. It was almost 2 a.m. but it wasn't far and, anyway, it wasn't as if I was on my own. We got into the car and I directed him to where we live. He takes me there, reverses tentatively into a spot outside our place and turns off the engine. I thanked him for driving me home and he reaches over to kiss me. I let him. I kissed him back. We sat there kissing for quite a while.'

'Why did you?'

'I don't know. I was embarrassed I suppose. It happened suddenly and I didn't know what to do. We'd been drinking. As horrible as it is to admit, older men . . .'

'Have always done something for you?'

'Have always told me what to do.'

'But he wasn't telling, he was asking.'

'Telling, asking, begging, it's the same thing given the situation.'

'The situation?'

'An older man, a powerful man, a nice guy, a man I had spent time with, worked with, wants something of me. I didn't think. I thought I'd stall for time.'

'By kissing him?'

'Not much of a plan, was it?'

Being judgmental must surely be one of the most joyful activities known to the species and it is cruel that other animals are denied this pleasure. But judging or perhaps prejudging her was likely to be the only pleasure I was going to get from this. Even just the mention of the name 'Gerard', especially coming from Amanda, the perfect mythical remembrance of things past, had me spluttering into my napkin. From there I was off on an endless journey loaded with premonitions of Amanda *and* Tanya, both of them together with Gerard in some kind of sick domestic arrangement in a North Fitzroy warehouse, all of it too horrible to contemplate. Except that I had already begun to contemplate it. I thought better of being too hard on Roger Schauble, the company secretary, an older more mature family man who already had one ex-wife to his name. 'Ex-wife' allows at least for the possibility of a return to relative calm, a beach after a shipwreck. I could probably do business with him.

'I'm sorry, Amanda. I am sounding judgmental. I don't mean to.'

'No, you're right,' she said with the instant self-reflection of a 1970s telemovie. 'I've been really stupid. And there's more.'

'More?'

'Yes. Can I tell you?'

'Well, yes, if you think it will help anything, but really, Amanda . . .'

'You're very sweet, Eddie,' she said taking my hand before continuing. 'I got to the front door and fumbled in the dark for the right key. Roger was still out there in the car, in the dark. I crept inside and, as quietly as I could, slowly, trying not to disturb anything, I got undressed, garment by garment, placing them softly on the chair, listening out for Roger's car. I remember just standing there, naked, watching Gerard sleep, terrified that Roger was still outside, that he wasn't going to leave. Eddie, you have to imagine it.'

Why did I have to imagine it? Why was I even there? Was it all a random event? Was it chaos? Was chaos random? I thought of the 'butterfly effect'. A butterfly flutters its wings somewhere in Japan, there's a tidal wave off the coast of Miami and a few years later some meteorologists from MIT win the Nobel prize. Every nine and a half years, it seemed, I see Amanda. I was to be married to Tanya in four and a half weeks and Amanda had the tips of three fingers of my right hand inside her palm. The mischief of Japanese butterflies is proportional to the proximity of my marriage.

Somewhere in Princeton, or maybe Cambridge, there are some very dedicated people on the verge of discovering what Amanda Claremont was doing in my life, orbiting me every nine and a half years. I have been completely unable to help them and they, just like Amanda in her effort not to disturb the admirably sinewed Gerard, grope about in the dark comforted only by the knowledge that any physical system that exhibits periodic behaviour should be predictable. For all I know, they might have already formulated the dynamical equations and just not be aware of my sensitivity to the initial conditions of our first meeting when I was nine and a half.

'I carefully slipped under the covers and into bed so as not to wake Gerard but he was only half-asleep. He turned over and placed the palm of his hand on me softly, just below my belly button. I remained deathly still. Gerard is a very solid man. His palm is heavy. Can you imagine! I still had Roger's saliva in my mouth and Gerard is stroking me with a heavy hand. I couldn't sleep. I felt just awful. I wondered what it meant about my feelings for Gerard. What do *you* think it means? I really appreciate you helping me like this, Eddie. As I said the other day, I've been thinking a lot about you lately and I've been wanting so much to talk to you, to see you, to see what you look like. And now here we are! I mean, what were the chances of running into you out of the blue like that the other day?'

'About one in nine and a half times three hundred and sixty-five,' I replied, wondering at the vacuous Mills and Boon cum *Vogue* world Amanda belonged to, and how you go about joining.

'I didn't sleep at all that night. I suspected that Gerard knew something. Not that there was really anything for him to know. But I was incredibly edgy. In the morning I felt he was looking at me in the shower. Perhaps I was paranoid. Do you think I'm an idiot? The next day at work Mr Schauble calls.'

'Mr Schauble?'

'Roger Schauble.'

'Oh yeah, the company secretary, sorry.'

'Roger calls and wants to see me. I told him I didn't think it was such a good idea. We were both involved.' Amanda sipped her wine.

'With other people?'

'Both involved with other people and had to work together and everything.'

'And everything?'

'I told him I thought it was against company policy.'

'Was that a joke?'

'I don't remember. I was stalling.'

'Again?'

'Yes. He told me to check the manual.'

'Was *he* joking?'

'I don't think so.'

'Does the company have a manual covering that sort of thing?'

'Yes. It covers everything from Alluvial Mining to Maternity Leave all the way to Zirconium.'

'Zirconium! I'll bet that section of the manual gets a thorough thumbing.'

'More than the page on Maternity Leave.'

'So was he joking about you checking the manual before giving him an answer?'

'I don't think so. A week later he called again to ask how my investigations had gone.'

'The manual?'

'Yes. He said that he'd wanted to call me every day but had kept putting it off. He said he'd been afraid. He sounded so vulnerable, Eddie.'

She squeezed my hand.

'Did you stall for time?'

'No, I agreed to meet him that night, just for a drink. I'm a fool, I know. Do you think badly of me?'

Did I think badly of her? It was more true just to say that I thought of her. I had, on and off, for almost twenty years. But what did I actually *know* about her? We had lost touch since my parents' wardrobe.

'No, Amanda. I'm not being judgmental, especially not about you, my dear old friend.'

'Wait. There's more. Drinks became dinner and over dinner he told me he had feelings for me, strong feelings. He said he'd had them for a long time and was never going to say anything but the fact was—he was ill. He asked if I'd heard the rumours. I said I hadn't; I lied. I don't know why. It just seemed like the best policy. He was so sweet. He has cancer, Eddie. I felt terrible. Then he grabbed my hand and kissed it.'

'Where?'

'In the restaurant, sitting just like we are now.'

'No. Where's the cancer?'

'In his prostate. He said he was due to go into hospital and that he wanted to go to a hotel with me. Just once. I don't normally do this sort of thing but it seemed like the right thing to do, the moral thing.'

'So you went?'

'We took a room at the Regent.'

'What about Gerard?'

'Eddie, it meant nothing to me. If I didn't say anything to Gerard, if he didn't know or doesn't ever find out, then where is the harm? I really mean that.'

'That's a question, Amanda. Do you really mean to be asking me this question?'

'I have done a good turn by a sick, probably dying man. I have made him slightly happier without hurting anyone and it was such a simple act. I have never done anything like that before. I don't know what I was expecting but it's really quite straightforward. No one at reception asks any questions about luggage or anything. It's as though the entire hospitality industry is giving you a wink. Have you ever done anything like this?'

The closest I had ever come to doing something like that was agreeing to have this lunch with her and permitting her to take my hand.

'I'm not sure I see it that way, Amanda,' I said removing my hand. 'What we're dealing with is a question of trust. I'm not sure that the issue is simply a matter of what he does or doesn't know?'

'Who?'

'Gerard.'

'Look, it might be wrong but, in the heat of the moment, that did not seem to be the issue,' she confessed.

'Now I'm really not being judgmental, Amanda—'

'I just knew you wouldn't be.'

'Really?'

'Yes,' she said taking my hand in hers again.

'Well, remember I'm just thinking out loud, coming at it cold, as I do, 'cause I can see your point, but—'

'Would you like another drink? I'll see if I can get the waiter's attention. You were saying . . .?'

'Getting back to Gerard, as a concept I mean, any particular act of infidelity or unfaithfulness, which the other person might not ever know about, is a breach of an agreement with the other person—'

'You mean Gerard.'

'Yes, in this case . . . Gerard . . . he's the other person here and while he might not ever know about your . . . indiscretion—'

'We were discreet but go on . . .'

'Well, you've explicitly or implicitly agreed that he—'

'Gerard or Roger?'

'Gerard, he is your partner until further notice and he expects you not to be with—'

'Not to sleep with?'

'Not to sleep with anyone else. I haven't put this very well at all have I?'

'Not really, Eddie. Although listening to you, I felt a bit sorry for Gerard for the first time ever. You see the truth is we're having a few problems, nothing to do with Roger. Sadly, tragically, Roger is dying and won't really enter into it.'

'What if he doesn't die?'

'He will.'

'But if he doesn't?'

'Then I'm in deep trouble.'

'Why?'

'I told him I'd marry him.'

'Really?'

'Just to give him hope, Eddie. The patient's attitude is a very important factor, perhaps even critical. I've read some of the literature and even heard from some of his doctors.'

'How do you know who his doctors are?'

'He told me. I've been on a party line when he's called them. There's consensus. He won't survive the financial year.'

'That's terrible.'

'Yes. Isn't it. But my problems with Gerard are a separate matter. Sometimes I think they're separate from Gerard.'

'What do you mean?'

'I don't know, Eddie, not exactly anyway. I seem to be having problems with everybody, well, with my family anyway. I feel very removed from them. My father started making a lot of money when I was in my early teens, you've probably read about him, and from then on we saw less and less of him. The more money he made, the bigger the houses and the dinner parties and we'd just get wheeled out for show and to pass around the hors d'oeuvres. I'm serious. One Christmas when I was sixteen my mother threw a Christmas garden party for my father's business associates and their wives and a man there, an investor or important shareholder—I forget his name—*fondled* me, in front of his wife and in front of my father. My dad just laughed.'

'Your father—he's a chemical engineer—isn't he?'

'By training yes, but he hasn't worked as a chemical engineer for around twenty years or more.'

'Hasn't he?'

'No, he's a mining investment adviser, he's on several boards of directors and he has his own consultancy business. Plays the market mainly. Mergers, acquisitions but all from a consultancy base.'

'Really?'

'Yes. He says consulting is the way of the future, sell your knowledge and experience. No overheads.'

'Right.' Suddenly, I started to cough, fit-like, inexplicably. People at nearby tables looked around at me with the mildest irritation.

'Eddie, are you alright?'

'I'm fine,' I said in a wheeze. 'It'll pass. Something went down the wrong way.'

'But you'd finished eating. Do you want a drink?'

'No. No. I'm okay but I'm going to have to get back to work. Didn't realise the time . . . We're so much older now.'

She took her bag from under the table and from her purse she took out a business card for me and a credit card for the waiter. I was breathing normally by the time I stood up and when I went to shake her hand she used my outstretched arm to pull me closer and kissed my neck about where my jaw and ear could share the experience equally.

'Now, you'll call me, Eddie? There's still so much to say. You haven't told me anything about *your* life. And it's your turn to buy *me* lunch—or dinner if it's better for you.'

CHAPTER 12

There were, in all, three visits to Maria-men's-formal-wear-can-I-help-you, the third with Tanya to collect the altered dinner suit and accoutrements in which I was to be married. So full of good tidings and optimism was Maria that Tanya and I left her the deposit with such hope that my attenuated first appointment for a fitting was all but forgotten. From then on Tanya took it upon herself to organise everything. I was just following orders.

We were married by a civil celebrant in the old Mint Building on the corner of William and Latrobe Streets opposite Flagstaff Station. I had suggested everyone take a train there to reduce our expenses, but the humour in the remark was not made welcome.

It was a small wedding. Tanya described it as quaint but it was small, pathetically small. I had asked Paul to be my best man, not so much because I considered him to be my closest friend, although perhaps he was—men who grow up in times of peace (and in times of war, but the aetiology is different) often find themselves short of close friends. I asked him to be my best man because Tanya was fully occupied as the bride and could not be both.

My parents stood so close together, holding one another by the arm, it looked as though they were one being, a small and fragile one. My father wore his blue suit with a white carnation and his shirt was so crisply pressed he might have been anyone's father. He had taken the day off work. My mother was an animated floral arrangement. She wore a stupid little hat that made me want to protect her. As happy as I was to be finally marrying Tanya, to see my parents, joined to each other as they were, and so newly small, gazing upon us both with their radiant eyes like shiny wet marbles, filled me with a profound sadness that made it unbearable to look at them. But they had got me there. From childhood they had got me there, with small walks and vanilla slices when it rained, hanging onto my father's tie, and he in his woollen cardigan, her story-telling, their nocturnal monitoring of the influenzas they promised would go away soon: they had taught me how to love Tanya. Nothing my sister and I had done at any time in our lives had ever displeased either of them for more than an hour. They loved us to within an inch of our lives, but within that inch there was room to move, to grow, to make mistakes and then come back. My mother had always been active in voluntary organisations, working for them quietly without ever shaming those she knew who could not give of themselves without needing payment for it.

'Some people cannot do it,' she once told Kirsten and me.

'Because they have too little?' my sister had asked.

'Yes,' she said. 'Or else because they have too much.'

Now she stood in the old Mint Building for my wedding, unencumbered by religious or political convictions and physically attached to my father. They had wanted so little and yet had always managed to get a little less.

After the ceremony we all went back to Kirsten's place

where her two children were waiting as super-heroes for the occasion, Batman and Batman, two of the same to keep the peace. Tanya's mother had prepared marinated chicken wings and my father found more praises for them than any chickens have a right to expect. Tanya took him outside onto the verandah for a while. When they returned she had her arm around his shoulders and he was trying to fold his handkerchief with one hand and return it to its pocket. With Tanya's brother, Marty, Paul shared the responsibility for alternating the Creedence, Supertramp and Chopin records every twenty-two and a half minutes while Kate cut her pavlova and her orange cake inequitably for all. A third cake, an iced chocolate cake, had not made it to the reception. In her haste she had iced it incorrectly and was not willing to serve a cake that read *Eddie and Tanya—Just Marred*.

We put off the honeymoon because Tanya had papers to mark and because the landlord was planning an inspection in the next few days. Besides, we were unable to choose one Flag Motor Inn on the Mornington Peninsula over another. Such was their uniformity, it really came down to the smoothness of the table-tennis table of one over the charm of another's serving of rice bubbles in the morning through the gap in the door. There was really nothing in it.

The landlord and the real estate agent visited us one evening while we were eating our take-away chicken curry. After they left we decided to try to save for a deposit on a place of our own where strangers would have to be invited to come and see us living like refugees (albeit not from another place).

———————

The decision coincided with what was tantamount to a promotion, perhaps even a vote of confidence in me from above. This made the saving of a deposit seem more attainable but more than that, there is something about a newly married man who has just been promoted and given a pay rise, however trifling, that makes bank managers want to stand up and sing the national anthem. This is what we thought as we left the bank manager's office one ripe autumn morning but in hindsight it was not just the leaves which were gold; this was the mid-eighties when people found it as easy to borrow money as they would find it to lose their homes a few years later.

The promotion was a mixed blessing. It meant my duties were quite radically altered. I was required to travel a lot and prepare on-site reports for someone else to read. The travelling itself was not bad at all. I got to say 'good morning' to people in parts of the country I had never been. But it meant leaving Tanya and neither of us liked that. She said that as soon as I left home the place started to look a mess. Socks walked out on each other citing irreconcilable differences and stains took such advantage of Tanya's innocence in the natural sciences that she was certain the cottons were conspiring with the synthetics to humiliate her.

It also meant checking in on the fluctuations in the 'all ordinaries' index from far away where it seemed that much harder to talk the market up. Tanya's mother had been spending more time with us since we were married and they often ate or watched television together while I was away. The difficulty was that Tanya's mother could watch nearly anything, while Tanya wanted to read, which her mother found a little anti-social.

'But you're not studying anymore,' she would say.

Tanya's mother had been an actress before she was married.

This was where Tanya had got her love of the theatre and particularly of Shakespeare. But her mother had also been a dancer, maybe even a showgirl, and in her advancing years the rumba was more fondly remembered than any soliloquy.

'Eddie, you've got to come home,' Tanya had said over the phone.

'What's wrong? Are you alright?'

'Everything's wrong. I miss you, I want to put my mother in a home. I can't think of a topic for my PhD thesis. I'm not interested in anything anymore. Our house is too small. We can't afford the mortgage repayments. There's talk of interest rates rising to seventeen and a half per cent. I want to have a child . . . should I go on?'

'Sure. The Department's paying for the call.'

'I hate the university. I want to be a florist. I have to have a PhD to keep my position. I'm stupid. I sound hysterical and I hate myself for almost everything I've just said and the way I said it.'

'Sweetheart, you mustn't hate yourself for wanting to put your mother in a home.' There was silence. 'Tanya, I'm joking. You just need a bit of a hug of the kind I'm going to give you in two days when I get home. There's really nothing wrong.'

'What if I can't wait two days?'

'Why don't you call your brother?'

'He doesn't understand anything.'

'No, but he could fix the right speaker in the lounge room.'

'What if he can't even do that, Eddie?'

'Then we'll put him in a home with your mother.'

'Eddie, will you please take this tantrum seriously.'

'I'm sorry, sweetheart, when I get home we'll have children and put your family in a home. I promise.'

When I got home, Tanya was out. I deposited my luggage in the bedroom, threw the laundry in the washing machine and went to check the mail. There was a letter from the bank. Tanya was right. Interest rates had gone up to seventeen and a half per cent. It was not just talk. There it was in black and white signed by a machine impersonating the signature of a highly placed bank official we had never met. They had actually started charging us the higher rate ten days earlier but there had been a delay getting the letters out and the bank apologised unreservedly. The cost of the letter would doubtless be absorbed by the increase. Underneath the signature the bank had decided to place a message of encouragement:

> *By depositing your savings in a loan trimmer plan account you have reduced your loan interest by $1.71.*

The mail contained advertisements: for a new gym specialising in fitness for men *and* women, home-delivered pizza from Cyprus, the Good News Bible, an encyclopaedia of entomology and a letter from our local member of parliament with a range of handy hints that would have Tanya fuming and vowing to put him in a home before the next election. Although he had misspelt our names, I had no reason to doubt the genuineness of everything he said. It was his belief that Tanya and I, as a household, could save up to a hundred and sixty dollars a year in energy by sealing gaps around doors and windows, using heavy curtains and maintaining our heaters regularly. We had only one heater so perhaps we would have to revise down this estimate but it was, nonetheless, a salutary reminder of the economic advantages of maintaining our heater.

He also recommended Tanya and I undertake regular fire

drills replete with an escape plan that has been followed blindfold by everyone in the family at least once prior to the time of an actual fire. There was no mention of the government's slashing of funding for education but he did remind us that he could arrange messages and telegrams for residents in the electorate celebrating a special occasion such as a fiftieth wedding anniversary, or, for those celebrating one hundredth birthdays, a message from the Queen and Governor-General. Without an escape plan or a blindfold we decided to try to have children.

Paul and Kate got married completely expectedly. His family had decided that the great virtue in denying him thus far his share of their not inconsiderable assets would soon ripen and then rot into a collective clannish shame. He had reached in their eyes the stage of life where the state of his furniture and the age of his car was a reflection on them. The first sprinkling of their largesse, in the form of Paul and Kate's wedding, was a public tribute to the purity of their sound business sense and sternly gentle cash-register-side manner over two generations of pharmaceutical service to the good people of Hawthorn, Camberwell and Mont Albert. With the assistance of the family's long-standing and now fragile vicar, and allusions to ideologies I was confident Paul had always rejected, they were married in the presence of two hundred and fifty people at a particularly fashionable bend in the Yarra River.

Paul had two brothers and so, although I could not escape the bridal party altogether, I was not required to make a speech that steered that fine line between deference to the vicar and deference to the macho success with women *de rigueur* for the groom, a success Paul had not known. In truth, he was lucky to be marrying Kate. As much as I liked him, she was better. Tanya knew this too but was kind enough never to make me have to hear it. Despite her fondness for him, I think Tanya always suspected something about him, something not wholly admirable. She was asked to be Kate's matron of honour and we were hoping that by the time of their wedding Tanya's belly would be swollen with child and we could insinuate an inelegance into the proceedings. But having spent so many months trying unsuccessfully, Tanya seemed about as likely to get pregnant as win the Eurovision song contest. So both of us looked on by the river, barren and speechless, as Paul and Kate with the stroke of a platitude and an injection of pharmaceutical funds, lapped us in one go and flowed with ease and prosperity into the hardening arteries of middle-class matrimony.

There had been rumours among certain of Tanya's academic colleagues that the university administration was trying to broker a 'takeover' of a neighbouring College of Advanced Education. The rumours were consistent with changes to the government's funding policy with respect to universities and tertiary education across the board. Universities were to be allocated funds solely according to the number of students on their books. In order to secure or increase funding, universities adopted a range of tactics which included the 'vertical broadening' of entry requirements and the annexation of any institution south of the Sudetenland that did not move faster than the Earth around the Sun.

Tanya and many of her colleagues began to fear the effects of any proposed merger on their security. No one was offered tenure anymore and every little tin-pot recreation hall that had been giving classes in pottery, yoga and the bottling of certain fruits added a class in International Relations, Marketing or Supply-side Economics and became an only too willing object for takeover by a predatory university and instant elevation to the status thereof. With the characteristic wisdom, sensitivity and foresight attaching to much of the managerial ethos that began to govern people's lives just prior to the collapse of Communism, the merger was initially 'rumoured', then 'likely' and ultimately 'inevitable and a great opportunity' for the university to increase the number of road signs that mentioned it in passing. Tanya's need for a PhD increased exponentially with the arrival of each new instant expert in the departmental tearoom. She started losing sleep with the fall of the Berlin Wall and by the time everyone knew the meaning of 'collateral damage' she had mastered the art of waking up five or six times a night having fallen asleep only once.

'I'm going to have to do something big, Eddie,' she said in bed one night following another of my by then many ill-conceived attempts to help her conceive.

'Just what you usually do would probably be sufficient.'

'I'm sorry, sweetheart, I just don't feel like it. I've got too much on my mind and I'm exhausted from not sleeping.'

'No, that's fine, Tanya, really,' I said, turning to one side.

'I'm going to have to do something big to solidify my position within the department.'

'We could have a child and donate it to the library,' I suggested.

'I'm going to have to write a book, you know, turn the thesis into an authoritative monograph, a controversial work that I'll be forced to defend at conferences and on daytime television.'

'You could even submit a funding proposal to the department and at the same time seek an advance from a publisher—two sponsors for the one baby.'

'Hey, that's not a bad idea.'

'Thanks, Tanya. Who needs to procreate when I can bask in such fulsome praise?'

'But what am I going to do the thesis *on*?'

That night signalled a turning point. From then on Tanya began to apply herself furiously to the idea. She buried herself in all the academic journals and monographs she could lay her hands on, historical, political, economic and sociological; she did not restrict herself. She was looking at the twentieth century from all points of view. But she would not tell me the topic until I told her that such intense euphoria could only be explained by the presence of another man in her life. She laughed and threw her arms around me, kissing me. We fell on the bed and she told me I was crazy.

She explained that her thesis was going to be about the eschewal at the end of the twentieth century of all political economic ideology. I thought it a hugely ambitious undertaking and when I told her so, she was even more delighted. She began to take off my clothes, explaining her central thesis between the kisses.

'The death of political economics, hey, how's that for a title, with the subtitle "Back to the Jungle",' she said, removing her bra.

'Every institution, including and especially the nation-state, and this is a global phenomenon, is now in crisis due to either the profound failure or the wilful abandonment of every previously conceived political economic doctrine, unless you count completely *laissez-faire* economics with nearly zero government intervention as a doctrine rather than the *absence* of a doctrine and a return to the jungle.

'What is being peddled in their place are panaceas devoid of all reason and humanity, religious fundamentalisms, be they of the market kind—the market delivers all socially desirable outcomes—or theist varieties.'

Her breathing was becoming heavier and her voice more stentorian.

'There is currently no policy so absurd that you could be confident that no economist would advocate it. There is no policy so cruel that you could be confident no politician would implement it.'

'My God, you're so absolutely right. There's not much hope, is there?' I asked her as we became one.

'I don't know yet.'

That night Tanya became pregnant.

CHAPTER 13

Once again we shared the same dreams: a child made in our image with the best attributes of each of us and none of the worst from either of us. Felt pictures of the dish running away with the spoon and the cow jumping over the moon started appearing in the house. Sometimes we bought them, sometimes we made them. It seemed to bring us even closer, sharing absurdly far-off plans for the future of the son or daughter we were going to have, sharing everything but the swelling and the vomiting.

Tanya continued to work on her thesis with an enthusiasm I had never before seen her direct towards her career. Perhaps for the first time she could see what it was she was going to be when she grew up: an author, an academic, a mother and a wife. It delighted her.

'What about names? We haven't really discussed names.'

'Tanya, we've got three and a half months.'

'Yes, but you don't want it to be a panicked decision, a name hastily chosen because they're cutting the umbilical cord? You'll probably have been sent to some remote open-cut mine and be trying to name your baby from a coin-fed telephone in the public bar of the second-best hotel in all of Mt Tom Price.'

'Probably, and if that happens I'll suggest the name of the barmaid.'

'What if it's a boy?'

'Then I'll ask her her husband's name and if she can't remember I'll go for the name of the last man she slept with.'

'No, really, Eddie. Let's go through this methodically.'

'What do you mean *methodically*? By starting with our favourite writers and working our way through philosophers, artists, photographers, actors and musicians? What about politicians? Think about it. Politicians are a rich source of distinctive names. Nixon? Disraeli? Menzies? What about August Kubizek?'

'I like the name August. Who's August Kubizek?'

'He was a boyhood friend of Hitler's. Eventually they lost touch. I think Mrs Hitler thought he might be a bad influence.'

'Maybe not August then but, all jokes aside, we should go through each letter of the alphabet and compile a list of names for each sex. I've actually started my list already.'

'You have?'

'Well I haven't got very far and it's only for girls.'

'What letter are you up to?'

'A,' she said, unabashed.

'Well, now the pressure is really on me. What names have you come up with?'

'Not many.'

'Well, let's hear them.'

'Amelia, Anna, Amanda, Aurora.'

'*Amanda!*' She couldn't be serious.

'Wait. I haven't finished. There's more.'

'We can't call our daughter Amanda.'

'Why not?'

'We just can't. It's one of those . . . names.'

'What's wrong with it? It's a very pretty name.'

'Oh it's . . . plain and yet . . . suggestive.'

'Suggestive! Suggestive of what?'

'Suggestive of . . . an insidious . . . plainness and vulgarity, no class, a completely unmemorable name liable to ruin everything we've worked for.'

'Take it easy, Eddie. Relax, I don't know why you're so passionately opposed to "Amanda" but it doesn't matter really. I'm still only on the "A"s. I don't have any special attachment to "Amanda".'

'No? Good. Neither do I.'

With each new sunrise as I counted down the coming bravery of fatherhood, I tried vainly to imagine my father's thoughts at the approach of my birth. When I asked him he laughed and reminded me that he already had Kirsten by the time I was born. And as he waited for her to be born? It was a long time ago. He did not remember but I would be fine, he assured me. Was this what he had been whispering subliminally to me since birth? 'You will be fine.' And do I whisper it to my child from birth despite all the empirical evidence to the contrary in the form of the tortured and tortuous river of humanity which crashes past us with such frightening violence on its way to somewhere none of us can ever see?

What about *him*? Had someone whispered it to him? Had he believed them? Was it true? Was he fine? Before the birth, and with great apology because it *was* before the birth, my mother and father sold the house in which my sister and I had grown up. Having never missed a payment, it was almost all theirs by then. My father had retired from the council. It had been shedding staff and, having discussed it with my mother, he decided to accept a *package*. By this time a *package* was already not what it used to be. From the end of the nineteen eighties the word took on a new meaning. A *package* was no longer a surprise and one accepted it as you would accept a blindfold, reluctantly and inevitably. They were going to take the package, their share of the proceeds of the house and their savings, such as it was, and move to the Gold Coast.

They told us one evening when Tanya and I went over there for dinner. Tanya was in the kitchen talking to my mother and I found my father in the study. The door, which had been kept open all the time I lived there, was closed. He said he had closed it to keep in the heat and pointed to the small heater by his feet under the desk. The cone of light from the desk lamp reduced the temptation to look at the rain outside. He was studying the options.

He welcomed me but his eyes were not the smiling eyes they generally were. There were glossy brochures scattered on his desk and he spoke in a language he had never used before. He wanted investment advice. His early termination and superannuation payments were *parked* in an Approved Deposit Fund. Should he invest it in a fixed term annuity or an allocated pension, and in which one? Whatever the tax advantages offered by any particular option, they could not be relied upon to continue indefinitely. The government was threatening changes but nothing was specific. This was the only money they had. The government was said to be looking for ways to limit early retirees' access to lump sums in order to reduce their Social Security benefit claims. What if they needed money in an emergency? Should he split his payout fifty/fifty or sixty/forty? What did I think?

I told him I barely understood what he was talking about but that they had two healthy adult children whom they could depend on in an emergency. Tanya and I were having Kate and Paul over for dinner later that week. Paul was a rising star within the corridors of the largest bank in the country. If he couldn't advise us himself, he would be able to recommend someone who could. I took my father's hand as Tanya's voice came to us from the kitchen inviting us to eat. He stood up slowly and I whispered to him, 'Don't worry. You will be fine.'

It still is not clear to me how it happened and I don't think it started when Tanya and I got married but some time after that, just a few months after, it was already firmly entrenched; dinner-parties had come upon us stealthily, imperceptibly, like winter and old age. It was not that we were invited to so many. We were not. Occasionally some-one from the university would invite us and two or three other couples to sit around, pat their children, admire the staining of their floorboards and listen, even if not with our concurrence, to their views. But dinner parties take hold of you like a virus and before too long you are a pregnant cou-ple admiring vases and crystal decanters in shop windows and discounting the monetary cost of candlesticks because they are so lovely and because no one else will.

It might start with a vase but it progresses to china dinner services or silver cutlery and soon you are contemplating a personal loan to knock down one of the many walls you are having trouble paying off in order to install a brick fireplace because other people's lives seem so augmented by having one. No longer did we meet Kate and Paul at the pub for a counter meal. Indeed, it became impossible to eat with them without the combustion of tallow taking place at the centre of the table. We tried to glove our austerity in a kind of politi-cal correctness, to pass off our straitened circumstances as environmental friendship or third world interior design. It was never discussed between us, it just came about naturally, possibly because everything we had was cheap and tawdry.

Paul and Kate owned nice things. They knew out-of-the-way places where you could buy a one-off this or an antique that. We knew places where you could get things slightly damaged but unless you held it up to the light you would never know and whenever people visited us we would turn off the lights and attempt to create an enchanting evening our guests would never forget in the candle-lit semi-darkness of their memories and our junk. But Tanya quite unintentionally broke the candle-lit spell early one evening when she brought up the topic of my father's forced retirement and what it would do to him.

'I understand you seeing it that way but public utilities have to be responsible to the public just as corporations have to be responsible to their shareholders,' Paul said.

'Oh, cut it out, Paul. You're not at work now,' I said.

'No really, Eddie, I'm serious. The days of public instrumentalities being havens for the inefficient are over. How else are we going to compete with Asia?' Paul countered. I wanted to put him in a home. Tanya wanted to kill him.

'Eddie's father worked thirty-five years for the Springvale Council. He doesn't have to compete with Asia.'

'Look, I'm not talking specifically about Eddie's dad, but the principle is the same.'

'What principle?' we snapped in unison.

'Its need for efficiency. Our nearest trading partners can do things so much more efficiently than we can. We have to free things up. If the service can be provided at a lower cost then the cost must be lowered for the good of the country.'

'But the country *is* Eddie's father and over a million like him that have been retrenched. Who is this being done for?' Tanya asked.

'Paul, how can you say this? People are being thrown on the scrap heap. The costs you speak of lowering are always and only labour costs. Nothing else has to cost less. You're saying people, people like my father, have to work for less or not work at all,' I continued.

'No, no. You're seeing this as all negative. It's not just labour costs that'll be lowered. The cost of everything will be lowered if trade is deregulated and countries are free to produce cheaply and on-sell to other less efficient countries.'

'But no one here can buy those cheaper imported goods because they're all out of work or waiting to be and they don't have any money because real wages are falling so that we can be more competitive.'

'Oh, that's a bit of an exaggeration,' Paul scoffed. He sounded like a younger version of Amanda's father.

'No it isn't. Why is it? Only people who don't make anything or don't offer any really useful service have money anymore. And they have lots of money to buy all the cheap imports that have taken away everybody else's jobs, except that *they* wouldn't be caught dead buying things that are too cheap lest their dinner-party guests get the wrong impression.' Tanya was getting a bit too personal. How I loved her when she insulted people. Throughout all of this Kate had said nothing and, in retrospect, it spoke volumes. But that night she just sat there.

No one has ever sliced eggplant so thinly.

CHAPTER 14

It is well known that things tend to fall. And when they fall there is something in some of us which makes us say that they have fallen into place, almost wherever they land. This is less known. Hospitals often have corridors of misunderstood quiet around pockets of shouting and, in maternity wards, of celebration. I took her there and did not shout myself although there had been no better time to shout that I could remember. We shout at traffic jams and at sudden changes we cannot control or foresee. There was never a more appropriate time to shout than when Tanya went into labour, the punch-the-air shout, the things now beyond our control shout.

I had still had questions, so many of them, all useless because any answers to them would not be enough to make me feel ready, really ready to be a father. The contractions were beyond her control, let alone mine, and I held her hand and dabbed at her forehead just as I had seen good men do in the movies. Perhaps there was still time to learn something before I had to know everything.

How had I managed to get this far and was it true that the success or failure of my life up till then would be revealed at any moment in the health or otherwise of this child?

Nothing else mattered. It was the only thing I knew, had ever known. Wet and crying. There we were, now three of us, wet and crying and struggling to breathe. We knew that no one else had ever done this before but the medical staff were kind to pretend otherwise.

When she came she was Abigail and gypsy-dark like her mother. I had known her forever. Cleaned and wrapped and entered in a register, Abby shunned the lights and begged to be alone for just a little while longer. But everything was alright, first cut and then dried as the obstetrician had promised. I still had all those questions but it did not matter anymore that I didn't know anything. When I held her I gained the simple strength of an overwhelming love, an irrepressible euphoria. Tanya was exhausted. She looked up at us and smiled. Everything had fallen into place.

From two thousand kilometres away there was no mistaking my parents' delight as they kept apologising for not being there. I told them we were lucky *I* was there. My trips away were becoming more frequent. I chose to take this as a vote of confidence from those above although perhaps it was just that I was easy to push around. Now that I had a child I had moved up another rung on the persons-unlikely-to-be-asked-to-leave-town scale. In *theory* single men were asked first, then married men and then married men with children. I was now at the tertiary stage of domesticity, the ideal person for a tax break, a re-financed mortgage and slippers on Fathers' Day.

But the kind of money spent on mining and mineral exploration and the size of the balance of trade ramifications if anything paid off, led the department to whistle to the companies' tune. So child or not, I had to go. On the other hand, the environmental lobby had already swung one election and the government needed to be seen to be policing the transnational mining companies. That was my job, to ensure that the public interest was being safeguarded. I could hear about her initial weeks of parenting over the phone. She will be fine.

There had been talk around the office of a particularly big and sensitive project, possibly involving direct advice to the Minister. In the face of the challenge and without inhibition or quickened pulse, I took to leaving work as early as I could to see Tanya and Abby. Whatever it said about me, there was no competition between Abby and the Minister. I did not give it a second thought. Paul might have said that I was letting the country down in the face of competition from the Asian 'tigers' but I was sure the best of them left work early to be with their cubs. The worst of them came here on trade delegations and bought golf courses and stuffed marsupials.

Paul would never come at the idea that, if we all agreed through ASEAN, APEC, NAFTA, the EC, GATT and the IMF to knock off work early and be with our children, no one in the world would have a competitive advantage. He said there was no way of policing it (an objection easily overcome if parents were compelled to clock in as soon as they reached the nursery) and, anyway, he was all in favour of competitive advantages. So he stayed a little longer at the office each night. Kate was usually at our place with Abby when he got home.

I could never understand parents' slack-jawed obsession

with their newborn babies when they had known since they themselves were children that they would one day have their own children, that it was *a* if not *the* purpose of their union; when they had watched the proof grow daily to the mother's discomfort for the best part of a year; and when the newborn child, through no fault of its own, could do nothing to compete for interest with nocturnal tree possums out for a night on the town. But Abby was not a baby, or was only technically so. Her hair was dark and thick. I liked to watch her breathe. I found myself always talking to her. If she was asleep, I just spoke more quietly. And she grew. She understood everything. She would grow to be understanding. Tanya would have hated the focused outpouring of attention I lavished on Abby if she had not been in love with her too. We took it in turns to breast-feed her in the middle of the night. Sometimes we got up together and sometimes I let Tanya feed her alone.

Kate was teaching English in a high school on the other side of town and between her end of the day visits to Abby and Tanya to share between them chocolate hedgehogs, coffee and a breast, and Tanya's mother's morning sojourns there was no gulf of carpet-staring adultless hair-tearing solitude for Tanya to endure. We had been worried that, as much as she would love the person that turned out to be Abby, Tanya might crash in the period immediately following the birth. She did not, and even managed to make some progress with her reading for *The Death of Political Economics.*

One warm Sunday afternoon in Kate and Paul's back garden Paul asked Tanya the title of her thesis. Abby was asleep under an umbrella in a transparent womb of mosquito netting. We sat beside her on their teak garden furniture eating grapes, Dutch cheese and drinking one of the dry whites Paul always had chilled, the smooth lubricant that helped him slough off opinions that conflicted with his.

'What are you saying in your title?' Paul asked. 'In what sense is political economics dead?'

'The political and social conventions, traditions, laws, practices, mores that developed in the nineteenth century and flowered briefly in the civilisation of the twentieth century, albeit with periodic relapses into barbarism, are in the process of being abandoned,' Tanya explained.

'What *was* that civilisation? How do you characterise it?'

'Okay. I'm talking about Western civilisation—'

'Of course,' he interjected.

'Not "of course" Paul, but she *is*,' Kate volunteered.

Tanya continued. 'The economies were capitalist, the legal systems were essentially liberal and the states either republics or constitutional monarchies. Most of them invoked the separation of powers between the executive, the legislature and the judiciary. Science, education and increasing material prosperity were all accepted as universal goals for each nation-state and sometimes even for their colonies. True, there was a relapse. The period from the outbreak of the First World War to the end of the Second World War was a recidivation which culminated in the first tidal wave of fascism, the abrogation of fundamental civil liberties and finally the death camps.'

Tanya's passionate delivery could be mistaken for anger if you did not know her.

'People's fear of change and their despair at the lack of certainty in any area of their lives, particularly where the social and the personal meet, that is with respect to their jobs and their income, if it lasts long enough, will lead them to abandon reason, to be suspicious of it and to look for scapegoats and simplistic solutions. The wisdom or correctness of a government's decision will scarcely be discussed but instead attention will be focused on the strength with which the decision was made, the apparent certainty, the conviction with which it was implemented.

'People will long to have someone remove the uncertainty. They will admire the way the government summarily dismisses any opposition to the decision. A climate will develop wherein critical and analytical thinking, unpractised arts already, will be seen at best as irrelevant and, at worst, as treasonous, threatening the certainty for which they have traded everything else. It will be the fall of the Weimar Republic revisited.'

There were times when Tanya was irrepressible. Admiration is not love but it can be part of the equation.

'And you're saying all of this happened in the thirties and forties and will happen again?'

'I'm saying it is happening now.'

Paul leaned back and smiled. 'You'll find it hard to convince anyone looking down at us here on this beautiful summer day, your daughter sleeping peacefully, all of us working professionals sipping the fruits of our labour in a quiet which is disturbed only by the rumble of distant lawnmowers, that there is anything faintly resembling a crisis here. Your reading public, if you publish your thesis, will not believe you, although there will always be some academics who will.'

Kate got up, turning her back to the conversation, and went over to watch Abby sleeping. Paul continued, unaware or unaffected by his wife's relocation.

'Really, Tanya, I can understand the need to make a splash with your thesis and I hope more than anyone that it's a huge success for you. Certainly I'll be able to claim a PhD among my closest friends. But aren't you just taking the clapped-out quasi-Marxists' alarmism of our undergraduate days and seeking to transform it into something both academically respectable and marketably chic? There is, I'll admit, probably a fortune to be made by the people who write these searing warnings of the next global catastrophe; the hole in the ozone layer, over-population, de-forestation. But it's so . . . tiresome.'

Paul opened another bottle and refilled our glasses.

'Paul, everything you've just listed is a genuine problem,' Tanya replied, 'and none of them are diminished in their seriousness by the fact that they first entered your consciousness as an undergraduate and have departed your consciousness since you graduated and started providing economic advice to a bank. But they're not really what I'm writing about.'

'Yes. I know you've chosen fascism. And you might be right in terms of the market.'

'Paul, are you only pretending to be Genghis Khan?' I asked.

'I hate to disappoint you two but I meant only that Tanya's thesis might be the first to tap the "fear of fascism market", though you'll have to do more than just frighten the minority who listen to the ABC.'

'I'm not concerned with the *marketing* of the thesis, Paul. I don't know what makes you say these things. Are you taking this at all seriously?'

'He is,' Kate called. 'He doesn't mean to be insulting.'

'Not only do I not mean to be insulting, I'm not *being* insulting. Tanya, I think you're one of the most intelligent people I know and I really believe you've got an angle.'

'Paul, this is not an angle. I'm talking, *writing* about the abandonment of government intervention in the economy, the deregulation of just about everything, the removal of protection from competition from third world quasi-slave labour—and complete and absolute reliance on the morality of the market, which is the morality of the jungle.'

Kate returned to the table. She looked less uncomfortable but more absent.

'I'm writing about an unprecedented confrontation between the ever-increasing number of disenfranchised, not just politically or socially but with respect to jobs and accommodation, about a confrontation between a growing underclass who inherit joblessness from their parents, and the tiny never-wealthier elite who, like you, will see everything in terms of market share, the cult of the MBA, and managerial theory, and the supreme majesty of Adam Smith's misunderstood *invisible hand*—until one dark night some other invisible hand drags you by the throat down the stairs and out the door into the reality you've been ignoring. But it will be too late then because there'll be no one to help you. All the instrumentalities of the state will have been sold off or run down. It will be everyone for themselves and then you'll really get the feel of a truly free market.'

'God, you *are* a Marxist!' Paul exclaimed. 'This is going to be one hell of a thesis cum book. Bugger the ABC. If you can perform like this they'll get you on one of the commercial networks. But you're going to have to have an answer. You'll have to offer a solution. Hope is the grabber. What's the tonic?'

This was the question I had hoped would not be reached. We had talked about it privately many times, long into the night between feeds and it distressed Tanya that she did not have an answer. I tried to comfort her, suggesting that a ruthlessly well-written delineation of the problems of the world, and how we got there, really should be enough, maybe not to save the world, but for a PhD thesis. She had been only momentarily comforted. I did not know whether she had anything to say in response, but she did and she said it slowly and with a quiet certainty.

'If we are to avoid the laissez-faire chaos we are rushing headlong into, the polarisation into the very wealthy and the very poor, the risk of complete social breakdown and the possible emergence from that wreckage of an oppressive and brutal neo-fascist regime . . . oh, for Christ's sake, don't smirk, Paul, it can happen here too. It's happened before and in a more cultured place than this. . . if we are to avoid all this, government policies need to be driven by a compassionate concern for the well-being of *all* the people. By a genuine concern for their well-being *now,* not by a bogus concern for it in some mythic ideologically posited but empirically untenable long-run when we are all dead and our children wish they were too.'

'So what policies are you advocating specifically?'

Kate was staring at her hands, playing with her ring.

'Well, the restoration of full employment by protection of manufacturing industry from low wage imports and the restoration of pre-Reaganite, pre-Thatcherite, pre-economic rationalist levels of funding for public health, education, welfare and public infra-structure works.'

'Ah, and where would the money for all this beneficence come from?' Paul interrupted.

'It would come from the decreased cost of unemployment benefits and from the increased taxation revenue that the bigger income earning base would contribute. And I'm not a Marxist, Paul. All I'm advocating really is a return to the Keynesian economics of the forties, fifties and sixties.'

Kate looked up and then at me. We smiled. My wife, her friend, was trying to save the world.

This was the eloquence and the intolerance of unfairness I wanted Abby to inherit. But what did I have to transmit to her but the solution of differential equations and an insight into which trains went via the city loop and why. On my death bed and with my last breath, all I could offer her would be: 'Abby, my darling daughter, remember this: no matter where you are or what time of day it is—avoid Punt Road.'

I had to offer her more than this. But there was no guarantee she would imbibe even this let alone any of Tanya's clear-sighted reformist zeal. Perhaps she would rebel and grow up to become the manager of a commodities trading house. She would earn a fortune, buy up all of her old neighbourhood in a fit of nostalgic extravagance and evict her parents. I could not really see this happening but it was getting harder to predict anything, much less control it. And if this was true in respect of our daughter, how much more so was it true in respect of economic policy.

CHAPTER 15

Abby was already walking by the time of the next crash. How early children can pick up on these things is not known with precision. Some say it is as early as the womb. I have no difficulty believing she was never unable to distinguish solemnity from cheerfulness, laughter from grieving or her grandmother's arms from those of her mother. When I came home one early evening from yet another interstate trip and the house was darker than it usually was at that time, I knew immediately that someone was fighting a thing darker than any room.

Tanya's mother was sitting in the half-light of the television with the sound turned down rocking Abby to sleep. I dropped my suitcase and the thud it made reminded Abby that she probably ought to cry again.

'What's wrong? Where's Tanya?'

'Nothing's wrong. Nothing. Nothing new. She's in the bedroom. Everything's alright. Isn't it, Abby? You show your dad that everything's alright.'

I went over and picked her up, rocked her and cooed to her, more for myself than for her. She was dry and clean. She had been fed and when I could finally put her down to sleep Tanya's mother told me that Tanya was in a bad way and had gone to bed. The need to stay in bed, the inability to leave it, I had seen it before. Tanya's mother and I sat alone in the lounge room and she spoke in a quiet voice.

'I know this is nothing new to you, Eddie.'

'She gets lonely and frustrated when I'm away.'

'She gets depressed.'

'It's not uncommon in new mothers.'

'It's not uncommon in Tanya.'

'I know.'

'I know you do, Eddie, and I know how much you love her. But there are some things you don't know, some things you couldn't know.'

I had never heard her voice sound so tired, so tinged with resignation, so old. She too was exhausted and for the first time, I knew that I loved her too, not just out of some sense of duty, but in a way that rendered me incapable of helping her. She continued.

'You couldn't know, Eddie, because *she* doesn't know what I'm about to tell you. It's about her father.'

At this stage I got up and went to the kitchen to pour us both a drink. We had only Scotch and vodka in the house so I poured us both one of each.

'Do you know much about Tanya's father?' she asked me.

'I know he was an actor and that he died when she was eight and Marty was eleven.'

'Not just an actor. He was a musician, a director, a story-teller, a bit of a poet and a devastatingly handsome man. We were in a theatre company together. That's how we met. We went on tour to all the regional cities and the country towns. His name was Eduard. Did you know that? But it wasn't spelt like your name. He was Czech so he spelt it E-D-U-A-R-D.'

'I had no idea.'

'No, well he Anglicised the surname when he got here after the war. He was a socialist and a Jew. It wasn't enough for him to be a bit unusual, he couldn't help but be unique. A professional dreamer, he could make you dream his-dreams with him wherever you were or whatever you were going through. Women loved him and . . . he loved them. But sometimes, even while he was still alive, I had to dream his dreams for him, without him. You see . . . he suffered from depression as well.'

'As well as what?'

'As well as Tanya. I see so much of him in both the children but more in Tanya than in Marty. You love her for many of the same things that made me love him, their humour, concern for the world, quickness of mind, the music that is always in them even at times like tonight when she is lying on her bed in the dark with a slow dirge churning away inside her. But Eddie, this isn't post-natal depression or whatever they call it now. This is Tanya. You have to know that and try to help her. You won't be able to get her completely well but you have to love her anyway, in spite of it. It comes with the territory and, please, don't ever . . . leave her, no matter what she might say.'

'Leave her! I couldn't leave her. She has been my life since I was seventeen. There is nothing more important to me than her and Abby. I am not me without them. I know about her depression. Perhaps I'm naive but I haven't given up hope of a complete cure, but even if that never happens I won't be leaving her. I love her too much. Hers is the voice that's always inside me when I'm at work, when I'm away because of work, in the car, always. It's because of her and Abby that I really do consider myself the luckiest man in the world. I'm not just saying it. I appreciate your concern but if you really knew the extent to which she *is* my life you wouldn't feel the need to say any of this.'

'There's more. What has she told you about her father, about her father's death?'

'You were away on tour. She and Marty were being looked after by friends of yours, or neighbours. It was very sudden, a heart attack. She has said that she always felt cheated of the chance to say a proper goodbye to him. She had thought he would only be gone for two weeks. As a young girl, for years after his death, she kept expecting him to come walking in again with some stuffed toy, a kangaroo or something that he'd promised her, as though you had made a mistake and he wasn't really dead but only lost like one of the inland explorers she'd been learning about at the time you, he, went away.'

'Really? Is that what she says?'

'Yes. She's said that.'

'We were away on tour with a play, something . . . I can't remember. It was Shakespeare, but I can't remember which one.'

'I can only imagine how painful this is. You don't have to tell me about it.'

'No. I think I do. We were away. It was the first time he had put up his own money, *our* money. There were no backers, no investors. We had gone to the bank, made out a case and borrowed the money in our own names. Eduard had long wanted to start his own theatre company, one which would travel the country offering a mixed repertoire of light comedies, drawing-room farce and, of course, Shakespeare. He thought that Shakespeare was the font of all wisdom, a wisdom he could help disseminate. Being the kind of man he was, he was always falling out with the sorts of people we depended on for work. Whenever I tried to temper his enthusiasm for pointing out their shortcomings, he would tell me life was too short to swallow all of the truth himself without leaving people that part of it which concerned them. This was how he talked.'

'Sounds like Tanya.'

'I know. It does, doesn't it,' she said moving from the vodka to the Scotch.

'We were staying in one of those grand country hotels— you know, the kind that sits proudly on the main street of every country town next to the post office, police station and municipal offices, with a different bar for every street aspect and a public dining room with mirrors on the wall and a piano in the corner. Eduard and I were treated like royalty by the staff, the original Larry Olivier and Vivien Leigh. We had dinner several times with the manager and with members of the local chamber of commerce . . . Between them they must've owned half the district. Apart from the injection of culture, it seemed we were good for business. They even offered to take Eduard rabbit shooting one night. I should've known something was up then.'

At this, she tilted her glass indicating that it was empty. I went to the kitchen, brought back the two bottles and refilled both her glasses. I looked at her with a quiet sympathy. Thinking of this once very attractive young actress who had fallen for the archetypal dark stranger in her midst only to be left suddenly alone with two young children, I was unable to escape the melancholic fallout of my own inarticulacy. She spoke with that tenderness so regularly born of exhaustion, the exhaustion of years of subservience to an often mocking hope that one day something either circumstantial or incarnate might have pity on her.

'Eduard had lost his family in the war. He had seen his parents and siblings taken away at gunpoint by the Nazis.

He himself couldn't kill an insect yet he had agreed to go
rabbit shooting with the mayor and some of his friends,
and, I later found out, with the mayor's daughter. They
really did go rabbit shooting. I saw the pelts. Afterwards they
drank into the morning and Eduard managed to get himself alone with the mayor's daughter. And he wasn't used to
drinking heavily, he was epileptic.

'Eduard was always far too easily flattered, he said so himself. Anyway, I don't know exactly where they were, how
drunk he was or how far they'd gone but it was far enough
for the mayor, when he caught them, to be in no doubt as
to what Eduard was doing with his daughter. The whole
town knew about it by lunchtime the next day and we were
immediately evicted from the town hall auditorium we had
been using for a theatre. We had the wages of the cast and
crew to pay and Eduard had just stopped our cash-flow with
one drunken night's indiscretion. Instantly we went from
being celebrities to foreign aliens, in Eduard's case quite literally. People made racist remarks in the local shops when
they saw him. There was talk that he had stolen someone's
shotgun. Some people even refused to serve anyone connected with the troupe, including me. But worse than any of
this for Eduard was his guilt for the pain he had caused me.
He had told me his life with me was the life he was meant
to have had in Europe and he felt he had destroyed it.

'I know I sound quite objective about it now. That and
arthritis are what time can do for you, and anyway, whatever
he did or didn't quite do with the mayor's daughter almost
twenty-five years ago has paled into insignificance. The silly
bugger thought I'd never forgive him a quick roll in the hay
with a country mayor's daughter. He's more than paid for it
and I've forgiven him for that too. I forgave him years ago
but I don't know whether his children ever will. Tanya

couldn't even forgive him for not keeping his promise to bring back a toy koala . . . or was it a kangaroo? I think perhaps it was a kangaroo. You're right. I'd forgotten.'

She paused, as if seeing it all.

'He spent the next day and a half in bed in the dark. He wouldn't eat because he didn't deserve food, he said. I was furious till he took it all away with a gun they probably used for rabbits and foxes. He shot himself in the bridal suite of the Grand Hotel. It was two days after the night he had accepted the mayor's invitation. I was downstairs at the time holding a crisis meeting with the cast and crew who were by then understandably mutinous . . .

'I never stopped loving him, Eddie, because it wasn't selfishness that made him that way. It was an illness from which he would alternately gain and then lose reprieves. I've always been afraid that Marty and particularly Tanya wouldn't understand this, that if they knew the whole story they would hate him and I couldn't have that. He loved them dearly and was so proud of them. He didn't forget her kangaroo you know, but when they took away the body they didn't clean up everything, only what they had to. It was with him, it was there in the room when he did it. And I couldn't look at it. So I had to let him disappoint her.'

We sat in the dark and let her words hold the air. My first thoughts were of her courage. Who was there to love her after this tragedy, the one that those she loved most could never know about? Hers was a platinum fidelity, rare, quietly durable, and fusible only at a very high temperature. For nearly twenty-five years the pain would have fed on itself; the trivial callousness of his infidelity, the horror and senseless brutality of his own reaction to it, her forgiveness twice over that went twice unacknowledged, the necessary but painful perpetuation of a lie fundamental to the well-being of her children and then, of course, the unmitigated loneliness that was always there, gently holding her hand like the vaguely familiar cousin of an approaching death once or twice removed.

I thought also of Tanya and how she must never know. There could be no haggling with the truth in a circumstance in which it could not help but be too costly. If Tanya believed she had inherited even just the stigma of her father's illness then she would take to her bed as if it were her birthright and she would be powerless to fight it.

Finally I wondered why her mother had told me this. Did she really think I needed to know it or was it a combination of this coupled with her need to say it? From within my arms she whispered, tears still falling down her cheeks.

'He's with me you know. I still talk to him, I always have. I never stopped. I tell him about the kids. He would be so happy you love her the way you do. It's the most we could've wished for.'

———————

By the time (or perhaps because) Abby had started to say 'Mama' with a new discipline born of understanding, Tanya had begun to resume her place upright in the world of open curtains, breakfast dishes and newspaper editorials written as if for liberal excoriation. That it was in no small part Abby who had helped her up nurtured my hope that there was an integrity in our feelings for each other which might just see us past whatever shapes our fears would take when they crystallised. She had taken maternity leave which delayed the expiry of her two-year contract with the university, and then upon resuming, she was offered another two-year contract. This also helped. Her PhD thesis remained far from finished but most of the time that did not matter. Abby went to creche at the university, and regional conflicts in the Balkans, the Middle East, Africa and the Indian sub-continent kept us all fairly happy.

'The end of the Cold War was meant to usher in a new world order but since 1989 national, ethnic or religious differences have resulted in military operations in Liberia, Angola, the Sudan, the Horn of Africa, the former Yugoslavia, the Caucasas and the Transcaucasus, ex-Soviet Central Asia, Afghanistan, Iraq, Kuwait, Israel, Lebanon, East Timor and Burma. Is this order? Is it even new? The New World Order is one of those magnificent calming, grandiose and meaningless terms coined by some bright young thing who, upon deserting the Bush administration, was immediately in a position to cash in on the riches of the lecture circuit as the coiner of the "new world order". Imagine coining phrases as an occupation, Eddie, taking living words and snap freezing them into cliches. Eddie, why are you smiling like the cat that swallowed the cream? Actually cats don't smile, do they?'

My baby was back. Abby and I breathed a sigh of relief.

CHAPTER 16

It did not require the end of the Cold War and the implosion of the state that had given the Stalinist brand of Marxism a more than fair try for the cry of the mutant child of Friedrich von Hayek and Ayn Rand to seep in under the doors and spread throughout the length and breadth of the Department of Planning and Environment. It began with meetings, a series of them at all levels and at all times. Each of us was asked to prepare a 'mission statement'. Since I had never heard the expression before, it did not occur to me that it would put so many departmental noses so far out of joint when I wrote that I had too much work to do and that an *emission* statement would mean very little to the general public, in my opinion, and that only the policing of strict legislation would have any effect on the oil companies and car manufacturers. But, in principle, I was all for them.

I was requested to go downtown to the Ministry offices for an interview.

Was I serious? they asked me. 'Hardly ever,' I answered.

'Things tend to run more smoothly that way, I've found. This is true not merely in the work environment but in nearly all human interaction, even in the parent–child interaction. I'm not what you'd call an expert on this sort of thing, although I am a parent. I'm the father of my wife's child. My daughter has just turned three. Do you have children? I think I have a photo of her in my wallet. I could show you.'

Was I a team player? they asked.

'Oh, God no. Whenever I pair up with my wife against our friends for scrabble we always fight. Usually it's about the role of slang in educated discourse or which Latin words have become part of English. She's had problems with *animus*.'

The distance between what you say in a daydream and what you actually say to a superior at your place of work is proportional to the number of adults unsuccessfully seeking full-time employment.

I was requested to go downtown to the Ministry offices for an interview where I was told to prepare a mission statement. Forsaking sanity, I complied with that MBA-inspired direction.

There were rumours of the appointment of sub-departmental managers. I had heard these rumours, as one does, in the post-industrial economy's version of a market place, the staff tea-room, but despite their increasing frequency, I had not believed them. The internal mail was a bit slow, it was true. And there was a tendency for people to leave their coffee mugs soaking in the sink rather than making them ready for the next person, but I had always taken this to be one of the unalterable traits of the species, something that could be observed and noted but not changed without first isolating the gene responsible for it. Also, soft-centred biscuits were without fail the first to go, but as with the other problems in our organisation, it seemed the even smoother running of things could be implemented without recourse to more

managers simply by invoking the time-honoured 'suggestion' box.

But in these times other times were not honoured. A
colleague, Chamberlain, approached me furtively in the tea-
room and began a conversation in whispers.

'Have you met him?'

'Who?'

'The new guy, the manager.'

'No. When did he get here?'

'This morning. Wants to meet everyone one by one.'

'That's nice of him. Is he an engineer?'

'No.'

'A chemist?'

'No.'

'Is he a scientist at all?'

'No. Apparently he wasn't even a bureaucrat till last year
when he finished his MBA, but he does have a computer
background.'

'I thought you said he wasn't a scientist?'

'No, he isn't. He used to import computer software and
before that he just imported things . . . generally.'

'What things?'

'I don't know. But he did write a book on cyberspace.'

'On cyberspace, a book?'

'Yes.'

'Before the MBA or after it?'

'I don't know but I'd better go—he might be coming.'

'Are you kidding?'

'Well, he wants to meet each of us personally.'

'You mean individually, separately, alone.'

'Yes, and he's already met me and he'll probably come
around here to see you. I don't think it would look too
good if he saw me . . .'

'A grown man whispering to his colleague in the tea-room.'

'He's not so bad I suppose. Well-built guy, solid.'

'What's his name?'

'Gerard . . . something. He'll tell you to call him Gerard.'

———————————

Incredulous is the wrong word to describe me or my state of being upon hearing that name, attached to that position, being introduced back into my life. At no time did it occur to me either that this new manager might be someone other than the ex-Tanya, currently cum Amanda, Gerard, or that he had changed for the better in the interim (and I was proved right on both counts). Indeed, such was my incredulity that on the way home that day I decided, without knowing why, that I would not mention it to Tanya. This was tantamount to an acknowledgement, at least to myself, that it was true. Of all the two-bit departments of planning and environment in all the world he had to walk into mine.

The reintroduction of Gerard in our lives, his reincarnation as a dangerous escapee from a graduate school of business management, would have to be at the top of the how-was-my-day news broadcast when I got home. It would have to be a headline. So I crept into the house that night, in an attempt to avoid the headlines altogether and come in unexpectedly at the weather.

Tanya was bathing Abby and they were deep in conversation. A few months earlier we had made the mistake of telling Abby she was four and a half that particular day. She had wanted a party upon hearing the news. We explained that people did not celebrate half birthdays but she insisted that some people did. When we inquired who these people were,

she said they were at kindergarten with her but she had forgotten their names. Whatever their names, if Abby could
remember them when she turned five, she could invite them
to her fifth birthday party. Since then there had been much
discussion about a fifth birthday party and birthday parties in
general. Did we have a party the day she had been born? No.
Then maybe we owed her one. I expected to hear something
along these lines but it was not quite like that.

'Mum. Is there an Elvis?'

'What?'

'There's a boy at kinder, Ricky Thurston, who said Ricky
isn't his real name. He said Ricky is his knicked name and
that his real name is Elvis. He said he was named after the
real Elvis. What's my real name?'

'Abigail.'

'Is Abby my knicked name?'

'It's nickname, but you don't have a nickname, sweetie.'

'Why do you call me Abby?'

'We just call you Abby 'cause we love you. It's not a
nickname.'

'What about "sweetie", is that a nickname?'

'Nope, sorry. That's another name we call you just 'cause
we love you.'

Abby thought for a moment. 'So nicknames go to people
. . . without love.'

'Good try but wrong. All we really know is that "Abby"
and "sweetie" go to people with lots of love.'

This seemed to satisfy her for a while. I took off my tie in
the other room still listening and still undetected. There
were only washing sounds, water interacting with soap and
sponge, for a while. Then Abby spoke again.

'Mum, do you believe in Elvis?' Tanya took in and then
let out a deep breath. I could almost see it. 'Do you, Mum?'

'You know how every night Dad or I read you a story?'

'Sometimes in the day too.'

'Yes, sometimes in the day. And the stories are always *about* something, a boy or a girl or a dog or a cat—'

'Or talking fruit.'

'Or talking fruit. And in these stories something always happens to the characters, the boy or the girl, the dog or the cat—'

'Or the talking fruit . . .'

'Yes, and sometimes what happens in the story is more important than any one person in the story?'

'Why?'

''Cause it's the story itself that makes us feel happy or sad or makes us think and then it doesn't really matter so much whether the story is true or the persons in it are real.'

'But do you believe in Elvis, Mum?'

'There probably was someone called Elvis who was born a long, long time ago and who sang songs and danced in a new way. I'll show you how he danced later when Kate gets here, but now the whole story of Elvis has become much bigger than the real Elvis. You'll have to make up your own mind about what you think of Elvis as you grow up.'

'Mum, did he shoot TVs?'

'Yes.'

Again there was another silence, possibly another moment for my daughter to grapple with existential questions in the bath. With the renaissance of Gerard I had forgotten that tonight was the night to light the candles in the centre of the table, turn out the lights and have Kate and Paul over to dinner. There was no doubt about us, we were a functioning family unit.

'Mum?'

'What, sweetie?'

'Do you believe in God?'

'No, Abby, I don't.'

'Can I?'

I waited to hear Tanya's reply. This was something we had never discussed *vis-à-vis* Abby.

'You probably can for a while but sooner or later it might get too hard and you might have to stop. If you do have to stop it'll be okay because Dad and I will still be here. But if it doesn't get too hard and you don't stop, that's okay too.'

We sat down all five of us at the table, Tanya and me, Kate, Paul and Gerard. No one except me could see Gerard sitting there. He sat between Kate and Paul and opposite Tanya. I drifted in and out of their conversation, occasionally hearing but seldom participating, in order not to let him out of my sight. Here we all were, approaching the resigned years of our thirties when hope is consigned to your backlist, a time when we had already had most of the conversations we were going to have, a time when future conversations would just be reworked versions of past ones. We had already cooked all the meals we were going to cook. I had made conventional meals, roasts with garlic and rosemary was about as far into the art as I was going to get. Tanya had exhausted her more exotic repertoire and the culinary semioticists could have told our guests then and there that they ought not to have come if they did not like eggplant and that if they *had* ever liked eggplant we were going to give it to them until they did not.

I already knew that Kate was intrinsically more interesting than Paul. I already knew that she was brighter than him, disappointed in him, that she wanted children with someone and that she was showing signs of advanced teacher burnout. I knew this from everything Tanya had told me. I only saw Kate at variants of these candle-lit egg-plant soirées and Paul was always with her. And at these she was only a shadow of her former self. Usually I watched her flicker on the wall, remembering her from university, imagining *that* young woman screaming in horror at the absence of exhilaration in her mid-thirties self. It was too simple and therefore inaccurate to say that she cared nothing for Paul's money and recently exalted status in a world so desperate for high priests that it rewarded the neo-classical librettists of macro self-interest with nouveau mandarin status. For if she cared so little for it why didn't she leave? Maybe it was upon all of this that she pondered while her husband wrestled yet again with my wife over her PhD thesis.

'No, of course not,' I heard Tanya answer.

'Then you should be completely in favour of unrestricted international trade. It would enable the poorer countries to catch up to the wealthier countries or at least to come closer to them.'

'Paul, you know that doesn't happen.'

'Yes it does. How can you ignore those third world miracles of deregulation, all of them industrialised via successful export-driven economies?'

'Now, let me guess. You mean Singapore, Taiwan, Hong Kong and South Korea?'

'Yes.'

'They represent less than two per cent of the third world population. They're repeatedly trotted out by people with no real concern for the small people who have to live there and who have no voice, no rights and no money, by people with an ideological commitment to deregulation that no empirical data can shake.'

'That's not right,' he shook his head in lieu of a counter proposition.

'Well, if empirical evidence could oust the dogma, why do you ignore the absence of benefits to India, Pakistan, Burma, China, Vietnam, Thailand, Cambodia and the Philippines?'

'Each of those countries has their own special set of circumstances, they're separate cases. Some, like China, are at the early stages of liberalisation and haven't yet reaped the rewards of the trickle-down effect.'

'The trickle-down effect! Cut it out, Paul, the only thing that ever really trickles down is sewage. Look, when we get rid of protection here, we send business off shore, increase our indebtedness overseas and export jobs. The people who get those jobs are usually women and children who work till four in the morning for a hundredth of the wage remembered so fondly by our new permanently unemployed. The employers of these overseas workers certainly get rich but the workers themselves remain abjectly poor. And the swelling ranks of our unemployed become ever more vulnerable with the attacks on the health system and on social welfare, not to mention the privatisation of public utilities. Every time an aged pensioner wants to make a cup of tea some crony of the party that offered the biggest tax cuts makes a handsome profit. In the meantime, real wages fall because there is now a reserve of desperate unemployed waiting to take the jobs of the employed if the latter dare ask for a rise to keep up with the cost of living. Everyone is disillusioned and afraid of what's coming next. They know in their hearts that the government hates them.'

'That's a bit strong. What evidence have you got for that bit of hyperbole?'

'This government is suing the fire-fighters. The ambulance drivers have been forced to strike.'

'Nobody is forced to strike.'

'Paul, you cannot accept that it is possible to so reduce the conditions, safety, wages and the self-respect of ordinary people that they have no choice but to do the only thing they can do, withdraw their labour.'

Both Tanya and Paul knew that they would never change the other's opinions but they went on regardless. She always rose to the bait and he always seemed to get an excitement out of her vehemence which I found distasteful to contemplate. This should have been the time for me to sit next to the flickering Kate as she toyed with extinguishment and be her friend as she had been mine. But I didn't because I was too busy watching Gerard. He also enjoyed Tanya in full flight and remembered it from other times. I could see in his face his memories of her, which he could summon at will. What spark had he ever carried that showed him, even briefly, in a good light?

I will never know precisely what combination it was of Gerard's intervention and my earlier interview with the gentlemen from the Ministry that led me to be chosen to work on that special project which had, over almost four years of rumour and speculation, attained the proportions of the Manhattan Project. I will probably never know this just as I will never know why it was first mooted four years earlier only to be periodically shelved and revived and shelved again until I was assigned to it.

When he called me into his office it was just as a headmaster summonses a student, except, of course, that he had slept with my wife. That she was not my wife then made no difference to me because I had known then that she would be and she should have known too. In this way, without too much effort, I could be cuckolded retrospectively. In any case he was, when I thought about it, the last man she had slept with before me—and the last man she should have slept with. And I *did* think about it, on the train, in the tea-room, lying next to her at night breathing in that mixture of her natural scent and that supplied by moisturiser manufacturers intent on convincing her that she could, with their help, stay the age she was when she had slept with Gerard. And I thought of it as he asked me to sit down in his office.

He had new furniture, leather. No one else in the building had new furniture, let alone leather. No one even had new pencils. I sank deeply into the leather armchair, gravity coming down firmly on top of me. His office had ducted gravity. Perhaps he did not know that I had married his ex-girlfriend, that Tanya was my wife?

'Eddie, we're offering you a great opportunity,' he told me with a smile that was denied by his eyes. He knew. I could see that he knew. It was not an offer, which is something one can accept or reject. It was not even a challenge. It was malice but it was dressed up hastily, awkwardly, coming undone at the back, and enough of it was exposed to shatter any illusions.

There was a project, he told me, for which I had been *specially* chosen. He did not divulge who had chosen me but I was to prepare and submit a report directly to the Minister and, in consultation with him and the Head of the Department, to advise on the drafting of appropriate legislation. The matter was highly controversial and so all my work was to be strictly confidential.

The government was considering entering into an agreement with the owner of some coastal land it had sold off a few years earlier at a controversially low price. The land had been sold within a few weeks of an election and guarantees had been given to the public that, although the land was being sold to a private concern, it was a condition of sale that no new or expanded mining activities could take place there without an environmental impact statement being obtained which would then be incorporated into regulatory legislation. Now, four years later, the owner wanted to put the land to the use for which it was bought, to massively expand an existing smelting facility for heavy metals. This was where I came in. I was to determine the environmental impact of the expansion and recommend necessary controls and safeguards with respect to marine and atmospheric pollution in particular.

'Where is this place?'

'It's been in the news, or at least the owner has, in fact I used to have a personal connection with the owner's family myself.'

'Where is it?'

'South-east Australia.'

'Could you be less specific? What's it called?'

'Spensers Gulf. He bought the island too, Spenser Island. He owns the whole area. Claremont. Perhaps you've heard of him?'

Perhaps I had heard of him? Facetiousness became Gerard. Eczema would have too. I already knew of him when Amanda and I were still small secret wardrobe sitters and I was, unwittingly but quite clearly in Mrs Claremont's view, posing an enormous threat to the future cultural, social and possible psycho-sexual wellbeing of Amanda. I must have known of him not that long after he had first turned his mind to lead, zinc and gold and their more base equivalents. And I had always found it difficult to imagine, as I lay on my bed in the years ten through seventeen, that Mr Claremont, a man whose first name was, I thought, *Mister*, would have himself been the engineer of my banishment from the realm of his daughter. There were several grounds for thinking this. Firstly, we had barely met. Secondly, I was not so bad and I felt that a chemical engineer would have known this, a man of that calling being possessed of in-built Geiger counters which measured other people's intrinsic worth objectively, without regard to the creases in the shirts of their fathers.

I had laid our enforced estrangement all at the feet of the mother out of whose mouth came hairpins, sit-still admonishments and the most elegant cruelty a child could hope never to hear. And if I had not entered the father's consciousness *then*, I would certainly not have entered it in the subsequent years of accumulation during which he so successfully jettisoned his engineering career for more public mercantile pursuits, years that began with the rejection of the ten-year-old me by her mother and concluded with the rejection of her mother and her father by the adult Amanda.

But if Mr Claremont had hardly registered my prepubescent existence he would certainly have registered the existence of the splendidly redoubtable Gerard, management's gift to God. After all, it was Gerard with whom Amanda had lived during those troubled and searching years of the middle period somewhere between *Achy Breaky Heart* and the completion of the Uruguay round of GATT talks. Mr Claremont would not have liked Gerard. He would have mistrusted both his aesthetically motivated athleticism (naturally-occurring testosterone should have been enough) and his New Age attempts to be open-minded, which meant, in practice, rejecting nothing. If Amanda was, before the fall of Gerard, impersonating the black sheep of the family, then any partner of whom her father disapproved should have been all the more favoured by her, all the more desirable, given the realpolitik of filial rebellion and the alliances made with one's enemies' enemies. But obviously something had gone awry because it seemed that Amanda and Gerard were no longer together.

I could not imagine Gerard blaming himself for their parting or accepting it with equanimity. Nor could I imagine him not being acutely aware that Mr Claremont disliked him. I thought I could see why he had picked me for the job. He blamed Amanda's father, at least in part, for their separation and he wanted to wound him where he was most sensitive, right in the smelter. And I had the reputation in the department of being obsessive about the control of industrial pollution. At best I could stop the project going ahead, with a long list of objections and uneconomic pre-conditions (assuming the Minister listened to me) and, if not, at least he would have exercised arbitrary power over me, shifting me back and forth around the country to the dismay of Tanya and his successor with respect to her, me. He was risking nothing. This was obviously what was meant by a win/win situation. He wins twice. He was clearly worthy of his MBA.

———————————

'Why did they have to choose you?' Tanya asked. I still had not told her the name of the manager of our unit in the department. She was feeling besieged enough as it was. By the time I had returned from my fourth trip to Spensers Gulf there were only eight months to go before her contract with the university expired. The thesis was not going to be finished in eight months and she was concerned about her position. Soon Abby would be starting school. On hot days the car begged to be put out of its misery and on cold days it behaved as if it had been. Tanya said it had entered its autumn years, the years in which it could only be relied upon to move in autumn. It was my first and our only car. We'd had sex (front and back seats) and eaten Nepalese food in that car, sometimes in reverse order.

———————————

One Saturday morning while Tanya and Abby were out shopping, a woman who was surveying people in the area for a polling company knocked on our door. She asked if I would mind answering a few questions. It wouldn't take long. It was hot so I invited her in and offered her a cold drink. She started asking the listed questions. How many people lived here? Was there a biological family here? If an election were held tomorrow who would I vote for? Which of the following issues was more likely to determine my vote: law and order, unemployment, health, foreign policy, interest rates or the personalities of the party leaders? It didn't take long for her to agree that the way the questions were framed made the answers to them close to useless in terms of their predictive capacity. She was an undergraduate psychology major trying to earn a little money on the side. I could see a wave of distress splash across her face when she learned how educated my wife and I were and that we were still thinking of trying to earn a little money on the side. Was education a waste of time? Was that what I was saying? 'No, of course not,' I said, leaving us both unconvinced.

We returned to the questionnaire. Where did we go for our last holiday? How far was it from where we were living at the time? How did we get there? How long ago was our last holiday? What proportion of our income did we spend on accommodation (in rent or mortgage repayments)? How often did we buy clothes? What proportion of our income went on food, on insurance, gas, electricity, on entertainment? When would we be upgrading our car, within weeks, six months, two years, five years?

I was looking at the kitchen floor. Abby had lost a glow-in-the-dark space monster. It had a name. She knew it. I didn't. It came from the cereal pack. She had only needed eleven more to have the set when this one went missing. Now here it was at my feet under the kitchen table. I had found it for her. She should want for nothing. Nobody ever wants for nothing.

The undergrad psychology major repeated her question about upgrading the car. Her voice was measured as she went through the options for me again, slowly, all her training thus far enabling her to gently massage my growing inability to answer her questions or deal with the concomitant realisations. She should not have been asking these questions, not of strangers. We were no one's target market. There was nothing to be learned from my answers, no valid extrapolation to be made. If an election had been held the next day, Abby would still have wanted the other eleven glow-in-the-dark space monsters and Tanya would still not have finished her PhD thesis.

Bathroom tiles were lifting in the shower recess. For days I had valiantly ignored them but Tanya had seen them too and now we had to face and even discuss the lifting of the bathroom tiles in the shower recess. I didn't know what had caused them to lift, the category of person that corrects the effect nor the identity of a suitable person within that category. As both a man and an engineer I should have known more about this than I did, should in the sense of everybody's expectations, perhaps Tanya's expectations. But I didn't. I would've called my father but he was in Queensland, Tanya's father had died a long time ago, and anyway, in our thirties we were meant to be omnipotent, at least in matters of grout and seepage, insurance and financial planning. But I had no doubt that if I ever did determine the appropriate category of tradesperson to fix the bathroom tiles problem, I would not be able to afford their services. The psychology major looked at her printed material and then at me with slight horror as if to say: You can be impotent but you cannot be indigent.

Out of necessity, we would get somebody to fix it and pay for it, like other essentials, with an already laden credit card. I would never be able to pay off the credit card. Not ever. My salary had not increased for four years. I just flirted with the debt, servicing it, like a prostitute, never leaving it fully satisfied, simultaneously contemptuous and in fear of what it might do. In the meantime my daughter would be growing up and we would try to shelter her from the debt for as long as we could. This was my plan.

And there was no time, not six months, two years, five years or ten years when, according to the plan, we would be ready to upgrade the car. This was true whether the car manufacturers named the new models Galaxies, Meteors, Novas, Supernovas or Blackholes. I myself was a professional male in my mid to late thirties with no prospect of appealing to the market. The market and I just never met and the greater the primacy of the former the more marginal I would become. Every alternate week the bank automatically deducted sixty-two per cent of the previous fortnight's pay packet for the mortgage.

So I looked down at the kitchen floor with a tightness in my throat and the young woman, this potential psychologist who must have wished she had never knocked on my door, absorbed my silence. I wanted to tell her to go away but none of this was her fault. If she had given it any thought though she would have realised that she too had a pretty good chance of ending up in a kitchen in her mid to late thirties looking down at the floor for glow-in-the-dark space monsters without a prayer of a hope for a new car in the time allotted for that purpose by her current employers. But it was Saturday morning and she probably had a date that night which she thought might just make everything alright. They were going clubbing. They would trip till not only was there no tomorrow, but till there was considerable doubt about today. She was going to forget that we ever met, and having failed to get a response to the question, 'Are you alright?' she would creep out of my home thinking how weird some people are.

CHAPTER 17

On the night of my return from my fifth visit to Spensers Gulf, Tanya had fallen asleep by ten o'clock. She had set the dining table for two and left my dinner in the microwave oven but when my plane was delayed she gave in to sleep. It was Abby's swimming lesson day and Abby had complained that Tanya's mother had been taking and picking her up too often and that she drove 'funny'. She had asked why Tanya couldn't pick her up if she really loved her more than work. When Tanya's explanations incorporated the proposition that she was only human, Abby responded that this was good because she was a human too. I heard all this over the phone but by the time I had closed the front door behind me the show was over and the central protagonists were fast asleep. There was a note on my pillow. *Welcome home, my dear one. Wake me if you like. Love Tanya.*

But she was sleeping so soundly I did not have the heart to wake her. I took off my shoes and went to look in on Abby. Fortunately she was going through the stage of needing to sleep with a night-light on or I would have tripped on a wide-eyed wooden bug whose lashes fluttered when its wheels moved. Abby had named it Alexander. Tanya had bought it for her even without Abby *needing* it. (Abby had recently replaced *want* with *need* in her vocabulary.) It, that is to say, Alexander, had been made by members of one or other oppressed minority.

Tanya was a sucker for goods that were marketed as the products of a cottage industry staffed by people whose problems made her feel guilty for worrying about her own concerns. It seemed that these people could see her coming because we kept accumulating variants of Alexander which generally found their way into Abby's imaginative world and from there onto her bedroom floor.

All that was required was for the oppressed manufacturers of Alexander and his friends to realise how far they could go in provoking Tanya's guilt. If they made her feel too guilty she would have to turn her back on them, their problems and their products. She might even feel a little angry at them for so brazenly invoking perspective to trivialise her problems. There were, no doubt, schools of commerce that propagated the law of diminishing marginal guilt, a law that holds that, after some point, further increases in the quantity of guilt induced yield smaller and smaller sales.

'Dad, are you home now?' Abby whispered from beneath a horizontal wall of soft toys. 'Mum said she'd wake me up when you got home.'

'She's asleep too, sweetie.'

'Shall we play, just us then?'

'Sure. As soon as you wake up.'

'But I'm already awake,' she yawned.

'Then I'm too late. I've missed you waking up. You'll have to go back to sleep so that you can wake up when I'm home.'

'Dad, after swimming today, we went to the beach.'

'Did you?'

'Yes and I've started a rock collection. Do you want to see it?'

'Yes I do. As soon as you wake up.'

Abby's growing body, swathed in flannel, soon yielded to the call of the hour but it was a different proposition for me in our bedroom. Tanya slept as if made for a tomb while I lay beside her, tired but not sleepy, alternating my focus between the ceiling and the digits of the clock radio, the same one that had alarmed Tanya first thing that morning so many years earlier when it had broadcast the fluctuations in the all-ordinaries index for the first time.

I knew well one of the possible causes of her need for sleep on these early nights. Her thesis seemed as far from its conclusion as ever and her need for it to be finished, and successfully so, was pressing down on her. She took to talking about her horror at the prospect of not finishing the thesis, not turning it into a book, not retaining her position at the university and ultimately waking up to one morning after another, each with nothing but its own afternoon. But the more she worried about it the further its completed form retreated from reality and the further it invaded her imagination.

There was a financial aspect to it as well. When budgeting for Abby's ever-increasing needs and the maintenance of the mortgage, Tanya's income had always been factored in. I couldn't do it alone. We had discussed this and Tanya had, depending on her mood, immediately characterised our situation as hopeless, or else offered an as yet unpromised advance from an unknown publisher for immediate banking. The latter would follow a good day's work or a positive meeting with her supervisor.

'He thinks it's going well and so do I. I know it will be

something publishers will be interested in,' she would tell me over the phone when I would call at night from Amanda's father's heavy metal rich gulf. When she asked me about my work I would resist telling her all of my concerns just as I resisted exposing her optimistic plans for publication of her thesis to the hard cold light of reality. But it was becoming inescapably clear to me that Mr Claremont's smelter project could not go ahead as planned without causing extensive degradation of the environment and killing off certain types of fish, birds and plant life.

Why should this have affected me? Surely once I had reported my findings, and perhaps attempted to steer the legislation accordingly, my stake in Spensers Gulf, Spensers Island and Claremont's lead smelter, zinc smelter and sulphuric acid plant would revert to that of any other member of the public? My job was to make recommendations based on my research. Whatever my social or moral concerns, my professional interest stopped at the recommendations. If they wanted someone to write the kind of report they were looking for, irrespective of the findings, it would not have been difficult to choose someone else for the job, someone whose scientific integrity stopped short of personal courage.

Ageing quietly beside the sleeping Tanya that night in our historiography-laden bed, watching the clock impart the neutrality of time as only a clock can, it occurred to me that it was not ridiculous to contemplate the predication of courage, or of its absence, with respect to somebody in the circumstances in which I found myself. Whatever the clock might say to the occupants of the bed between one event and the next during the term of our tacit agreement to sample these two particular versions of a life together, these were not neutral times.

Public servants, of which I was one, had become servants of hidden and private fiefdoms, publicly funded till the next economic 'reform' by the government and the eventual onset of rigormortis in the body politic. In this instance, I worked for Gerard and he worked, at least in part, to settle an old score with Amanda's father. It had been rumoured that his contract of employment specified that any increases in the department's productivity, which meant any reduction in its operating costs for the financial year, were to go directly to him as a bonus. If my recommendations were looked on with disfavour by the Head of the department or even by the Minister himself, there was nothing to stop me being dismissed and the consequent reduction in the Department's operating costs going as a bonus, in several senses, to Gerard. Then one or other colleague of mine would be asked to try again, being free, of course, to draw on my earlier work and the knowledge of my experience.

If I did not write a report that was favourable to the smelter project, in whose interests would it be to keep me around? And if I were dismissed, who in the hierarchical pyramid would find this sort of blatant interference with public service objectivity and outright intimidation of a servant of the State so improper, so grossly offensive that he would have to speak up? Would it be the Minister or the Head of the Department? Would it be Mr Claremont or Gerard?

At night the helicopters moved above our home. I listened to them churning up the sky. What were they looking for? Could it not wait until the morning? This never used to happen. I didn't remember helicopters in the night skies of my youth. Tanya and Abby stayed sleeping and if I was to join them I had to make peace with the helicopters. There was no sense in fighting them. Turning my back on the clock, I repeated to myself, slowly, all that I knew.

At night the helicopters moved.

I woke the next morning to intermittent sunlight sneaking up on me from under the blinds of our bedroom. Tanya was up already. My half-emptied suitcase lay at the foot of the bed. The intermittence of the light was not due to any fault in the sun but rather to the jagged horizon I collided with when I moved from my supine position in bed. Whichever way I turned, the pillow had become hard and coarse and smelling as of the earth's beginnings. I hoped I was not fully awake and that this was only what you faced when your subconscious kow-tows to the helicopters in the bargaining for a few short hours of sleep that no one else is using.

But this was real and only made explicable and bearable by the studious creeping about of my daughter, wrapped in her dressing gown and wearing her rabbit slippers. She was carrying the rocks of her new collection and delicately arranging them in a circumference around my head.

'Hi, Dad,' she whispered. 'These are my rocks, the ones I told you about. Are you awake?'

I picked her up from the side of the bed and held her tightly to me with my eyes closed, tempted to believe in God just to have someone to thank for her.

'Dad. You're squishing me! Why are you crying? Are you crying?'

'No, sweetie. It's just lovely to see you. Are these your rocks?'

'Yep. The ones I told you about. You said you'd see them when we woke up.'

'And I have.'

'Do you like them?'

'Abby, I love them.'

Tanya had squeezed fresh orange juice for all of us. We had breakfast and then it was agreed that I would take Abby out shopping and let Tanya have the morning to work. It was not the time to discuss the things that had kept me tilting at helicopters in the hours I had borrowed from another day. I looked at them both sitting at the kitchen table in the morning dishevelment and thought how far I had come.

I took Abby to the old neighbourhood by the beach where Tanya and I had spent our money and our youth together almost half our lives ago. For a moment Abby had thought that I meant that she would see us there as we were at seventeen. It was not a flaw in her understanding but a flaw in my expression coupled with her almost tangible desire to see us in the olden days. She was disappointed that the supermarket where I had met her mother looked just like today's supermarkets and she wanted to see the exact aisle where we had first spoken. (She had heard the story of our meeting many times and loved hearing it, so much so that she could tell it to us, and she would correct us if we got something wrong.)

I explained that everything was much faster these days. Groceries were scanned, bar codes were read and prices were totalled instantly by computers. If this technology had been around back then Tanya and I might never have met and she might never have been born. The thought horrified her and didn't do much good for me either. It had been hard enough meeting Tanya *then*. It would be impossible now. Everything happens too quickly to be understood while it is happening. Analysis is impossible until the event is over. Nobody seems to mind this. It is never commented on, except in a manner of speaking, by Abby.

With all the rhythmic shifts in one's pulse that accompanies a second order emotion like nostalgia, I took Abby into Old Man Williamson's Cards and Music. It had changed in ways Abby could not imagine. By the corner opposite the counter there stood a forlorn display case half-filled with second-hand LP records, the very gold of my youth when pocket money was measured in inches of vinyl. Abby picked one of them up and examined it.

'What's this, Dad?'

'That's Elvis, sweetie, on record, vinyl.'

She seemed excited by this. 'Really?' she asked.

'Uh-huh. From his Las Vegas period, by the look of it.'

'It's really old isn't it, Dad,' she said looking at it with new reverence.

A very young man, fashionably close to bald was manically slapping plastic CD covers along the wall from A to Z to keep them from leaning forward. I had never done anything that fast and I was not likely to.

'Excuse me,' I said to him, having just then, in that instant, acquired my parents' displacement from his part of the century. 'Excuse me, is Mr Williamson around?'

'Who?'

'Mr Williamson. I thought I'd say hello. Is he around here somewhere?'

He looked at me blankly but not with the blankness of someone failing to understand. This was the blankness of a young man with a cold head, who had spent too many hours preventing CDs from inclining uncommercially head-first toward oblivion and who wanted nothing more from a career.

'The owner, Mr Williamson,' I repeated.

'Oh right. He's dead.'

'Dead!'

'Yeah. Been dead for years.'

'Like Elvis, Dad,' said Abby, at my leg beneath the counter with a vinyl recording of the King under her arm.

There was no reason why Old Man Williamson should not have been dead. If he were 'Old Man Williamson' almost twenty years earlier it was likely, even proper for him to have died. It was just that in calling him 'old man' Williamson we had not meant to imply then that he was old, just that he was older then we were and unable to distinguish aurally between Joy Division and The Clash (which is why he filed all New Wave records under 'T').

But I was not ready to stop thinking of him as 'Old Man Williamson' because if I did my father would be next in line to be the old man that some seventeen-year-old factors vaguely into the outskirts of his consciousness as the personification of what used to be but no longer is. And this would mean that I would soon be forty which, of course, I could not be. I was still seventeen, or perhaps eighteen, and had just stayed that way for twenty years.

The bald young man struck up a conversation with Abby without any trouble. Perhaps it was easier for them to talk *because* they both knew that he'd had trouble talking to me. When we left Williamson's Cards and Music I was still acclimatising myself to Old Man Williamson's death, remembering his not unfriendly gruffness, particularly in the summer I had met Tanya. I held Abby's hand as we made our way back into the street. Her other hand had *Elvis in Las Vegas*. The young fast bald man had given her the album on the condition she let him know if she saw Elvis appearing anywhere in her travels.

So 'Old Man Williamson' was no longer alive. Was there

something I would have said to him? This was ridiculous. I had made no imprint on the pages of his life. But his business was a large part of his life and I was a regular customer, albeit not a regular purchaser. People like me and Tanya had helped that business survive and keep the same name, if nothing else, till the prime of the young bald man. We had known the rules and were respectful in our discourtesy. I pulled out of the car-park thinking that perhaps, merely as a representative of my peers, I would have told him what had become of me and maybe thanked him for taking a chance on the soundtrack to my youth. Abby was strapped in the back seat singing to herself between bites of a donut.

'*So let me see . . . your teddy bear.*'

On the spur of the moment, I drove to Tanya's mother's house. It was only a few streets away and it was in keeping with our excursion through nostalgia. Tanya's mother, who could not do enough to be part of our lives, especially Abby's, was delighted.

'What have you got there? Elvis Presley?'

'Yes,' said Abby before drinking her cordial, 'but we can't listen to it 'cause it's not a CD.'

'Really?' said Tanya's mother.

'No, it's an LP record from the olden days, isn't it, Dad? LP stands for *long playing.*'

'Would you like to listen to it, Abby? I have a record player. It used to be your mother's and Uncle Marty's.'

'*Could* we? We could dance in the Elvis way. Nanna, do you know the one about the hound dog?'

When she had made the two of us a cup of tea, Tanya's mother played *Elvis in Las Vegas* for Abby and the two of them danced to it in the lounge while I went down the passage to change a light bulb in the ceiling of her bedroom.

The house managed to be both small and empty. I had not

visited it often enough recently for its dimensions not to have changed. It was not sufficient to have Tanya's mother over to our place even once a week. Looking at the photos on her dressing table of a younger Marty, Tanya, Abby and of Abby, Tanya and me, I realised that we had to take time to visit her at her place so that it was not just a museum. I stuck my head into Tanya's old room where she had started all her thinking so long ago, where Antigone had wrestled with a temporal and spiritual conflict of interest and where Tanya and I had practised the begetting of Abby to the strains of Marty's band paying homage to Creedence.

In the lounge room Abby and her grandmother swivelled their hips to another Elvis recording that had found its way like a Gideon Bible into a cabinet by the silver tea set. Together they sang Abby's song about the dog.

'*You said you're in my class . . . that was just a lie.*'

It was Abby's choice next. We would do whatever she wanted to do. She chose the beach in order to add to her rock collection. I could help, she told me. We drove to the beach, not far from Tanya's mother's house, where Tanya and I used to walk and make love between the beach-houses. I didn't ask but suspected that Abby knew it was a destination in keeping with the sort of day we were having. We parked in the car-park at the top of the cliffs and made our way down the steep path where the ti-trees had been cleared, singing and giggling what became a medley of Elvis tunes. I found myself encouraging this Elvis exegesis.

'*Don't be cruel to a heart that's two.*'

Abby ran to the water's edge and back again towards me as the waves gave tired chase to her feet, just going through the motions and letting her escape each time. I held her shoes and socks until I was forced to drop them when she ran full bore into my lap while I was standing fully upright.

Something about the beach brings out the philosopher in my daughter or perhaps it is just being around water, because she's prone to matters ontological in the bath too.

'Dad?'

'Yes, sweetie.'

'Are there more grains of sand in the world than drops of water?'

'You mean in the whole world or just at this beach?'

'Dad, I'm serious. Be serious!' She had learnt this response from her mother.

'Abby, that's like asking how long is a piece of string.'

'Why?'

''Cause, for one thing, it depends on the sizes of the drops of water and, like a ball of string, a drop of water could be any size.'

'What about a ball of wool?'

'Same thing.'

'But wool comes from sheep, Dad, and if we knew how many sheep there were in the world we'd know. *You* could work it out. You're a scientist. You could work it out with science couldn't you, Dad?'

Whether her faith in science was more misplaced than her faith in me was sometimes hard to say. I managed to get her away from balls of wool and string, drops of water and grains of sand by showing sudden enthusiasm for her rock collection. It took us to the rock pools where she squealed at the starfish, the minnows and the sea anemones. But it was only a short reprieve from the metaphysical.

'Dad, do you want to talk about God?'

'Didn't you talk to Mum about that?'

'Yep, in the bath. But that was ages ago.'

'Well, I suppose things might've changed. What do you want to talk about?'

'Dad, do you think I believe in God?'

'I don't know, sweetie, I've been away for a little while. I might be a little bit out of touch. *Do* you believe in God?'

'I don't know yet,' she looked up at me with her mother's eyes. 'Is that okay?'

We put the rocks in a box in the boot of the car and I picked her up in my arms.

'Abby, like you, that's perfect.'

I placed her in the back seat and snapped shut the buckle of her seat belt. Before I had turned the key in the ignition she was singing again.

'*I still want to see the tigers . . . but tigers ain't the kind you love enough . . .* Dad?'

'Yes, sweetie.'

'Why did Elvis say "ain't" instead of "are not"?'

We stopped for a Dairy Queen and a Flake on our way home. It was almost dinnertime so Abby had to promise she wouldn't tell her mother. As I wiped the last vestiges of our indiscretion from her fingers and her mouth, she confessed that she might be able to keep a secret but that she wasn't sure. Could she just see?

The sun was setting behind our neighbour's hedge as I carried the shopping and the box of Abby's new rocks from the car to the house where Tanya had had the day free to work uninterrupted on her thesis. Abby's exuberance at returning home to Tanya was heightened on seeing her sitting in the lounge room drinking coffee with Kate. She flung herself onto Tanya and burst out for both of them with machine-gun rapidity selected highlights of her day: Elvis and Nanna, the beach, some new rocks, a Dairy Queen and a Flake. When I came in from the kitchen Abby passed me to find *Elvis in Las Vegas* which was standing upright on the kitchen table between a bag of broccoli and a box of Coco Pops. Some habits die hard.

There were four coffee cups in the kitchen sink suggesting a more than social intake of caffeine. A box of tissues by Kate's side in the lounge room suggested a crisis. Tanya confirmed that suspicion privately a few minutes later in the kitchen when we decided it would take two of us to make a fresh pot of coffee.

'She's left him,' Tanya whispered over running water.

'Really?'

'Uh-huh.

'Is it a fight or is there something . . . deeper behind this?'

'Both. Why? Don't you think she's done the right thing?'

'Well, I don't know anything about it. Did you know it was coming?'

'Sort of.'

'Sort of?'

'Eddie,' she whispered over the whistle of the kettle, 'she's left him for good. I hate to see her like this.' She pressed one side of her face against my chest. 'Did you have a good day? You were gone such a long time.'

'We had a fantastic day,' I said running my fingers through her hair. 'We even visited your mum.'

'Oh, that's great. Was she delighted? I bet she was.'

'Yeah, took it rather well. Listen, shouldn't we get back out there? Abby's probably got her dancing to "Jailhouse Rock".'

'You couldn't guess all the places we've been to today,' I said, carrying the fresh coffee into the lounge room where Abby sat on Kate's knee. Tanya came a minute or so later.

'Oh yes, I could,' said Kate bouncing Abby on her lap as though her life were not falling apart.

'I told her, Dad.'

'Oh, well then it's not guessing. Do you know Williamson's Cards and Music?'

'Near the beach?' Kate asked.

'Yes,' I said pouring the coffee.

'Oh, Eddie and I used to *live* there when we first started going out,' Tanya volunteered with a smile.

'*Did* you, Mum? Did you and Dad live there?'

'No. Not actually *live* there, sweetie.'

'Yeah, I think I might know it,' said Kate.

'Well, you might remember the old guy that used to run it, Old Man Williamson?' Kate looked vague. If it didn't come flooding back she wasn't going to trowel for it.

'Yeah, what about him?' asked Tanya.

'He's dead,' I told her.

'Really? Dead!'

'Yeah, only physically, the business is still there.'

Abby went to bed after dinner but even before then it was clear without anything being said that Kate would stay the night with us. Over dinner we had limited ourselves to conversation that was consistent with the common adult charade that we are just dangerously large children; the conversation was not about that which absorbed us to the exclusion of everything else. Strangely Abby did not ask where Paul was or why he was not there, children being so often more adaptable to change than adults. Or perhaps it was just that Kate was her friend as well as ours, whereas Paul and Abby had always tacitly agreed not to bother each other. Abby was an example of what Kate wanted that Paul would not give her and Paul was one of those adult outlines that was coloured in only after Abby went to bed. (She had grown up falling asleep to the sound of Paul and Tanya disagreeing.)

CHAPTER 18

There is always a last argument, the one that permits us to be tempted at some later time into thinking that if only we had not said, seen or raised some issue or other then things might not have ended as they had and always would have.

We listened quietly, vacillating between apprehension and resignation, as Kate told us of the straw that broke the camel's back.

He was my friend, best man at my wedding and all that, but what did it mean to call him my friend? He was someone that I saw and he saw me. Our wives saw each other and we went with them most of the time. We were responsible for their knowing each other. We followed each other's progress with an interest that seemed largely motivated by a desire to see how it ends. There had been camaraderie there once, at the beginning. But it dissipated as a result of some combination of the effects on him of his parents, their money, his job, and the times which made powerful and arrogant buffoons out of little people who might otherwise have spent their whole lives misguidedly waiting for the realisation of a potential they did not have.

Kate had married my friend from university and Paul was

not that man anymore. Neither of us could have known that he would change in the way that he did but she was the one that had married him. We were all like peas in a pod in those days except that Paul was only trying it out, just visiting. He did not have to stay in the pod. We stayed there and ripened only to be thrown into an industrial-sized cauldron and turned into pea soup for a chain restaurant. His parents owned the franchise.

Paul had not understood why Kate was walking out. She said it was bad enough that he tried to allay her fear of losing her job with his usual cant about economic efficiency and the over-supply of teachers. He had no idea of how things were on the ground, of teacher-student ratios, or of the provision of opportunities for disadvantaged children. But worse for her than any of this, he had only a limited understanding of her need to work. How could he defend policies that stopped her from working? Did he not appreciate how much passion there was inside her to get out and do something in the world? Did he think she could be bought off with the range of Lancôme products?

He had become enraged, infuriated, that she did not want to stay home and be looked after. He threw a lamp, not at her, but near her. There was money. He would take her out. Why did she have to turn everything into a critical issue when things could be so easy? She threw a wooden box of pot-pourri. It hit his leg. She didn't have to struggle, to get up early every morning and fight her way through the traffic, he argued. Wasn't that what every woman wanted?

'I was bored,' she told us, her face half in shadow and warming the palms of her hands. 'I had been bored for a long time. You must have known that?'

She looked up at us sitting next to each other on the couch like children and we looked back sheepishly, as though we had known all along and failed to do all the things it was not in our power to do. In her pain she had grown smaller in the shadows.

'But I thought if it was just boredom you can live with it, find the spark somewhere else, friends, work, reading, movies . . . children. He kept saying he wasn't ready for children. What's the point of being shackled to the prick if he won't even give you children?'

It was at this point that she began to cry. Tanya went over to Kate and took her in her arms. I had not made up my mind whether we should be comforting her by pushing the you-are-so-right line or whether we should be comforting her by gently suggesting that she might feel differently in the morning. Then, of course, there was the question of disloyalty to Paul.

Kate was right, Paul had become an unmitigated prick but didn't we, or at least, didn't *I* owe my nominal best friend something other than encouragement to his wife to leave him? Was it really in her best interests anyway? And what if they reconciled? In the honeymoon of a reconciliation people tell each other everything. They name names. I could recall instances I had read about. About the only worse thing a friend could do would be to try to make a move on her himself.

I decided to be firmly noncommittal with respect to the correctness of her decision in a there-there guise, with perhaps a subliminal I-understand timbre to it, while we waited for the fallout from what she had done. This was until at least I could see which way Tanya was going to go. Prudence told me to wait for a sign from her, although it was difficult to imagine her saying anything in Paul's favour.

'What are you going to do? What do you *want* to do?' Tanya asked our sad friend.

'Well,' she began between sobs, 'I thought that I would delay telling my parents for a little while. It'll only upset them and . . . I don't know . . .'

'I know,' Tanya offered sympathetically, 'it somehow makes it more real when you start telling people. You need time for it to sink in first. You know you can stay here as long as you like.'

Kate looked up and smiled at Tanya with something approaching gratitude, then at me and then they both looked at me.

'Oh yes, of course. Of course you can stay here as long as you like.'

There had not been any time since my coming home from Spensers Gulf the night before that Tanya and I had been simultaneously alone together and conscious, apart from the brief joint venture in the kitchen to make coffee. This made it almost ten days. Tanya fixed up the couch for her with the coffee table doubling as a bedside table on which she put my bedside lamp, while I went to hide in our bedroom. I could hear Tanya whispering to the sounds of Kate getting undressed.

'No, don't be silly, sleep in the raw if you're more comfortable. Feel free to put your toothbrush and toiletries in the bathroom. Just make yourself at home. Wake me if you can't sleep. You might feel better in the morning but don't be upset if you don't.'

I was exhausted from a full day playing with Abby and a full night of sympathetic listening and silent bipartisanship. Tanya had washed her hair and so had the scent I had often tried to recall during the many nights alone in my hotel room at Spensers Gulf. I nuzzled my way towards her ear but she barely responded, preferring instead to face the ceiling. After so many years together one learns the meaning of 'no' without it being said. It's just that I wasn't sure what she was saying no to. Such was my tiredness that I was not up to the robust lovemaking that was usually induced by the department's need to send me out of town. But the dreamy kind, in the rhythm of the slow motion hair-in-the-breeze turning through one hundred and eighty degrees of shampoo commercials, would have been nice. The kitchen was closed.

'What do you think?' I said, joining her on the ceiling.

'I don't know. It's not going to be easy but . . . I suppose she *should* leave him if she feels this way. They don't have kids. God knows she *ought* to feel this way. Can you imagine living with Paul? I find it difficult enough being his friend, or at least the wife of his friend.'

'Which is it? Which do you find hard, being his friend or his friend's wife?'

I wasn't trying to be funny but it seemed better not to point that out. I was trying not to be scared of all those things I had not yet named, things in Spensers Gulf, things in the department, in our *flexi-account* and in the answers I had given to the undergraduate psychology major when I could see no further ahead than a glow-in-the-dark space monster at my feet.

'Tanya, he wasn't always like this.'

'I know. I've seen him get worse over the years. What is it about the passage of time that makes the present so much worse than the past?'

'It's a law of the physical world that things tend from order to disorder. It's called the Second Law of Thermodynamics.'

'A law with no appeal. It's . . . even been happening to us,' she said.

'What do you mean?' I sat up slightly, with a twinge of newfound lower-back pain.

'We used to be progressives. Now we look back with

almost religious fondness to the past. This is a distinguish-
ing characteristic of conservatives.'

I sat up further, suppressing anger, more back pain and a
desire to shake her, to wash her mouth out with hope. 'Hey,
we're not conservatives. Don't be so simplistic. That's
stupid. *We're* not tending towards disorder. It's just that our
friends look like they're splitting up. Now maybe they
should and maybe they shouldn't but either way *we're* not
conservatives.' I took a breath. Now that Old Man
Williamson was dead breathing would become a talking
point in the endless conversation I had with myself.

'Well, do you think she should leave him, start again?' she
asked.

'I don't know,' I said yet again. 'I mean, if it's just a matter
of ideology maybe she should think again.'

Tanya sat up.

'What do you mean, *just* a matter of ideology? It comes
down to some pretty fundamental issues like core values
and respect. If his cores values are so corrupt and repulsive
then she can't have any respect for him and if she doesn't
have any respect for him she can't love him.'

'And if she doesn't love him?'

'What do you mean *if she doesn't love him?* Isn't it obvious
what she should do if she doesn't love him? Otherwise
she'll become like everyone's parents.'

'If she doesn't love him should she leave him? *Must* she
leave him? What if she liked him, could learn to like him, re-
learn? They have years of shared memories. She is financially
secure with him. She could go back to study, look for another
job, have children sooner or later with him. Is she lonelier
now than she will be pushing forty and trying to meet unat-
tached men, with the spectre of unemployment, and with all
the promise of a rented one-bedroom flat and the intermit-

tent whisper of regrets as the years pile up like the English and History textbooks she will no longer have room or need for? Think about it, Tanya. Should she leave him?'

Tanya slowly took in a deep breath through her nostrils and let it out rather less slowly through her mouth before answering.

'I don't know, Eddie. I don't know.'

The paint on the ceiling was flaking. It had been flaking slowly before our eyes every day but we, or at least I, looked at it only at night in the dark. When the light was on I was either reading, making love to Tanya or fumbling for a book or the light itself, or the semi-conscious button of the clock radio that had silently kept the beat of our inner lives, or else I fumbled for my wife, sometimes to hold her, sometimes to find her and sometimes just on her behalf. But we had been talking with the light off. (My bedside lamp was in the lounge beside the sad and naked Kate.) Nonetheless the paint on the ceiling was visible to me and therefore probably visible to Tanya. It had reached such an advanced stage of disrepair that our night-eyes could not ignore it. That is what lay above us while, yet again, at night the helicopters moved looking for something less likely to be found by day.

'Tanya, how important is ideology to you? I mean, would *you* leave *me* if our ideas on the important things were not the same?'

She turned from lying on her back and rested her head on my chest.

'I can't begin to imagine it, Eddie.'

'Leaving?'

'Your ideology changing. It's so much part of you, your strength, your integrity.'

'But what if you found that I'd compromised my integrity?'

'I can hear your heart beating. Listen!'

'I can't hear it. Tanya, what if you found that I'd compromised my integrity?'

'You wouldn't. You *are* your integrity.'

'No, I'm not.'

'Yes you are.'

'I'm more than that.'

'I know that, darling, but your integrity is one of the things I admire most about you, along with all the other things of course.'

The helicopters were closing in. When the paint was ready it would fall on my hair. Perhaps I would breathe in minute flakes of it till I was ready to meet Old Man Williamson. He would want to lecture me like all old people did, especially once they're dead. But what could I have done differently? Could I have loved her more or fought harder to prolong the sweet childish days when our immaturity guaranteed non-cognisance of any of the things that could happen to us?

'What if I compromised my integrity, say, for the sake of my job, if I made false findings, wrote false reports, something like that?' I asked again.

'Why would you do that?'

'I wouldn't but what if I did?'

'Why would you?'

'To keep my job.'

'Oh, you wouldn't do that.'

'No. I know.'

'You'd be the last person in the world to do that!'

'After you?'

'Mmm . . . maybe even after me. I'm more pragmatic than you,' Tanya declared.

'You think so? You would do it to keep your job?'

'I doubt it.'

'But you *could*? You can't rule it out?'

'I don't know. Maybe.'

'What if *I* did? What if you found out that *I* did?'

'Well, I wouldn't *find out*, you'd tell me.'

'And if I did?' I asked.

'I'd lose respect for you.'

CHAPTER 19

In the morning I awoke to find myself alone in bed once more. My wife, who knew the bed in all its moods, was up with a purpose. She and Kate were preparing a lavish breakfast and Abby was leafing through a book, primarily concerned with tigers, in the warmth of the couch that had been Kate's bed. From the bedroom I could hear the festive sounds of capable women teasing out their destinies over the random clatter of morning domesticity, a sort of tertiary pyjama party. One of those inarticulate night-time fears which are meant to evaporate on contact with the morning was hanging on valiantly despite the sounds of human activity: the fear that Kate and Tanya had come back almost full circle to Freud's latency period, and that if they had they would virtually ignore me and only read books by women authors.

I crept out of the bedroom into the bathroom which had been swiftly and painlessly colonised by Lancôme. Being a male felt a lot like being alone. I wondered who my male Kate was and remembered Paul. He was an idiot. I did not want him sleeping naked on my couch.

In the vanity mirror my teeth smiled back at me under sufferance, tobacco-stained from too much tea and coffee. The bathroom had its attractions. I could shower and shave.

But the bedroom contained my clothes. Each room was a beach-head with its own distinct advantages and disadvantages. I felt the need to meet the activity of the rest of the house only when I was fully prepared. I took off my pyjamas, and while waiting for the water under the shower to become anaesthetisingly warm, I noticed the bathroom window was slightly ajar. Fresh air had been invited to join forces with deodorant, soap and perfume in the war against steam and the products of our bodies. I looked irresolutely through the window along the side of our house, and out onto the street. Several dogs had nothing to do.

Why do we love? It gives us hope of escaping a solitary existence. When I was clean I wrapped myself in a towel, shaved and sneaked back to the bedroom to dress for the breakfast party. I put on corduroy pants, an innocent face and, quite alone, went to join them.

There can often be an air almost of euphoria after fundamental changes in people's lives, even when these changes are to their detriment. In the days surrounding the death of a long-term chronic sufferer of some debilitating illness, family members or very close friends who have made a pilgrimage to the scene will often finally give in to exhaustion and laugh inappropriately until the gravity of the situation returns to chide them. No one had died at our place but there was that same slightly surreal festive atmosphere. There we all were making the best of it like stranded campers, Kate utterly spoiling Abby, or helping Tanya in the kitchen and everyone, myself included, generally diverting themselves after their unanimously acknowledged hard day at work.

There was a tacit understanding that although we had discussed with Abby the origin of the species, sex, death, God, swearing and not swearing for tactical advantage, racial prejudice, the dichotomy between equality and freedom, and involuntary peristalsis, conversation concerning divorce and even trial separation was not on. In this way we maintained the campfire ambience and ignored the future which included the end of this unplanned series of days. Kate had still not told her parents nor had she spoken to Paul for four days. It was almost time to change the sheets on the couch.

It was also approaching the time when I could not any longer in good conscience put off speaking to Paul. It did not have to be a matter of taking sides or of providing aid and comfort to the enemy. He was, after all, my friend of nearly twenty years and his wife had just left him. That day, the fourth, I decided I'd call him at work. He said he was fine and he sounded fine.

'Kate's been staying with us,' I said in an exhaled apology, like an unpleasant confession.

'Yes, I know.'

'How did you know? I thought you hadn't spoken?'

'We haven't.'

'Then how did you know she was staying with us?' I was both peeved and relieved that he knew.

'She told me on Saturday that that's where she was going. Listen, Eddie, you've got me at a really bad time. I've got back-to-back meetings all afternoon. How's she doing? Is she taking it okay? Oh shit! I didn't realise the time. I'm gonna have to call you back . . . mmm, being realistic it's gonna have to be tomorrow at the earliest. I hate to do this to you.'

'She's fine, Paul.'

'You take care of her. I'm sorry you guys have become involved.'

'Paul, it's okay on *us*. That's the least of . . .'

'Yeah. Okay,' he called out to someone on his side of the phone. 'Gonna have to go, Eddie. Take care of yourself and . . . yes, okay, coming! . . . give my love to Tanya.'

The really difficult part of being Paul's friend, I realised as he put down the phone, was that I, unlike his wife, could not leave him. There was probably a duration after which he would notice that a period of time had elapsed without our having spoken but he could never really be sure that I had left him and in order properly to leave someone they have to know about it. Kate had left him and adopted us. It was unequivocal. She was lucky.

I did not tell Tanya about my conversation with Paul or even that I had called him. I'm not sure why I kept it from her. There is something addictive about keeping things to yourself. It started with Gerard's managerial role in the department and then with his managerial role in my life. Since I had managed successfully to keep from her the identity of the persona that was sending me to Spensers Gulf every other day, it became almost a challenge to see how much I could keep from her before I was keeping something of myself from her. Then it became obvious that in keeping from her my concern about the effect on my career of my report on the Spensers Gulf project, I was already keeping back part of myself, but it was an anxious part that could only have exacerbated her periodic sense of our impending doom. Actually it had started way before any of this. Tanya had never even heard of Amanda.

The weekend arrived and still no one had discussed Kate's leaving, not her leaving Paul, not her leaving us. The first week had gone and she had finished the novel she had been reading when she came and was ready to start reading something else by my bedside lamp. The three of us agreed there was something sad about coming to the end of a good novel and that each of us tended to remember the year in divisions delineated not by months or seasons but by what we were reading at the time.

She had the night before just finished *Tess of the d'Urbervilles* and saw herself, naturally, as Tess and Paul as Alec d'Urberville. I was afraid to ask who in her life was the romantically idealised, apparently progressive but fatally flawed Angel Clare. Hardy's tragic heroine and her tale had made a deep impression on Kate. She wanted everyone to read it.

'It's so beautiful and so very sad,' she said. 'It would have changed my life . . . but it's already changed.'

That dangerous hour was upon us when the sun is leaving and you have not yet capitulated to the night by pulling the curtains across and turning on the lights. We had started a new cask of red (we drank by the cask since Kate had moved in) and I looked at her and it seemed that Tanya and I were thinking the same thing; how special she was. Like so many other people, when you looked closely at her, she was manifestly precious and in need of protection.

'You know,' Tanya said, already onto her second glass, 'I used to think there were two kinds of people in the world; people who read novels with no plot, about horses in beautiful rugged landscapes, and people who read other things but—'

'No, that's not right,' Kate interrupted. 'There are two kinds of people; people who read books and people who deal in the short-term money market.'

'No, no, you're both wrong,' I volunteered. 'There are two kinds of people in the world; people who divide people into two kinds of people and people who don't.'

Kate threw a pillow at me. She laughed and the two of

them made Oh–Eddie noises. I was scared for her and thought perhaps the best thing for her was to sleep naked on our couch next to my bedside lamp reading Hardy for the rest of her life.

It was decided that we would all stay in and that once it was really dark and much colder I would walk up the street and buy some take-away curry. (Tanya and I couldn't very well go out and leave Kate to babysit Abby even though her offer was no doubt sincere.) Because I had spent the last part of the day vigorously impersonating a Sri Lankan tiger in the back yard with Abby (a tiger *per se* was insufficient, she needed to know its ethnicity before we could play), it was agreed that I should shower before walking up the road to collect the food.

Once again, alone in the bathroom, naked, I looked at my untouched body, untouched because it would have been insensitive of us to express affection for each other in front of Kate, and unnecessarily dangerous to make love in our bedroom when it was so close to where Kate was probably still wide awake with Tess and Angel Clare. I looked at my face with the shower running. I was getting older. I always had been but it was visually unmistakable now and only steam on the mirror could conceal it. If only steam could be counted upon in the street and in offices. The bathroom window was slightly ajar again and I peered through it along the side of our house, and out onto the street. It was too early for the helicopters. Under the street-light two dogs had nothing to do.

CHAPTER 20

Tanya had phoned to order our take-away curry. All that was left was for me to collect it. She was to give Abby a bath and Kate would read before dinner. And with this makeshift civilisation in place, I set off on the three- or four-block trek to bring home the *bhutuwa*. There was barely time for my mind to come to rest from checking for my wallet and keys when it was claimed by a man a little further down the road.

He wore a tight pink t-shirt which showed a well-developed upper body and firm biceps unambiguously veined. He was pacing, his eyes threatening impatience. Clutched to his chest was a small dog with white fur and tight curls and a little shaggy beard between the lower jaw and its neck. Both the man and the white dog held to him looked down at another larger dog, brown with a white patch between its ears, that seemed to have, or wanted to have, some connection with them. It barked at them intermittently and intermittently the white dog replied. As they moved the brown dog moved with them so that the distance between them never increased. The man, who could not have been much past forty, kept shifting his attention from the imploring brown dog to me and back again as I approached. A thin film of sweat filtered down from his own dog-like brown curls to the top of his forehead and I could see from the overwhelming despair which had long ago found a home on his face that the ordinary no longer ordered him around.

'You live around here?' he asked, not without some menace.

'Yes, I do.'

'Do you know who owns this dog?' he asked pointing to the brown dog with his free hand.

'No, I don't. I've seen it around, I think, but I don't know who owns it.' I had seen both the dogs from my bathroom window and only recognised them now from their evident friendliness with each other, the two dogs who had nothing to do but look blindly at me looking, through the steam, at them looking.

'So you don't know who owns this dog?' he said, still clutching the white dog to his chest. 'Fuck!' he said under his breath, his eyes filling and he not wanting me to know.

'Are you alright?' I asked in the manner we ask people who clearly are not. He continued moving with his white dog attached to his chest, rocking it as one rocks a baby, the brown dog with the white paw-print on its head watching them.

'What would *you* do?' he asked. 'It's not my dog.'

'*Not* your dog?'

'No. *This* is my dog. That,' he said nodding at the brown dog, '. . . is someone else's dog. I can't look after it. I can't keep *two* dogs. This one belongs to someone else. You don't know who. I just can't understand. It's been dumped here. Someone's obviously dumped it. It's been coming around to my place playing with my dog and it won't go. I can't keep it. But you know what will happen if I call the pound. He'll be dead inside ten days. You know that. *They* knew that, whoever it was that just dumped him here. I don't know how someone could do it, you know. I can't keep him but he keeps coming round. Should never've fed him in the first place. You can't kill him. What would *you* do? I've been walking the streets with him hoping to find someone who might know the owners, who might've seen him dumped or maybe someone who might be able to take him in but there's no one bloody around . . . just me. What would *you* do?' He was crying. There were cuts on his hands.

'I don't know. Maybe you could put up some signs in shop windows, asking if anyone knows about him.'

'Signs . . . in shop windows?' he repeated under the street-light without trying to hide his contempt for the perfectly reasonable and practical suggestion that was at once, of course, of no use. We stood there for a moment on the corner under the street-light, cars going by oblivious to us, the little dog tucked under one arm and pressed against his chest, me not knowing what to do, the larger brown dog in the cameo appearance of its life and the man with paw stains on his pink t-shirt trying to brush away tears with his free hand.

'You're doing everything you can, you know,' I told him.

'You think so?' he asked, not cynically but as if starving for redemption.

'Yes, I do,' I answered. 'Are you okay?' He was silent for a moment.

'It's just that I can't take him home, you know. Can you take him?'

I looked briefly at the stray brown dog. 'No,' I said with a firmness which surprised me. 'No, I just can't. But I'm sure someone will if you can just hold on till daytime.'

'People shouldn't be allowed to do these things. I'd take him but I've already got this one and it's not fair on my mother. I'm staying with her, with my parents, for the time being. It's hard enough on her having one dog.'

'What's your name?' I asked. He looked in shock and his

eyes, red and moist, stopped darting around for the first time
and fixed on me before he answered.

'Nick.'

Slowly I put out my hand. 'Nick, I'm Eddie.'

As I extended my arm he could see in my eyes my realisation that I was going to be taking his cut hand in mine.

'It's alright,' he said. 'I don't have AIDS or anything. You
can shake my hand.'

'Pleased to meet you, Nick,' I said coming closer and taking his cut hand in mine and adding quietly to both of us,
'It's alright. Is there anything you would like me to do for
you, Nick? What would you like me to do?'

At this he started to cry uncontrollably. The tears were
those of a child. Embarrassed, he awkwardly took out his
wallet with his free hand and placed it in mine. As I held it
he reached in with his fingers and took out a torn and
crumpled photograph of three children and pointed to
them.

'They're mine. Two of them for sure. But they're with
their mother now. That's her,' and he pointed at a woman's
body that ended where the photograph had been torn.

'I'm an alcoholic. You can probably smell it on me. I'm no
good to them, no good to anyone. I was on the wagon,
clean for almost a year and half, loading crates at a pub in
Richmond, and I was still clean. But I got laid off without
a word of warning. She took it bad. The kids started crying
when she started going out. You know what I mean, Eddie?
That's right, Eddie, isn't it?'

'That's right.'

'So I started drinking and then . . . I don't know myself.
I've hit her. I'll tell you that. She was screwing around,
thought I didn't know and then she didn't care after a
while. Now I'm living with my mum. She only lives up

there a bit, Eddie, and she can't take two dogs. It's bad
enough as it is, man. It's killing her.'

'Is there anything you'd like me to do, Nick, anyone I can
call?'

'Why're you being like this? Why're you doing this?'

'What? I'm not doing anything. I was just on my way to
pick up some curries from there and I saw you. You seemed
like a good guy. I thought maybe there was something I
could do.'

'But why?' He cried harder. 'Why would you want to do
something for me?'

'I don't know, Nick. You know the way it is. You seem like
a good guy. Maybe you'd do something for me one day if I
needed a hand. We're neighbours, practically neighbours.
You'd help someone out, wouldn't you? Wouldn't you, Nick?'

'I don't believe this. You're like a dream. Why are you
doing this?'

'I'm not doing anything. Just talking. You seem like a
good guy.'

'Why? Why do I seem like a good guy?'

'I don't know. You care about both of the dogs, the one
that's yours and the one that isn't. You don't want to hurt
your mother and you miss your kids. I know all of this
already and it's more than enough.'

I could see that it was the first time in a long time that
he'd been shown a kindness and he couldn't believe it.

'You're incredible, man. I don't believe this.'

'I'm just a guy, Nick, just a guy on his way to pick up
some curries, a guy like you. And we talk to each other. It's
no big deal, Nick. It's what distinguishes humans from other
animals. We don't do it enough but we'll get there. It's still
early in the day.' Nick looked up at the street-light. Insects
fought each other under it. 'Early in the evolutionary day,

Nick. You know what I mean? I think you're okay now. Don't you think?'

'Let me get you something. I only live up there.'

'Nick, it's okay. I don't want you to give me anything. Take care of those dogs for just one more day. You'll be doing the neighbourhood some good. I can't take either of them. It's a real help. Lucky you're around.'

'This is incredible, just meeting you like this. Two weeks ago I was on my way to an AA meeting in Oakleigh and three guys jumped me, carved a swastika in my chest with a screwdriver, I'm serious. Look!'

He lifted up the top of his t-shirt to show raw flesh disfigured in the shape he had promised, just above the white dog's head.

'Let me get you something, Eddie. It's only up the road.'

'Thanks, Nick, but I've got to get my curries. Really. They'll be cold.' I started to walk on and we called to each other.

'Shit, man! I won't forget you, Eddie, wherever you're from.'

'Take care of yourself, Nick. You'll be fine.'

He walked up the side street occasionally turning back to face my direction, still holding the white dog. Its larger brown friend with the white between its ears followed them both back to Nick's mother's place. I was exhausted from the encounter and from trying to make him believe in something neither of us could see, from trying to steer a fine line between unintended condescension, credibility, hope and an unwanted dog.

Abby was going to bed with Tanya's assistance when I returned. She had reluctantly eaten about a fifth of a hastily prepared dinner of eggs, toast, and junket. Having complained of feeling hot she had to be begged, bribed and coerced into eating the little she finally ate. The bribe involved the next instalment of a story Tanya was making up each night as she went along, a story about a beautiful and sensitive mouse that lived in the woods and was having trouble finishing its thesis.

Kate was with Thomas Hardy or his successor in what used to be the lounge room and I stood in the kitchen thinking of Nick and the two dogs, the three children and his headless wife, and the three men that jumped him in Oakleigh leaving a swastika on his chest. Absent-mindedly, I snapped the lid off the plastic containers of curry and tasted each dish.

Was the worst part of the encounter his incredulity that I would stop, ask his name, shake his hand, talk to him and offer assistance or was it the fact that I had really provided none? Would he wake tomorrow hungover, missing his two or three children, seeing his mother pained at what she saw when she looked at him, and he still with one more dog than he required? Had he been cheated, misled, conned by a smokescreen of liberalism? I had left him with only the two dogs with which he had started; anything else would evaporate quickly. From Oakleigh he took away something he would never forget, something which will be under every t-shirt he would ever wear, sober or not, something they will, sooner or later, bury him with. The anaesthetic I had provided was cheap and unreliable. It goes like the warmth of a winter sun. Intangible anodynes, the words run out of steam—the steam that won't come with you from the bathroom and out into the street. And no one else would offer him even this. That was the worst part.

I should have taken the dog, the taller brown one with the white paw-print marking on its head. This is what I was thinking when I surprised Tanya, who looked at me quizzically as I stood motionless at the table, with my coat on, silent with watery eyes and a fork in one hand.

'What kept you? Hey, are you alright?'

Some other time. I would tell her some other time, or never. Was I alright? I would be. I would be fine.

'The curry . . . it's really hot. Never been like this.' She looked at me in silence. The fluorescent light was gently strobing, humming, flickering like an eyelid over pepper.

'Tanya . . . it's never been like this.'

CHAPTER 21

Two days later Abby's non-specific 'hotness' had ripened into a flu. Tanya had to be convinced that she was not being a bad mother not to cancel her late tutorials and to stay back later for a seminar delivered by a visiting overseas expert in international relations, a big time mega-luminary of the circuit who had managed the cross-over from academia to late-night television panels where he had critically informed us for years via satellite, with only one earplug, about everything; a big man, the Elvis of international political economy.

Kate had at that time taken to picking Abby up from Tanya's mother whose job it was to pick her up from kindergarten, in superb displays of tag-team parenting, the parenting of the 1990s which permitted the biological parents to simulate world's best income-earning activity without the child ever suspecting that non-charitable childcare was beyond the means of most definitions of the average family. But with Abby ill, feverish and aching, I came home at lunchtime, enabling Tanya's mother to explore with an appropriately qualified young man why she was retaining fluid in her legs.

Abby slept fitfully. I had read her stories but she fell asleep before each denouement. I kept her temperature down with analgesics but I could not interest her in food at all. At half-past three she was asleep and I was sitting on Kate's bed in the lounge room when the mail was delivered. It still arrived by bicycle but the whistle was not blown anymore. Was there no one who had a breath left in them to spare? Perhaps they had lost faith in what they were delivering or in themselves? It is more likely that whistles were being phased out. Recipients of tangible mail would no longer learn, Pavlovian-style, what time the mail arrived.

I went out to the letter box just when the postman arrived, as though I had structured my day around his arrival. It was a big day for us judging by the quantity of mail. I began opening it before I had even reached the house again, an impatience left over from childhood when the mere existence of a letter addressed to me was good news irrespective of its contents.

Envelopes with windows were the most strongly represented. The bank issued a periodic reminder that, as things currently stood, Tanya and I would own the house outright by the time Abby was thirty unless interest rates increased or unless we defaulted one fortnight by having less in our account than the bank automatically deducted to service the loan. If this happened the bank was entitled to sell our home forthwith, without providing advance notice of the sale in writing. This is called a mortgagee sale and we had agreed to it at the time we took the home loan. Unlike many other customers, I read the small print. The bank had not wanted me to, which is why it made the print so small, but I took the document to work and had it enlarged on the photocopier. Everything was as it was meant to be. The smaller the print the greater the liberty that was turned into license upon our signing.

What else? There were several accounts from the then recently privatised statutory authorities. At the time these authorities were privatised much was made of the Government assurances that the newly privately-owned bodies would remain subject to the strictest principles of accountability. And they had. Under the new corporate logo and colour-coordinated company banner of the power supply company was the full and frank disclosure that we had been charged zero point seven per cent more than for the same period the previous year. There was no breach of accountability in this and the print, or at least some of it, was much bigger. Disconnection would follow if this account remained unsatisfied after twenty-eight days.

I unwrapped an unsolicited newspaper that had been slipped inside our letter box between our sanitised debts and felt at once disconnected. In white lettering through a purple mast the *New Citizen*, a publication of the US far right conspiracy-peddling LaRouche movement, had made its way into my home and no doubt into the homes of my neighbours. A black-and-white photograph showed its founder, Lyndon H. LaRouche, behind a podium with his right arm unbent and outstretched, reminiscent of another time no longer so long ago. I wondered which of my neighbours were as chilled as I was to find such hard-core scapegoating conspiracy theories dressed up as salvation infiltrating their homes without any warning bells having been sounded, attempting to catch our fears and uncertainty like a wooden splinter against the flesh of a finger. And once the splinter is caught, it is more painful to dislodge it than to leave it there. Many leave it there.

I wondered what Nick would say to the *New Citizen*. He was a man as much as anyone in need of someone to blame. But because of the strange freedom which we champion at all costs, the freedom to intimidate, to promote fear and pre-existing mistrust, there would be nothing to stop him taking to the street at night with fear and pain and with whisky on his breath, nothing then to stop him setting fire to someone's bed. Then the helicopters would go looking for him and when they found him his mother would be left forever with two dogs, a small white one with tight curls that looked like her son and another larger brown hybrid with a white paw-print marking on its head. I had seen Nick's eyes, smelt his breath, touched his bloodied hand. There would be nothing to stop him if the time came, nothing to stop him but him.

Finally there was one letter with my name and address written diagonally, in a familiar hand. Thank God for her. My mother had written to me from Queensland. I missed her a great deal and her handwriting reminded me that I did. It was embarrassed handwriting. Its strokes were unconfident, first taught so long ago. Although much practised, it suggested that she would not have been surprised if the style were now so archaic it would be looked down on. It had taken her some time to get used to calling long-distance. She'd had a lifetime of not calling long-distance before moving up north. It was only Abby, and Kirsten's children, that forced her to call at least weekly. They could not afford to fly down very often and neither they nor their car would survive the drive down to Melbourne, so she gradually got used to the telephone calls down one half of the eastern coast. Why was she writing?

Dear Eddie, it began, the tentative downward strokes already apologising . . .

> *I am sorry to be bothering you but I didn't want to speak to you about this in front of your father. The fact is that he hasn't been feeling quite himself, a little flat and a*

little tired. Although neither of us are getting any younger, your father seems to have stopped getting younger with a new and unparalleled vigour.

For the best part of a month now I have tried to get him to see a doctor, but you know your father, he refuses to acknowledge that anything is wrong or even that anything might be wrong. I was hoping, if it was not too much trouble, that you could fly up and see us. I know it would do him the world of good just to see you, even if you were also unable to persuade him to see a doctor. A few days might be just the ticket, two, if that's all you could spare.

And speaking of tickets, if I could pay for it, you know I would, dear. I had actually started putting a little aside for just this purpose but I'm afraid I'm just not progressing with it at the rate your father is, well, unravelling. I don't mean to alarm you, Eddie, but I have been rather concerned about him and I didn't want to worry your sister, what with the children and everything.

Of course if you are unable to visit us I will understand perfectly. I hope everything is well with you and that your job continues to be satisfying without being too stressful. How are those wonderful girls? Give them both my love. I know you share everything with Tanya and you know I think that's wonderful but I would appreciate it if you didn't say anything to her about your father, or to your sister. I am aware that it is possible that I am being perfectly silly about this. Please come up if you can and tell me that I'm just being silly.

As always,
Your loving mother.

P.S. Tell Abby I've found a picture of Elvis Presley in one of the magazines and I've cut it out for her. Does she still

*like Bananas in Pyjamas? Give her a big squeeze from me
and one for yourself while you're at it.*

Mum

The children and everything. What did this mean? It meant my
sister had more than one child and, reading between the
lines, that my mother found Kirsten's marriage to be shaky,
of the kind where one needs to hang on. Kate would not
hang on. Perhaps my mother knew more than she was saying, about my sister *and* my father, about everyone but me,
Tanya and me.

We had one child and we did not permit long-distance
reading between the lines. On the phone we bombarded
them with questions about the weather and what they'd
been doing. We described every one of Abby's steps, her
words, her thoughts, her every observation. There were
sometimes as many as five separate people living through
Abby. We blurred the lines. How *was* my marriage going?
I felt in no position to tell at the time, not really the best
person to say, a bit close to it. And anyway, with what
frequency should the question be asked? We were fine three
weeks ago, three days ago, I think. But yesterday? How are
we today? How was my marriage this morning?

I walked to the study with the letter after rereading it.
Tanya's regional conflicts, spread out on the desk, waited for
her return the next day. I sat at her desk and wanted to tell
her immediately, not to whisper it either, but to shout it in
the child's panic that comes from nobody knows where.
My father was sick. With a wink and a nod he had moved
north and started taking instruction from Old Man
Williamson. But she was not coming home that night. She
was going to stay over at her mother's place after the late
seminar by the mega-luminary. Her mother had a doctor's

appointment the next morning and Tanya wanted to go with her.

On the desk, barely conspicuous, jutting out of some papers on the history, tactics and ideology of the Tamil Tigers of Elam, was a letter to Tanya from the head of the Politics Department. So she had been keeping secrets too. I was not prying when I read it. I was hiding from my own dark thoughts when I came upon her dread captured so plainly under the university's logo in its standard font and in the standard language used for these now standard things. The laser printer treats *regret* just as it would treat *love*.

It is with deep regret. It is with regret. We regret.

I could not have said it better myself and since I knew her so well, I knew that they could not have said anything worse. It is with inadequate understanding of Tanya's capacity to enthuse other people and to enlighten them in ways they would never forget, and with disregard for the consequences to her financial and emotional well-being, that the university regrets it is unable to extend her contract of employment. They would like to take this opportunity to offer her grave self-doubts and to employ a meaningful cliché towards the bottom of the letter, without fond sincerity, without gratitude for past service, so that the printed words on the page, when viewed in the middle distance through unfocused eyes, generate the image of an upside-down Christmas tree.

Placing the letter back slowly as though nothing had been disturbed, I realised that before she could be made to believe it, I would have to believe that she would again laugh uncontrollably, in that completely liberating way, even between unsuccessful applications for jobs that were beneath her. I would have to convince her that she would again feel her own strength when catching her daughter in her arms; that she would not ever have an emotional understanding of hunger; that she would not *be* whatever she was forced to do for a living nor would she become what had been done to her that went unseen by those she thought would always look down on her. And that she need never ever feel alone. But how to convince her of this when I had not been told what had happened?

Why had she kept this to herself? I had kept things from her, it was true, but that was for her sake. For a start, we had a long tradition of not talking about engineering or anything connected with the natural sciences, that stretched all the way back to our student days. I thought this was because, while I was interested in her subjects, she was terminally bored by mine. The pressure of a mass of ideal gas multiplied by its volume is equal to the mass of the gas, in terms of its molecular mass, multiplied by the universal gas constant, multiplied by the absolute temperature of the gas. It seemed we never got around to discussing something even as basic as this. I took it for granted that she knew it, or if she didn't know it, that she didn't want to know it. Since beginning work on her PhD thesis she had started reading a little about the history and philosophy of science and she knew that any survey of the twentieth century could not escape scathing criticism without acknowledging the impact of science on technology and of technology on almost everything else. Pure science was left untouched, abandoned religiously, by almost everyone.

Within this tradition of my sharing most of her interests and views on literature, history, politics, cinema and music, this tradition of monitoring, with her assistance, the highs and lows of her all ordinaries index, there seemed to be no room for the vicissitudes of my career and neither of us had minded. 'Those bastards' in the Department sent me away too much. We agreed on this but, by and large, we both just accepted it. Perhaps we even suspected that my trips away gave us a regular heightened longing for each other that most other longstanding couples could only watch versions of on video and simulate on wedding anniversaries. So she had no idea that the temperature of the environment in which I worked was steadily rising. I had not given her any idea. Was this because it would only make her anxious, because I did not want to hear her enthusiastic advocacy in my defence, or was it because I had no wish to remind her of Gerard, a man for whom she had once left me, a man who was paid an extravagant stipend and who could, with the imprimatur of the State, tell me what to do? Yes, yes and, to be honest, yes.

But other than this, what had I not told her? The helicopters. They were there at night above her as well but she slept through them. She was able to sleep through them. I was up, I stayed up, the family's satellite dish receiving messages from the outside world and filtering them, sanitising them, swallowing them whole, so that she might sleep undisturbed by helicopters, by Nick's torn snapshots, stray dogs, by the heel snapping of flexi-accounts, acid rain on the horizon and all the visiting collateral damage of the new world order which came disguised as mail. She slept but I was on call against the world, twenty-four hour call. And if the news from the world was not good and likely to alarm her, I let her sleep through it. Her daughter got through uncensored. It was only the world coming down on us that I kept from her, that I had only ever tried to keep from her. That was all . . . And Amanda.

But if she kept things to herself and I kept things to myself, if we hoarded enough of them to pave a once grand city of deserted streets, thinking there was some prize for this kind of protection of each other, then we were alone.

Kate was in the kitchen deeply involved with pieces of veal, tomatoes and white wine. She poured me a glass and told me to go and tend to my daughter. She knew where everything was and had discussed the preparation of the meal with Tanya the night before. When I returned to the kitchen, glass in hand, explaining that Abby was asleep, she agreed that it was probably the best thing for her. Of all the people one could love, Kate had to have been one of the easiest. Her eyes were round and large, betraying in a glance an innocence that experience had not yet been able to shift and, at the end of a long day, her hair tied back with a bright red ribbon, no one could have denied her a belief in the possibility of other things. She said something to herself about roma tomatoes, refilled my glass and hers before banishing me good-humouredly from the kitchen. She was enjoying herself, the cooking, the mildly ill, adoring and adored, sleeping child, the man with a glass of wine reading in the other room and Chet Baker playing softly. Had I really wanted to set things off for her, I might have filled a pipe and lit it, preferably an heirloom.

No longer was she assisting merely with Abby, she was also tacitly helping Tanya look after me. Perhaps this was not purely to enable Tanya to attend late-night seminars, dinners with visiting international academics or even to spend time with her mother. Was it a coincidence of wants, just for a night: Tanya takes a twenty-four-hour leave of absence and we do not yet have to discuss the evaporation of her teaching position or the limbo her thesis is about to be cast into, while, at the same time, Kate steps back into a past she has never known? Through the kitchen door I could see her adding chopped garlic to the olive oil, warming it in the cast-iron pan. She had chosen the Chet Baker accompaniment and the songs infiltrated the time, marinating it, making memories of what would have been blank moments but for her quiet industry, the wine, the scent of garlic changing states, the diminishing light of sunset and, of course, Chet Baker's songs programmed on the CD player in an order other than that chosen by the record company. One by one they told their separate stories, making one long story: 'The Thrill Is Gone', 'I Get Along Without You Very Well', 'Just Friends', 'Let's Get Lost', 'My Ideal', 'I've Never Been In Love Before'.

'Where did he get her from?' she asked me rhetorically of Hardy and Tess as we sat at the dining table with more wine, veal and a tossed green salad before us. Between us, erect but leaning, were candles bought one Sunday afternoon on the St Kilda esplanade but made in a country Tanya had variously categorised as third world, developing, less developed or fourth world. (Candles from the fourth world would not burn. They were the only things from there that wouldn't. Consequently, the third world was making a killing. Candles were not made locally any more. Few people here were aware of that.)

I was blanketed by an exhaustion under which my father, the bank, Lyndon H. LaRouche's outstretched right arm, Tanya's job and my problems at work all huddled together, fighting for space There was no room at that instant for my mother, for Abby's influenza or the earth-shaking crash soon to be but not yet reflected in the all ordinaries. When stocks are low it is time to buy, to reinvest. Everyone knows that. But not everyone can. It presupposes that you have something left to invest. I was tired without constraint, *laissez-faire* tired, deregulated world's best practice tired. In the glow of a nineteenth-century interior, Tess was talking about Kate and how Hardy was written all over her face. The veal was tender and I realised that between half a day at work, making useless hot lemon and honey drinks for Abby and reeling from the mail, I had not eaten since breakfast.

Kate was alive, quietly alive, that is, positive and animated, without tipping psychophysical VU meters over into the red. She refilled our glasses, we kept draining them, opened a second and third bottle and all the while I tried to remember how it was I came to be dining in strangely familiar and unfamiliar circumstances, comfortable at the end of the day with my freshly ribboned, wide-eyed old friend, talking about Thomas Hardy and his most tragic heroine just like the good old days we never had.

'Where did he get her from?'

'She is a creation of his deepest hopes,' I answered unhelpfully, distracted, exhausted but not daring to hint at my condition for fear of hurting my friend.

'But he loved her. Hardy loved her as though she existed. When you read it . . .'

'She seems so real?'

'Well, actually, she is a little *unreal*, too noble to be real. You don't get that mix of nobility, intelligence and beauty in real life, just the tragic ending,' she smiled wistfully.

'No, that's not right. Look at you, noble, intelligent and beautiful.'

There was a silence. I had shocked us both. She said something about the veal talking but I had meant it when I said it. It was just that I had not meant to say it.

'You *are* noble, intelligent and . . . um . . . beautiful.' Repeated, it sounded worse. It had, in my head, seemed like a suddenly revealed truth in need of saying but now, propped in the air, it sounded like shameful flirting, the whole thing made worse when I added oafishly, 'So is Tanya.'

'Oh yes, *she* is. That's true,' Kate agreed. We both felt better. We drank to Tanya.

'There was outrage when it was published.'

'What year was that?'

'Eighteen ninety-one.'

'A big year for outrage.'

'It's hard to believe something so pure could be the subject of scandal.'

Provoked and unprovoked by the alcohol, I was still sentient enough to be able to evaluate the likely effect of my candle-lit words, but sadly not until they already had lives of their own, belonging to me only in respect of their origin. They fell out of my mouth and threatened to rebel against the established order even before they had reached their adolescence.

'Were it not so beautiful you could say it was a black-and-white morality tale, pure and simple,' Kate suggested.

'But don't you think some of its beauty resides in, or stems precisely from its moralistic nature?'

Whether or not there was any validity to my response, it needs to be remembered that I was a well and truly soused chemical engineer with certain personal difficulties all competing to bring my world to an end. I was doing well to remember who I was let alone what we were talking about.

'You might be right. As Alvarez says, there's a tendency to be so moved by Tess's fate that the beauty of the book, aesthetically and in terms of its language, is perhaps . . . overshadowed.'

I tried to repeat her words in my head. I was incapable of determining whether she was agreeing or disagreeing with what I had just said. I could not remember what I had just said. I couldn't remember what she had just said. I caught only the bare beginning.

'Really, Alverez said that?'

'Yes, in his introduction to the Penguin edition.'

'Mmm . . . Penguin.' The cavity where most people stored their tact, poise and memory was, in my case, filled with lead. I thought I was about to collapse.

'I'm sorry, Eddie. I'm boring you.'

'No, no, no, no. Not at all. No.'

'It's just that I knew you'd read it and I thought it was fantastic. I loved it. I loved *her*.'

'No, no, no, no. Not at all.'

'I'll shut up about Hardy. I promise. I love him and that's it. Enough said. *Too much* said, probably,' Kate said, diffidently.

'Of course. I love you too.'

'Eddie, are you okay?'

'Not at all.'

'Why don't you lie down for a second. You look really beat. Do you want to? Come on. Over here.'

She got up and I watched her guide me from the table to the couch, her makeshift bed. I could smell her perfume or moisturiser on the pillow. With her arms she levered me gently to a horizontal position. She took my shoes off and I heard the *clunks* as they dropped to the floor seconds apart. With each clunking sound I felt my head lift as if it had bounced off a marble surface, thick marble in slab-form, the kind used to enshrine a dynasty of forebears. A light went out and it was quiet. But it was the dark and quiet of some other world. I lay on the family vault at Kingsbere. Tess had gone.

There was a scratching sound close by, like someone scraping or clearing moss or some other stubborn and simple life-form from around the marble edges of the family tomb. As my eyes accustomed to the scene, it became clear that there was someone tending the vault. It was Old Man Williamson. He was chiselling away, with an instrument of crude form, at the periphery of the grave. He worked with solemn diligence before noticing me.

'Hey, remember me?' I called out to him.

'Yes, of course I remember you.' He looked up through the mist. It was not clear whether it was with slight anger or just tired recognition.

'What are you doing?' I asked him.

'Clearing things, keeping order, preparing.'

'Preparing?'

'Preparing for your father.'

'Preparing the tomb for my father?'

'Yes, and for you.'

'For me? Why for me?'

'We all go the way of our fathers or our forefathers. Have you learnt nothing from Thomas Hardy?'

'But my dad's going to be okay. He's not coming *here.*'

'How would you know? You haven't seen 'n since afore the harvest and now you can't afford to see'n at all. Well, you'll see'n soon enough, I can tell you that.'

'Wait a minute! You were never a malevolent old man.'

'No more'n any and I'm not particular so now. Whatever 'tis there was always there. You just n'er noticed it, 'tis all. I was always too old for the likes of you to pay me any mind.'

'Are you saying that if I visit him I can keep him from here?'

'Answer yourself then. How can you visit'n if you ha'nt any money? That's in the first place. In the second place, how can *you* of all the hayfarers and dairymen to walk the district keep'n from the final place? Have regard t'yourself. If e'r you could do't you cannot do't now. You know't in your heart and you cannot fight it. The best a sort of man like you can do is to know it, store it, file it under "T".'

'Under "T"?'

' "T" for The future. Your future is as dark as this here night that hides all but the very hand you see before you but, as a fact, it is as plain as this as well. You cannot come to your father so he will be coming here. You yourself, in what others may call your prime, live from week to week, scrimpin' and savin' and always at the beck and call of an ass of a man, an ass of a man who knew your wife. Your wife knew him even though she had knowed you a'fore 'n but it did not stop her calling on'n then. And in those times she had all ahead of her, or so she thought, and her frail constitution had not yet set in. How can y'not admit the possibility that she might know'n again, he never having been so much taller than you before, she ne'er afore so much needing to be raised?'

'But she'll find other work. She was just tutoring. And I will help her. I'll help in every way I can.'

'No doubt you will and there's the sadness t'is the mark of your current self. Just a tutor, you say! There be cut-backs in these dark times till even the best of *students* are turned away. Remember Jude Fawley, as fine a man as *you'd* ever want to be, was turned away in the darkness at Christminster.'

'Jude Fawley? Was he at Monash? I'm sorry, I don't remember him.'

He exhaled slowly and with time-honoured exasperation muttered underneath his breath, 'Bloody engineers. Tanya'd remember him. He was a stone-mason, a strong man. Ask Tanya should you find yourself speaking with her.'

The sound of someone making their way through the foliage arrested his animation.

'Someone's coming,' he whispered, as though no one was meant to see him, but I did not want it to end there. I called to him with increasing desperation.

'I can help her. Why don't you believe me?'

He continued in a low but urgent whisper. ''Tis not your will be lacking but you're surely no full man at all.' He stood upright with his scraping instrument in hand ready to flee whoever or whatever was approaching and continued in a hasty whisper, looking around as he spoke.

'It might be Tess or someone else who comes here now but no matter to you, son, you who are at once too young to know what's missing in you, or the price of it, and too old to grow up and acquire it.'

With that he went past me with ghostly speed. I grabbed at him to keep him there but missed and caught only his parting whisperings, of a nature somewhere between advice and admonition.

'In the night streets of the town they're carving swastikas into the hearts of stray dogs but still you and your wife keep separate counsel. Have regard t'yourself. Could *you* be assisted much less attracted by someone in your position?'

Then he was gone and Tess it was lay down beside me in the mist seemingly unaware of my presence on the tomb, at least initially. She was wearing a red ribbon in her hair and freely gave away the recently familiar scented invitation from the Lancôme products in my bathroom and from all manner of things around the lounge room couch. She looked tired beyond sleep and had been crying.

'Tess?' I asked tentatively. 'Is that *you*?'

She was shivering and did not seem to hear me. I could not even make myself heard in the darkness. The moon had set and there was nothing to be seen of her outline anymore but a pale nebulousness which represented the white terry-towelling dressing gown she had borrowed from Tanya and which was now all that separated her desperate form from the leaves underneath her and the vapour above. I called her name again but she did not stir. I could not move her.

Darkness and silence ruled everywhere around. Rabbits and hares were about, birds rested above us but no guardian angels were on hand to keep us from a closeness born of need, born of cold. Then tenderness closed the gap, the hungry gap in the terry-towelling and in both of us. In closing it another opened and, even before it was over, I was crying. What had I done?

She had my face in her hands and was wiping away tears, my tears.

'It's alright,' she said. My heart was beating with more force than was good for it. I rested my face against her chest, my nose was in her cleavage, that other lacuna of hers I had never before known. One ear was warmed between the terry-towelling and the exposed mammalian face of our malversation.

'It's alright, Eddie,' she whispered. 'You must have been dreaming.'

She turned on my bedside light, the one that was serving as her reading lamp.

'It's okay. You're awake now.' But she was only partly right.

'Oh my God! Was I calling out?'

'You'd fallen asleep. I'd just finished the dishes and was tiptoeing around you undressing for bed when I heard you.

'What was I saying?'

'It was nothing.'

'No. Kate, what was I saying?'

'Nothing. You . . . you were crying.'

'Oh shit, I'm so sorry. That's so embarrassing.' I sat upright.

'Hey. Eddie,' she offered with warm understanding, 'you can never be embarrassed in front of me.' She was stroking my face. 'You've been so good to me. You're such a good man.'

Her stroking hand ranged from my cheek to my hair. She combed with her fingers. When I closed my eyes there was still some moisture there that had not seen the light of that night. She held me to her and squeezed, rubbing my back.

I could hear her breathing. This was real and when I looked up our mouths were joined and neither of us could speak.

It was the first time in our married lives that either of us had kissed someone other than our spouses in that way and we could not stop. I ran my fingers through her hair and the ribbon slipped off. Tanya's dressing gown came untied revealing a sweetly scented naked woman who had my head in her hands, who wanted me in a way I had forgotten and was bringing me to boil with her caress. But it was not Tanya. It was not even Amanda Claremont. And it was all wrong.

'Eddie, this is madness. We've got to stop,' Kate said without much breath. I pulled back in a way that I am sure she will always remember and whenever she does it will hurt her. I was appalled by my own weakness. And in the shock of the simultaneous arousal, comfort, guilt and furious regret, I was unable to control the violence of the movement. It was as a result of the eventual triumph of one of the many voices in my head screaming wildly at me that I heard my bladder begin to complain about the wine.

'It's not your fault, Kate, these things happen, these . . . mistakes. I was drunk, *am* drunk and barely awake. I hope you can forgive me. Forgive and forget or just forget. Either one. Up to you,' I called, leaving her undone on the couch and racing to listen to the complaints of my bladder.

The unambiguous sound of that part of the wine which had no use for me hitting the water at the bottom of the bowl did not drown out the thought of her thoughts in the other room. What was she thinking? What could she think of me? She would be right to think it, more right than she was aware unless, of course, she already knew of Tanya's pending unemployment. Did she know? Perhaps Tanya confided in her the way she should have confided in me, the way she used to confide in me. If this were so it was likely

Kate reciprocated with confidences of her own and what could be more confidential than what has just happened. Or could that be categorised under the rubric of 'not to be divulged to Tanya for Tanya's sake'? No one rationalises better than an unfaithful husband nor is there a more receptive audience for the result of that process. How sophistical I had become. How sophistical *had* I become? I looked down at my visage in an attempt to answer the question but the wine, once a dry white with just a hint of mischief, sabotaged the attempt with a two-pronged blitzkrieg of obfuscation, shaking inside my head and shaking the image of my head inside the bowl. I flushed for redemption but the cistern contained only water.

'Are you okay? I am so sorry.' I could not look at her, uncomfortable with both the guilt and the arousal.

'Eddie, I'm as much to blame. You really shouldn't . . . It's probably best if we get some sleep. I really think I should get some sleep. I'm sure it will all seem . . . in the morning. You sleep well and don't worry about anything.'

From the passage I called in a whisper. 'Goodnight, Kate. Can I get you anything?' Always the perfect host.

'No, it's okay, Eddie, I know where everything is.'

Our bedroom door had never been so light, never been so easy to close. I pulled off my clothes and threw them onto the chair. I chose my thickest pyjamas. It occurred to me that I should never again allow myself to be alone in the same suburb with a woman other than Tanya.

Hiding under the covers in the dark, it was the sweetness of what had nearly happened that scared me the most. On trains and buses, in queues and at traffic lights, it would always be there to call on, and if call on it I did, far too much of me would remember it fondly. It was the knowledge of this which discomforted me the most. I had to get to sleep. Tomorrow this would have happened yesterday. Or perhaps not at all, perhaps it was a dream most of which I would forget. I was slowing down again, imagining calm made a reality of it. Perhaps it *was* a dream, *her* dream. I would not condemn her for her dreams. My eyelids grew heavy with forgiveness for her. Sleep, for once, took a liking to me. I thought I could hear the distant sound of Kate brushing her teeth, but, as if conscious of my need to court sleep, she seemed to brush softer and softer. The bathroom moved further and further away, *Gonna wash that man right out of my gums.* Even the helicopters were silent, discreet. It would be fine.

What had happened mocked the hitherto firmly held conceit that my fidelity had always been far more than the product of inertia. Perhaps I was just another of the many faithful men whose cringing fidelity was a habit with them like shaving, flossing after meals or remembering rubbish nights.

How long had I loved Tanya? Since before I knew what love meant. Still unsure, I knew that it was whatever I had felt for her since, more than half my life ago, I first spied her in the supermarket from my vantage point deep within fresh produce and nominated her for my wife. My gypsy girl, my own dark storm with her eyes so round and black, always hunted by the shock troops and standard bearers of line-toeing mediocrity, of conformity, haunted like her father before her, I wished her with me. I wanted her, to show her I would fight the bastards for her until she was able to fight them with me.

'Eddie.'

I could hear her calling me.

'Eddie.'

This time she was afraid.

'Eddie.' The call was insistent.

'Eddie.'

It was not her voice.

Kate's calls broke through the door. But we had to sleep this thing off. Sweet Kate, don't make it any worse. I did not answer, burying my head under the pillow. She would tire soon and be thankful in the morning that I had stayed asleep.

'For Christ's sake, Eddie, wake up will you!'

She pushed open the door and switched the light on. My clothes fell from the chair and lay on the floor against their will.

'It's Abby.'

CHAPTER 22

The longest part of the longest night began with the seconds it took me to rouse myself and follow Kate down the hall and into Abby's room. In those seconds I had begun to drown. Still in the dark of her room I was now fully awake. She lay on her back snoring through clenched teeth. It was a sound I had never heard her make before, like the feeble erratic running of a small and unreliable engine moist on the inside through a design fault, gurgling in stops and starts.

'Is she dreaming? Abby? Sweetie?' Kate found the light. I became frightened at what I saw, sickly afraid as I had never been. She bounced. She appeared to be bouncing. Her back was arched unnaturally and her arms and legs stiffened and then relaxed arrhythmically. It was no rhythm at all but a violent madness in her, no rhythm I could recognise.

'She's fitting,' Kate said. 'I think we should call an ambulance.'

I said nothing. My daughter was bouncing. She had bounced out of sleep and into unconsciousness. Her eyes were open, the pupils rolled upwards as if drawn by something inside her. Then they rolled down a little and then back up, flitting up a little more, then down then up again, and all the while her arms and legs waving as if in panic, as if she shared my panic. How long had she been like this? How long would it last, so much like Abby but not like her. At times, there was nothing but white in her eyes. She slapped the mattress with her arms, kicked it with the back of her legs.

And it would not stop as the half-remembered half-hatched treatments from a lifetime of charts on the walls of doctor's surgeries echoed in my head: *roll her on her side, stop her from swallowing her tongue, find the blame, call an ambulance.* Her moist snores kept coming from the back of her throat. Let her *sleep.* But she was not asleep. She was deep in battle. *Let her breathe. Clear the passages. Press the blame tightly against the father's chest.* Was she breathing?

'Call an ambulance!'

It wasn't stopping, it wasn't slowing. She kicked. Her muscles tensed and untensed alternately.

'I called one. Has this happened before?'

'No. I don't think so. I don't know. I don't know what this is.'

'She's fitting.'

'I know. Can she breathe?' I touched her head. 'Is she breathing? Abby, what are you doing?'

'She's fitting.'

'I know. Will you stop saying that and call a fucking ambulance!'

'I did.'

'When will it be here?'

'Five or ten minutes.'

'Ten minutes! She's not breathing. Kate, she's not breathing!'

'She *is* breathing. She's fitting. What are you doing?'

'Turning her on her side.'

'Why?'

'So she won't swallow her tongue.'

'You don't need to do that with children.'

'Are you sure? You do when they're fitting.'

'I don't think so.'

'I'm doing it. Will you help me? Should we hold her? Ring them again. Ring the ambulance again. She's having some kind of fit.'

We turned her on her side.

Because neither of us thought to leave the door open the ambulance officers had to ring the doorbell like friends dropping in for afternoon tea. Kate let them in. They looked at Abby dancing on the bed. One stayed at the bedroom door, the other approached the bed.

'How old is she?' he asked firmly, routinely and without panic, an older man with thinning hair.

'Six,' Kate said.

'Six and a half. She's had the flu. For a couple of days. Temperatures.'

The younger man at the door ran out of the house as if to get something from the ambulance. The older man stayed by her bed. It was just after four in the morning. He stooped over her slightly and laid his hand gently on her head. The government and certain editorial writers thought this man had it too good in his job.

'Are you her parents?'

'I'm her father.'

Kate pulled the flanks of Tanya's dressing gown closer together. The ambulance officer kept his eyes on Abby.

'She's fitting. Has she done this before?'

'No. I don't think so.'

'How long has she been like this?'

'About half an hour,' I said.

'We don't know exactly. We found her about ten minutes ago, just as she is now,' Kate said.

'Is she breathing?' I asked.

'Yeah, she's breathing,' he said calmly. 'We're going to have to call a MICA.'

'What's a MICA?'

'Mobile Intensive Care Ambulance. We're not equipped for this.'

'For what?'

'She needs valium. A MICA unit will treat her with valium to stop the fitting but she'll need to be hospitalised for diagnosis and in case she fits again.'

'Why can't *you* give her valium? I think we have some. My wife has some . . . unless she's taken it to her mother's.'

'No, it's given rectally. My partner's gone to call a MICA unit. I'll stay with you till it gets here. She's okay.'

'Is she really okay?'

'She'll be fine.'

She did not look fine. I had never seen her look less fine. She looked angry, furious to the point of madness. Bouncing involuntarily on her little bed, gurgling, frothing, she would not look at me. Her body was trying to rid itself of what it knew and no words of calm from the uniformed older man with the thinning hair could take away my fear as we watched the storm inside her, her flailing arms and legs signalling a frenzied protest against her health.

'It's never happened before,' I said looking for some sort of comfort. But still she would not stop, and still the fever burned as bright. I had previously always been able to stem her tears and sweeten her rare bouts of ill-humour but by her bedside now I was alone, deserted by all my previous selves, useless against this insult to my child's reason. She danced this repulsive dance in front of us without embarrassment and without showing any signs of stopping.

'Will she stop?' I asked him like a child.

'Oh yes, it'll take its course. These things have to take their course. The MICA boys will be here any minute.'

The arrival of the MICA unit, the continuing need for it and the idea of these things taking their course seemed mutually inconsistent. Did it mean that without it she would not stop?

'But will she stop?'

'Oh, she'll stop alright. That's them now if I'm not mistaken.'

But what if he *was* mistaken? Would she stop? Kate held my arm.

There were now four uniformed men in my daughter's room. The two MICA men tended to her. One of them held her as still as he could. The other prised apart her cheeks with one hand and inserted a catheter into her anus with the other. Something was being done at last. The MICA men had come to penetrate her with valium and take her to hospital. I sat beside her with one of them, a younger man, and together we rode the ambulance to hospital. Abby slowed her dance but would not wake up. Her spasms weakened their resolve, their intensity and their frequency. I wished the older man had come with us.

Abby and I were as one with the trolley. She was strapped in. I grasped its handle with such pointless intensity that my hand whitened and petrified in its grip. In this way MICA-the-younger wheeled us both into the Emergency Ward. He parked us in a queue a little way in from the doors and then left us in order to translate his version of our situation into something the system could rank. Abby was in a deep sleep now. She did not stir whenever her trolley was assailed by the passing traffic of other people's traumas or by the crying or random screams which lit up the room like an audio pinball machine and penetrated the thin partitions separating each trolley's panic, fear and regret. My little girl slept calmly through it all.

The turning points of so many lives had come together under the hatching fluorescent light of this confined space as if for a convention. The partitions lent an air of privacy to each case, but above, beside or through each partition misery did out. A young man let out cries of such distilled pain behind a partition slightly deeper into the ward that an older woman unacquainted with English was forced to interrupt the tragedy inside her own neighbouring partition to get some help for him. He had screamed the loudest of us all, his howls being interrupted only by dry retching. This had been his fifteen minutes. They gave him something through his arm and he went about his waiting quietly from then on.

A crisp, confidence-inspiring woman, a nurse, still young but ageing by the minute, came over to us with a pen and clipboard in hand. She went through a barely audible drill with the man from MICA. He told her all she needed or had time to know about us before nodding to her then to me and finally riding off into the sunrise.

'Abby, is it?' she said to us.

'Yes.'

'Doctor will be with you as soon as possible,' she said in a tone which meant the system was apprised of our existence so there was no point making trouble.

Trouble came here ready-made. It followed no pattern, it could not even be relied upon for its own rhythm. Sometimes there was no beat to it at all. Two orderlies greeted each other over a sheet-covered trolley. I listened to them as Abby continued sleeping.

'Internal bleeding,' said the one pushing the trolley.

'And he was so well behaved. Undetected?'

'Yeah. S'pose so. But what would I know.'

A woman with thick black hair on her sagging head thrashed about in a motorised wheelchair unable to communicate except through a small computer. She combined with the whirring sound of the wheelchair engine to produce an angry, frothing grunting hum. Mobile at right angles to everything, she would not take her disability lying down. She looked to be in her late twenties or early thirties. Her animal sounds protested against her indignity. Finally calmed she had the attention of one of the older nurses who spoke to her as one speaks to boys who cry wolf.

'This is a busy time. You know that. There's nothing wrong with you today.'

Then the nurse read the woman's typed response.

'Just call Sylvia? I can't stop to make telephone calls for you. Look at this ward! It's happy hour. Anyway, you'd wake her up at this time of night. Who's Sylvia anyway?' The woman typed a response and the nurse's tone changed.

'Your mother?'

A tall stooped scrawny man, hollow and jaundiced, outdid the grunting woman in the wheelchair. By a surgical strike of invective the nurse's attention was wrenched from the woman's computer to all the narcotic-induced problems this man's physiognomy would soon bequeath to the makers of the beautifully photographed cult movies he would never see. It was his back. He wanted everyone to understand this, not just but especially his back. Pethidine would do it and then he would go away. It was as simple as that. And she was not to mistake his intent.

Abby was asleep.

There was a television mounted high on the wall in a corner of the room. A fifteen-year-old hospital drama was coming to a close for the night. It was followed by a string of advertisements. A man resembling one of the television doctors, all teeth, tan and haircut, had come upon the ten points which distinguished successful people from the rest of us. He had managed to get these points down onto six cassette tapes which had already changed the lives of literally millions of people across the United States. Some of those people happened to be near his swimming pool and were willing to testify to the beneficial effect these tapes had had on their lives. Previously they were us but now, after owning these tapes, they were them. The television doctor came back. He said that if we phoned the number at the bottom of the screen with a credit card ready, we would also receive his easily-assembled book based on the actual tapes at no extra charge. Even the limitation period on this offer did not diminish his smile.

Then a woman in her underwear appeared speaking softly to us from beside another swimming pool. At first it seemed that she was one of the literally millions of people whose lives had been changed by the six cassette tapes and/or the actual book. There was still a phone number at the bottom of the screen but it became apparent she was limiting her invitation to men and was not promising to change our lives unless we were lonely and wanted to talk to her or one of her fungible colleagues. After she had reiterated the point in each of several different attitudes it was time for *Beany and Cecil in a Bob Clam-pitt cartoo-oon.*

Tanya looked exhausted. She touched my arm and kissed Abby's sleeping head. Kate had called her at her mother's place after the ambulance had left and Tanya had woken from stretching her father's cardigan once too often to a formless nightmare she could only imagine from the half-heard words of a panicked friend. For most of her life the

fears with which she lived were no more than private imaginings; this was an intersubjective nightmare with its own
car-park, reception desk, public address system; people
caught taxis to this place. People died here. This was the
public's address.

'Oh my God. Is she sleeping?' she asked running her fingers through Abby's hair.

'Yes,' I seemed to whisper. My futile reply was drowned
by the television, the persistence of restless trolleys, the
high-pitched vehemence of the dark-haired woman's
wheelchair and the shouts of the jaundiced scarecrow convinced of his democratic right to pethidine.

'It's the back, babe! I'm serious,' he called to another
nurse. 'You come here and feel it for yourself.'

Tanya held on to me for support. Her face was white over
my shoulder. A small particle of sleep looked out from the
corner of her eye. I knew her so well. The particle was new.

'What happened?'

'She had a fit.'

'What kind of fit? Did you find her? That must've been
awful.'

'No. Kate saw her first and got me . . . alerted me. I was
in bed, asleep. You can't imagine, Tanya, it was . . . horrible
. . . just horrible seeing her like that and not being able to
do anything, not even knowing what it was.'

'What *is* it? What did they say it was?'

'You know as much as I do.'

'What do you mean?'

'We're in a queue.'

'Hasn't anyone seen her?'

'Not properly, not a doctor, just the ambulance guys.'

'Eddie, for God's sake! How long have you been here?
Why didn't you get someone to look at her? You smell, you

reek of alcohol.' We talked over each other. We looked like the stereotype of a couple under stress.

'I don't know—half an hour maybe. I couldn't leave her here by herself. What if she woke up while I was gone?'

Tanya panned slowly around the ward till she came back to me.

'This is hell, isn't it,' she said looking over at the scarecrow who by rotating his head on an axis gave everyone within radius, including the woman without English, a turn at thinking he was shouting at them.

'Feel it, babe! Come on. I can take it. I can take it, you fuckwhipped mongoose tight-arse!'

'Well, okay. I'll stay with her now and you go and get a doctor. Look at her, Eddie, sleeping through all this.'

'They gave her valium.'

'Really!'

'Yes, they gave it to her rectally.'

Tanya winced. All over the city millions of people were sleeping, unaware of the subtle changes in an Emergency Ward between five and six in the morning. Firstly there is the light. Around the edges at least, near the windows, nightmare and dawn come to a tacit arrangement on the floor. Coffee competes with antiseptic for your memory and a barely perceptible slowing, like a wind-up toy turning itself in, comes over the players. It is as though they all suspect that the music of the place, the cacophonous sound-track made by aggregating the misery around each partition and each petitioner, is about to stop abruptly and no one wants to be caught out. They get ready to give in to the day, to catch a break and be sharp for the qualitatively different daytime suffering.

The public address system did not address the public. It found the static, quarrelled with it and broadcast the whole

thing so that as I made my way from Abby who slept and
Tanya who watched, past partition after partition looking
for a doctor, I knew that someone who knew more about
the workings of the place than I did was also looking for
doctors. And this person was amplified and could name the
people they were after.

A hand caught my shirt. It belonged to an old man. He
lay on a trolley and had the pallor of children covered with
talcum powder playing old people in a school play. He had
a young man's grip though, and it took hold of my shirt
with determination, just above my waist.

'Excuse me,' he said with a dry mouth and as much dignity
as he could prise from the situation. 'Excuse me, but . . . Can
you help me?'

'I'm sorry, I'm not a doctor.'

'No, I know you're not a doctor. My name is Alfred Price,'
he said raising his head slightly from the trolley and releasing
his grip to form his half of a handshake. I shook his hand.

'Eddie Harnovey.'

'That's an unusual name.'

'Well, I'm not usually here.'

'No, neither am I, as it happens.'

'Alfred, I can't talk to you now. My daughter is unwell
over there and I'm trying to find a doctor for her.'

'Oh, I am sorry to hear that. How old is she?'

'Six and a half.'

'And what's wrong with her?'

'We don't know. She had a fit.'

'A seizure?'

'Yes.'

'Epilepsy?'

'We hope not.'

'I hope not too, Eddie,' he said gravely and then added,

'but epilepsy can be controlled with medication nowadays, to a large extent anyway. They used to say prophets were epileptics, or was it epileptics were prophets?'

'Alfred, I have to go.'

'Yes, you do, Eddie. I'm sorry I've kept you. I have a son like you. Oh, I'm sure everybody says that. I mean that he is about your age. If I could get up I'd call him. He's often up this early.

'Eddie, listen. When you have found a doctor and when the doctor has examined your daughter and when you are satisfied that she will be fine, that everything will be alright, please would you be kind enough to return to me and take whatever you find in the contents of this bag? It's a small bag. I had it with me when I took the fall, my hip you see. I can't get up for a while. Would you take some money from the bag and buy me something to eat. I cannot seem to get their attention. Everyone is more important than me, your daughter legitimately so. But when you are done, please would you return? In fact, take the money now. Go on. Then you will return. I know you will if you've taken the money. They have their hands quite full with that man over there, don't they. Perhaps he's dangerous? Take the money for me, Eddie, and fetch me something to eat. I don't care what you get. Would you hand me the bag please?'

I did as he asked. Anything just to get away. He rummaged. 'Even a drink, orange juice, if it's all you can manage. I'm so hungry. Isn't it the damnedest thing.'

Having reached inside the bag he placed some coins in my hand. I walked away before he had a chance to say anything more, not knowing whether or where to buy food there, but counting the coins so, at the very least, I would be able to return the exact amount. I walked looking into my hand avoiding the traffic as best I could. He had given me three dollars.

CHAPTER 23

Medical administrators have managed to keep the passing of the Factory Acts from the young men and women in their charge for the biggest part of two hundred years by snaffling up anyone who showed an aptitude for chemistry in the final years of secondary school and a burning desire to rote learn the phone book, putting them in white coats in Emergency Wards and not letting them out until the laws are repealed. Soon to be released, the young man we cross-examined assured us he was a doctor and a doctor he actually was. He looked as though he had not slept for some days which made it easier to coerce him into examining Abby slightly ahead of hell freezing over. Doctors came with acne now. This was not possible when I was a child and remains impossible on television to this day.

He said that it was too early to tell whether Abby's convulsion was the onset of epilepsy or what he called a febrile convulsion, a childhood condition of epilepsy-like episodes which they usually grow out of by seven. By *too early to tell* he meant that he did not know and when this became clear Tanya's face told me that she thought he should be back in the school for uncertain young doctors who had not yet learned omniscience when confronted with sick children. But the pustuled kid's uncertainty made sense once we had given him a chance to defend himself. Abby had been fighting a high temperature, a common pre-condition of febrile convulsions. On the other hand, he explained, it is highly unusual for a child to have her first febrile convulsion as late as six and a half. She was fine now, he told us, and we could take her home. He seemed to miss or dismiss attributing causal responsibility to the father.

We caught a taxi home, our own car still resting on its laurels in the driveway at home, Abby and I having caught an ambulance to get there and Tanya having caught a taxi from her mother's place. Both her mother and Kate had offered to drive her to the hospital but she had declined their offers. We huddled in the back seat of the taxi, the three of us. It was around six-thirty in the morning and in the pale light our post-traumatic dishevelment made us look like refugees from one of Tanya's regional conflicts. The taxi cruised, glided silently, hushing the poor and wretched occupants over the wet streets to a sanctuary. Abby was cocooned, still in her pyjamas, between the two of us. She was not unhappy, just a little confused about the adventure in which she was the central protagonist. It all seemed a little unreal to her but she wasn't afraid, just mildly cross with herself for remembering so little about it. It was Tanya and I who were afraid.

The instruments on the dashboard quietly registered changes down to a tenth of the units being displayed in large green digits all clearly identifiable from the back seat. We took corners on average at fifteen point one kilometres an hour. Warm air seeped comfortingly into the immaculate cabin sustaining an ambient temperature of nineteen point five degrees Celsius. Even the indicator was muffled in its acknowledgement of our turning. Had it taken us much longer to reach home we would all have been asleep. But Abby was starting to stir. Would she get to go in an ambulance again? She would be sure to be awake next time. The young doctor had told us that we would have to wait to see if she had another seizure when she did not have a fever. If she did she had epilepsy. It was best not to do anything that might mask her condition, at least until she had been examined by a paediatrician. We would have to wait to see if she had epilepsy. Just wait, he had said, watch and wait. In the meantime, I could not let her go.

Tanya's mother was waiting for us with freshly squeezed orange juice. She had made everybody's bed and tidied the lounge room. The couch was no longer a bed and my reading lamp had been returned to my bedside. Kate had gone. All traces of my nocturnal near involvement had disappeared with the vacuum cleaning, dusting and general straightening.

'Where's Kate?' Tanya asked her mother.

'She helped me tidy the place and then packed up her things and left. She said she wasn't going to be in the way anymore, not if Abby was unwell. She'll call you.'

'She was never in the way, Mum.'

'Her words, not mine,' her mother defended herself.

'Where's she gone?' I asked.

'To her home, to her husband, I suppose. I don't know. Where else should she go?'

Tanya's mother made us breakfast. Relieved that Abby was alright, she was pleased to be so needed again. Neither of us was capable of much. Looking at Abby, watching her pick off the cracked shell from her soft-boiled egg and recount her experiences to her grandmother, it was difficult to believe that she might not be alright. Tanya and I sat lifeless at the table, sipping our tea and letting the steam hit us between the eyes. What was she thinking?

'They put me on a bed and it had wheels on the bottom,' Abby explained.

'That must've felt special?'

'No, everyone had them.'

Was Tanya thinking of the waiting she had in front of her in all its different hues? She was waiting for her daughter to escape epilepsy altogether or else wear it forever, a blemish on her perfection. Influenza still resonated inside our daughter but it was clearly on the retreat. She was hungry again. But epilepsy came from Tanya's father. He had left it like a promise. Was this what she was thinking?

Was she thinking of her thesis, which need not have been more than she could chew, but tasted ridiculous to her now? Intellectually it was not beyond her but, emotionally, defrosting the soup was a touch-and-go proposition. To create something from nothing requires an anchor that Tanya had but kept leaving raised. Was she waiting for the remaining weeks of her current employment to peter out until that one day when she would come home, close the door, unpack her briefcase and never go back to the university again? She could see this day coming, had rehearsed it in her mind as a pilot might rehearse an engine failure, only in each of her imaginings she did nothing to prevent it happening.

Was she thinking that it was never meant to be—and had not ever been—like this for she who had lost her father at eight and had read Sophocles on her break in the car-park of the supermarket. It never ended like this for the bright students in the BBC dramas she had kept faith with on the Sunday nights of her youth when hope was still warm with cocoa, a blanket and her mother.

It was not that she loved the university. On the contrary, as time went by she had become increasingly critical of universities, their acceptance, as she put in her more mordant

moments, of Departments of Hospitality and Tarantino studies, or Hairdressing, whatever brought in fee-paying students. She railed against the intellectual weakness of the
students and the moral weakness of the staff. The universities seemed to her at the vanguard of society's unravelling.
But I knew better because I was not there. They were not
the first to retreat from what they had once stood for, they
were not the first to turn their backs on any notion of the
common good and to prostitute themselves, they were not
the first to promote a meaningless language designed to preserve their own pseudo-cultural and economic fiefdoms,
they were not the first to willingly, enthusiastically and
blindly, destroy themselves. But if the universities were not
the first neither were they the last. And Tanya was in and of
one and so had expected more from them. The last time she
was not in a university she was stacking fabric softener on
the shelves in a supermarket.

Was she thinking of me while I was thinking of her thinking? If you have ever loved your parents, if you have ever
been able to talk with them, then all you really want from
life is someone you can talk to when your parents die. That
is the unarticulated goal at the back of your mind when you
choose a partner, at least for your first marriage. You might
think that you are looking for all those other things, shared
interests, values, goals, shared folk memories, sexual com-
patibility, the same taste in taste. But all of this, if you are
lucky enough to have been loved as a child, is just a smokescreen that you put up as you crawl between the trenches
of your life, a smokescreen to hide the need to find just one
person you can always talk to after your parents have died,
one person whom you can tell your employment contract
has not been renewed.

It must have seemed to her a ghastly trick to find us as we

were then, because for so long I had been that person for her. Coming up to our twentieth winter together, we had watched each other's bodies change, we had nourished ourselves on the other's preoccupations, laughed together at the things we had been expected to remember, sighed at all that everyone else seemed to forget. We had made a little girl and both of us loved her more than we loved ourselves. Coats we had bought for each other had engendered a greater warmth than had ever been dreamt of in the design of the manufacturer. She had crashed before, gone liquid on me without warning and sold herself short in bed for a few days at a time. But I had always managed to get her out of the dark just by talking.

There had been nine years between her losing her father and finding me and ever since then, with a short break for Gerard and Hamlet, we had not ever really stopped talking. Even in the curtain-drawn days there had been some exchange. There had always been some exchange. Until then. Perhaps the letter from the university made her feel as though her father had died again.

But why hadn't she told me? Was she ashamed or was it that the telling of it made it more real? It was real alright. I had read the letter myself. Perhaps that was it? I was meant to find it. Maybe she had let the document tell me what she could not tell me herself? This was not talking, not where we had come from. Whatever my failings, whatever I had been unable to do for her, to bring her, to give her, it had been no small joy to me that since we were seventeen I had tended a small fire in the cavernous station of her solitary existence. Now it was out.

This was what I was thinking watching her after breakfast as she brushed her hair.

CHAPTER 24

Gerard had been patient with me, patient as a cat with a mouse. It was up to me to decide how many field trips I needed to make before I felt confident enough to report on pollution containment at Amanda Claremont's father's gulf. Budget cuts had been felt throughout the department. Familiar cleaners had disappeared. There were no presentations of gold watches, no novelty-sized cards signed by all the gang, no two ninety-nine spumante and cream sponge cakes. No one said a word. Staff received memoranda reminding them that retirement seminars had been scheduled at very convenient times. They would keep being scheduled until no time was inconvenient. The supply of pens, pencils and paper dried up but still I was not questioned about any of my trips to Spensers Gulf.

The way I got there and back changed however. Initially I had been permitted to fly there, then I flew part of the way and had to take a train the rest of the way, and finally it was just train all the way. You took them and they took you. They ran away from suburbs as fast as they could, past the backs of people's houses, people who once had not known whether it was good or bad to live on a train line and now had no choice but to know, past the farms and pastoral properties to the nothingness between the pastoral properties and other pastoral properties. Children had occasionally been held aloft by smiling adults to wave at the trains. But already in the short time I had been taking the train to Spensers Gulf I had noticed the change. The children were gone and so were their bearers.

Much of the area rests on crystalline basement rock. To the east there is a zone of instability, the Shatter Belt. Sediments harking back to the Palaeozoic era were folded by movements of the earth that people around there prefer not to dwell on. The fault lines had become active again in later periods and occasional earth tremors are still recorded along them. But even at the desert margins to the north-west, the people take pride in what the land puts them through, in what it does to them. In the north-west it often starves them. But it is theirs, they will tell you unasked. Their faults, but not their minerals.

In the north-west it gets redder. The shrub is light and sparse and what is there is fully appreciated. I don't know why I kept wanting to go there. I did not need to. It was not technically part of my brief. There is something attractive about margins. I get seduced by them. But margins require hubs, cores, kernels, nuclei, hearts. Perhaps I am seduced by that area where the heart's jurisdiction is dubious? By 1870 it seems a snake's tongue of settlements had sprung up as far as the western plains, these settlements constituting the north-west frontier of the time. Thus the margin.

The settlements petered out where the mallee became too thick and difficult to clear. I sometimes drove out there in secret—in secret, that is, even to myself—in search of the very last property before the desert proper. And what would I have done had I found it and its inhabitant, an old character from *The Petrified Forest*, Walter Brennan maybe, sub-sisting where it was impossible to subsist? Did he know when he arrived that he was never going to be other than marginal? Did he only live this way because he was not yet fully dead? Did I accord him a certain beauty within my own mythology?

The east and south-east was more hospitable to grazing and crops. Moving eastwards you find wheat, sheep, then dairy cattle and vegetables, even wine. Copper was found thereabouts one hundred and sixty years ago bringing with it ship-loads of money and men to a colony then barely old enough to have earned the crisis it was in. The quarries deepened into cuts until the hunger for copper grew so large there was not a hill to be found that was not sucked dry. The ore was carried south to the sailing barges in the time before the railways arrived and by the time they did the hills were exhausted and one mine after another was closed as a result. The railways were late. In recent times there had been talk of opening up the copper mines again. Amanda's father was behind it.

Just before the turn of the century a succession of unusu-ally wet years pushed the wheat frontier further and further north. Perhaps this was the time Walter Brennan's ancestors got wind of the desert blooming and staked their claim on a sure thing. The drought was four years coming and stayed for six.

After all the trips I had made the area had become dear to me in a way I would never have expected. Brought up in the suburbs, I was always suspicious of the bush bal-ladeering sentimentality of, say, the Jindyworobaks and its more recent socio-political manifestation, that type of often unyielding, unscientific, dogmatic, and bombastic environmentalism that does for society's habitat what the followers of Foucault and Derrida did for the promotion of literature as a source of sustainable enjoyment. It takes the people out of the equation and leaves it that much the poorer. But the area around Mr Claremont's gulf became quite known to me and knowledge of a place often leads to affection for it. How else can we account for the specialness of all the world's home towns? I collected information about it that went beyond anything that was likely to be important to me professionally.

The people in the east and south-east would almost boast over a beer about their early use of superphosphate and subterranean clover to boost wheat yields.

'So that was *you?*' I returned.

These were the people you heard about, the people who took perennial droughts, floods and heatwaves in their stride. When you watched them up close you could see they were limping. They had been limping for generations, ever since white settlement. The remains of the former wheat frontier too could be seen in the landscape if you knew what to look for. Sheep grazed among the ruins of stone houses. Crumbling tiny churches and chapels offered themselves for advanced civilisations to restore or at least chronicle, Jesus being for now a captive of the gun lobby. Grand stone railway terminals dwarfed their users' requirements. They had been planned in the good old years when the unbridled optimism stemming from four consecutive bountiful harvests had given the civic leaders ideas above their stations.

But it was the lead, silver and zinc mines that put the place on the map and brought more than twenty thousand people there in the last decades of the nineteenth century and it was the smelter that brought me there in the last gasps of the twentieth century. Because I never got to know any of the local inhabitants well, because nobody there knew me in

Melbourne and because nobody I knew in Melbourne knew anyone there, my visits to Amanda's dad's place constituted a rare opportunity not to be me. It was not that I affected a different personality there, it was just that I was able simply to observe without having to interact with anyone. For a few brief moments I was not responsible, or at least did not feel responsible, to or for anyone but myself.

Often when I was at the gulf I would imagine taking Tanya and Abby there some time for a holiday but to imagine when and how this might happen would bring me back home faster than any train and faster than I wished. We could not afford to fly there and the car, in its 'autumn' years, would never have agreed to a return trip. Accommodation in a hotel or motel or even in one of the more reasonably priced guest houses was out of the question. We found it difficult enough paying the bank for our accommodation in Melbourne. We had no savings, no surplus, nor margin of error. Still I was attracted to the margin, to the error.

I thought how much they would enjoy the walks in the National Park. I imagined Abby on my shoulders and the three of us making our way along the creek beds beside the old river red gums, sugar gums and white cypress pines, admiring the fringe myrtle with its dense blossom and singing 'I feel like chicken tonight' and other television commercials of the day that Abby liked. The list was constantly being revised and updated.

This was probably the best place to explain to Abby how it was that a certain section of the population came to be singled out for the worst of everything. She could look out across the plains of the former wheat frontier and among the stone ruins where sheep now grazed, and form impressions, imaginings, backdrops to the stories we would tell her, most of which would evaporate with age but some, or at least one, would remain to flesh out a child's feeling for what had been done to these people. She would not remember the dates. Depending on when I took her there, perhaps I would not even mention the dates. What would the eighteen-forties mean to a little girl? But she would not forget the story of the pink people from Europe whose sheep ate the native plants relied upon for food by the brown people who were already here. She would understand the theft of sheep to feed a family, punishment, servitude, abandonment of home and then death. If she could just see the sheep on the ridges she might never forget the rest. One day, I thought. Tell her about it in the sun on top of an abandoned copper mine but watch out for snakes.

In clear weather the flat top hills stand out in sharp relief. I wanted to bring Tanya there to show her everything I had noticed, all the small things, so that she might notice everything about me all over again. I wanted to show her the endless variation of plant life with aspect or availability of water, but living in spite of the conditions. Goat turds are slightly longer and more olive-like than sheep turds. I know because I had to investigate what it was the goats and sheep refused to linger in.

At home Tanya walked between pockets of cold, turning off lights that Abby had felt she needed, between pockets of cold where the heating we could afford stopped dead, tracing thermal maps around us that showed the regard in which we were held by the market. She found that she was warm in bed. If, if I had just had a little money!

If Amanda's father had bought all of this land twenty years earlier would I have ever seen it? Probably not. I had guarded the suburb while she had been kidnapped and forced to play French cricket with her brothers at Coff's Harbour. And when they got back her mother had quickly arranged a cordon sanitaire between the house of the starched and pleated white shirts and the house of the cotton polyester drip-dry variety.

The men who operated the relatively small-scale smelter already in operation knew me by sight after a while and a few of them would even say hello. But the few who did were admonished by the cold looks of disgust on the faces of their colleagues. I was from the government and not someone warranting civility. My presence there would threaten jobs, or so they seemed to believe. Management, though, had no qualms about me. To them there was a quaintness about me pottering here and there as innocent as a mockingbird. I was taken around and shown everything everywhere and as many times as I liked. 'Just having another look,' I would smile. But certain things were clear.

Lead sulphide and zinc sulphide are separated in these types of operations by means of a flotation process in which air is passed through a mixture of the crushed ore, water and various frothing agents. Nothing wrong with that. Sulphur is removed from the separated lead sulphide by roasting the lead sulphide in the air. When the sulphur combines with the oxygen in the air it produces sulphur dioxide. This is not of itself a problem because the sulphur dioxide can be contained. In fact it is deliberately trapped in many places around the world to produce sulphuric acid for commercial purposes.

The problems arise when it is not trapped. When sulphur dioxide is dissolved in water, say in clouds, fog, streams, rivers, dams or even the sea, it becomes sulphurous acid which is rapidly oxidised to form sulphuric acid. From here we get acid rain. It is as simple as that. You can see its effect on the vegetation even with an untrained eye. The affected plant at first takes on a grey-green appearance. This is known as a marginal necrosis. Then when the tissue dries out it becomes bleached ivory in colour and lined along its edges in brown or red or sometimes black. Eventually the dead areas fall out giving a ragged misshapen form to the foliage. No one will want to eat it. It will not be possible to sell. No one will even want to touch it.

At each stage of the lead and zinc refining process particles of lead, zinc and even arsenic are emitted in a spray of dust into the outside air. And while Gerard might not have been aware of the precise inadequacies of the existing regulations with respect to the control of lead pollution in the region, even that steroid-enhanced neuronally-challenged Buddha of organisational psychology must have heard the rumour about the toxicity of arsenic. He would have known that I would have to recommend far more stringent controls and safe-guards and a regime of monitoring the entire operation if the smelter were to be massively expanded. To do otherwise would have been grossly negligent of me, a legitimate ground for dismissal and possibly for hanging.

I boarded the train for the return leg of my final trip to Spensers Gulf prior to the completion of my report wondering if I would ever get to bring Abby and Tanya there to see the small things of this other world, things too small to take home for them but large and strong enough to have affected me. I wondered how it came about that most people have no problem with a state of affairs in which they are as likely to get hit by a meteorite as to accumulate wealth on the scale of that of Amanda's father. Is it that they do not comprehend the odds or is it that they do but would rather hold on to the one chance in several billion that it will happen to them? They will die for that one chance. They will live for it too, paying their taxes without recourse to avoidance, not parking anti-socially on a dual carriageway, never stealing enough to worry the one in a million guy who owns half of everything and who factors in their petty theft as an operating cost and is not bothered about it or anything else much except social security and taxation, both of which he sees as grossly distortionary.

But exactly what is being distorted? I certainly could not tell anymore. Even my guesses were no longer educated. From somewhere further along the train I heard raucous laughter, then beyond laughter, sounds far removed from anything recognisably human, as though cattle had been smuggled on board a passenger train and were revelling in their triumph, wishing to make a habit of it, a convention.

I knew about acid rain. I knew about lead, zinc and arsenic dust. I could see the faces of the people I had met there, the shrewd hoteliers, avuncular publicans, restless barmaids, the itinerant cleaners. I could see the suspicious faces of the men at the smelter, the exhausted faces of the farmers whose children now hid from the trains or else put boulders on the track and then kept an uncivilised distance. Not one of them had been consulted about any of this. I was the closest thing they had to a voice in the councils that determined the future of the place in which they did everything they were supposed to, keeping their side of the social contract without giving it a thought. As the train made its way from there to nowhere and from there to regional shopping centres, to the backs of display houses and then to the real houses with display families, my recommendations began to write themselves.

When I returned home I took my Capraesque enthusiasm into the study to let the report continue to write itself in there. The room was unused because it had always been Tanya's domain. She was the scholar, the writer, researcher, compiler. I, on the other hand, almost never brought work home, adhering to the adage that made the Soviet Union what it was to its dying day. *They pretend to pay me and I pretend to work.*

In clearing space for myself, I could not help noticing that some notes on the Tamil Tigers of Elam in Sri Lanka—she was looking at the connection between poverty and social conflict—were still on top of the pile of her notes and journals. Tanya had stopped. The thesis hovered around us but any progress in it was impossible to detect with the naked eye. Why had she been unable to tell me that her contract was not going to be renewed? I understood lead, zinc, arsenic and acid rain but had only a tenuous grasp of my wife.

She saw me collect her work into several piles, placing it to one side, and said nothing. I worked day and night with unusual but troubled diligence for perhaps two weeks making recommendations, mapping out a process for monitoring the so-many-parts-per-million of toxic dust in the air and watercourses, suggesting the establishment of an independent team of engineers and technicians who would report both to the Environment Protection Authority and, quarterly, directly, via the Minister, to Parliament. The engineers and technicians were to be paid by the government which would levy a charge on the smelter per unit of output to cover the cost. Limits, both to output and discharge, would be set and non-compliance would be subject to proportionate penalties. A percentage of the operation's pre-tax profit would be held on trust by the government for the payment of wages in the event of closures. This percentage itself would be exempt from tax and interest earned on it would go back to the owners of the smelter.

In addition to the general recommendations, I drafted specific and detailed procedures for inclusion in the requisite legislation, a precise regime not one elected representative would ever read let alone understand but which would, in my opinion, balance the country's need to exploit its resources with its need to preserve an environment conducive to the welfare of the local flora, fauna and human inhabitants. Such an environment would include jobs and a small levy for the maintenance of local public works and services.

For the first time in a long while I had the feeling that my work might contribute to some larger social outcome that, years later, my daughter could tell her children about and say, 'Your grandfather was partly responsible for that.' My wife, however, showed no interest in it. It was not that I needed to bore her with tales of effluent, particle extractors, scrubbing towers or ion exchange but the social goals of the report were, in a way, concrete examples of the very things she said had so wrongly been abandoned.

That I had taken over the desk was not even discussed. The desk, like our bed, where she periodically hid from the world and then, increasingly, from me, was just a piece of furniture, old and not intrinsically attractive in itself. But like the bed, the desk that had for so long supported her PhD thesis acquired its *meaning*, for her and for me, through our subjective responses and not through anything built into it. It was a product of someone's simple design, of sanded wood and nails and of our perception of it. I had not meant to take it over and Tanya had not meant to abandon it.

I put off telling her that I knew about her job until I had finished drafting my report in its entirety. I put off everything until then, promising myself that after it was in, I would write to my mother, speak to Kirsten about one of us somehow getting up there to see them and get to the bottom of my father's stoic and silent unravelling. I put off trying to contact Kate and I put off considering how Tanya would find work, whether any work was better than no work, whether she could continue her thesis while working part-time in a job she would find demeaning and how we would live without debts on one income. I knew I could always find the time to rank our debts, each one snapping at our heels, competing for attention, like small terriers.

I could not put off waiting for Abby's next convulsion. At Tanya's desk I waited. In the office at work I revisited the unforgettable dance and at night in bed, as the paint told of its disaffection with the ceiling, I waited too.

CHAPTER 25

In a sense the completion of the report was the return to the paper cuts, itches and inexplicable sprains and bruises of normality from which we long to escape but cannot for very long. This is why orgasms are exalted and idealism is so comforting. But the ordinary is persistent and tyrannical. On the first Saturday after the report was finished, I rose early and crept out to do the shopping while Abby and Tanya were still asleep. Abby almost always woke before we did so the fact that she was asleep when I left meant that she had already woken, played a bit and then gone back to bed.

Not more than two hours later when I returned she was sitting in her dressing gown cross-legged in front of the television watching a series of rock clips and trying to sing along with the commercials between them.

'Hi, Dad.'

'Hi, sweetie.'

'Have you been shopping?'

'Sure have.'

'D'ja get anything for me?'

'Are you kidding? A rotten kid like you!'

'Dad!' she squealed.

'Everything in here's for you. Let's see what we've got here. There's some bathroom tile cleaner for you. Toilet Duck, that's especially for you.'

'But I've been good. I've got my dressing gown on.'

'What about your slippers?'

She looked down at her bare feet and answered coyly. 'No slippers actually. That was a close one.'

'A close one?'

'Yeah, I nearly put them on.'

'Where's Mum?'

'Still in bed.'

'Any stirring sounds, signs of life, that sort of thing?'

'She went to the toilet during the cartoons but that was ages ago. It was wee. I listened. D'ja want to carry me to my slippers? I know where they are.'

'That's about what I most want to do in the world. Let me just put these bags down in the kitchen. For days I've been wanting to carry you to your slippers but I thought you were just too busy.'

'I have been busy, haven't I?'

At that I picked her up, hugging her to my chest as she squealed and cycled her feet in the air.

'Shh! You'll wake Mum.' We made our way through the hall to her bedroom.

'It's time for her to wake up now anyway. We're awake. *I feel like chicken tonight. I feel like chicken tonight,*' she sang with a sudden burst of enthusiasm.

'Do you?'

'No, it's just a song. I'd like some toast.'

I left her putting her slippers on. Tanya stood in the kitchen with 'Tess's' dressing gown fastened tightly around her waist going through the plastic shopping bags. I went to kiss her as she emptied the bags item by item placing every-thing in its proper place.

'I've done the shopping.'

'Yes, I can see.'

I watched her unpacking and she looked up to find me watching her.

'I'm sorry, Eddie. Thank you for getting up early and doing the shopping.'

'That's okay. Did you get some more sleep?'

'Yes, on and off, sort of fitful.'

We looked at each other following her choice of words, just as Abby came into the kitchen now in her dressing gown and slippers.

'Any treats? Hey, Mum's not wearing any slippers, Dad.'

'Not even one?'

'No.'

'Then it's no Toilet Duck for her.'

'Eddie, could you go into the lounge room and turn the television off if no one is watching it?'

'Sure.'

'The noise . . . it's so inane. I don't want to live in one of those houses where the television is always left on as if it were the refrigerator.'

'Where are those houses, Mum?'

Just as my finger hit the off button I heard her call my name with a mixture of disgust, contempt and outrage from the kitchen doorway.

'What?' I called back cautiously and defensively.

'Edam!'

'What?'

'You bought Dutch Edam!'

'So? I like Dutch Edam. You like Dutch Edam. Everybody does.'

'Do *I*?' Abby asked from behind her mother, her voice gently filling one of the plastic bags.

'It's too expensive, Eddie.'

'We can afford it once in a while.'

'No, we can't. Anyway, it's imported. We should be supporting local producers.'

'That's the principle but Edam tastes better.'

'No, it doesn't. Australia makes some of the finest cheeses in the world,' she continued, now in the lounge room.

'Yes, but that's not the crap *we* buy. We buy yellow soap that's labelled "cheese". It bears no other relationship to cheese. It's a complex blend of many organic compounds but none of them is cheese. Its active ingredient is not even cheese but a type of sodium dodecylbenzeasulfonate. We don't like eating it which is why it sits in the fridge maturing, waiting for a disease it can cure to justify its cheesey existence. Granted, its moisturising and conditioning agents make it gentle enough for the whole family but—and this is an important qualification for a cheese—it is not cheese.'

'It's no use.'

'It has a use. I'm sure it has use, just not as a cheese.'

'Why do you have to turn everything into a fucking joke?'

Why did I? How quickly it became obvious that it was no joke. There wasn't a joke to be found. Suddenly it seemed they had all been harvested and none replanted. Jokes were packaged for export or else saved for the tourist market and no one was visiting us.

'Tanya, it's okay. It's not important, we're talking about cheese. It's only cheese, more or less.'

'It's money. I'm always trying to save it, to cut back, and then you have to shop like a complete idiot. She needs clothes, Eddie, and you're buying imported fucking cheese—when we can't afford to buy her a new coat. She'll freeze if she keeps wearing the one she's got. She'll bloody freeze and get the flu again. You know what I mean, don't you? How about some imported milk next time, from Belgium perhaps?'

'We'll get her a new coat. If she needs a coat we'll get her one.'

'With what? Shall we barter the cheese? We're rich in cheese. Actually, you don't even get much for what they charge you. Bloody EC.'

'Tanya, there's no point buying cheese we don't eat and, anyway, the difference in the cost of local cheese and the cost of Edam isn't going to make the difference between a new coat and no coat.'

Why couldn't I shut up?

'It all adds up. The interest on the credit cards, the phone, gas, electricity; they all add up but never the income. The car is dead. We don't have a car. We have a car-shaped shrine to mobility, physical and social. It's going to cost us to have it moved. What are you thinking of doing about it? 'Cause you're going to have to do something for once in your fucking life besides relying on me.'

'Tanya, it's not that bad.'

'Yes it is.'

'No it's not. We'll be okay. We'll be fine.'

'Stop saying that. You don't know the half of it. We will not be fine. Already I'm not fine. I am not fine.'

'Overcast?'

'Downcast. Each Saturday I go down to the supermarket, the place I'm destined to return to and . . . I wait.' She swallowed.

'Wait?'

'Wait. At the end of each Saturday, standing there by the meat counter, pretending to look at the different cuts. But they know. How long can someone stare at raw meat? They know why I'm there and I know that they know so I can't look at them. I wait till the first of them starts rinsing the drip trays.'

'Tanya,' I said quietly, 'what do you wait for?'

'In the afternoons, Saturday afternoons, they drop the price of whatever cuts are left over. That is what I wait for and it's going to get worse.'

'Tanya!'

'Eddie, don't *Tanya!* me, you dear sweet useless bastard. Go back to Spensers fucking Gulf because this is the real world and you can't save it. How do you think we can afford to eat meat at all? I buy what the bankers, consultants, systems analysts, news readers and chief executive officers' families won't touch and then I put it in a big pot with a lot of water, tomatoes and pepper and we eat stew.'

'Casserole.'

'It's stew, Eddie. It's fucking stew. We're in the bog and it's stew. And I can't see any way out of it. My biggest challenge is to disguise the meat once I've cut off the parts they've camouflaged with packaging. If I had a big enough pot . . .'

'Tanya,' I went over to her, 'please stop it.'

She turned away from me. 'Why? What are you going to do? What do you ever do? I don't think you realise we're in big trouble. I've tried but . . . I'm out of options.'

'You'll finish it.' I closed my eyes. Her voice cut through me.

'No, I won't ever finish it. I'm tired of it. I'm tired of everything.' Then something caught her attention in the kitchen.

'What the hell is she doing? Abby!' She rushed into the kitchen and I ran after her. Abby was sitting at the kitchen table with a knife in her hand cutting up the cheese into shapes. The unpacked shopping formed a semi-circular wall on the table around her but she had limited the sphere of her activity to an imposition of her will on the cheese at knife-point.

There are moments when you see something happening so slowly it still has not really happened before you have finished seeing it and yet you are completely unable to alter it, or are unable to intervene. In the same way and with the same grace that clouds drift across the two-dimensional reduction in television weather reports of the places in which we live, Tanya flew at Abby, knocking the knife out of her hand and striking her with the hard side of a not quite open palm. The terror in Abby's eyes as she saw her mother coming toward her prefaced the return to normal transmission at life's usual speed. The first thing we heard was Abby's scream, high-pitched and composed in equal parts of pain, shock and humiliation. The knife hit the floor and bounced once on the linoleum. We heard it even though we were too close to see it.

Abby cried in horror.

'Mum.'

There was genuine and distilled disbelief in her voice. An unknown dam behind her eyes burst on the contact with her mother's hand and she ran out of the room leaving the cheese figures on the table alone with her parents. I took Tanya not in my arms but, for the first time ever, in my hands, one hand on each arm just below the shoulder, and I shook her in an instinctive tribute to all this refined pain. Is it ridiculous to say that the cut-up cheese on the table made me love my daughter more? The sight of it made me angrier with Tanya.

'Leave her alone. Are you mad? What the hell did you hit her for?'

'I didn't hit her. That knife is very sharp. She could've cut herself. It's the sharp knife.'

'Maybe she just wanted some cheese?'

'She could ask. It's dangerous for her to use that knife. Will you let go of me?'

'Tanya, you can't take it out on her.'

'She was making a mess . . . and destroying the cheese.'

Tanya listened to her words and surveyed the kitchen in its brand new disarray with the knife lying accusingly, bizarrely on the floor. She tried but seemed unable to process what she saw and how quickly it had all happened. Then she began to cry and I took her from my hands into my arms.

'Oh God, Eddie. I've seen this happening in other people's lives.'

'Sweetheart, she's innocent.'

'I know. I can't believe what I did. I'm not innocent. She is. I . . . can't believe this is happening.'

'We are all innocent. It'll be okay. We'll get through it. It's not so bad.'

'Eddie, you don't know the half of it.'

'I do. I know everything.'

She looked up. 'What do you mean?'

'I know everything. The only thing I don't know is why you couldn't tell me.'

Now she cried seriously, rhythmically, the cavity inside her chest collapsing and expanding as if from oxygen depletion.

'How did you know?' she asked between staccato breaths.

'I saw the letter. You left it on the desk. Why didn't you tell me they weren't renewing your contract?'

'Why didn't you say something if you knew?'

'I was going to but Abby . . . got sick and then I had to go away again. Why didn't *you* tell me? Tanya, you can never be ashamed in front of me. You know that.'

'You're wrong. I can.'

She did not look at me. Now I held her up, her body having gradually given up the need to remain vertical, no longer wishing to aid and abet the chronicling of her despair. Even with our daughter crying on her little girl's bed, part of the smallness of her still warm from her mother's hand, there was no sadder person than my wife. On noticing Abby looking in at us from half in and half out of the room Tanya began to cry with renewed fervour.

'Come in, little one,' I entreated. 'Mum's just a bit upset.'

Abby took the smallest steps towards us.

'I am so sorry I hurt you. I got a shock to see you with that knife. You know you should ask someone if you want a piece of cheese,' Tanya said apologetically.

'But I was making something for you.'

'For me?'

'Yes, a surprise.'

Tanya picked her up and lifted her to her chest, the two of them looking like different-sized, tear-stained versions of the other.

'I'm so sorry, sweetie. Really sorry. Show me what you were making.'

'Tigers,' Abby said pointing to the table.

'Tigers? Out of cheese?'

'*Your* tigers. The ones you like.'

'*My* tigers?'

'Tamil tigers . . . of Edam.'

I picked the knife up from the floor and took it to the sink to wash it.

Abby had no better friend and no softer touch than Tanya that day. Pink and blue ice-cream dripped down several cones in several parks and sticky hands were wiped off nonchalantly with a flick of the wrist. Ribbons, tiger picture books, jacks and petals encased in transparent rubber balls were bought with money Dutch dairy farmers could have used to visit us. Abby got to stay up late that night and watch 'The Bill'. Nothing more was said about the blow but in the middle of the night I turned to find I had our bed all to myself. Tanya was sitting in Abby's room watching her sleep, waiting for another seizure.

CHAPTER 26

At work I waited to hear the fate of my report. The longer I waited the more it seemed to matter to me. While its implementation might displease Amanda's father I did not think anything in it would disconcert the Department. The Minister could trumpet it as a tribute to his commitment to environmental responsibility. He could make political mileage out of it without having to spend an extra cent. It was, after all, 'revenue neutral' which was the most important quality any government initiative could have. Each time I came back from Spensers Gulf I noticed small changes, small absences around the office. A biscuit tin, a water cooler, soap and paper towels in the men's room, a secretary, and timid colleague after colleague; they were quietly disappearing.

One day Gerard called me into his office to tell me that the secretary of the department wanted to see me. He could have communicated this over the telephone but that would not have necessitated my walk down the corridor, the brief knock on his door and the inquiry exquisite to his ears, 'You wanted to see me?' which enabled him to answer, 'Yes, Harnovey. Come in and close the door behind you.'

He often addressed me by my surname even though we had been in the same year at university. It was not simply that he had appropriated one of the devices that had been used to dehumanise him at boarding school. I had married someone for whom he had felt as deeply as it was possible for him to feel. Despite his inability to register even the unsubtleties of his life and of the world which had spewed him up and out like mud at a New Zealand tourist attraction, he had nonetheless grasped the magnitude of his loss when Tanya became the one that got away.

Even though Amanda had also yearned for a sunrise in the company of someone other than Gerard, he would never see Amanda as the one that got away. For that she would have had to have left him by the side of the gutter with his head in his hands, waiting for the moon to howl at, with a saxophone far off in the distance. Amanda did not leave him that way. She left mid-morning in a taxi while he was at gym.

I had been to Head Office only once before, maybe twice, back when I was asked my view of mission statements and of being a team player. It was an office, plusher than some, but just an office all the same, one that housed top people, mostly men, who had served the public so well and for so long that they were rewarded with the market value of my house every three months. They wasted little time getting to the point, which was that all references to heavy metal pollution in my report should be deleted, and, in their opinion, new legislation was unnecessary.

They praised the report for its thoroughness for which I was to be commended although exactly how and by whom they did not say. None of them looked embarrassed. No tea or coffee was offered, nor any explanation. I crossed my legs as I listened. It seemed the right way to sit listening to them. I examined their faces for a flicker of a smile to indicate that they were joking and that really all reference to heavy metal pollution in my report should *not* be deleted. No, I had it right the first time. The gentlemen were efficiently untroubled by the passing of this information to me. They wore expensive suits, one a houndstooth, one a pinstripe, one a plain black flannel, and while I myself did not wear a suit, owning merely one and not being required by the daily conventions of my employment to wear one, we all four of us wore ties and so had our top buttons done up. So it was not as if we had nothing in common.

When I left them and was back in LaTrobe Street I tried to work out the extent to which I had been praised, criticised, admonished or simply informed. There was an element of each and in each an element of equivocation. It was not even clear whether the report was to be shelved, edited or revised till it was something else and, if so, by whom. I had come away understanding only that what I had drafted in its original form would never see the light of day. The gentlemen had their quite serious reasons, obviously, otherwise I would never have been summoned. They would have just put in writing whatever it was they thought they were telling me in person.

———————

At home the tiles just below the taps in the shower recess continued to lift. I noticed this at least once a day when I took a shower first thing in the morning. I would choose to turn my back on it and look through the window we always left ajar, the window through which the steam escaped and through which I had seen the two dogs doing nothing under the street-light. Both the origin of and the solution to the tile problem were a mystery. I felt confident that water was behind it but from there all confidence deserted me.

In addition to two of the tiles lifting further and further away from the wall, other adjacent tiles had begun to make a hollow sound when tapped. I resolved to stop tapping them. It was likely that rot and mould were involved. Somewhere around there things were growing, primitive life forms that were prepared to put up with dark, dank conditions which I felt powerless to change. The soap in the soapdish took on the role of a stop-gap protection against imminent infestation. Plastic shampoo containers acquired a slimy film coating making it clear where their allegiances lay. Each morning I glanced at the problem, noticed that the tiles were still at least partially attached to the wall then turned my back on it.

I was not prepared for war with primeval slime. But did it have to be war? Although close to the most primitive life-form imaginable it was, nonetheless, a life-form and if it could not see reason, if cognition was still a few tiles above it, perhaps it could be tamed. Could it be educated into some sort of a Hobbesian civilised slime with Tanya and me as its teachers? Probably not. One should not put too much faith in Hobbes. After all, he held that sovereigns cannot commit injustice. I knew better. Having made some inquiries I learned of a confidential agreement, brokered between the government and representatives of Amanda's father, to the effect that no new limits were to be imposed on heavy metal discharges at Spensers Gulf. Given the proposed size of the planned operation this would lead to an environmental disaster.

Hobbes never denied, as far as I am aware, that sovereigns can be immoral but, and this is where he leaves us all dripping wet and powerless in the shower recess, he did deny that the immorality of sovereigns can be punished. For

Hobbes believed that to punish sovereigns for their immoral acts could serve as a catalyst for civil discord. So what do we do with these immoral sovereigns? I wrote directly to the Minister of the Environment and received no reply. I wrote a second letter enclosing a copy of my report, its recommendations and an outline of the confidential agreement between the government and Claremont that I had heard about. He, it appeared, wrote back directly to Gerard.

Once again, Gerard called me into his office, but not before making me wait outside.

'You've been writing to the Minister.'

'Yes, I know.'

'You've gone over my head.'

'I know that too.'

'Why did you do that?'

'To be honest, I didn't feel comfortable taking up something as big as this, running with it and stopping at your head. Out of concern for you, I felt I had no choice but to take it over your head. I felt better with it over your head.'

He told me that he appreciated my honesty and asked me why I was so concerned. I explained what would happen to the whole area around Spensers Gulf if the proposed mega-smelter were permitted to operate, to all intents and purposes, unregulated.

'Not *un*regulated, *de*regulated,' he said. 'There's a difference.'

I asked him how he saw the difference.

'*Un*regulated suggests we haven't looked into it. *De*regulated means that, after detailed analysis, we've decided to free everything up.'

'Free it up from what?'

'Regulation. Over-regulation.'

I asked him whether he saw a difference between regulation and over-regulation and he asked me what I meant.

'Isn't it possible for something to be under-regulated or regulated to the right extent?'

'Harnovey, these are semantic games and *de*regulation is the name of the only game in town. We don't play semantic games here.'

'Where do you play them?'

'It was a figure of speech, Harnovey. I was using words in a colourful way to illustrate my point. You've got to understand that writing directly to the Minister is not part of your job and that your work at Spensers Gulf is over.

'I see here from your file that your recommendations concerning the shifting of that chemical storage facility were ignored. You seemed to be able to handle that. The report you co-authored with Chamberlain found that a chemical accident there was highly probable and that such an accident, seven kilometres from the centre of the city, posed a toxic threat to a large part of the metropolitan area. According to your report, the facility housed styrene, propylene oxide, acrylonitrile and . . . acrylates . . . what are they?'

'They're used in paint.'

'Are they? Good. Your views were bypassed and you offered barely any resistance . . . a few telephone enquiries and a one-paragraph memo to . . . oh, it was to me . . . and yet you go directly to the Minister just because your Spensers Gulf report was ignored. Frankly, Harnovey, no one wants to hear any more about it from you. Do you understand that?'

I explained that there were many levels of understanding. I left his office and wrote a third letter to the Minister. After another two weeks of silence I lost patience and anonymously sent copies of my report and the letters to the newspapers.

Hobbes wrote that the goodness of actions consists in

their furtherance of peace while evil actions were related to discord. But then Hobbes was ultimately an exponent of ethical egoism and I was, with Bentham and Mill, a utilitarian. The tiles kept shifting, slowly and relentlessly, and it did not help anything to suspect with near certainty what was behind it. With the walls crumbling around us and only the most ignoble of life-forms prospering, Tanya was right to suggest that we needed more than that to forestall the threatening deluge.

―――――――

Failure rarely announces its own appearance. It creeps into your life unobtrusively as if to say, 'No, no, don't get up. Just go about your business. I can wait.' But like a bullet in flight, it cannot wait. Failure is impatient.

Not long after my anonymous leaks to the newspapers, we were all informed via individually named computer-generated memoranda that the department was to be restructured. My position was to be restructured out of existence. The memorandum did not mention me by name but showed, diagrammatically, that following the restructure there would be fewer chemical engineers than were currently employed. I sought out Gerard for confirmation of the obvious.

'Who's going?'

'It's still being decided,' he said, tapping the palm of his hand with his letter opener.

'Who's going?' I repeated.

'Probably you.'

'Why do you say that?'

'It's a gut feeling I have.'

After lodging a grievance appeal I was told to see a departmental management consultant.

'It's to determine your future within the Public Service,' he explained.

'Gerard, I'm a qualified and experienced chemical engineer. Is it to determine where in the Public Service I should work or whether I should work in the Public Service?'

'Yes.'

CHAPTER 27

The all ordinaries had dived hitting the ground digging. As I made my way from the station to the front gate beside which rested our late but not yet departed car, now a sanctuary for flora and fauna previously thought to have become extinct, I could see that the bedroom curtains were still drawn. They were either still drawn or already drawn and I knew which like I knew the back of Gerard's hand. Not content with hitting any rock bottom, Tanya had kept going past the sediments of the Palaeozoic era all the way down to the Archaean rocks she had never known before. This was not the time to discuss the ebbs and flows of my career.

Abby was with her grandmother. Tanya was alone and still in bed. I walked into the darkened bedroom and placed my briefcase down by the foot of the bed. If she was awake she was too ashamed to speak.

'It's me,' I said quietly. 'Sweetheart, it's me.'

I bent down to kiss her and suspected that she had not showered. Withdrawal was both a consequence of her condition and one of its defining characteristics. I took off my shoes and lay down beside her. She had her back to me.

'You don't have to say anything,' I said rubbing her back.

I rubbed and rubbed for warmth, she inside the bed, me, in my clothes, on top of it. The digital clock on my side of the bed said nothing to us, silently doing its job as it would till the day the new owners of the city's newly privatised power supply decided we were not worth supplying. It had displayed to Tanya every minute the day had on offer but not one of them had recommended itself to her as a fine moment for rising. This was all the clock that had for so long known us so intimately would do, give each minute a minute's display and then silently move on to the next minute with an efficient neutrality that was, on reflection, a breach of the promise, on its packaging and on the display in the store from which it was purchased, that it would show us a good time.

There are thoughts that cannot grow in that by then standard darkness, thoughts that are fed by the sun. I needed the sun to rouse the buds of those thoughts planted once by a joke, a piece of music, a film, by her daughter and maybe, albeit some time ago, by me. I persisted even then in thinking that she was not beyond hope, just beneath it. I touched her face with the side of my hand. It was newly wet. She cried when confronted with the outside I had brought in to her, humiliated by the preponderance of those unbanishable thoughts which Wordsworth said *do often lie too deep for tears*.

'Don't be afraid, my darling,' I whispered. 'I'll get you out of this.'

What extraordinary promises one makes.

I had thought that I knew her affliction and not merely the fact of it. It was no stranger to me. I understood it emotionally, empathetically. But I had only ever touched down at its airport. She was a citizen of its vast interior.

'Why didn't you call me?'

'The phone is over there,' she said softly and, without turning over, she pointed behind her toward my side of the bed. I held her through the covers and listened for the involuntary sounds of her breathing. We stayed this way for a period to which not even the clock could affect indifference. My eyes were closed when she began to speak slowly, in a half-whisper.

'If you stay in bed for long enough the sheets and blankets take on your own smell . . . but not all of it, not the whole of your smell, just the saltiest part. From inside the bed it seems that the air around the bed takes on your saltiness too. After a while it's hard to know whether the sheets and surrounding air are making you smell that way even more than you're making them smell that way. I'd never thought you could smell salt but you can when it's a person's salt. It's a strong and intoxicating saltiness.'

She paused for a while.

'I thought that perhaps a chemical engineer like you could find a way of distilling it, bottling it, making cars and all sorts of machinery run on it. Could you do that? Then it could be sold. It could be useful to people, the saltiness of me. It could be valuable. I figured something out, just today, in bed, about value.'

'What did you figure out?'

'I think that I am not worth my salt.' She turned more into the pillow.

'Tanya, do you know how much I love you? Maybe you don't.'

'I do. I think I probably do . . . but it's not about that. It's not your fault but . . . you're not getting it. I don't think you can ever get it.'

'Maybe not. Maybe I'll never get it completely but you've got to help me get it as much as I'm able. I promise I won't ever stop trying to get it.'

'Okay,' she sighed, 'let me try to . . . even though I'm like this, I'm *in* it *now*, it's still like trying to remember some-thing. Does that sound mad? I'm trying to remember for you . . . how it is now.

'I can't stand this. I can't stand this person I've become. I mean it, I am exhausted these days just from loathing myself. It gets so freezing cold inside and out. There is . . . it's like a block of ice at the core of me and when I move it rattles inside of me. I can feel it. But it never melts, never goes away. And there is no colour to anything, just grey, and no flavour to anything. Nothing has any taste to it. I know that what started it this time is the job, or more precisely the losing of it, not having my contract renewed. But it's bigger than that, bigger than the thesis or my career. That was just the catalyst. I feel such a fraud, such an idiot. Maybe it does go all the way back to the death of my father but I don't think it really matters anymore. I mean I don't think it mat-ters where it comes from. The fact is—it *is*.'

She made herself smaller under the blanket.

'I cannot ignore it by reading or watching television. It doesn't go away even if I manage to get dressed or make breakfast. It's many things—I feel anxious, agitated, foggy, unable to concentrate on anything, even when I've slept the night before. If I haven't slept the night before I want to sleep all the next day, as though that would do it, as though everything would be alright if I could just catch up on sleep. But it's much more than sleep.

'And I blame myself for only being able to face the ceil-ing and not the walls. I hate myself for not being able to get up and have a shower let alone go out and get another job. I know better than anyone from my work on the thesis that there are no real full-time jobs out there. Every-thing is contracting, everything is imploding. I know how much we need the money and this only makes me feel worse. I can't go back to some shitty job and even *they* are hard to get. I used to think they were below me but I can't even make it out of the bedroom so who am I kidding. I admire you so much just for being able to go to work and face the world. And I hear Abby singing her little song . . .'

'Her song?'

'From television, *I feel like chicken tonight*. I used to hear her sing it and run to pick her up, to thank her for the joy she gives me with every little song. Now I can't. I still hear her but . . . the song infiltrates my consciousness, slowly winding me up like an old watch, and then I'm singing my own altered version, catching it in my head—*I feel like nothing tonight . . .*'

'I know that I must be hell for you. I'm so proud of you, of the work you do, the way you love us and keep us all going.'

'I've always thought it was *you* that kept us all going . . .' I interrupted.

'No, it's you. It's always been you. I see myself getting short with you—and I hate myself for that too 'cause I do love you incredibly. That hasn't changed. But sometimes, Eddie, I just can't do anything. I've nothing to give and I have no hope or joy in anything. I know that most of the world is far worse off than me but it doesn't help. I can't bear it when the phone rings. I hate speaking to my mother or to anyone 'cause I know I'll have to put on the facade of being . . . *involved* in the world. When I stopped working I thought, "Okay then, that's it, I'm not playing anymore. I'm out of it. World, you're on your own." I thought it would be a relief from the facade, from the pretence. Yet I feel so unbearably . . . alone.'

I waited for her to go on.

'I feel like I've lost the person I used to be and I'll never get her back. Nothing gets me excited, or happy, or content. Nothing matters anymore. No one can offer me anything to look forward to, even things I've always loved: Mahler, Thai soup with coriander, choc-tops with you on a Sunday night at the Astor watching a new print of *The Grapes of Wrath* or *It's A Wonderful Life*, the short stories of Lorrie Moore, Arthur Miller's plays, "The Singing Detective", Art Blakey's "Moanin".'

She was struggling to remember.

'Anything by Elvis Costello, Ella Fitzgerald, the childlike paintings of Paul Klee, a long hot bath, sex with you in clean sheets, Harry Nilson singing "Without You", Everything But the Girl before they got a drum machine, taking Abby to see the tigers at the zoo, Atticus, Jem and Scout, Macedon in autumn, Abby anywhere . . . and you, sharing everything with you, reading the paper on Sunday mornings with you, holding you, watching you with her—Eddie I hate myself for it. I'm telling you all this because you want me to help you get into how I am—into how it is that nothing reaches me. I feel so alone. Eddie, I was going to do so many things. Now there's too much involved in rolling over. I just want to sleep and . . . I'm so sorry to be like this.'

She had energy only for hating herself. I continued rubbing her back through the bedclothes. It was clear to me that what she most needed was to integrate back into the world. Whether I could bring this about on my own I did not know. I doubted it. And I had other doubts too. Each fortnight the bank automatically extracted a mortgage repayment from our joint account. If ever the account were empty or there were insufficient funds to meet the payment, the bank could legally treat the shortfall as a breach by us that entitled it to sell our house.

After the first rumours of the restructuring, and even

before that, during my attempts to contact the Minister, I had wondered at home, on the train, in the supermarket, anywhere I went, whether the bank would actually go through with it for one missed payment. Would it sell our house because we had missed one fortnightly payment when we had paid in full every fourteen days for the last ten years?

It could. It was entitled. The small print that no one ever bothered reading let alone understanding was the bank's entitlement. Someone gets up in the morning and decides that your house should be sold. They get paid for the decision. They go home. They pay off their home with the proceeds of many such decisions. If the account were completely empty it would be because neither Tanya nor I was working. How many payments would we miss? How many would we need to miss? I remembered the mortgagee sale of my uncle's home and what it had done to George and Peggy.

I could not begin to devote all my efforts to helping Tanya until I had secured my position, any position, our house. Even then I would need time off to help her. I thought that perhaps she should see someone professionally. But would she ever agree? I was afraid to put it to her. She mistrusted psychology. It was not the mistrust of the unsophisticated. On the contrary, her mistrust was born of an appreciation of the still comparatively primitive state of psychology, its relative lack of well-defined and effective therapeutic procedures, and ultimately its reliance on the *verstehen* of its practitioners, be they psychiatrists or psychologists. And the majority of them, she thought, were much too—what had she said?—dumb, facile, lacking in wisdom, or screwed-up—to help her. Anyway, she would feel that to see a therapist of any kind would stigmatise her forever, in her own eyes and in the eyes of the rest of the world, as someone mentally ill, someone to pat and give coins to in the market beside the giant panda on the edge of the car-park.

Nor would we be able to keep it all as completely hidden as she would want, want as much as a cure. At the very least we would have to let her mother know in order to enlist even more of her services with Abby before and after school, at least if I were working. Her mother knew the problem was latent. As long as it remained that way she could put it to the back of her mind. But if she saw her daughter incapacitated by it would she be able to help us or would she only compound the problem for Tanya? I had no choice. I needed her help. I needed someone's help. Perhaps I could ask my own mother?

I had not yet written back to her, not even the usual requests for information about the weather up there. I sat down and wrote a perfunctory letter mentioning nothing about the crises in our own lives, asking in a roundabout way for more information about my father and explaining that I was trying to get some time off work. I enclosed some crayon works from Abby's Elvis period.

CHAPTER 28

Before my appointment with the department's management consultant I took my letter and two of Abby's drawings to the post-office nearest departmental headquarters. Abby's artwork needed more than standard postage.

It was the same post-office I had always used when sending parcels and packages to my parents from work. The people there had not seen me for a while. They seemed embarrassed. They seemed older and fatter. Some of them had died, first their hair, then their positions, then their vital organs. But dead or not, if their employment contracts were still current, there was no way they would take a package. They rotted, slowly, patiently, each nine to five, till the public stared but no longer asked, 'Are you alright?' or 'Can I help you?' We just waited quietly. Embarrassed from waiting, we waited some more. There was no way they would take a package, neither mine nor the standard weapon in the downsizer's arsenal, the tax-free early retirement payment based on length of service.

Somehow your perception of the number of people ahead of you in a queue is inversely proportional to the number of people behind you. If there are six people ahead of you in the queue and nobody behind you, you might consider leaving. If there are six people ahead of you and six people *behind* you, you will not leave the queue. You cannot. It would seem like a tragic waste of a precious resource even though, as you stood there in the queue, you would not be able to name the resource.

I was only slightly late for the appointment with the management consultant. It was important to me to get the letter off, and anyway, I couldn't walk into the appointment with two large crayon portraits of Elvis. The only alternative was to quit my place in the queue, ditch Abby's pictures and shove the letter itself in a regular-sized envelope and post it like any normal letter. But I could not leave Abby's drawings abandoned in the post-office. I could just see her drawing them at kindergarten or at home on the kitchen table. So I stood there and thought, 'How much longer can they be?' Thus I was slightly late for the management consultant.

His office had its own gardener. If it didn't, it should have had. There were plants everywhere, lining the walls of the room and in between the sink-down-as-low-as-you-can-go furniture. It was a manicured jungle. I apologised for being late and he responded gracefully. It had, he said, given him an opportunity to reacquaint himself with my file. He had already acquainted himself with my file but my lateness had afforded him an opportunity to reacquaint himself with it. He had it in his hands. It was thick and grey and bore the legend *Edward Harnovey—Department of Environment and Planning,* a barcode and some pink and yellow sealing tape. I was obviously a code pink-and-yellow case.

He seemed younger than me, or perhaps he was my age, and the darling of a reassuring credit facility, the kind that whispers sweet nothings in your subconscious on a monthly basis. Paint stayed on his walls no doubt. Bathroom tiles never threatened insurrection. His car moved, initially from Europe to Melbourne, and then quietly and smoothly from the underground car-park deep within the basalt of LaTrobe Street all the way to the renovated terrace in South Yarra via Sothebys where he would meet his wife who was well and truly ready for that late dinner, exhausted from a full day auctioning the children.

'Now, Mr Harnovey, do you mind if I call you Edward?'

'Not at all, Giles.'

'Edward, what made you want to come here?'

'I didn't want to come here, Giles. I was made to come here.'

'Why do you *think* you're here?'

'Let's see—I'm here because my position has been terminated as part of the Department's general restructuring and I was given the very clear impression that, whatever might be my chances of remaining in the Public Service, they would be zero if I didn't keep this appointment with you.'

'You're a . . . chemical engineer.'

'Yes, I know.'

'There are still chemical engineers employed in the Melbourne office aren't there?'

'Yes, three.'

'Three . . . I see.' He made a note of this.

'This is twenty per cent of the number employed when I started.'

'Which is what—twelve or thirteen years ago?'

'Something like that, yes.'

'Let's recap, Edward, on where we've got so far. Some of the Department's chemical engineers are still there following the restructure, some are not.'

'Most are not, Giles.'

'And you yourself are one of the ones who are not, Edward.'

He began leafing through my file at a speed which would have made it impossible for any information to have been absorbed from the activity.

'Can you think of any reasons why you're not one of the ones kept on?'

'I had a seventy-five per cent chance of not being one of the ones.'

'Is there anything about you that you can think of that makes you a more likely candidate for not being kept on?'

'No, but perhaps you can.'

'Why do you say that?'

'Your attachment to my file.'

'Do you think there is something incriminating in your file, Edward?'

'It's hard to answer that, Giles.'

He looked seriously at his hand for a moment. 'To be of any use, I'd like to see you again. I'd like to conduct some tests.'

'Tests? What kind of tests?'

'Perhaps I'm premature.'

'Well, there's certainly evidence of *some* kind of birth-related trauma.'

'What do you think you would find in your file?' he asked with textbook earnestness.

The world was in the hands of animated self-parodies delivering Dale Carnegie wisdom to the bewildered from the mountain of their own banality. I exhaled once slowly, for old times' sake.

'Giles, please, out of deference to that long distinguished line of management consultants from which you descend, please come to the point. Are there any positions for someone with my experience or not?'

'Why do you say that?'

'Say what?'

'Mention management consultants.'

'I was appealing to your professional pride, or attempting to.'

'Edward, I'm not a management consultant.'

'What do you mean?'

'I'm a psychologist.' He chuckled at my misconception. At this my head fell involuntarily into the palm of one of my trembling hands.

'A psychologist?'

'Yes. Why does that surprise you? Perhaps now you can relax a little and answer some of my questions.' He smiled uneasily from the same textbook, the eighties' edition.

'Giles, I've been had. Is there really any point to this?'

'That's up to you. I'll ask you again, what do you think you would find in your file?'

'A psychologist?'

'Yes.'

'They didn't tell me my appointment was with a psychologist.'

'Do they generally try to keep things from you, Edward?'

'I don't know. They're so good at it.'

'Does it bother you that I'm a psychologist?'

'Well, it's just that they said you were a management consultant attached to the Department.'

'Are you sure that's what they said or just what you heard?'

'You're not being serious, are you?'

'Do you think you have problems, Edward?'

'I know I do. I have a wife and daughter to support and I'm out of work. Aren't I? Giles, am I out of work?'

'Are you afraid of your problems?'

'Yes, I am. I am afraid of losing my house. I am afraid of being out of work. But that doesn't make me ill or disturbed. This is how healthy people feel in unhealthy times.'

'Do you feel other people are responsible for your problems, Eddie?'

'Oh, for God's sake!'

'What do you think you would find in your file?'

'I've no idea. I've never read it.'

'Well, speculate.'

'Couldn't begin to.'

'Would you like me to help you?'

'Oh yes, please, Giles. Why do I suddenly feel that your name is Dr Spivvey and I'm R.P. McMurphy?'

'It details your employment history, work-related travel, et cetera. It also says that you've been somewhat difficult.'

'Difficult?'

'Yes. You've shown a resistance, even a hostility, to change. You're not a team player. You refused to co-operate in the preparation of a mission statement, those sorts of things.'

'You're not serious?'

'It also says that you take instruction poorly, that you've leaked confidential information to the media and that you have failed to declare a conflict of interest.'

'What conflict of interest?'

'You worked over a long period of time on the Spensers Gulf report, didn't you?'

'Yes, so?'

'Before commencing the work, in fact throughout the entire period, you failed to disclose that you had gone to the same primary school as Claremont's daughter. You were also at university with her, it says here.'

'Barely. What has this got to do with anything?'

'Since you know a member of the Claremont family

socially and were going to be privileged to price-sensitive information, it was thought by the Department that you ought to have disclosed the relationship.'

'There *is* no relationship. This is insane. We were children. There's someone in the Department who's had much more recent social contact with the Claremont family than me.'

'Furthermore, it is possible that the objectivity of your report was compromised by your association with the Claremont family and, according to the department, that is another reason why you should have disclosed your association with it.'

'Firstly, my report was completely ignored.'

'I understand its implementation was adjusted for bias.'

'Secondly, my report sought to impose stringent conditions on the whole operation. How could this possibly be seen as bias *in favour* of Claremont?'

'The Department attributes the leaks to the media to you. Once the report is in the public domain, the publicly listed share price drops and Claremont's private company buys up the public company's shares at a discounted price.'

'What new fresh hell is this? Did this actually happen? Did Claremont's private company buy the public company's bargain-priced shares?'

'The department doesn't know. But the fact is that your failure to disclose and subsequent conduct made it all possible. The department notes your inexplicable determination to have your recommendations adopted.'

'You're all mad, completely mad.'

'Is everyone mad, Edward?'

'Quite possibly, Giles, mad, malicious or both.'

'Malicious?'

'We can't rule it out.'

'Well, you'll be pleased to know the department has decided not to take the matter any further.'

'Any further?'

'Yes, it's not seeking any internal disciplinary measures.'

'They can't if they don't employ me. They'd have to keep paying me in order to punish me.'

'Neither are they recommending that any charges be brought against you.'

'Charges? What charges?'

'Well, if you had leaked price-sensitive information to the media, you would have been in breach of certain sections of the Corporations Law. Criminal sanctions apply. Then of course there's the Public Sector Management Act you'd have breached by expressing your own opinion about a matter of public importance in which you have expertise, in a manner contrary to government policy. Something like that. I can't tell you the provisions off hand. I'm a psy-chologist, not a lawyer. As part of my brief though, I'm obliged to prepare a report on you and to submit it to your Department as well as to the Department of Personnel and Industrial Relations.'

'Sounds like a lot of work. Would you like some help? Do I get a copy?'

'Yes, I'm required by law to supply you with a copy on request.'

'Well, treat this as a request, Giles.'

'Fine, but I would like you to agree to complete some psychological tests for the purposes of my report.'

'No.'

'Would you prefer not to, Edward?'

'I would prefer very much not to, Giles, because either way I'm going to have to leave this hothouse of conspiracy theories and insanity. One day, perhaps many years from now, when the world has turned often enough to have shaken off its malaise and its slavish adherence to pseudo-science, managerial psycho-jargon, economic insanity and efficiency worship dressed up as the great Western quest for individual freedom and prosperity, I will run into you somewhere. It might be in a supermarket queue or in the foyer of a cinema or maybe in a soup queue. You might be there with your wife and perhaps your adult children. When I do, I undertake to use the utmost restraint and not come up to you, your wife and your children, to remind you, in front to them, of what it was psychologists were doing during the occupation.'

I did not have to wait very long for a copy of his letter. He must have started drafting it as I was leaving the building. It was a strange sensation opening a letter perfectly addressed, my name perfectly spelt and finding a 'with compliments' slip attached to a document likely to be the closest thing to my own death certificate that I would ever see.

He concluded: *Mr Harnovey does not exhibit any psychotic symptoms. He does, however, suffer from an obsessive-compulsive and paranoid disorder. He also presents as someone likely to regularly invoke Departmental grievance procedures for insufficient cause. It is a benevolent employer who hires him.*

———————

Gerard had privately confirmed that twenty-five per cent of chemical engineers were to be kept on but that I was not going to be one of them. Nothing had been communicated officially to me. I did not know anything about the others who were not going to be kept on. Either they were waiting at home to be formally terminated or else they were still at work and keeping a low profile. I clung to faint hopes.

Perhaps, and at times this did not seem too ridiculous to me, if nobody saw much of me, didn't see me come in first thing in the morning, leave for lunch or go to catch the train at the end of the day, then maybe they might just keep me on inadvertently, by accident, by mistake. Perhaps they were dismissing only the first seventy-five per cent they saw?

There was no work for me to do when I crept into my office. I had considered leaving the lights off but it occurred to me that I would have a problem explaining it if someone came in. So I sat in my room with the lights on but the door closed, trying to make my desk look messy. I spread out old memos in a manner calculated to give the impression of industrious chaos, the chaos they reward. Even as I did it I knew it was a hopeless strategy. It was not strategy. It was madness.

I thought of calling my parents but was unsure of how long I could keep up the pretence. My mother would hear it in my voice and if she did I would not be able to think fast enough to satisfy her with anything but the truth. Several times I picked up the phone anyway and put it down again. I had nothing to do. I wanted to talk to them. I looked at the desk calendar, a distant relative of the digital clock radio in the bedroom. What was going on with my father?

I had the receiver in my hand and had even started to press the area code when, fortunately for my parents, I was interrupted. Gerard opened the door and walked in a few paces. There were two men in suits behind him who stayed at the doorway. His voice was uncharacteristically friendly, almost affectionate. I realised that this was probably because there was no sport left in me for him. But nonetheless it was strange: that he came to my office instead of summoning me, that he came unexpectedly with two men I had never seen before and that he spoke in that voice, a voice he had probably used with Amanda.

'Harnovey, come on, old son. You know the score.'

'Well I haven't actually been . . . haven't received any for-mal—'

'But I told you personally.'

'Yes, but I still expected—'

'It's in the mail.'

'Oh I . . . there are entitlements, aren't there?'

'You mean the ETP?'

'The what?'

'ETP—eligible termination payment.'

'Yes, aren't I entitled to a termination payment, after all . . .'

'It's all dealt with in the letter. Should be at your home . . .' he looked at his watch, 'should be there today. But from mem-ory, most of what you're getting is tied up.'

'Tied up?'

'In superannuation.'

'What about the rest?'

'I don't think there is going to be all that much left, not after the disbursements had been recovered from you.'

'What disbursements?'

'Well, when you were at Spensers Gulf, you frequently went over your allocated travel allowance, planes, hotels— that sort of thing. Given the number of trips you made, you ended up owing the department quite a bit. Nobody knows quite how much. There will need to be a departmental investigation to determine your precise net entitlement. It will take some time. We will let you know the results.'

'I don't believe this,' I said involuntarily, *sotto voce*.

'Look,' he said almost sympathetically, 'Harnovey, one door closes . . . You know the saying. One never knows what's behind the next door. Let's make a clean break of it. There's a good chap.'

'What, right now?'

'I think so. Better that way. Do you need any boxes? We could get you some boxes, different sizes if you like.'

Of course there have been other periods, not merely in this century but in earlier, far worse-recorded, though now often fondly remembered centuries (the rights to the more recent of which have been sold to Merchant-Ivory) in which shallowness and moral vacuity went out together one night in the pitch black of unreason and dancing cheek to cheek very quickly spawned grotesque idiot children, children whose incapacity for self-doubt enabled them to push the concerns of honest people (or at least the concerns of those who would not ape them) off the front page of the times and gradually back through the world, beyond the weather, finally making sport of them before using them to wrap up something dead. Then they were thrown away. Gerard must have felt I was beyond sport. But I was not yet beyond the weather.

CHAPTER 29

Winter, always so generous with its time, had come early. I waited in William Street outside Flagstaff Station with a number of different-sized boxes which in aggregate contained my career. The wind found the unsecured papers from inside the boxes. I chased some and let others go. I was not waiting for a train but for an idea. How was I going to get the boxes home? How was I going to explain coming home so early? How was I going to keep from coming home early every day from now on? How much sadder could Tanya get? How was I going to find the money for the next mortgage repayment? How did the young Orson Welles manage to finance *Citizen Kane*? Did he mean us to know what 'Rosebud' meant? Did he care as long as we talked about it? And who was it who first conceived of a deity whose indifference knew no bounds, whose ill-temper begat so much pain? I would never in a million years have done to one person what he did every day to so many.

The station hummed. How much of my life had I spent at this station? Days, but it felt like years.

What was I going to do *that* day and then on the days after it? By the banks of the station I sat on one of my boxes but did not weep. I attracted very little attention. After all, just across LaTrobe Street there were men who *slept* in boxes in Flagstaff Gardens, or at least they did in the warmer months. In winter they all moved at least five hundred metres or so past the Customs Office building to the Salvation Army hostel in Wills Street.

The ignore of the passersby induced the illusion of freedom. But in what sense was I a free man? I did not know what to do but it occurred to me that whatever I was going to do was, or had been, determined by previous events beyond my control. Everything had been. A woman, about my age or a little younger, with long straight dark hair, was walking a brown dog. She had him on a lead but the dog was leading her. She had red lipstick, black jeans, a purple jumper with matching scarf. They passed me as they sauntered down William Street heading for the gardens. Everyone else was dressed for their business. Walking her dog was this woman's business. As I watched them cross LaTrobe Street heading away from me, I thought that I was a chance to cry.

A gust of wind hit me in the face and took a few nascent tears to another place. I was not even free to cry. Who is ever free to cry? There are always people around, people who might turn a blind eye to a man at that station of his cross, his career in boxes, but who would not be able to resist the visual feast of a *crying* man being blown about in the winter of his discontent. But neither were they themselves free to take in the spectacle and return to their places of business to cry lest they be seen by their colleagues crying at their terminals. The last one to cry is the winner. We all know this. Children know this as an article of faith. Adults can no longer articulate it but they know it instinctively. So no one is free to cry. No one except Tanya.

It occurred to me outside the station that it is possible that no one is really free, not merely where tears are concerned, but with respect to anything. If one event or situation determines or causes another, in what sense can it be said that we are free to do or not to do anything? If our behaviour is determined by every factor from our genetic structure to the type of birth we experienced, our perception of the love, attention, material comfort we received as children, all the way up to our current blood sugar levels and immediate exposure to the prevailing weather conditions, then in what sense is our behaviour free?

And even if we could calculate the effect of all these factors and predict our behaviour, we would still not be free. For to be able to predict a future event does not make it possible to influence that event if the variables that determine it are beyond our control.

I watched more papers fly from one of the boxes.

There is, of course, a sense in which our behaviour can be regarded as free even if it is completely causally determined, indeed only if it is determined. We can regard our behaviour as free if it is determined by *our* will or choice. What we do is surely free if it is determined by what *we* want to do, given all the external factors operating. My tick on a ballot paper is free provided its position on the paper is determined by my will.

The question is, is there a sense in which our *will* is free, presuming that it too is causally determined? But perhaps it doesn't matter.

So why talk about it? Why even think about free will? Well, for a start it delayed having to think about what I should do to save my family and, anyway, it made me feel better. If Kant and I both wrestled with the problem then perhaps I was more than the sum of the boxes. Actually Kant had never given the issue a thorough going over in William Street, outside Flagstaff Station. But I was sure that if he had he would have reasoned that neither of us was free to do anything about these boxes, especially me. Neo-classical economists have succeeded in getting most people to accept as an axiom that it is preferable to forgo a guarantee of the things we need in order to survive than to forgo free choice. But then von Hayek never addressed the purchase of a little girl's overcoat or a mortgage repayment.

I had problems but the problem of free will was not one of them. And that was precisely why thinking about *it* was so attractive.

It was growing increasingly overcast. As I saw it, the only real use we could have for free will as a concept was in an ethical or moral sense. Free will, although we really mean free action, is the construct we have to use to assess whether or not an action is an appropriate candidate for an ethical judgment. For, it seemed clear to me, it is the purpose of an ethical judgment to influence the psychological states of people in such a way that they choose to do the things a system of ethics prescribes and not to do the things it proscribes. And if a person's action is not determined by his or her will or choice, if it is not a free action, then affecting the person's will will not affect his or her action and hence there is no point to subjecting it, or the person, to an ethical judgment. Only if an action is the result of a person's will or choice is it a candidate for an ethical judgment. And so long as an individual feels free from other people's coercion in his or her *choice* to do or not to do something, it does not matter that innumerable previous and present events have determined which choice the individual ultimately makes. For among the causal events will be past ethical judgments and the present expectation of future ones. Such an understanding of free will makes it possible for us to describe people's behaviour as moral or immoral. Without it everyone is amoral.

I wondered how Kant and Hume and the others did this stuff without the benefit of a railway station.

The woman with the purple jumper and scarf had let her dog lead her past me and my boxes again, only this time they were going away from the gardens, and still I had come to no conclusions with respect to any of my problems, other than perhaps the problem of free will and much good that would do me. I watched the woman and her brown dog. I knew them or wanted to. I wanted her to talk to me. I wanted to pat the dog. I smiled at them as they passed but neither of them noticed.

What dogs do is not undetermined either. They lap water from a puddle. The dryness in their mouths causes them to. Why are their mouths dry? They have been running. Why were they running? At a particular moment the chemical state of their brains was such as to cause them exuberance. How did that chemical state come about? I didn't know. Would it ever again come for Tanya? It was possible, at least theoretically, for these things to be known even if I did not know them.

The purple-clad woman with long black hair stopped because the dog had stopped. One thing determined another. The dog stopped because it was thirsty. Sitting in front of him watching him drink, I understood why he was drinking. But why, when he was through, did he turn around and stare at me? There had been no sudden loud noise, no onset of cats, no delivery of prime-grade mince. What suddenly compelled this stare in the middle of William Street from a brown dog with a white patch on its head?

I needed the attention. I needed more than that. With self-doubt, the great cancer of the psyche, whispering to me above the trams and the traffic, I needed help, I needed an answer. I looked around. Everyone was moving, on their way to somewhere, on their way to nowhere. The only person relatively motionless was a one-legged man propped up against a pillar of the station selling magazines. Even he kept shaking his head involuntarily every few seconds or so. The coins in front of him stayed still but the pages of the magazines would not keep to the topic. *I'm too fat* alleged Elle Macpherson, then *Trust Your Stars* urged the staff astrologer at the whim of the wind. If it were true that the fault was not in the stars but in myself then I was indeed back where I had started, with ten days, by my reckoning, until the next repayment was due.

I left my career unguarded and took the escalator further into the station, to the next level down. There were three empty telephone booths. One of the two with an *Out of Order* sign still had the Yellow Pages of the telephone directory. Under *Employment Consultants* I found that the agency with the largest share of the page was in William Street, not far from that very station. The first available appointment was for the following morning. I wondered then whether this might not indeed be the best of all possible worlds, and if it were, whether that was the ultimate in pessimism.

CHAPTER 30

It took three round trips with arms full from the station nearest our house to the front door to get all the boxes home. Dividing the load into three, I had left the boxes I couldn't carry with the station master. Once home for the third time I relied on Tanya's reticence in social intercourse to enable me to ensconce them in the study, the room which had become a shrine to our respective professional futilities. It was the room wherein my Spensers Gulf report had been stillborn and where Tanya's Tamil Tigers were stacked on top of each other waiting under the cover of dust for liberation.

Once that was done I went in to see her.

'Eddie? Is that you?'

'Yes, my dear, I am afraid it is me, now that you mention it—would that it were something more.'

I sat down on the bed. She had her back turned. It was dark. The curtains were drawn. I knew the drill.

'I thought I heard you.'

'Heard me?'

'Heard the sounds you make coming home. But then it wasn't you and I drifted back to sleep or somewhere near it. Then a little while later I thought I heard you again and again it wasn't you. It wasn't anyone. I started thinking—imagining that maybe you were not coming home. I mean—what must you think as you make your way home? What do you think as you walk to Flagstaff Station? After the second false homecoming I wondered why you would want to come home at all. I felt sure that sooner or later you wouldn't.'

'Home is wherever you are, the two of you. It's not the place that matters. It's not the place that's important, is it?'

'It just couldn't be today.'

'What couldn't?'

'It couldn't be today that you didn't come home.'

'Tanya, I'm always coming home. I may never leave it again.'

''Cause I decided to do something.'

'What?'

'To try . . . Eddie.' She began to cry.

'It's alright. We're . . . you're going to be fine. Tell me what you did.'

'It started with Kate.'

'Kate?'

'She came over this afternoon after school in quite a state. She's been calling for days, you know, leaving messages on the machine. I just haven't been up to calling her back. Finally, she just came over. She said she was worried something terrible had happened to Abby after the night we took her to hospital or else that she'd done something wrong, something that had really hurt me, and that I wasn't speaking to her. She really is a good friend.'

'Yes. Yes, she is,' I agreed without enthusiasm.

'She's gone back to Paul. I think she wants to have a child.'

'That'll solve everything.'

'Who knows? Maybe it will.'

It was good to hear Tanya talk about someone else, some-one other than herself, even in that tiniest of voices, not that her depression had given her any great insight into herself. She had bypassed the familiarity that breeds contempt and gone straight to contempt. She had found it the way some people find God. Having always been predisposed to loathing herself, full-blown self-contempt would have seemed like a revelation. I looked at my hands and then at my shoes.

'She's wanted children for a long time, long before she left him. Paul didn't want them or not yet, not then. What does she think has changed? You don't create human life by blackmail, for Christ's sake.'

'You sound annoyed with her, Eddie. Are you?'

'No, of course not. Why should I be annoyed with her?'

'Maybe not annoyed then, jealous.'

My pectorals were tired from carrying my career around the city. 'Jealous! Jealous . . . of what?'

She took her time answering, more time than I needed her to take.

'That . . . they're okay.'

'They're not okay. Shit, Tanya! People don't just get *okay*. They have to be born okay and no one's born okay.'

'Eddie, what's wrong with you?' she asked sympathetically.

'Me? There's nothing wrong with me but don't go thinking that they're okay. It's just like people at kitsch weddings, every-body assumes that the marriage of the two cutesy kids must be a good idea because somebody's given half their house to the caterer and the other half to the florist. No one's got the guts to say "you're both making a huge mistake".'

'Eddie, what are you talking about? Kate is trying. We should support her even if you think it's . . . stupid to try. Do you think it's stupid to try?'

'What?'

'To try to . . . make it work.'

I looked at the clock again. The room was dark. Tanya had her back to me throughout all of this. There was only the clock smugly marking time, fluorescent neutral, refusing to mix in.

'We're not talking about . . . what we're talking about, are we?' I asked her.

The same word will have a cognitive *and* an emotive meaning to us simultaneously. Perhaps this was why it was funny when Groucho Marx said that words beginning with 'k' always get a laugh. It never failed, he said, urging us to consider, for example, 'chicken'. Not only did I always laugh at this but I've never stopped trying to figure out why I always laughed at this.

'Eddie? Eddie . . . what are you thinking? Say something.' She turned over. There was the smell of peppermint on her breath.

'I feel like chicken tonight.'

'Eddie, listen, something happened today.'

'I know.'

'I decided I'm going to try—'

'Yes, you said.'

'I mean it. After Kate left. We'd had a long talk.'

'Shit, this is with a woman who thinks she can save her life by creating another one and inflicting hers on it.'

'I reached the other side . . . I reached the other side of the bed . . . the phone, Eddie.'

'Yes.'

'I picked it up . . . and I called a number she gave me.'

'Who did you call?'

'A doctor. A psychiatrist, a woman Kate recommended. Then she left the house saying she'd be back in ten minutes, after I'd made the call.'

'Did you speak to her, the doctor?'

'No, I spoke to her nurse. Said they couldn't fit me in till November.'

'November? What did you say?'

'I said they had to. She asked why. I couldn't talk properly, I got all . . . like I am now and . . . I cried . . .'

'Like you are now?'

'Yes . . . she asked why and I said that I thought I was . . . depressed.'

I held her in my arms and squeezed tightly trying to keep Tanya from seeing my eyes in the light of the clock. Neither of us said anything for a while, letting the clock do its work in silence.

After a while in the dark your eyes make their own shapes, shapes you cannot understand. They don't stay still long enough to conform to the contours of any daylight object you can recall. It is pointless to curse them just as it is pointless to regard them in any way as meaningful or as the shapes perhaps of things to come. At night, in the dark, when we are temporarily unashamed of incoherence, when we are robbed of the daylight proportions conferred by our senses, sounds can flesh out, can amplify the shapes. That night in bed as Tanya slept a chemically-induced sleep, I tried to ignore the shapes drifting just above my face. Born out of the lines of cracked paint on the ceiling they had left home early that night to be the things we can only see ourselves. And closer than ever this time, separate but still part of them, like water and its surface tension, came the sound of the helicopters.

Though she had been having increasing difficulty greeting the day vertically she had no trouble waking up. Indeed we normally took being awake in unspoken shifts. I had trouble falling asleep and later waking up. Tanya had trouble staying asleep and getting up. Throughout almost all of each night there was always one of us fighting something. During the first shift, the one in which she slept and I was harassed by the circular mechanical motion of airborne tadpoles, I took my suit, my only suit, out of the wardrobe in the bedroom and hid it somewhere in another room. If Tanya had seen me dressed for work in my suit she would have questioned me about it and the clock would have given me at least two minutes of lying time. I would not have been able to sustain it that long.

Why was my only suit blue? The thing about green is you never know when it's going to really set you off or when it's going to make you look pallid and sick. It has this in common with brown except that brown can be relied upon with far greater confidence to make you look pallid and sick. Grey is sombre, funereal or intimidating, which really left only blue. My father had a blue suit.

Everyone on the train that morning looked as though they were dressed for a job interview. One had to impress, to impersonate someone you were not, all for the hope of ill-defined security. For this hope, unspoken of for the most part, older women and their daughters wore short skirts in winter, having been shown how never to menstruate by teenage girls who had fasted their way out of chronically under-funded schools and into glossy magazines.

The women knew two types of men: the men they were looking for and the men who had left them. Both types were on this train. One could pick the men who had left them. They had left them because on their return home at the end of many frightened and uncertain days at work their partners were still not home from long hours bending over backwards to keep *their* jobs. When the women finally did get home there was nothing teenage about them but their clothes, and the men, whose mothers had never made their fathers defrost anything, needed more than ever to escape with one of the kids from the magazines. These men, both before and after they abandoned their partners, kept voting for parties strong on traditional family values. They felt in their hearts that no one understood them and that there was nothing wrong with leering over someone's shoulder on a train to catch a glimpse of a skinny girl-child in a very short dress. After all, their ex-wives used to dress like that.

It was cold. Men wore coats obscuring all but their shapes. I was not in a coat. In the middle of the night, at the time I had taken advantage of Tanya's sleeping to steal my suit from the wardrobe in our bedroom, I had not thought to take my coat. In the morning when, shivering, I had remembered, it was already too risky to creep back in for it. Tanya might have been awake and seen me. So I stood exposed on the train between the men in their coats reading newspapers with headlines, *Telstra Sale Jobs Go, Magpie Chief Lashes Out,* and the women in short skirts reading various magazines all with the same hair care product advertisement on the back, *Your hair is as individual as you are.* Nobody spoke.

This was an express train to the City via Richmond and the City loop. I would be early. I wanted to be early. That was good. Early was good. Everyone on the train would be early for my appointment. Our hair was as individual as we were. But we were ninety-eight per cent water. Or was that lettuce? We share ninety-eight per cent of the same genetic material with apes or is it ninety-eight per cent of the same genetic material with each other? Or is it apes *and* each other? Our brains certainly differed from those of apes. Unlike apes our brains have ten billion nerve cells; even mine. Banks were owned, managed and staffed by people with ten billion nerve cells per brain. I tried to take comfort in this. And yet, of all the people I could see from where I stood on the train as we entered the underground loop tunnel, the men in their coats, the women in their stockings and short skirts, I felt certain that I had the most in common with lettuce.

I got to Flagstaff Station early. The train was on time. Everyone else hurried off and up the escalators as though the train were late and lateness terrified them. But if they wanted to feel differently why didn't they catch an earlier train? Had they considered the night before how they would feel in the morning hurling their bodies toward William Street, and then opted for more sleep anyway? Or did they fail to factor-in the fear and instead lived each day like the day before, in the style of the sleepy rats that led a despondent Pavlov to dogs?

I got to William Street in no hurry, realising that we were just as subject to evolution as were rats and microbes, viruses and the slime behind the bathroom tiles. Although there was still some time before my appointment there was not enough in which to evolve further. I was a slow walking man in a blue suit and where I had got to had to be enough.

Between the station in William Street and the Metropolitan Hotel I found a coffee shop I had overlooked each day for more than ten years. There are at least fifty known neuro-transmitting molecules capable of carrying impulses from one brain cell to another and this was the first time this place had moved any of mine. It was not that I had a choice. The aroma of freshly brewed coffee can so enslave a coatless suited lettuce of a man in winter as to make a mockery of any notion of free will. It was fortunate I had the time because even from the street the coffee provided greater comfort than I was capable of resisting. Come in, sit down, inhale my charred sentiment. Warm yourself, feed yourself. Welcome to this vaporous charity. I was in heaven's debt.

There were old magazines by the register and even older suburban newspapers no one had wanted to steal. Having ordered a coffee I picked up one of the latter. *Locals not the culprits: Police.* Other people were to blame. Beside this article was a small photo of an elderly woman. I took her to be a victim of whatever it was the locals had not done but as the coffee kicked in it became clear that she had a small article to herself. What had this fragile old woman suffered to earn a place on the front page of this inner city newspaper? In black and white she trembled in my hands.

She had lived and lived and lived. *Elizabeth May Amery has done it her way for one hundred and one years and has no regrets, although she does regret her loss of personal dignity. Page two for details.* I was not going to turn to page two. Was there someone in a coffee shop on the Gold Coast drinking coffee over a community newspaper with a photograph of my bewildered father on page one? *Upstanding retired man opts out. Page two for details.*

Living too brief an hour we seldom make it to the front page. Had she died a long time ago, Elizabeth Mary Amery would only have made the death notices towards the back and even that would have required the assistance of some interested intermediary. But she kept living until there was a small space open for her on the front page. What temptation there must have been to pack it in at any time over the last five decades, during the long years when the exigencies of her life were no match for the lotto results or lost cat notices.

But was it worth it, Elizabeth? She had done it her way for a hundred and one years with no regrets save for the loss of personal dignity. Is there any greater loss, Elizabeth? Perhaps it would have paid me to see page two for details but the steam from the coffee robbed my eyes of the acuity I was by then decreasingly taking for granted. With little but the steam in sight and the loss of Elizabeth's personal dignity in mind, I pictured my lovable father retiring, contracting, shrinking, no longer crossing things off his life's list of things to do, engaged only in lonely contemplation of what to do with the list now that he feels no need for it.

Was he angry that he could not pin down the days that the rest of the world insisted he had accumulated? I hoped he did not look to me to be the measure of those days. I, who had arrived at a point where nothing would have pleased me more than to fall through the steam and to dissolve, body and mind, in the contents of a polystyrene cup, I tried to remember the last time I had hugged him. Once I had the roof over our heads firmly secured I would make it my business to renew a tactile acquaintance. Still in the grip of the steam I could feel him then, his touch. What were my hands feeling that was so like him when I was in William Street, face down over a steaming coffee for which I was still to pay and he was up in Queensland. Face down, it was my own face I was feeling.

I might have stayed that way forever had a chair not taken advantage of an elderly woman by failing to deliver on its promise of structural permanence. It crashed to the floor one way and she to the other. Shaken, she lay there momentarily, legs askew, wondering if perhaps she had not died and gone straight to the scuffed linoleum floor of a coffee shop which, unlike her, had not seen its best days. She looked over at the upturned chair as if it might reasonably be expected to explain, if not apologise. She could remember apologies.

'Are you alright?' I asked her. It made her look up at me and she closed the bent scissors of her legs, one bandaged, the other like a stick of tinned asparagus.

'Are you alright?' I asked her again, bending down to help her up.

'I think so. I'm . . . not really sure.'

'Come and sit down. You just had a bit of a fall.'

'Yes.'

'Would you like a cup of coffee?'

'Sorry?'

'Would you like a drink?'

'Thank you—a cup of tea, please,' she answered, still in a daze.

'You should have something to eat, you know. Something a little bit sweet maybe. What do you think? How about one of those blueberry muffins with your cup of tea?'

'Well, I have an appointment.'

'Is it far from here?'

'No, not really but . . .'

'When's your appointment?'

'Quarter to eleven.'

'Oh, you definitely have time for a muffin. Let me get you a muffin.'

'Thank you, that would be nice. Actually, what I'd really like is some aspirin. Do you have any aspirin?'

'Let me check.'

I ordered the tea and the muffin but they were out of aspirin. The nearest chemist was a block away in Lonsdale Street between Queen and Elizabeth streets. It was cold so I ran. I don't know why I ran. I ran, I suppose, for her because she had an appointment, and for myself, because I could and had not for so long. I ran clumsily. The street was crowded, even though it was past rush-hour, people everywhere and I the only one on a mission, for aspirin. The street was wet with rain and everyone around me shunned it hurrying. I turned up the collar of my suit and ran.

When I had left the coffee shop it was only drizzling but by the time I had paid for the aspirin the rain was angrier and it was not just the passing office workers and shop assistants who fled the wet but construction workers too who found crevices in Lonsdale Street I had never known existed. At least the rain did not bore them. Knocking down the walls of government offices and chipping away at the edges of the Peter MacCallum Cancer Institute seemed to leave them cold. They lit up cigarettes and watched me try to run past them uphill and into the rain. Why I too did not shelter none of us knew or thought much about but they had nothing to prove and no aspirin to deliver.

My eyes made their own moisture when faced with the head-on confrontation with the weather. I wondered what they could reasonably expect if I looked only ahead from then on. They could look forward to focusing becoming so difficult that I saw better what was behind me than what was ahead. My skin would become thinner and whatever muscle bulk there was beneath it would become soft. I would stoop. It was coming, Lord. The discs in my spine would wear down and I would shrink, just a little. I would not be able to move as much air through my lungs and less oxygen would get into my blood. My prostate would enlarge and I would have less control over my micturition. As my skin became less elastic my testicles would droop. I would shrink, just a little.

The rain and the hill slowed me down but did not stop me. I ran. The construction workers sheltering from the rain stood like honour guards and watched surprised. They watched as I slipped and fell, saved from hitting the ground only by some protruding wire fencing that had caught my jacket. It also saved me from thinking of anything but the tear.

I heard the tear and could think of nothing else all the way back to the coffee shop. How big was it? Did it reach the lining? Could it be seen? Of course it could be seen. All the world could see it, *would* see it, but I could not look at it. Even under cover back in William Street in the entrance of the coffee shop I could not look at it. But I had heard it, just as I had heard the tile smash on the floor of the shower recess that morning.

These sounds syncopate the soundtrack of our lives, the soundtracks we bring with us into the world without even knowing. They start off pretty enough, sometimes even beautiful. You hum them to yourself. This is your internal melody, more than a wake-up call, it is a sound which prevents you from ever hearing nothing. Even when you are alone, when you have woken without realising that you are no longer asleep, the melody is there.

After a decade or so of this inescapable melody that no one else can hear, you start to tire of it. It bores you, shames you. There is nothing you would not do to be free of this dragging melody but it clings like a sick man's pyjamas. There seems nothing you can do. But sometime in your late teens or early adulthood you learn to jazz it up. Where, in your early years, it used to swing over a moderately fast four-four beat punctuated even more by the steady bass thump of your birthdays or the end of the annual exams, now you modify it to keep insanity from the orchestra pit of your mind. There you are, improvising your way through sporting teams and early romance, driving tests and alcohol all over the familiar chords but modifying its simple root by adding extra notes here and there. The melody is enriched. The little changes keep you interested.

But after a while even this won't do. It too starts to drag. The decisions you have made or failed to make leave you wanting more, *needing* more. But you only know one tune, the one that never goes away, the one you hate. You hit thirty or thereabouts when you learn, out of necessity, to scat. *Bibbidee-be-be-be..do-wha-.* . . You close your eyes and swivel your head on an axis like windscreen wipers over that tired old melody. Approaching forty you scat with the best of them. You still have a version of your life's theme and impulsively, unpredictably, you run through it now and see yourself overturning conventions of timing and phrasing. Only you can't help it. Your every certainty is scattered. Anything goes. You thought you had rhythm to accentuate the positive but you've got plenty of nothing. It's noisy, vague, devoid of meaning. It's too *out there.* You try to look back but all you can hear is *bibbidee-be-be-be..do-wha-.* . . You want to rest on the accents, make plans for the coming semi-quavers but it's too late. The soundtrack of your life has become far too unpredictable and even though you don't get around much anymore, it no longer means a thing cause it ain't got that swing.

The elderly woman was sitting where I had left her, still bewildered. She had finished her tea and half the muffin was gone as well.

'Here you are,' I said handing her the aspirin between breaths.

'Thank you,' she said, oblivious to my panting and drenched appearance.

When the man to whom I had earlier given both my order and hers saw me with the aspirin he approached us with a glass of water and placed it in front of her.

'Thank you,' she said to both of us. 'You don't work here, do you?'

'No, I don't.' I smiled. There was an idea. 'You'd better take the aspirin now. You'll be late for your appointment.'

'I didn't realise you didn't work here. I'm sorry to put you to all this trouble.'

'You didn't put me to any trouble,' I lied. She swallowed two aspirin tablets and got up, a little unsteadily hanging onto the back of the chair.

'Let me give you some money for the aspirin before I pay for the tea and muffin.' She began to reach into her purse and I watched her spotted hands work the clasp before it plunged into the black hole of all the things she thought she needed.

'No, don't worry about it. Forget it. I've already paid them for the tea and muffin and the aspirin . . . wasn't expensive so . . . really . . .' My hands fanned away her fake crocodile-skin handbag from where her long-serving wrongly-convicted money had just emerged weaker than it had gone in all that time ago and badly in need of rehabilitation.

'Please take it. I have to go now. Please take it. You've been so kind.'

'Thank you but . . . really . . . You go to your appointment.'

She looked at the watch at the end of her spotted left hand and it gave her a start. She turned toward William Street, walked two steps to the door and then turned to come back again.

'Why did you do this?'

'Sorry?'

'Why did you do this for me?'

She had me there. I felt stupid. I had behaved aberrantly, ridiculously. The construction workers knew it. Uncertain what to answer but clear that she would have preferred to be late for her appointment rather than miss my attempt, with a long shame left over from the bottom of my school bag, I opened my mouth like a goldfish.

'My father is sick.'

I did not know where or with whom her appointment

was and could only hope that she ultimately arrived there in time for the advice, the procedure or the news for which she could not be late. It was likely someone at the other end asked her to please take a seat. Hopefully it was just a dental appointment, a check-up which revealed no need for intervention and that all the gleaming sterile instruments of her interrogator could wait untouched for the bent bicuspid of someone's anxious offspring.

CHAPTER 31

The proprietor of the coffee shop who had seen it all from behind the counter was moved to meet me on the other side as I was leaving. He wore the white smock of a dentist and examined the tear in my jacket, thoughtfully, gently, as I stood abjectly still.

'Hmm. There might be something they can do.'

'Who?'

'There's a place down the road. Do you know the AMP building, corner of Bourke and William?'

'That's the BHP building.'

'No, they were opposite but they moved uptown. Anyway, that was years ago. Have you been away?'

'Uptown?'

'Well, there are these tailors in the AMP building. They specialise in repairs. They might be able to do something for you.'

'Thanks. Should I tell them you sent me?'

'No, they've never heard of me.'

I found the tailor in the cavernous arcade as promised. There was no one at the counter but upstairs were three young Vietnamese women, almost children, hunched over sewing machines. I made those cartoon throat-clearing sounds to attract their attention but they had not been raised on cartoons. I punched a small bell on the counter and still they did not look up. Eventually, a portly middle-aged woman came out of a back room looking slightly peeved. She had been interrupted. I took off my jacket for her to examine, not having surveyed the damage first myself and she said that she needed to examine it closely which seemed to mean taking it backstage whence she had come.

She left me alone to watch the three girls or peruse the surrounding rolls of fabric. The girls continued working without stopping to look at me or even at each other. The radio news was just finishing. A man in Moscow had been sentenced to four years' imprisonment for setting his dog onto any passersby who would not give him fifteen thousand roubles which was, the announcer said, equivalent to three dollars.

When the portly woman returned she still looked irritated. Her expression was of someone in pain from gastric hyperacidity.

'We could do something for you,' she managed to offer, in a threatening manner.

'Can you repair it?'

'Yes, of course. It's a question of *how*.'

'Isn't that what you do here—in the usual course of your business?'

'There are three possibilities.'

'That's good, isn't it? I've been lucky to get *one* lately.'

She continued as though her words were the last to be spoken. 'There are three possibilities: hand darning, grafting and weaving.'

'What's the difference?'

'They are different methods for achieving the same end, the repair of this . . . sadly torn jacket.'

'It is sad, isn't it?' I said more to myself.

'Without the repair you have no jacket and without the jacket you have no suit.'

'Hand darning, grafting and . . .'

'Weaving . . . as I said, different methods for achieving the same end.'

It occurred to me that perhaps her normal working day was not usually filled with this much portent. She was not handling it well.

'The same end but at a different cost,' I ventured.

'Precisely. A different cost to both of us,' she asserted.

'Are you going to pay for this too?'

'They are not equally labour intensive,' she snapped.

'Weaving . . . that's the killer isn't it?'

'It's painstaking work but it achieves the best results,' she said crossly.

'How much will I have to stake this pain?'

She looked at my sad jacket. The tear smiled at her as she shifted its jagged pure wool lips from inside the lining.

'It's one hundred and fifty dollars for the weaving.'

'A hundred and fifty?'

'Yes, far less than the cost of a completely new suit, especially one of this quality,' she said, unable to hide her admiration for my suit.

'Let me see if I understand the situation in all its aspects.'

She said nothing; having trapped some oxygen somewhere between her neck and her waist she was loath to tamper with her body's precarious gaseous equilibrium.

'There are three possibilities, hand darning, grafting and weaving. Each method would see the jacket repaired. Weaving would see an exchange between us of one hundred and fifty dollars. Each of hand darning and grafting would require a smaller exchange. Is that right?'

'To be frank, sir—'

'Please, *be* frank.'

'To be frank, anything less than a weaving would not be worth it.'

'Worth it to whom?'

'To either of us.'

'But there *are* three possibilities. You said there are three possibilities.'

'There are—in theory.'

'There are three possibilities in *theory*. Have you ever read *The Trial* by Franz Kafka?'

'No time for reading. I've got a business to run, as you can see,' she said impatiently.

'I do understand, it's just that there is a scene in *The Trial* in which an accused man is told by the Court painter, a man who makes his living from the painting of judges, of *his* three possibilities, three possible outcomes to his trial. There is a definite acquittal, ostensible acquittal and indefinite postponement. Kafka was writing this in the first quarter of the twentieth century and yet . . . do you see my point?'

'Well, we all have our trials, I'm sure. Anything less than weaving this jacket,' she said holding it in the air disdainfully with one hand, 'and your entire suit . . . would not be worth three dollars.'

'So you advise against hand darning and grafting?'

'Strenuously—but it's entirely a matter for you.'

Juggling a checklist of our debts and a request for examples of all three methods, I heard myself say: 'Weaving it is then. One hundred and fifty dollars, and when will it be ready?'

'Two weeks Thursday,' she said without hesitation.

Greeted rudely in my shirt-sleeves by the wind when I

got outside, I tried to huddle inside myself. I considered what I had just done and that perhaps I had felt as warm as I would ever feel. I had no money on me. My last coins had gone to pay for the blueberry muffin, the aspirin and what my mother would have called beverages or *cups of kindness*. I would have to take out some money from the automatic teller machine closest to the employment consultants or else enter their offices on the verge of vagrancy. Touching my ribs through my shirt with vaudevillian panic I realised that my wallet was still in a pocket of the torn jacket.

This was good. It meant that I had no choice but to go back to the tailor's to retrieve my wallet. It was warm there. I could postpone the repair on the pretext of the weather and maybe even call Tanya from their telephone just in case she was able to turn over two days in succession and would try to call me at work. I could quite honestly tell her that I just called to see how she was but that I couldn't talk long. I had a meeting. As long as the Vietnamese girls stayed quiet I would be home and dry.

The woman with gastric reflux was not pleased to see me. When I told her that I had left my wallet in one of the pockets she looked quickly toward the ceiling and then down again without moving her neck, suggesting, with her eyes, that I was too stupid to live. But I was not yet that stupid. I realised that she was more likely to let me use her phone if she thought I was still a 'weaving' customer in a hurry rather than a half-suited procrastinator. I might even have been pleased with myself for this inspired commercial reasoning had I not been so thoroughly sick of being me.

As she handed back my frayed wallet, heavy as it was with other people's never-wanted, never-needed business cards, I asked her as if it were an afterthought, 'Oh, do you mind if I use your phone? I'm running a bit late for an appointment.'

'Local call?' She eyed me suspiciously. Perhaps it had happened before that a 'weaving' client had discussed the three only theoretical possibilities of weaving, grafting and hand darning, then left her establishment only to come back through the door minutes later in order to call Madagascar. Perhaps experience was her teacher and not a mindless penny-pinching meanness she had inherited genetically along with hyperacidity.

The line was busy. Tanya was talking to someone, a sign of progress. This really was the best of all possible worlds. I looked at my watch to complete the impersonation of someone who was taking a liberty with someone else's telephone only because of a lack of time. The watch ticked loudly and went along with the whole charade, helping me out in a way that the silent red numerals on the clock radio in our bedroom would never have done. It went along with it so well I realised that I would very soon be late in real life if I did not take steps to prevent it. At the last minute I could not bring myself to ask the woman for my jacket back. The employment consultants' offices were not far from there and, anyway, how would it look to them if I presented in a torn jacket?

As I punched my personal identification number into the consciousness of the automatic teller machine, the wind started harassing me again, questioning my judgment. Would I have looked better in a torn jacket than in no jacket at all? Perhaps they would not have seen the tear. And even if they had seen the tear, the gaping parting of the strands in all its prodigality, this was not a job interview. They were not my potential employers. I did not have to impress them. Or did I? They were there to sell me. They existed only to sell people. This was what I wanted from them and they would do it better if I impressed them. The absence of my jacket would not impress them. Was that how it worked? Were they meant to *sell* me? But I was not a product, was I? Yes, I was a product of many things. I was a lettuce of a man in a shirt and tie being tossed about by the wind.

The automatic teller machine beeped three times. I looked at the display terminal. A sad clock face appeared above the words *Denomination Not Available. Please Try Again.* What denomination? What did this mean? The machine made a whirring sound consistent with post-industrial epilepsy and spat out a transaction record. There it was in purple and white. I had three dollars.

———————

At what stage in their development did certain children realise that they were going to make a career in interior design? When dirt became mud for them and when mud became clay, and that led to finger-painting, why did it not stop there? If parental encouragement is the secret ingredient that makes of their children closet interior designers how do the parents know what to encourage? When all I know to tell Abby is that there is never a good time to take Punt Road unless she wants her car windows cleaned at some critical intersection by stick figures as desperate as her father was when she was still a little girl, how did *these* parents know that there was so much money to be had from interior design? Why were there never too many of them?

In Europe between 1980 and the mid-1990s, of the order of ten million jobs were lost in manufacturing alone. What enabled this to happen without massive social unrest, without blood in the streets? It must have been that all these people got jobs in the newly developing industries the neo-classical economists had predicted. And when careers could not be found for them in desktop publishing or marketing, the world of interior design welcomed them with neutral tones and casually draped arms. They became interior designers. Of course, if they were really brilliant they became management consultants.

The carpet in the waiting area on the twelfth floor beside reception needed a shave. The chairs were matt grey and soft, and quietly and gently inviting. You sank into them without caring whether you ever worked again. You could check your spine in at the door when you entered. There was no call for it in these chairs. The walls were pale lemon and on them hung, alternately, the dot paintings on bark which the first Australians had waited forty thousand years to sell to consultancy firms, and large photographs of starkly rugged, barely hospitable landscapes. I knew this area. It was where the desert and the pasture met deferentially. It was like the edge of the habitable land just in from Spensers Gulf.

After waiting for a while I got out of my chair just to stretch my legs. There were no magazines visible so I went over to the reception desk where the brochures and corporate cards of the firm of employment consultants lay in two neat piles on top of the granite lip which demarcated the receptionist's private space from the shaggy carpeted common, the range over which roamed the anxious, perspiring, previously rejected people who had come for re-invention. I leafed through one of the brochures and picked up one of their business cards. Without thinking I put it in the breast pocket of my shirt. It was warm in there. My body was remembering great sleeps of the last thirty-eight years, a sort of involuntary 'This Is Your Life' of the unconscious. I stretched out Christ-like, while standing in front of the quietly busy receptionist and it was then and from there, for the first time, that I could see into some of the offices. It was then that I saw Amanda.

CHAPTER 32

The fourth time I saw Amanda she was seated behind a large granite-topped desk imported from Italy. At her back was a wall of window overlooking William Street. To one side of her desk was a half-filled drip filter coffee-making device, also from Italy. On the other side of her desk was a computer terminal and printer, intercom, telephone and fax machine. Because she was seated at the time I could not see her fully, but it appeared she was wearing a black pin-striped suit with a white blouse underneath. Her jacket, at least, was black pin-striped. Her long hair had been cut to shoulder length and she was wearing it behind her ears revealing small gold-coloured earrings encasing some polished stone I was too far away to identify.

Of all the firms of employment consultants in all the cities in all the world, I had to walk into hers. Had I missed something? Had some information, some data come before me during my thirty-eight years, information which to other people would have suggested that she was likely to be there in this capacity and that I, if I were not careful, was likely to be there, so shabbily, in mine? But I had been careful. When had I been anything else? Now she would see what had become of me. I had touched her leg so innocently inside my parents' wardrobe three-quarters of our lives ago, breathing in the scent of her hair, and yet nothing of her had rubbed off on me. Innocence, now there's the rub. Had I departed from it, not just with her, but with everyone and often, perhaps I would not have been that supine, crumpled shirt, over ninety-eight per cent water vegetable that was to be her next appointment.

Standing by the receptionist, an attractive young woman in cashmere who answered telephones without speaking, who should have been accustomed by then to desperate men from both her personal and professional lives, I felt oppressed beyond reason by the heat of the room. I thought of recantation, of withdrawal from all wordly pursuits, anything to avoid a re-encounter with Amanda in such sorry circumstances. Already during the previous hour or so, somewhere between the aspirin and the lecture on weaving *über alle*s, I had become accustomed subconsciously to being and remaining nothing. But it is one thing to wake up one mid-winter morning and be nothing and yet another to be served to Amanda Claremont on a silver platter, an undressed lettuce leaf looking like nothing so much as me, for her delectation.

To avoid this I was prepared to lose the house, all of it, including Tanya's share. She only needed the bed. In panic, with a damp forehead for cover, it occurred to me to bow down before the granite altar of the young cashmere receptionist who could silently patch anyone through to anyone else and to beg for the chance to do whatever was necessary not to be in this position. Then I clearly heard Amanda's voice coming through a small speaker positioned between me and the young receptionist. She was ready for her next appointment. Time was sick of me. Born so long ago with

her in the Eden of innocence, too young then to be blamed
personally for my family's non-success, now the carpet was
choked with weeds, perfect for any number of serpents, so far
were we from then. I had to go.

Past the receptionist, through the glass doors and down
into the fire escape ran the thirty-eight-year-old chemical
engineer, husband, father of one, former 'Joy Division'
scholar-in-residence, a son, a brother, a tax-paying citizen.
Back in William Street the ground was drying but the sky
was growing darker again. Why I had left or where I had
gone was not Amanda's business. I had left her business
premises and if she did not personally check the appointment book or page or wherever it was my name was
recorded, then she need never know it was me who had
enabled her to call someone unexpectedly and say 'Hi, my
eleven-forty just shot through.'

And back in the wintry democracy of William Street, as I
headed toward LaTrobe Street, I came very close to praying
that this was all I would be to her, the absent, nameless
eleven-forty who perhaps remembered that he had a job
after all. I huddled beside the grey walls of Flagstaff Station.
In addition to the disfigured vendor of magazines and the
self-exiled office workers whose need for nicotine out-
weighed their need for warmth, there were a couple of
strange-looking men in tweed and plaid jackets, checked
shirts and striped ties who stood beside placards invoking
users of the station to think more about Jesus and his father.
But I, who had almost prayed by the walls of the station just
to remain anonymous to Amanda in absentia, could ultimately find no comfort in the ontological commitment
they urged. Even in my chilly desperation, out of step with
the escalator and in no fit state to be let loose near the
underground platforms I knew so well, I understood that

secular humanism, liberalism and social justice had not abandoned me. Though I walked through the valley of the City Loop too early to go home, they had not abandoned me. It was just that everyone else had abandoned *them*.

In the Flagstaff Gardens I found the wind even more determined to press home its heartless advantage. It blew in fresh off Port Phillip Bay and it seemed that I was the first thing to stand in its way. I was also the only person in the gardens. The indigent and homeless welfare cheats whose artful greed had so sorely taxed the benevolence of successive governments were not to be seen and neither were the previously demented but now stable citizens whose urgent reintegration into the inner city was the only social programme to be taken up vigorously by those same governments. The trees shivered. At regular intervals the ground shook underneath me. The trains were running on time. Ominously, that had been accomplished on a number of previous occasions during the twentieth century. Alone, I stood shivering in my shirt sleeves at the edge of the central business district of the biggest small town in all the world. It looked like the place for a village.

When I could no longer stand the bare branches thrashing about in the wind in futile protest against their own loneliness, I crossed William Street and walked aimlessly down LaTrobe Street in search of life. At least then the wind was at my back. I thought of pneumonia. As a child I had once been publicly, famously unable to spell it and it saw me come second in the class spelling competition. Amanda had won. Could she spell it now? It came from the Greek, meaning completely and utterly miserable down to your lungs.

Next to the branch of the post-office I had personally supported ever since my parents moved north was the Customs Office. One of its most faithfully observed customs was the regular gathering of nicotine addicted staff around the perimeter of the building. Through the windows of the building you could see the contraband on display in glass cabinets. Beautiful items lay skilfully arranged for the passing public to admire. Gems, old coins, shiny muskets, stuffed snakes and even a leopard had been variously placed in different-sized display cases over the years. I had taken Abby to look through the windows once when the leopard was on display. She had trouble seeing it because it was quite a way in. Even when I had lifted her up she said it was too small to be a real leopard but remarked favourably on the shininess of the floor.

People from the Customs Office all wore uniforms and we could imagine that once they had finished their cigarettes they would be back on the job, hiding out at airports and roving the high seas in hot pursuit of leopard stealers. They were grinding their cigarette butts into the pavement when I passed. I stared but they would not meet my gaze, as though there was something in my eyes that might hurt them, something which they could discern from twenty paces might harm them more than any leopard could. A man in just a shirt on a day such as this is a man *in extremis*, in extreme poverty, distress or desperation or perhaps all three, and if they had met my eyes they would have found it difficult to be indifferent. Two small pools on the middle of a frozen face but in that tiny moist warmth there was a sea of despair which they were right not to look at.

Walking past Customs House I looked across LaTrobe Street at the high walls of the old Royal Mint Building in William Street. Once money had been made and stored there. Later when it was not needed for that, it housed the local historical society and the civil Marriage Registry. Tanya and I were married there. I had not looked across the street on our wedding day and seen my reflection in the window of Customs House. If I had I would have seen the reflection of a different person. I reached Wills Street, a tiny dead-end street notable for the number of derelict buildings boarded up with corrugated-iron sheeting. A group of men were warming themselves around a makeshift fire. So many things burn. Some others were kicking a football to each other. Here and there shuffled solitary men talking to themselves, some in anger, some with resignation. A small white dog craved attention by the side of the road.

I could have kept walking down LaTrobe Street but something told me that I would have to walk a long way before finding any other people who were so unashamedly not going anywhere. Though their clothes were ill-fitting, torn and filthy, I was drawn to them because they seemed to have time for everything except someone pretending not to be desperate. Timidly, I turned the corner into the dead-end street. Unlike the customs officers, these men had nothing to fear from seeing themselves in my eyes. Looking at them around the makeshift fire I had no idea how they managed to stay alive. Then I saw the Salvation Army Hostel a little way down from the corner. Walking past several groups of ragged men without staring at anything but my shoes, I looked inside and understood where the real growth in the country was. Large industrial-strength heaters, a city of vinyl chairs and a television high in the corner showing a woman making a cake with a mixmaster; all of which helped some of the men to sleep, others to play cards and others to fossick around in old satchels for something they had managed to keep in spite of everything they had managed to lose. The linoleum floor shone and reeked with pot-pourri disinfectant.

I did not want anyone to think I was staring so I walked back out hastily to the street not even pausing at the swastikas on the wall just down from the entrance. The men were still there in their groups, different-sized men, different ages, different shapes and at different angles to the street. Why did I know them? Why did I recognise them? They did not avoid the broken glass on the ground where they walked. Some shouted at their own shadows. Despite my erstwhile middle-class circumstances, I knew them. Some smoked. Some chewed gum. One group played two-up. I had never played two-up, never even seen it played and yet I knew them or needed to know them.

I walked back out feeling a fraud. If anyone spoke to me, my voice, my accent, would give away my parents' attempts to ensure that I would never have to associate with men like these. I did not belong there even though I sensed that I knew them. In the street I was so cold I thought of going back in to see how the cake had turned out. My tie blew around in the wind, a relic of a previous incarnation.

I was glad my father could not see me. I was not a prepossessing sight, not that anybody was looking. In that, my wife had a headstart on the rest of the world. She had turned her back on me days before. How prescient she had always been. A small dog came from nowhere, it was the same dog I had seen before, and started sniffing at my shoes.

'Eddie? Hey . . . Eddie!'

I heard my name called and though I knew it could not have been meant for me, it felt sadly comforting to hear it anyway. They were not of my world, the footballers here and the quiet talkers, the firesiders and the stay-insiders, men who had left their shame behind in another world. They had left it in my world. It had been my world once but now I was between worlds. Still, someone there had my name.

'Eddie? Jesus Christ! Will you look at you! I *thought* it was you. It *is* you, isn't it?'

'I don't know,' I said, not knowing if I could be who he wanted.

'It's you alright. I never forget a face, hardly ever. You don't remember me, do you?'

'Well . . .'

'You still eating curry?' he laughed. 'Don't worry about me, okay. Forget about me, but I'll be really insulted by you if you don't remember my dog,' he laughed again picking up the small white dog and holding it to him. It was Nick. I would have known his old dog anywhere.

'I still got her,' he smiled. There were a few moments' silence as he tried to formulate the question, gave up and asked seriously with serious no-nonsense empathy, 'What the hell happened to you, Eddie?'

He took me inside under one of the heaters, being careful no one saw his dog which he secreted under his arm. When I was seated and when he had made us both a cup of tea, he sat down next to me, sucking on a sugar cube and I started what I realised in the telling was really a story of post-industrial decline, the last convulsions of the middle class as the sun set on the second millennium. Over the steam from my tea I began from the beginning, at first tentatively, as though I did not know the story myself, and he sat there and listened patiently to every word. *Every . . . nine and a half years . . . I see Amanda.*

CHAPTER 33

I told Nick about Amanda, the four times of Amanda, about Tanya from the cradle of my civilisation to the bed, about Gerard and Kate and Paul and the joy of Abby, about the Department of Environment and Planning and Mr Claremont and his gulf, about epilepsy and my father and blueberry muffins and the primacy of weaving. I told him about employment consultants masquerading as childhood sweethearts and about the unadvertised sanctuary of fire escapes, where, more than at any holiday resort, you can really get away from it all. He got up without saying anything, checked to see that my cup was really empty and then took the two cups over to the sink where slowly he washed and dried them. I thought he had aged but then I had never seen him in the daylight.

'What do you want to do?' he asked on his return.

'I don't know. I'll have to get another job in the next ten days or we'll lose our house.'

'No, I mean what are you going to do right now?'

'I don't know that either. My wife's at home in bed and there is no food in the house.'

'You can't buy any?'

'I've got three dollars.'

He looked away into the distance thoughtfully, not saying anything, as he patted the dog who shared the seat with him.

'You like garlic bread?' he asked suddenly with a big smile.

'I've got three dollars. I shouldn't be buying garlic bread, Nick.'

'I'll get you the garlic bread.'

'No, really Nick, I couldn't—'

'You just listen to me for a while. But you've got to do as I say. We'll go over to Tiny. You can borrow a coat from him and he can look out for Helen.'

'Who's Helen? Who's Tiny?'

'Helen's my dog.'

Tiny was a big man, dark, drunk and sad. He was either Aboriginal or a Pacific Islander. I couldn't see his face clearly even though we went and stood right in front of him. He was sitting, rocking gently, in the swastika-decorated shuttered entrance of a dilapidated building. Wrapped in an old blanket he had four plastic bags beside him filled with old clothes, pillows and things he must have thought he might need.

'Tiny, this is my mate Eddie,' Nick explained.

I stuck out my hand and Tiny nodded.

'We're going out for a bit but we'll be back later. Was wondering if you wouldn't have a bit of a coat for Eddie here. Just something, stop him freezing his balls off. As you see,' Nick continued, hands in his pockets and gesturing at me with his head, 'he's just in his shirt.'

Tiny did not get up nor did he speak. He just kept rocking and we waited in front of him. Nick didn't seem at all concerned at the absence of a response. He just stood there as though we were waiting for a fax to finish its transmission while Tiny rocked in his blanket.

'Is he alright?' I whispered behind Nick, who closed his eyes and nodded slowly to silence my doubt. Then Tiny, still swaying, reached into one of his bags and pulled out what looked like a rolled-up army greatcoat. He held it up and now it was my turn for a delayed response.

'Take it,' Nick whispered.

'Are you sure you won't be needing it?' I asked, but Tiny said nothing and just kept rocking.

'We'll have it back to you by the end of the day,' Nick assured him and with that he handed Helen over to him, Tiny picked up the dog and included her in the inner sanctum of his blanket.

We made our way to LaTrobe and William streets and south down William past the station, the Metropolitan Hotel and the Courts, heading toward Bourke Street. Tiny's greatcoat swam around my body, the sky grew still darker and I didn't care much where we were going. On the way Nick told me about Tiny.

'Fact is he never talked much, not a great talker is our Tiny.'

'So he *can* talk.'

'Well, he *could* but . . . no one's heard him lately, not for about six days. Six days ago he was bashed by some NA skins.'

'What're NA skins?'

'National Action skinheads. NA skins come round the hostel at nights, sometimes buying drinks for blokes or bringing their own bottles and trying to get a bit of action.'

'Action?'

'Membership, rallies . . . attendance at rallies or meetings or whatever. Or sometimes just for fighting. It was those bastards done me. Remember?'

'No, I don't think so. I'm sorry.'

'Jeez, Eddie, you don't remember anything do you? And *I'm* the bloody alcoholic. You're the . . . what are you again?'

'Chemical engineer.'

'Right. Well, a month or two before we first met that night near the curry shop I'd been attacked on my way to an AA meeting by three NA skins. They called me "wog" and carved a swastika into my chest with a knife. I've still got the scar. I showed it to you that night. Some of the blokes at the hostel when they saw me in the showers accused me of being one of them.'

'One of what?'

'A Nazi . . . neo-Nazi or whatever they are. I said to the bastards, "Not me—No fear." I'm Greek, anyway, but there's still some in there that say I'm one and it sticks. And worst of all are the bastards who come up to you and talk about all that shit.'

'What, other residents in the hostel?'

'Yeah. Some of the young ones, not many, but one every now and then, will come up to me and want to see my chest and want to talk about getting rid of Slopes and Wogs and Yids and who else . . . oh yeah Abos, of course, poofs, Commos, fuckin' everyone, Eddie. These psychos want to get rid of everyone and they think I'm one of them. If you took them seriously there'd be no one left.'

'Do you think that's what they really want?'

'I don't know what they want. They talk about the Jew government that's robbed us of our own country, our own homes. One lot said the Queen's in on it . . . some world conspiracy. Christ, it's not the Jews or the bloody Queen, it's my wife that got a restraining order taken out on me. Can you believe that? Can't see my own children. What else have I got but drink? You tell me. Just Helen. My wife's not a Jew for Christ's sake and she sure as hell ain't the Queen of Eng-

land. But I'll tell you this, Eddie, a lot of the blokes listen to
the crap the NA skins talk and they're not all skins either.
Some of them wear suits and the full catastrophe. You've got
to take them seriously. They can look just like businessmen
. . . some of them. People don't take them seriously. I do.
Jesus, I really do. And Tiny does. He's not talking now.'

I wondered whether Tiny had been wearing the coat I
was wearing at the time he was assaulted. What chemical
changes had taken place in the brain of the first of his
attackers from the moment he had first noticed Tiny to the
last of the blows? I was hungry and tired. I listened in horror and in fear. I was jobless, unable to provide for my
family, desperate, but still I could not imagine taking
pleasure from assaulting someone, neither from the act nor
the effects of the act. Perhaps people like me would not survive. We were a young species still evolving. Would all those
who could not take even the smallest pleasure from inflicting pain on others die out? What would Tiny say?

Nick led us to Bourke Street and we headed east toward
the Mall. The darkness of the day, my hunger, exhaustion
and bewilderment mixed with Nick and Tiny's story gave
the day a confused night-time air of unreality. As we walked
I looked for traces of blood on Tiny's coat and, not paying
attention to where I was going, collided with a couple of
people heading away from the Mall. Just a few blocks the
other way the jacket to my suit was being painstakingly
woven by a girl from Vietnam. One block further up on the
twelfth floor Amanda was drinking coffee, looking out onto
William Street as she skilfully avoided the eyes of her next
appointment.

Nick and I were off to buy garlic bread. He seemed to
have a plan and assured me the plan had a point. We were
heading to the food department of one of the major depart-

ment stores in the Bourke Street Mall. But, in the way he spoke, the plan had greater possibilities than just the purchase of garlic bread. He wanted me to understand this but I didn't. First, he said, we had to find one of their empty bags which was why we had to scan the area around the Mall.

'It'll be quicker if we split up. It shouldn't take long to find one. People always take more bags than they need and it's easy pickings around here. Just watch out for the trams.'

'Nick, wait a sec, Nick. Why do we need a bag before we go in if we're going to buy the garlic bread?'

'You ask a lot of questions, don't you. It would be a lot quicker if you didn't.'

'Do we want Myer bags or David Jones bags?'

'It doesn't matter. They both sell garlic bread. Just keep your eyes peeled. Start with the rubbish bins. You might find a good one there first off. Raise your hand if you do.'

He saw the distaste on my face at the prospect of going to the rubbish bins.

'What's wrong?'

'I don't like the idea of going through rubbish bins.'

'It's not illegal.'

'No. It's dirty.'

'Oh come on, most of it's newspapers and plastic bags, fruit peel and old sandwiches. What are you worried about?'

'What about spit?'

'Who spits into rubbish bins? Can you name one person you know?'

I shook my head.

'Well that makes two of us then. The ground's for spitting.'

'But, Nick, it's filthy. I'm not going to do it. I can't.'

'You'd be surprised what you can do. You want to eat, don't you?'

'Not that much.'

'Yeah, well, I never said you were going to eat that much. But you've got to eat something, for your family's sake. They're depending on you. Anyway, there's nothing to be afraid of in rubbish bins. Most of the real dirt people take home with them.'

Amid the buskers, the jugglers, the lost children and the even more lost mothers, the bored skateboarders devastated by the realisation that their lives were not on television, neither in a Twisties commercial nor in a Generation X love story with Winona Ryder nor even in the heart-warming Disney story of teenage runaways screening at the special family time of seven-thirty, the spruikers, Japanese tourists, truant school children, truant office workers, tarot card readers, quasi-Gypsy violinists, quasi-South American nylon string guitarists, fire eaters and evangelical critics of the Family Court—amid all of this I kept an eye out for an unwanted plastic bag from one of the two major department stores. My heart was not in it. It wasn't just that I needed to know the reason for the bag. The reason for anything would have been sufficient.

I tried to imagine coming home. I would tell Tanya the whole story, about the legislation I'd recommended, the department, the employment consultants and maybe even all about Amanda. Then I would take off my shoes, get into bed next to her and the two of us would stay there until the bank had sold the house. Abby would have to leave school and go out and get a job. I had lost Nick somewhere among the trams and, somehow, hunting and gathering did not have the cachet of nobility with which it had been imbued by anthropologists who had never tried it.

Nick was right. He had no trouble finding an appropriate plastic bag. He had more trouble finding me but when he did, instead of taking me to the store behind the bag, he led me to a small pizza place in an alley off Bourke Street. I understood nothing.

'Is the garlic bread good here?' I asked with a childlike need-to-know.

'It's the worst, usually mouldy,' and with that he went inside and bought a piece. Then when he was safely outside again he unwrapped the garlic breadstick to examine its insides. Sure enough, there was mould.

'Great!' he said wrapping it again and placing it in the plastic bag of the department store.

In the food section of the department store I just watched as he approached a young man behind the hot bread counter.

'Excuse me,' Nick said with gentle politeness.

'Yes, sir.'

'I bought this bread here a little while ago. I'm not sure if it was you that actually served me but it seems to be off.'

'Off?'

'Yes. Mouldy,' and he gave it to the young shop assistant to examine.

'Oh yes, it is mouldy. I'm terribly sorry. Would you have the docket with you?'

'The docket?' enquired Nick innocently.

'The receipt.'

'I don't keep receipts, not for such small purchases. But look . . . it's still warm, it's in one of your bags and it's very, very, mouldy.'

The shop assistant looked gravely at the unwrapped garlic bread and, having had enough time for his own immediate future to flash before his eyes, he clearly decided to keep the customer satisfied.

'I'm terribly sorry, sir. Would you like a replacement or your money back?'

'Well, actually I don't really feel like garlic bread anymore. It's put me off it a bit,' Nick continued with polite concil- iatoriness.

'Certainly. Can I get you something else, sir?'

'I wouldn't mind two barbecued chickens.'

'Two barbecued chickens?' the shop assistant asked with surprise.

'Yes, thank you.'

The young man looked doubtful but he left us at the bread counter and returned shortly with two barbecued chickens. A slight crowd had formed in front of the bread counter by the time he had returned.

'Thank you, sir. Less the garlic bread, that will be thirteen dollars fifty, thank you.'

'Oh no, I didn't expect to pay any more for this. The bread was mouldy.'

The word 'mouldy' sent a ripple through the small crowd of potential hot-bread consumers. The young man, who seemed to be regretting his birth, cleared his throat to explain that he was not able to complete the exchange on those terms. With genteel upper-middle-class insistence, Nick insisted firmly and, when the shop assistant tried to explain with a dry- mouthed reasonableness that it would be an unequal exchange, Nick suggested the intervention of the manager.

'The manager, sir?'

'Yes. I think that is best.' Then he turned around and said to no one in particular of the gathering customers, 'It's the mould. You don't expect mould, not in your hot bread, not from here of all places.' They had come for bread and had gotten a performance thrown in.

The manager was even shorter than Nick. His shortness was accentuated by the passing of the years and the mod- esty of his success in retailing. If his sharp angularity and eyelash-strength moustache did not intimidate Nick at first sight, then it was apparent, even before he opened his gold-fish mouth, that he was likely to be the loser of any conflict between them. He looked as though he had been at this level of management for some time, having read trees and trees of memoranda, always noting them, but never writing them. He was tired. His tie was tired and his maroon cardigan had surrendered. There was nothing about him to suggest that he had recently warranted promotion. On the contrary, it looked as if it had been some time since he had known the wild exhilaration of moving up in the corporate structure, since the demands of fresh produce, multi-grains, French pastries and imported delicacies he could not pronounce had seemed the edge of greatness. The weekend casuals laughed at him. Now as he took Nick to one side I tried to maintain my perspective.

'I've only just heard,' he offered gravely.

'About the garlic bread?'

'Yes.'

'It was riddled with mould,' said Nick indignantly.

'Yes. I can assure you, sir, we will look into it,' the manager promised in hushed tones.

'I *looked* into it. It was riddled with mould.'

'In addition to our apologies, you may have either a replacement stick of garlic bread or a cash refund in full. It's entirely up to you.'

'Thank you. I'd like two barbecued chickens.'

'I'm sorry, sir, we can't do that.'

'Yes you can.'

'No, I'm sorry, we can't.'

'Why not?'

'Because the value of two barbecued chickens greatly exceeds the value of a garlic bread stick.'

'You mean the *cost*?'

'Yes.'

Nick nodded appreciatively. 'Look, I understand what you're saying . . .'

The manager looked relieved at last.

'. . . but it's the principle. A man comes here to buy garlic bread—'

'Sir, I quite understand,' the manager interrupted.

'I think I'd better have two barbecued chickens.'

'I'm sorry sir,' the manager continued in exasperation, 'the value—'

'The cost you mean. The value changes depending on who's talking.'

'The cost of two barbecued chickens—'

'But you can't think of such a small cost in today's terms. That would be wrong. What about goodwill? I'm a customer and—'

'We do value your custom and we do thank you for informing us.'

'Why?'

'Sorry?'

'Why do you thank me for informing you?'

'Well—it prevents it from happening again.'

'No it doesn't.'

'Oh I can assure you, sir . . .'

'Now if I call the Health Department—'

'Oh now there's no need for anything like—'

'And that Mike what's-his-name from the TV—'

'Really, sir . . .'

'What's two chickens then? It's a bargain at two, wouldn't you say?'

The chickens were heavy, wrapped in foil, they steamed in plastic bags as we made our way back through the miscellany of life that ebbed and flowed in the Bourke Street Mall. Nick put both of them in the one plastic bag and threw the other away. 'Why waste a bag?' he said throwing it in the rubbish bin. 'May as well give someone else a hand up.'

I asked Nick what would have happened had the garlic bread from the pizza shop not been mouldy.

'They're pretty reliable there.'

'But they can't all have mould?'

'No, they don't.'

'Well, what then?'

'I guess we'd have eaten it, or you would've. I hate garlic bread. The whole thing is speculative, isn't it? But it's the only way these days. If you want to go home they might still be warm when you get there. Or your family can eat them cold. Lasts for a couple of days in the fridge. Otherwise we can eat them at the bus stop opposite Customs. Don't have to share them there. Not at this time anyway. Up to you, Eddie. They're yours.'

I was ready for an excuse not to go home, without realising that this was what I was looking for. Since Tanya felt nothing already she would feel no less on hearing about my day. What kind of day did I have, dear? Weaving was an art. And I could not even leave the house to register with an employment consultant without incurring a debt. There was another art, the art of the ridiculous man's autobiography: from children's parties where we all fall down to adolescent parties where only the lucky ones fall down. Most of the rest of us prop up the walls and tell ourselves that it's alright, that despite our palpably absent finesse, our leaking loneliness and incompatibility with *the story so far*, we will be fine in the long run. That all makes sense, more or less, between the last war and the next depression. But if you are already in the latter, why not fall down *ab initio* and be the life of the party?

Bring out the violins as soon as you smell a fire.

And what do you do if you have put your faith in a person whose pain is beyond understanding? Ultimately you will be left the loneliest person in town. She was not unwell enough yet to see how much I had let us down. They should never have given me a marriage licence. Unable to steer, I could only go in reverse. But was my love for my wife anything more than a feudal right to interfere with her mood? Was it outdated, past its use-by date? In the absence of fraud, was it worth less than two chickens?

CHAPTER 34

In the hostel a man was unsuccessfully trying to open a locked door to the dormitory. Other men walked past him.

'Left my medication in there,' he said as people passed. Nobody looked up. Eventually Nick told him to wait until there was someone at the front office. They would let him in. The dormitory had been closed since eight in the morning and the medication was very likely to still be there.

'But there's no one at the front office.'

'There will be soon,' Nick promised him. 'Won't be long at this time. Why don't you take the weight off your feet and watch TV for a while.'

The man made his way uncertainly to one of the vinyl chairs in front of the television and sat on the one with the least foam coming out of it. Within a couple of minutes he was back at the locked door.

'Left my medication in there,' he explained again.

I was still wearing Tiny's coat and holding the bag of barbecued chickens. Looking at Nick I realised that I did not know what had happened to him between the night we cried together separated only by two dogs and a curry, and that day, the day Amanda sent me to the Bourke Street Mall in search of a plastic bag. Did he sleep in the clothes he wore for rustling chickens? When did this become normal for him? How long does it take? He had not mentioned his children. How long does that take?

'Do you want to stay for a while?' he asked me as we watched a man spit expertly from within the hostel to the street. 'You could stay for dinner at least. Why don't you, Eddie?'

He marched to the opposite wall to read the noticeboard and called to me, 'It's beef stew. And . . . cream cake.'

I got out of the chair to join him as he stood there reading because I had no wish to refuse or even equivocate across the room. The noticeboard contained the house rules. *Dorm closes at 8 a.m., 9 a.m. weekends. Breakfast is 8.30 a.m. Bowling Thursday $1.00. Please note, it is an offence to sleep in the streets of Melbourne.* What was it Voltaire said, or was it Anatole France, something about the majestic equality of the law which forbids the rich as well as the poor to sleep under bridges?

The rest of the board was taken up with folded slips of paper with men's names written on the exposed sides. People would sidle up to the board, scan it, hands in pockets and leave with their eyes back on the floor. Nick took a while to give up, longer than others. Then he turned back to me as if nothing had happened or as if something had long ago.

'So what do you want to do, Eddie?'

'I probably should go, Nick.'

For the first time that day he looked sad and I remembered his eyes from the night we met. They pleaded with me to stay.

'I've got a wife and a child,' I answered.

'So do I,' he said quietly.

'Where's Tiny? I should give him his coat back.'

'He'll be around somewhere, probably hiding Helen. Takes good care of her.'

'What made you call her Helen?'

'That's my wife's name. I'll walk you to the station. You can wear the coat till we get there and then I'll see Tiny gets it.'

We passed the groups of men around their fires and the loners who had not yet discovered fire or else had already left it for dead and we made our way back to the corner of Wills and LaTrobe streets. But at the corner something made me turn around and look back at the place for a village, at the near silent activity.

'Hey, it's not a dead end is it?'

'What, Wills Street?'

'Yeah.'

'No. It's narrow at the other end but you can cut through.'

'Where does it get you?'

'You know, I've never been that way. Isn't that funny! I think it's the Vic Market. I must go there. Maybe tomorrow.'

As we approached LaTrobe and William streets I saw the woman with the dog again.

'There's Helen's friend,' Nick smiled.

'Does your wife know that woman?'

'No, my dog.'

'Your dog knows that woman?'

'No, my dog knows her dog. I know the woman. Well— I've met her. I sold her Helen's friend. She lives around here. They're still inseparable, Helen and that dog,' he smiled.

The woman walked past us and smiled politely at Nick, her progress impeded by Helen's friend's attempt to stop.

'What's your wife's name?' he asked.

'Tanya.'

'Tanya,' he repeated.

'Tanya.'

'Pretty name.'

'Yes, it is.' I pictured her in happier times.

'Do you think you'll tell her what's happened?'

'I suppose I'll have to.'

'You might as well try to,' he said and then, as if trying to imagine her, '*Tanya*. Very pretty name. Maybe Helen and I could visit you one day? Bring a couple of chickens?'

'That would be nice.'

We continued down William Street, me in Tiny's armour and Nick in a jean jacket with the collar turned up over a slightly torn checked shirt of red and black flannel. There had to have been a first time for the wearing of the shirt. How could he have known then? A man buying a shirt never thinks he will one day be wearing it while hunting in the street for empty plastic bags. He never imagines wearing it to bed and freezing nonetheless in a room full of other frozen men who cough and wheeze away the weeping hours meant for dreaming. Now, hanging onto himself with eyes squeezed shut and a clenched fist in his mouth to muffle the sound of the child in him, still disbelieving it all with every breath, he knows no words for all the pain, the real hunger and the side-order of shame, the isolation, the small cuts and the large wounds, the degradations unimagined by the captains of industry or even the corporals of nothing much at all. Does he lie awake and wonder whether there could ever be a poet with skill enough to move whatever powers might be to change something so that he might be reunited with his dreams, just once without all the pain? Or has he slept here so long that he has missed the tiptoeing exit of his old persona and now feels, with every fibre of his flannel shirt, that this has always been all he was worth?

'Nick, do you ever wonder if . . .' I tried to stop him with my stare. 'Is the fault in ourselves or in our stars?'

'What fault? What do you mean?'

Helen came toward us suddenly in small bounds from the sheltered plaza of the AGC building. Nick caught her in his arms from one last paw's kiss of the pavement as though she were a basketball bouncing naturally from the ground to his chest. Out came her small pink tongue as she licked his face and he responded with a quiet tender reassurance of his strong feelings for her. I turned my head away with instinctive embarrassment waiting for a lull in the reunion. Passersby ignored them.

'Tiny must be around the corner,' he said when calm returned. 'He comes here a bit.'

I did not know where the *here* was to which Tiny came. This was a street like all the rest. We turned the corner into the street from which Helen had come after she had presumably heard Nick's voice. There was Tiny sitting hunched up with his back against the automatic teller machine, a blanket over his knees and another around his head and the back of his neck.

'It's sheltered and they give off a fair heat, those machines,' Nick explained matter-of-factly as we moved toward Tiny. If you looked closely at him you could see he was a big man but at almost ninety degrees to the world, his bigness was not what hit you but his darkness and his need to be covered. People did not look closely at Tiny.

'Good on the kidneys, eh, Tiny?' said Nick, to which Tiny nodded almost not at all. 'Thanks for looking after her. Eddie's finished with your coat now.'

'Yes, thank you very much,' I said taking it off, putting down my bag of barbecued chickens and rolling up the coat to the shape it had when it was first offered.

How do we know when we are on our way to seeking warmth for our kidneys from automatic teller machines? Should it already be clear when we find ourselves still standing at them but with only three dollars? I picked up the bag of barbecued chickens and realised that the signs were probably there before that. Whether they were there at birth I was not prepared to say. Perhaps it will one day be possible to isolate the 'three dollar' gene. But even without that, perhaps the tell-tale signs were discernible to an ordinary person with ordinary observational and analytical faculties. When the consumption of food in your routine is no longer a kind of entertainment, then it is not impossible that one day you will seek out automatic teller machines only for warmth. Food as entertainment means it is not yet over for you. It was not yet over for me the night I had first met Nick. Tanya and I were helping Kate and this and the curry entertained us. Helping someone is also an entertainment. If I went home would Tanya find me entertaining?

Nick escorted me back to the station. It was the evening rush-hour. Only the buskers and the evangelists were not going anywhere. With office workers, insurance assessors, systems analysts, clerks, lawyers, shop assistants, receptionists, work-experience students, table-top dancers, short-order cooks, construction workers, cleaners, tea-ladies, dental hygienists and trainees from accounts all streaming past us on their way home, he proffered the hand that was not full with Helen.

'Good luck, Eddie. It's been good to see you. Tell her the truth. You know where I'll be if you need me. But you'll be fine.'

With that he turned abruptly and started walking the other way with the firm resolve of someone ripping off a band-aid. I watched him head back towards LaTrobe Street and, in the jostling crowd under an unnaturally dark sky ready to burst, with two chickens in a plastic bag and a blind busking violinist knocking into me, I lost him. He had walked away slowly, as if waiting for the credits to roll over his back. A few people stopped in front of me (thank God for the buffs!) but they were not waiting for any credits nor were they even watching Nick. They were looking at the sky and the blackest cloud they had ever seen.

Soon people to each side of me were looking at it, a cloud so much darker than the rest of the already too dark sky. Within minutes, everyone around me had slowed down to look at it, even if it meant missing their train. Traffic screeched to a stop when the lights turned red because at least half of the drivers were looking at the cloud. Had it ever happened before that a cloud had stopped people at the end of the day on their way home, uniting them, even if only momentarily, in speculation? They had never seen anything like it before. But I had.

I had seen it before. Or rather, I had seriously envisaged it. I had that advantage over the pedestrians, the drivers, the passengers and the holders of the weekly travel cards and zone two passes stopping all stations via the City Loop for Pakenham, Dandenong, Frankston and Glen Waverley. It was the expertise which had left me with three dollars that had me knowing. The others, burdened by more than three dollars, did not know that it was smoke blowing in from the bay. There was a fire at the chemical storage facility there. This was the fire I had warned them about in another report they had requested and then ignored.

Most people knew, within minutes of noticing it, that this was not a normal cloud, not the kind that was 'good for the farmers', but they were unable to explain it, its darkness, its suddenness. Almost none of them knew that there was a chemical storage facility on an island in the bay so close to them, waiting to burn, every day of their working lives. Someone, who knew what was best, forgot to tell them. Someone who could not reach them at this late hour, forgot to ask them if they minded. Soon it would be presented on the television news as our very own *Bhopal disaster, coming up after this*. The Minister would be unavailable for comment and reporters would go looking for someone fitting my former job description but, like the Minister, I too would not be contactable. I was last seen in William Street outside Flagstaff Station in my shirt-sleeves holding two barbecued chickens, watching my fellow citizens looking a little apprehensively at the sky.

The arrival of mobile television broadcast units would shortly enable the significance of our very own wind-assisted toxic chemical event to be grasped not only by them but by the good folk on the grassy knoll or in a book depository in Texas, or by someone in Tiananmen Square or the World Trade Centre or Srebrenica. The beauty of the global village was that, if my wife could make it to the television, I might just be able to buy another twelve hours and not have to tell her about my day, the part that was just mine and had not yet been syndicated.

I would have paid more attention to the group of skinheads that had emerged from the bowels of the station had I not been thinking of my father and wishing that he were there with me at that moment. I wanted to show him the cloud blowing from the chemical fire my report had warned them about. I had done all my homework and gotten it all right. I wanted him to see that it was right and then to tell me why it was they were not putting me up into the next grade.

A fine spray started to fall. It was then that I became aware of a commotion some little way behind me down William

Street, towards Little Lonsdale Street. I turned around and saw the skinheads that had come out of the station milling around the automatic teller machine outside the AGC building, shouting and pounding at something. Were they trying to destroy the automatic teller machine? They were bashing someone.

Once this dawned on me I had to get closer to see whether I was right. The rain was getting heavier and the shouting louder. I hoped I was wrong. What was I going to do about it if I wasn't, with my two barbecued chickens.

There were five of them. Two of them had baseball bats which they swung at a solitary figure in a greatcoat, his arms covering his head for protection. The other three kicked at the man who kept turning around to evade the blows but was slowed down by the parachute effect of his greatcoat in the wind. It was Tiny spinning in the middle of them with his hands over his head.

I called to them to stop. My voice came out soft and high-pitched like a child's. It was as though I had not called out at all.

'Fuckin' nigger,' one of them yelled as another leapt at Tiny and knocked him to the ground. Tiny tried to make himself small.

'Help! These guys are bashing him,' I finally managed. 'He's being bashed. They'll kill him!'

A few people turned their heads to look but nobody stopped. They were going home and did not want to know.

'Hey, cut it out,' I called, and in the few seconds it took one of the skinheads to turn, in genuine surprise to see who would make so futile a request, Tiny got up, grabbed the baseball bat from him and started swinging it wildly. From his eyes down, Tiny's face was covered by a sheet of blood with billowing sails and bubbles where he breathed. His lips were torn and swollen. He gritted his teeth and his eyes were wide, I had never seen anybody's eyes so wide, as he swung. The disarmed baseballer fell to the ground.

Tiny kept swinging but there were five of them. I rushed at the one with the other baseball bat but I was not quick enough. I felt a crack in my side. Spaces opened within bones. I was unable to breathe, unable to make a sound. The pain was worse than anything I had ever imagined possible. I clutched at my ribs as my legs gave way and I sank to the ground. I felt the moist air touch a part of my eyes that had never been exposed before. Another blow, this time to my head, brought a spreading numbness.

———————————

The rain was easing up. I let my face soak up the footpath. My head throbbed violently, brutally, and the pain in my chest was sharp and stabbing when I breathed. The attack seemed to have stopped. I could discern legs running away and other legs running towards us. I heard a man's voice, distressed, filtering through the noise of the traffic as more people gathered around.

'Leave him alone, officer! He went to check on the other guy. Just went to help the other guy.'

It was the second time I had witnessed Nick crying.

'Where's Tiny?' I faltered, but nobody heard me. Without moving I looked along the ground through the gaps in the forest of legs. Not far away two legs protruded horizontally from an old army surplus greatcoat.

I felt Nick's breath on my ear.

'Don't move, Eddie. You just stay there,' he whispered above the noise. He lifted my shoulders and put something soft and warm under my head.

'I'm his friend, alright. Just lay off,' he shouted at someone behind me. 'I'm his friend.'

Then he whispered, 'I'll come back, Eddie.'

Something warm and wet licked my ear and for the briefest moment took my mind off my ribs. It was raining softly. I remembered singing, as a child, '. . . long to *rain* over us' whenever it rained during outdoor assemblies at school. I blacked out on William Street with two barbecued chickens beside me in a plastic bag.

As you fade to black your life becomes a badly edited retrospective of unconnected and meaningless ten-second visual bites in which you play only a bit part, and unconvincingly at that. You have not even read the script. It's a huge ensemble piece and you workshop it repeatedly. Every now and then you are rained on in a foetal position, in the middle of a street coated with greasy dirt and you are clutching your ribs, fading in and out of focus.

CHAPTER 35

'It's alright, constable, I know him—a client . . . and a friend, an old friend.'

I looked up at her through slowly opening eyes, hoping she wouldn't see me. She cradled my head in her lap. The first time I met her I had touched only her knee. It seemed nothing about her had changed. Still dressed pristinely and still unafraid of getting dirty, still smelling like ripe strawberries, she hovered just above me.

'Hey, Eddie,' she whispered, 'don't fade out on me. Stay with me. Just breathe slowly. That's right. There's an ambulance coming soon. We'll take you to a hospital, okay. Your friend's trying to contact your wife. When did you get married, you sly old dog? You never tell me anything. Thought you could sneak out on me. *You* were my eleven-forty weren't you, handsome? Thought you could get away. Thought you could . . . now what is it? . . . *Be elusive but don't walk far.* Remember? Eddie? Eddie. Remember, Eddie?'

I was examined, x-rayed and sedated at the same hospital

Abby had been taken to, and after a few hours Tanya drove me home in her mother's car. That they met I would learn later. I had slept through it. Maybe even Nick was there. He had not known my surname, and not wanting to move me to get at my wallet, had obtained it from Amanda's office with the help of the card I had taken from her reception and placed in the breast pocket of my shirt. He had promised the night I first met him, the night of the two dogs, that he would never forget me.

Tanya sat me on the couch while she changed the sheets. Then she put me to bed. I dozed on and off but each time I opened my eyes she was sitting there, in the chair she had brought in from the study, watching me. I had missed her for so long. At around nine o'clock she brought me in a bowl of her mother's barley soup and fed it to me. Abby watched from the foot of the bed in total silence. Then, at Tanya's suggestion, she kissed me on the forehead and went to bed. Tanya took the bowl to the kitchen and went to kiss Abby goodnight. I heard her. Then she was back.

'How're you feeling?' she whispered. People addressed me in whispers now. It was her turn.

'I don't know.'

'I called you today.'

'Uh-huh.'

'At work.'

'Why?' I whispered.

'I saw all the boxes, Eddie. I kept calling and when you didn't answer I called the switchboard. They said you didn't work there anymore. I called Kate. I was scared . . . and guilty . . . so very, very guilty. Sweetheart, why didn't you say something?'

'I was going to.' My voice logged in and out. Some words went missing.

'When?'

'I don't know.'

'Oh . . . my poor Eddie.'

'Yes.'

She had my hand in hers and, even sedated, I could smell the soothing scent of the Lancôme moisturiser Kate had left behind.

'I was going to tell you, really . . . when I had something else.'

'You know we're going to be okay,' she told me.

'Yes. Are we?'

'We'll be fine, Paul said—'

'You spoke to him?'

'He called. Kate called him at work.'

'Does he know . . . everything?'

'Yes. He does. It's okay. He wants to try to get you a job at the bank. He said it's the least he can do given how we looked after Kate.'

'I don't know anything about banking.'

'I told him you'd say that. He said you could work in personnel, "Human Resources" he called it.'

'I'm a chemical engineer. I don't know anything about personnel.'

'I told him you'd say that too. He said he'd try to get them to start you off somewhere high. You wouldn't have to know anything.'

'But it's too late, I already know things.'

She undressed for bed as quietly as she could and held me gently, avoiding the bandage on my ribs, till I was almost asleep. Then she started to whisper again.

'Eddie?'

'Uh-huh,' I answered sleepily with my eyes closed.

'That woman . . . was very helpful.'

'Uh-huh.'

'She said she was a friend of yours . . . Eddie?'

'Uh-huh.'

'Is she a friend of yours? . . . Eddie?'

'Yeah?'

'Is she a friend of yours?'

'Uh-huh.'

'Meet her through work?'

'No.'

'You didn't?'

'Uh-huh.'

'You didn't meet her through work?'

'No.'

'Eddie?'

'Uh-huh.'

'How often do you see her?'

'Amanda?'

'Yes, Eddie.'

'Every . . . nine and a half years . . . I see Amanda.'

'You know who her father is? . . . Eddie? . . . Did you hear what I said?'

'Uh-huh.'

'Who's her father then?'

'He's . . . he's actually . . . he's a cross between Fred MacMurray in 'My Three Sons' and Fred MacMurray in *Double Indemnity.*'

Tanya turned off the light and we both fell asleep. I dreamed I was flicking through the records at Old Man Williamson's. Each album cover showed a still from my life and my whole life was there under 'T', 'T' for these things that happen. But at about five o'clock the painkillers had worn off and I crept out of bed, put on 'Tess's' dressing gown and turned on the TV in the lounge room, just quietly. The hospital show had been replaced by 'Heart-break High'. Progress comes in the form of repeats.

Within a few minutes Abby was beside me in her dressing gown and slippers.

'Hi, Dad,' she said. She sat down quietly and took hold of my hand. Then, just as quietly, Tanya came in. We sat together watching television, the three of us in the dark, none of us saying anything. Neither Tanya nor I tried to make Abby go back to bed nor did we ask her why she was up. Part-way through the cartoons that were on by then I could see the first tentative rays of light through a gap in the curtains. Maybe I would go back to sleep later. Outside a dog barked.